Myra Lost and Found

by

Vivian R. Delmonico

Golden Antelope Press

2011

D3598 m

ISBN: 978-0-9817902-5-1

Library of Congress Precataloging Number: 2011944782

Published by:
Golden Antelope Press
715 E. McPherson
Kirksville, MO 63501
(USA)
Phone: (660)-665-0273
Email: ndelmonico@sbcglobal.net
www.goldenantelopepress.com

In fond memory of

my beloved Jewish mother,

Rose (Hirschkowitz) Lucas

(1896-1988)

Chapter One

1930 — New York

Myra held her grandmother's hand and had to skip a little to keep up with her. She had no idea where they were going, or why Grandma had put her clothes in the suitcase that had belonged to her mother. She now carried it with her other hand. It was snowing lightly and a wet mist covered the curbing by which they walked. Myra didn't know why she didn't go to school this morning or why Grandma seemed so nervous. Myra loved her grandma and if there was one thing she had learned in her five and half years, it was to mind her grandma. Aunt Margaret once told her that Grandma would never let anything happen to her and Myra believed that with all her heart. So, when Myra was told to hurry and wash up for the day and put on her new coat and the hat Aunt Margaret had given her for Christmas, she did as she was told.

There were tears in Grandma's eyes as she buttoned up Myra's coat, and the hugs and kisses made Myra ask --- where were they going? It was not to school today, her grandma told her, but a trip on a bus with a very dear friend of Grandma's, a very nice lady that her grandma had known since they were young girls. Then Grandma placed her favorite old teddy bear in Myra's arms and told her to always keep it safe for it had been Grandma's bear since she was a child. Myra had called him Teddy from the minute he had been given to her although her grandma called him Mr. Bear. Mr. Bear would always remind her of her granny, she was told; but why would she ever forget her beloved granny? Myra lived with her grandma and they saw each other every day. It was confusing for a five year old. She felt something was wrong but as long as she held on to Grandma's hand, she was safe.

They waited at a corner for the red light to change, Myra remembered she had not been supposed to tell Grandma about her hurts. She had promised Jake she never would because he said he would hurt her more and also Grandma. But she could not help but to say, "Ouch!" when grandma toweled her off from her weekly Sunday bath. She let her grandma carry her to the bed and examine her private parts. The look on grandma's face was terrifying for Myra. Grandma's face was as red as the beets they sometimes ate, and her eyes so wide they could have popped out of her face, so Myra thought.

"Who did this to you?" Grandma asked. But Myra had promised not to tell. "Who did this to you?" she repeated. "Was it Jake?" she said. "Tell me who did this to you?"

"I promised not to tell." Myra said. Then, Myra whimpered, bursting into tears: "He said he would hurt you and me too."

Grandmother held her tightly and spoke softly. "No one is going to hurt you, my love. Just tell me the truth," she said.

Of course it was Jake, but Myra tearfully pleaded with her grandma not to tell him. It was done and over with, so Myra thought and that was almost a week ago. But was it? The next morning there was no sign of Jake or his old jacket in the closet where they kept their coats. He did not pick her up from school, and it was Aunt Margaret who met her when her kindergarten class let out at noon. Something about Aunt Margaret's mood kept Myra from asking why Jake had not met her as he had done since she had started school. She was, however, happy he wasn't there for now she was really scared of him and what he would do to her and her grandma.

The light had changed to green and Grandma pulled her along across the street. Grandma had every morning brushed and curled Myra's dark hair into Shirley Temple curls. This morning there had been no time to do so. Her natural curls were brushing against her face like a spider web although her bonnet held most of her hair in place.

Something was wrong. Was she being punished for telling on Jake? She had never in her young memory told a lie. Didn't the teacher tell her class about lying? How then could telling her grandmother the truth when she was asked cause the flurry that was happening now? She would question her grandma when they were on the trolley later, but now the excitement of the ride with Grandma erased all the worry she was feeling.

Myra didn't know how many blocks they had walked to the bus depot, but it seemed a very long way from their apartment. At last, they entered through a large door into a hall where many people mingled or sat on the benches lining the walls of the large room. Grandma stopped and looked around. Then she found an empty space on one of the benches and told Myra to sit there until she found her friend, Gerta. She placed the suitcase under the bench where Myra sat.

Myra was more than happy to sit and rest her legs. Her face and hands were cold and caused tears to rise in her eyes. She pushed the unruly hair off her face and blew on her hands to warm them. She hugged Teddy so as to warm him too. Grandma had disappeared into the crowd and Myra felt a little panic in her chest. She knew her grandma would not leave her there forever. She would just have to sit quietly and wait for her to return. It seemed like a long time for Myra but eventually grandma reappeared with another lady following her.

"Here she is, Gerta. My darling granddaughter, Myra," Grandma said.

"She is beautiful, Bertha. Just like your Mary at that age," the strange woman said.

Myra knew that name. It was her mother's name,

but Grandma never spoke of 'her Mary' very often. It was Aunt Margaret who told Myra what little she knew of her mother, now in heaven with the angels. According to the schoolteacher, angels were good people who protected men and women, so she knew her mother was in a very nice place.

Then, the situation became confusing for Myra. Her grandmother handed the suitcase to Gerta and a thick envelope from her purse. "It is her birth certificate so take care not to lose it. Also information she may need to know if anything should happen to me, God forbid."

As Myra watched the transition the panic in her chest started up. Why was this strange lady taking her suitcase? Why didn't Grandma have a suitcase? What was to happen?

"I will take good care of her, Bertha. I called Carl, too, and he was very reasonable about bringing her home with me. I am so glad you called my daughter before I left," Gerta said.

"And I was so happy you came to see me at my work in the laundry. After all these years, you still remembered me," Grandma brushed tears from her eyes. "It was a godsend, I know. We never really lost touch did we? But here you were just as I needed someone. Just like old times. How was I to know this would happen? I prayed, Gerta, I prayed so hard for help and there you were, just dropping in to see what the years had done to

"I had a strange feeling, Bertha. It is hard to explain but I felt the need to look you up in case I never got the chance to do it again. They say this Depression is going to get worse, as though the year hasn't been bad enough: so many people out of work, so many families torn apart. Carl insisted that I visit our daughter Katie and give her some moral support since we cannot give her much money. Her husband is considering signing up for the WPA program mentioned in the New Deal President Franklin D. Roosevelt is talking about. They have three kids now and another one on the way. It is a very sad situation for them at this time."

Myra watched her grandmother shake her head as she said: "I know, Gerta. I, too, may be laid off soon. But when this happened, I knew I had to get Myra away from here. I would not let them take her away, God forbid. I have protected her since birth. What they did to my Mary should not be forgotten. I thought we would be safe here in New York. I didn't think they would find me, but I know who told them."

Then Grandma bent down to Myra's eye level. She brushed Myra's face softly with her coarse hands and took her in her arms.

"Listen, Myra, my sweet. I love you very much, but you have to go with Gerta for now. She lives in a small town out west. You know, where the cowboys and Indians live."

"Indians?" Myra shrunk back a little, but her

grandma pulled her close again. "Oh darling, they are not dangerous any more. Greta's husband is a farmer and was a cowboy in his youth. They say the land is beautiful with trees and real animals that you can see everyday. They have dogs and cats like the ones in the stories I read to you. You will be happy and safe there."

"But Grandma, aren't you coming, too? I won't go without you. I love you. I will be extra good, I promise."

Grandma stood up and retrieved a hankie from her purse. "I love you, Myra, more than anyone else in this world and you are never bad, never. I can't go now. I have work here and I need to save up some money before I can join you. In the mean time, my friend here, Gerta, will care for you until we can be together again. Please, my little one, don't make this any harder than it is," Grandma blew her nose and wiped her wet, tear-stained face.

"Never forget me, Myra, in the time we are apart. Never. Promise me that."

"No, Grandma. Don't leave me! No! No!" Myra cried.

Then her grandma nodded to Gerta who took Myra by the hand and started to drag her towards the doors at the other end of the building. She looked back and saw her grandma rush at them again. "Gerta!" she yelled. "I forgot this. It belongs to Myra. It is her birthright. Please keep it for her." Then she gave Gerta a small white box and blew Myra a kiss. She turned around and ran towards the outside doors.

It was the last time Myra ever saw her.

Chapter Two

1941 — Boulder, Colorado

Myra was running as fast as she could to catch the lady running in front of her. How could a woman that age run so fast, she thought, feeling the energy drain from her own legs. The woman looked back at her and dashed down the subway stairs. Myra followed, but her legs seemed to move in slow motion. The woman's dark hair seemed to be the same color as Myra's and she always had her hair in a bun. What did she want of the woman? Why was it so important to catch up with her? Before Myra could reach the bottom of the steps, the woman boarded the train, and as the doors closed she called to Myra: "Always remember me! Always."

Myra opened her eyes and realized she had been dreaming again. It was always the same kind of dream, always Myra trying to catch up to the woman with the dark hair. Once, they were climbing a mountain with Myra in pursuit, but it ended when Myra felt she was falling and screamed herself awake. Another time, they were in an amusement park and the woman turned to Myra and held out her arms. As Myra was about to touch her, the woman changed into a man with crooked teeth, bloodshot

Myra

Waking from her dreams left Myra in a cold sweat. She couldn't remember when the dreams started or what they meant to her. As a child, Gerta would wake her and hug her tight and Myra felt the comfort of being in her arms. The dreams appeared and disappeared throughout her life like a movie replaying something from her past. Something she couldn't remember, before there was Gerta and Carl.

She swung her feet over the bed and noticed the bed across from hers was neatly made up with everything in place. That was typical of Diana, her roommate. It was a sunny day for December, but that was Colorado for you, snow one day and sun the next. She hoped Diana would have a nice day skiing. The ski areas usually got more snow than down on the flat land of the University of Colorado. It was Sunday, Myra reminded herself, and the housemother's day off. She would have to make her own breakfast. She could put on her blue jeans since there was no place to go that required a dress. She looked at the small clock on her nightstand and could not believe that it was almost ten o'clock. She wrapped her bathrobe around her and grabbed the basket that held her towel, toothbrush, toothpaste, soap and lotion and went out the door to the bathroom down the hall. It had two shower stalls, two toilets and one big bathtub for the ten girls who lived on that floor, but it was always clean. It was an old house, because all the V12 sailors being trained here had taken over the freshman dorms. Myra didn't mind, although no one knew why the V12's were being trained here; it was most likely for the war in Europe. America had yet to declare war, but there had been a lot of talk that it could happen soon.

The hot water on her body revitalized her spirit.
She scrubbed her long dark hair with the bar of soap, as
she could not afford shampoo this month. Her naturally
curly hair cascaded down her back in ringlets. They
would dry that way, too, as Myra preferred the natural
look even if short hair was becoming more in fashion.
Myra could never afford to be in fashion, and just surviv-
ing was one of her goals in life. Myra's reflection in the
mirror pleased her. She would never tell anyone she felt
beautiful, but she did. Her long, dark hair had red high-
lights in the sun. It was her skin under her curly hair that
drew attention. Pale for a brunet but appearing soft and
creamy without a blemish. Her facial features were in line
in every way, with her perfect nose and wide brown eyes
and high cheekbones all beautifully arranged. She could
be a model, but Myra never gave that a thought. She had
been approached as a young teenager for such a job. The
nuns quickly nipped that idea in the bud and Myra felt
they were right to do so. Saving her soul, they said.

She got the scholarship to the University of Colorado by studying hard, and working as a waitress in a
cafe' near the orphanage, when she was allowed to do so.
Of course, her stay at the Queen of Heaven Orphanage for
Girls where discipline was part of her life helped her understand that she was the only one who could make her
life coherent. With that thought, Myra told herself, she
would have to explore her past now as an adult. She
would uncover what she had forgotten before her life in
Salida, Colorado, with Gerta and Carl. She was tired of

pretending that out in this wild world, someone searched for her. She had to resemble someone. Deep down she knew her life had a tale to be told and she was going in search of it; it was her holy grail.

Myra toweled herself off and wrapped the towel around her hair. In her room she brushed her hair back and dressed for the day. She felt hungry, since she had studied late last night, trying to be quiet so as to not wake Diana. Saturdays and Sundays in the freshman houses, you had to eat on your own. Myra had forgotten to eat in her desire to get her assignments done for Monday morning classes.

Downstairs in the large front room, there was a small group of girls sitting around talking and laughing. A girl named Betty noticed Myra and greeted her warmly.

"There are some fresh baked rolls in the kitchen, Myra. Judy here loves to cook. Would you like some?"

Myra smiled at her. "Oh yes. I am starved and I overslept. Thank you."

"I bought some milk, too, if you would like a glass," Betty said. "It didn't seem right to eat the rolls without milk and we were out. Mrs. Wright doesn't order enough for the weekend, but as long as she can show she is under her budget with the school, she won't spend a penny more."

The roll was good and the milk nice and cold.

They filled a big void inside Myra's stomach. After downing another roll, she took her glass of milk and went to join the girls in the front room. It was interesting to hear them talk about their families and events that were never a part of Myra's life. She placed her glass of milk on the little table beside the couch and sat on the end corner.

"Oh Myra! There was a package for you yesterday. Mrs. Wright had to go to Denver and asked me to give it to you. I almost forgot," Betty said. "I put it on the piano. Is it still there?" She asked Judy, who was sitting on the piano stool.

"Sure is!" Judy answered and tossed it over to Myra.

It was a small package, about the size of a compact or a package of cigarettes. The return address was unfamiliar, too: an Yvette Levine of New York City.

"Is it your birthday, Myra?" Betty asked her.

"No, it isn't," Myra said, "and I don't know the sender." She turned the small package in her hand to wondering if it was a mistake. "How weird. It is from New York and I don't know anyone in New York."

"Ah, a mysterious present for our silent roomie," Judy laughed, and the other girls laughed too, while offering their views about the package.

"I have scissors in my room. I had better go up and

open it carefully in case it really is a wrong address," Myra said as she stood up and grabbed her glass of milk with her free hand.

"Let us know what it is, Myra," Betty called to her as she went up the stairs.

In her room, Myra once again turned the package over and looked for the best way to open it so she could put it back together if it were not meant for her. But there it was, in a lovely, hand-written script, Myra Grainger, her name, as clear as could be.

The scissors cut neatly across the sealed paper and at last a white box appeared. Myra slowly lifted the lid off the box and held her breath. Inside a silver star brooch with little glass stones lay on a piece of folded paper. It looked familiar to Myra but she could not remember where she had seen it.

She picked out the paper and saw that it was a note. She laid the brooch down and unfolded the paper.

Dear Myra,

You don't know me, but I was asked by a very dear friend to send this to you. It took some time to find you, but Myra is not a common name and my friend knew the area in which you had lived. That helped me in my search. I hope you are pleased to have it again.

Yvette Levine

Myra was confused. When had she had this brooch? Who was Yvette's friend?

Betty knocked on the open door and entered smiling, interrupting Myra's thoughts. "I just couldn't wait to see what it is, so here I am. Do you mind?"

Myra felt too numb to say anything and just stared at the brooch in the box. Betty took it from her and looked at it. "Why, it is a Star of David, Myra. Are you Jewish?"

"Jewish?" she asked Betty. "Not that I know about. Is this Jewish?"

"Of course, you silly girl. Haven't you ever seen the Star of David before? Oh look, there is some writing on the other side of the note." Betty read the words: "*I have replaced some of the diamonds as requested by my friend. Y.*"

Myra grabbed the note from Betty and read it for herself. "I don't understand. I can't remember when I ever saw this before or owned it. Yet the note indicates that it belongs to me."

Betty reached for the folded note in Myra's hand and asked: "Can I read it, Myra? Maybe there is something you are missing in it."

Myra handed her the note and walked to the window. The sun was bright and people were walking along the curved sidewalks of the campus. Bright blue skies and fluffy white clouds drifted slowly across the mountain view. The brooch reflected a bright light across her face causing her to blink. She looked down at it again nestled in its cotton pad like a crown.

"Diamonds? I thought they were glass. I was told they were glass."

"Who told you that?" Betty asked.

Myra turned towards her with a confused look. "What did I just say?"

Betty shook her head and handed back the note. "You said someone had told you they were glass and not diamonds. Who told you?"

Before Myra could answer, they heard a commotion coming from downstairs. Betty bolted for the door while Myra put the brooch and the note in the box in her nightstand drawer. She could hear a burst of noise from below and decided to go see what was happening. The package could wait until later.

As she stood at the top of the stairs, she could hear the radio blasting away about airplanes and boats and Pearl Harbor. Betty looked up and saw her. "We have been attacked, Myra. Come down and listen with us."

The radio announcer was going crazy. His words

were slurred at times and confusion reigned everywhere. There was already a war in Europe with Germany attacking other countries: Poland, Czechoslovakia, Hungary, Austria. And they were advancing on France. England was being bombed and now the United States? Were the Germans now attacking us?

"The Japanese!" yelled Judy. "It's the Japanese. They are sinking our ships in Pearl Harbor!"

Then someone asked: "Where is Pearl Harbor?"

"In Hawaii, you dope. They are bombing Hawaii," Betty growled at the girl.

Myra came slowly down the stairs. She noticed the calendar posted on wall in the front hall to remind the girls of their schedules: December 7, 1941. "A date that will live in infamy," President Roosevelt would later declare in his speech to the nation. He also said: "There is nothing to fear but fear itself," a phrase Myra would remember for the rest of her life.

Chapter Three

1941 — Colorado

There was a draft that took some very impressive students from the campus scene. Others, who knew they would be drafted, joined the service they preferred rather than waiting to be called. It was a traumatic time for everyone and Myra was no different. What would happen to her Boettcher Scholarship? Myra had heard from Sister Bernadette who wrote her in November that she would welcome her for Christmas break. That was before the declaration of the war and now Myra wondered if the invitation was still good. Her monthly allowance was disappearing fast due to the season of gifts. Although she spent cautiously, she felt a hankie, a five-and-ten piece of jewelry or something of that nature, would make her feel better when her housemates gave her gifts. At least she didn't want them to feel how really poor she was. The pride she took in herself and her character would not allow for anything less nor allow her to ask for any help from her house-mates. However, Diana had borrowed some change from her at Thanksgiving, and suddenly when Myra wished for some change, Diana remembered.

Myra plunked the coins into the public phone in their house and called Sister Bernadette. How happy Sister was to hear from her and of course there was an empty bed that Myra could have for however long her Christmas break would last.

It was Sister Bernadette who encouraged Myra to apply for scholarships and it was Sister Bernadette who almost fainted when one of the state's best scholarships went to Myra. Sister Bernadette had been Myra's lifeline while living at Queen of Heaven Orphanage. She was the only one to know how deeply Myra wondered about her unknown past. It was Sister Bernie, as the girls called her, who truly seemed to understand and give motherly advice to Myra. Once she told Myra that some day God would give her the answers, if only she believed. Myra had confessed that she had no faith in Jesus, but she did believe in God, though he never seemed to hear her prayers. She felt then and always would feel like a piece of timber adrift in a rough and wild sea, she told the nun. After making the sign of the cross, Sister Bernie said she would pray for her, but Myra must always remain focused because her guardians, Gerta and Carl, had baptized her, after all, in the Catholic Church.

That was true, but had she been born a Catholic? Gerta had told her they would tell of her past when she was old enough to understand, but she never got to be old enough. Carl had gotten sick and Gerta could no longer take care of her. She was ten years old when, clutching her old suitcase close to her, she waved a tearful goodbye through the back window of a Social Service car and watched as Gerta stood crying on the dirt road next to the farm house. She had another home before at last she was sent to Denver and the Queen of Heaven Orphanage. By then, Carl had died and Gerta had moved to California to be with her son and his family. The eleven year old gave very little thought to her past as she settled in to a new life.

Sister Bernie took to Myra like a lost daughter and that alone gave the young girl a reason to advance in her studies and achievements. She wanted to please this lovely lady. So far, it had paid off well. It would be nice to remember the good times Sister Bernie shared with Myra and even the bad times when storms of despair and self pity took her over. She had so much to be grateful for in having Sister Bernadette in her life. At least God had given her that much.

The bus to Denver was crowded and some riders had to stand. Myra was lucky in finding a seat next to the rear doors. It was finally snowing on the plains and the highway looked slick and wet. The bus-load of people seem to be in a holiday mood even if the war loomed like a giant black cloud in the background. She watched a couple standing by her as they kissed softly and hugged each other. Myra heard their words and knew the young man was going to Denver to enlist and the young girl was scared. Her eyes glistened with tears, but he wiped them away with his coat sleeve. It was a sad parting for them yet Myra envied them. How wonderful it must be to be loved like that. How wonderful it must be just knowing that someone loved you and needed you, even if only for a short time.

Myra

Myra had very little experience in romantic life. She had attracted many admirers with her outstanding beauty, but she could never fully accept their motives as genuine. Something inside her always shut the doors of her heart before she really understood why. She had been abandoned too much in her life and now that she was an adult, she wanted no one to have the authority to hurt her. She wanted the loneliness and hurt of her childhood never to happen again. If there really was a God who loved her, as she had been told most of her life, she was sure He would help her deal with the twists and curves of life as it came towards her. She would be prepared. She would be on top of her studies and she would gain a faith in herself that surpassed anything in her life so far. She considered herself a survivor.

The Denver bus depot was a beehive of activity. Soldiers and sailors in uniform were mingling in and out of the crowd, searching for bus schedules or saying their goodbyes to family and friends. Myra retrieved her night bag and walked out the door into a cold and driving snow. She had to walk three blocks to Sixteenth Street to catch street car Number 28 which would take her to Northwest Denver and her destination on Federal Boulevard. The wind seemed to blow right through her and she pulled her knit hat tighter on her head. Why did this seem familiar to her? --- she asked herself. She had not ridden the bus down to Denver since she left the orphanage to attend the university at Boulder. What was it that flashed through her mind as she sloshed along on the wet pavement? Was someone holding her hand? She stopped in her tracks and looked at her night bag. Who was carrying the old suitcase she had always traveled with since she as long as she could remember? What was happening to her? Her mind flashed like a photographer's camera. What was it she saw in the flashes? The cold chilled her body and she moved along, thinking she must have dreamed something like this and it had left an impression on her thoughts. She just missed Number 28 and wondered whether if she had not stopped for that brief moment, she would have caught it. Now she would have to stand on the corner and wait another fifteen minutes to a half hour for the next car.

She looked around and saw the Woolworth Five and Ten in back of her. She would go in there to wait because she would freeze to death if she waited outside. As she entered, she saw a phone booth next to the outside wall. She entered the booth and put her bag on the floor as she collected the nickel she would need to call Sister Bernie. Sister Bernie sounded relieved to hear from her. Sister would have hot chocolate and homemade sugar cookies waiting for her when she got there. It was such a warm feeling for Myra to hear Sister's voice, someone who really cared for her, someone who really loved her. The operator interrupted their call saying their five minutes were up, so after quick goodbyes they were disconnected. There would be more time to talk when Myra got there.

Myra hung up the receiver and opened the booth door. She walked over to the counter to look for a small gift for Sister Bernadette. She had a lace handkerchief she found in a gift shop in Boulder, but maybe a Christian brooch like a cross or a dove would also be nice. She did find a brooch with the statue of Jesus on a gold cross for a quarter. It would look lovely on Sister's black robe and it was something she would be allowed to wear. Just as she reached into her purse to pay for it, there was a tap on her shoulder. She turned around to find the smiling face of a young soldier holding her night bag.

"Did you leave this in the phone booth?" he asked.

Myra looked at the bag and felt surprised that she could have walked off without her bag. "Oh my goodness," she exclaimed. "Yes, I did. How stupid of me. Thank you so much," she said reaching for the bag.

The young man laughed and shook his head. "You remind me of my sister. She is famous for losing things: a bag, her money, and her head if it wasn't connected to her shoulders!" His smile was contagious: white, even teeth and soft, full lips. Myra could not stop looking at him. When she realized she was staring, she looked down and said: "Well, she is lucky to have a brother like you to set things right."

"Oh I wouldn't say that. She's never found everything she's lost. I am hoping that now she is in college, she is more careful with her things."

Myra nodded and looked up at him: "Well, thank you again." She counted out her change and paid for the brooch and put it in her purse. The young man was still standing next to her and she had to pass him to get to the door. He noticed her movement and backed away for her to pass but followed close behind her.

"I am sorry, but you've done it again," he said, handing her bag to her again. "Maybe I should follow you home to make sure everything gets there."

"What am I thinking?" Myra said in surprise. She knew what she had been thinking: about the soldier with the glorious smile and twinkle in his blue eyes. His facial features were not bad either. It was as though they had been put together by Michaelangelo. He was indeed very charming and Myra was aware of her senses playing tricks on her. She had never been impressed by a man so suddenly as this before. She had to control her emotions or forget everything she had vowed to undertake in the quest for her holy grail.

"Do you have a car or someone to help you get home?" he said, smiling at her.

"No, I am waiting for my streetcar. It should be here in a few minutes. I just missed the last one and dashed in here to make a call." Myra felt like she was rambling.

He handed her the bag again and said: "Was it the Streetcar 28?"

Myra nodded her head and he laughed, "I missed it, too. Well at least we can keep each other company while we wait. Oh, by the way, my name is Eric Dawson. I am on my way to Little Rock, Arkansas. My aunt lives here and I thought I should stop by and spend some time with her. I think of her as my second mother"

Myra felt so comfortable in his presence that she felt free for the first time in her life to talk with a stranger. "I am Myra Grainger," she said, holding out her free hand to shake his. The electricity of his touch touched sent a thrill up her arm. "I am a freshman at the University of Colorado, down for Christmas."

Eric went on to tell her a little of his past. He was from Los Angeles but had spent several summers here in Colorado with his aunt and uncle who lived near Elitch Gardens in Northwest Denver. His uncle had died a few years ago and his aunt was a little lonely, even though she continued to have an active social life. She had taken him to concerts at City Park and the operettas at Cheesman Park. He loved fishing with his uncle for trout in the mountains near Idaho Springs and down south in the Platte River.

The conversation took up the time faster than Myra would have wanted it to. This man enthralled her. But as the streetcar stopped at the corner, they both bolted out the door and boarded the it. They dropped in their coins and found seats together after Eric asked her if she would not mind his company a little longer.

"So, my fair lady, what is the story of your life? I have talked your ear off, now it is your turn." Eric smiled

Now Myra felt the door of her soul beginning to close. What would he understand of her life? He would ask her questions she didn't want to think about. He would find out what a plain Jane she was, someone who probably didn't belong in a university at all, though she was sure CU was exactly where she belonged.

She forced herself to ride the curve, "Oh, I have lived here for awhile. I got a scholarship to CU. Outside of that, there is nothing much interesting about me." Would that satisfy him enough to get him to continue about his own life?

"I don't believe that for a minute. Your parents must be so proud of you. What about brothers and sisters? Surely you have a sister as pretty as you at home." Eric noticed her features darkened at his comment. "Oh, I didn't mean to disturb you. I am sorry, Myra."

Myra had to stop his curiosity so she said: "Actually, I have no parents or brothers or sisters. I grew up in an orphanage, the Queen of Heaven Orphanage. It is on this route and I am going there to spend Christmas."

Eric's smile faded and he shook his head. "I am so sorry. I didn't mean to pry. I thought a girl like you, so poised and beautiful, had to spring from a heck of a family."

Myra managed a weak smile. "It's alright. I'm used to it. I do appreciate your kind admiration of me, but I am not really worthy of it yet. Some day I may be, but not yet," she said from her heart.

"Will you be with other orphans? Are you allowed back in to the graces of the nuns after you leave?" Eric asked her, not smiling now.

"My closest friend and mentor is Sister Bernadette. She invited me to come down for my first Christmas alone. She is like the mother I never had and so here I am. I was buying her a small gift at Woolworth's. Yes, there will be children there, but Sister Bernie has plenty of help to care for them during the holidays. She will be alone in spirit. That is why I am here. Just to be with her." That said, Myra thought they had reached the end of subject. However, Eric wasn't finished.

"I have extended my stay here because my regiment won't be ready to form until after New Year's Eve, on January 3rd in Little Rock, Arkansas. I left home earlier so I could stay with Aunt Edna. What say if you and your nun friend have Christmas dinner with us? Aunt Edna has no children but loves to entertain. She always invites some of her distant relatives and friends who have no families nearby, and I know she would love to include you and Sister Bernadette. What do you think?" He was so serious Myra had a hard time saying no.

"I doubt that Sister Bernadette would accept an invitation from someone she didn't know. (Myra knew that wasn't true.) It is very kind of you, but I think we better not."

Eric would not take no for answer. "How do you know? You haven't asked her yet. Let her make up her own mind. I would like very much to see you again and what better way than in the company of two old ladies we love?"

"Please, Mr. Dawson, It sounds lovely and your aunt sounds very nice, but think about it. We've just met a few minutes ago. Even though it is Christmas, we hardly know each well enough for that."

"Look, there is a war going on, Myra. Time is short. And my name is Eric. Did you forget?" He smiled at her.

"My stop is next. Thank you again for the enjoyable conversation and the invitation. I wish you a safe tour of duty and a very Happy Christmas." Myra reached up and pulled the rope that sounded the bell.

Eric handed her bag to her and said: "This isn't goodbye, Myra. I will see you again. I think we are destined to get to know each other better. Until then, no goodbyes, please. Just see you soons."

With that, the streetcar doors opened and Myra hopped down from the platform and waved to Eric as the car moved on.

———

Sister Bernadette saw Myra coming up the steps of

the orphanage and opened the double doors for her. Myra swept in like a wet child needing a hug. Sister hugged her tight then proceeded to help her off with her wet coat. "You really must get a raincoat, dear. You will catch your death of a cold."

Sister Bernadette was taller than most of the nuns. Her bone structure was large and her round face had the spiritual look of an angel. Her cheeks always had a reddish glow just where a cosmetic rouge would have been painted, but on Sister, it was as natural as green leaves on a spring day. It was her warm smile that Myra first recognized about Sister. It was a true and compassionate smile that captivated everyone lucky enough to be in her company.

Her familiar words warmed Myra's heart and it felt good to be back where someone nurtured her. How silent and serene the main entry seemed now.

"Is there no one here tonight?" She asked the nun who was shaking Myra's cloth coat to expel any wetness clinging to it.

"Oh, a few of the children are already in bed, but some have been invited to stay in private homes for the week."

"Ah, yes," Myra said. "I remember those occasions. Where are the sisters?"

"Sister Theresa is in the kitchen making you some

cookies. I think Sister Maria is already in bed. You know how she values her sleep? Mother Superior is still in her office and asked that you come to see her before she retires," Sister answered her in a hushed voice. The echoes of their voices in the great hall might have disturbed the peaceful atmosphere of the building, Myra thought.

"Come dear," Sister Bernie motioned and led her down the familiar staircase to the lower level where the smell of cookies and incense mixed with other holy aromas that Myra recalled, and she felt safe and at home. Dim candle-shaped lights lit their way to the white doors at the end of the hallway. Myra wondered how many novice sisters-in-training there were behind the closed doors they passed on their way to the kitchen.

In the kitchen, Sister Theresa was placing a tray of hot cookies on a counter top. She turned towards Myra and held out her arms. "My dear, we have missed you so much." Myra gratefully received Sister's hug.

"I have only been gone since September, Sister, but is great to be back again even if for only a short visit."

"Let me have your little bag, Myra." Sister Bernadette reached for it. "We certainly made the right choice for your gift when you won that scholarship, dear," she said, putting Myra's wet coat on the back of a chair near the stove and the gift bag near the hall door.

Drinking the hot chocolate revived Myra's Christmas spirits. Before the Queen of Heaven Orphanage, the holiday after leaving Gerta and Carl had been a night-mare. It was only one Christmas, but she would never forget the horror of it. She wanted to forget it, but since that time every Christmas reminded her of that fearful Holy Night.

After finishing her chocolate and having a few cookies, she paid a visit to the Mother Superior. A knock on Mother Superior's office door led to a brief look-over by the Good Mother, and a short catch-up conversation (for which Myra was glad to report) marked the end of her long day. Or so she thought.

The brief body wash in the small room Sister Bernie had given her relaxed Myra, and she crawled contentedly under the wool blankets of the double bed. Sister Bernadette knocked twice and cracked open the door. "Do you have everything you need, Myra?"

For a minute, Myra wanted to pretend she was sleeping, but Sister Bernadette was as close to her as any mother could be. They filled the roles as mother and daughter which each dearly needed in her lonely life.

"I am fine Sister. Aren't you ready for bed?"

"I am, but I wanted to talk with you alone without the other sisters around."

Sister Bernadette stepped into the room and quietly closed the door. She pulled back the wool blanket and

"Talk about what Sister?" Myra asked.

"Your faith, my dear. I am worried about you. For a Catholic girl you seem to be so distant in your belief of Jesus. You turned away from his teachings and Father Lou noticed that. You're free now from our Catholic rites, but I fear for your religious spirit. If you do not follow the life we have shown you here, what will happen to you?"

Myra laughed: "Sister, you know I have tried. I just don't feel the same as you feel about the Catholic faith. Maybe something in my past is part of the reason. You know I can't remember anything before I was five and living with Gerta and Carl Grainger. They made me a Catholic. If I were born a Catholic, wouldn't I have been baptized before the age I was?"

"It doesn't matter now, Myra. Your being Catholic should sustain you for the life you have ahead of you. You are eighteen now and without faith in our teachings you could make wrong choices and be lost."

"What I want, Sister, is proof that I was born of Catholic parents. I have to know because I received something in the mail that makes me doubt I was." Myra had brought the brooch with her and now reached over Sister Bernie for her purse.

Before she could reach it, Sister Bernadette stood up and gave her the purse from the chair. "I don't understand, Myra. What did you receive?"

Myra opened her purse and retrieved the little white box. She uncovered it and held it up for Sister to see.

"This is what someone sent me. Do you know what it is?"

Sister grabbed her chest. "It's the Star of David, dear. Who sent this to you?"

"There is the note that came with it and another sentence on the back of the note too,'" Myra said, handing the box to the nun.

Sister Bernadette picked up the brooch and examined it closely. Then she took out the note and read it. Sister's complexion turned pale as though she had seen an apparition. "Oh Myra, what is this? I don't know what to make of it. I know nothing of your past except what came with you and your baptismal records from the St. Joseph Catholic Church in Salida. There wasn't a birth certificate."

Myra motioned for Sister to sit beside her on the bed. "I know, Sister, but are you sure? It could have been overlooked. Is there anything else here that I came with?"

"I am not sure. We were so excited about your scholarship, we may not have looked in the storeroom when you left. We could look tomorrow, if you want, but don't get your hopes up."

There was silence for a minute. "Are you still having your dreams, dear?"

"Yes, and I am still chasing the older lady with dark hair. It is as if she is trying to tell me something, but the only words I can remember when she faces me are 'Don't forget me, Myra.' And that seems to be the cue to wake up. Once in awhile, and I have never told you this before, a man with blood shot eyes, stinking of liquor and smoke, is chasing me."

"That had to be those horrible people who wanted to adopt you before you came here. I thank God every day that you had a teacher who realized something wasn't right with those people," Sister said, shaking her head in disbelief. "If their daughter had not been so disruptive and spoiled, the teacher might not have noticed. You would have been in a lot of trouble."

Myra didn't want to talk about that time in her life. "Sister, I am sure you are as tired as I am, so why don't we call it a day now. Tomorrow, I would like very much to see if anything of mine is still in the storeroom."

Sister Bernadette gave Myra the box and brooch and bent to kiss her cheek. "You are right. We will begin our search tomorrow. Good night, my dear girl."

Alone in the darkness, Myra wished Sister had not brought up the memory of the Carpenter family. She was sure that Gerta would not have allowed her to be adopted by a family that would abuse her. How was anyone to know? They wanted a companion for their Susan, not another a daughter. When Myra's school grades had out shown Sue's, the girl became malicious towards her: salt in her hot chocolate, hiding her clothes, and at times, destroying library books for which Myra was blamed. But it was Mr. Carpenter that scared Myra the most and brought the nightmares to her dreams. He acted as though he wanted to comfort her and would hug her tightly after an altercation with his wife or daughter. His hands rubbed up and down her body, and when he started visiting her bed at times when the others slept, he hurt her badly. It was the scratch on her neck and the bruises on her upper legs that alerted the teacher. Had the teacher not been there and noticed when Sue pushed her down on the gym floor causing her skirt to fly over her head, no one would have cared. When the family was confronted with the facts, they told lies about Myra being a misfit and having a horrible imagination. They canceled the adoption. No action was taken against Mr. Carpenter as people saw him as an upstanding citizen and family man who was trying to help an unruly orphan. It didn't matter what was true, for at last Myra was free from him and from living with them. Only Sister Bernadette listened to her story and believed her. Maybe Sister too had been in a similar situation because she said she understood and thanked God for Myra's salvation.

Myra did dream that night but not of the lady with the dark hair or the man with the blood shot eyes and foul breathe. She dreamed, instead, of Eric Dawson. His smile stayed lingered her memory and his spirit seem to reach out to her, filling her with warmth for a man that she nev-

Chapter Four

Myra woke up feeling rested and at peace. It was nice to be back in a familiar place knowing Sister Bernadette was there for her. She recalled yesterday's encounter with the young man named Eric. How nice it would be to spend part of the Christmas Season with him and meet his family. However, it was not possible. Sister Bernadette would never leave the orphanage for her own pleasure. The children left behind for the holiday needed to know they were loved and cared for by all the sisters.

Myra sat up and yawned stretching her arms high above her head. She found the long robe Sister had laid on the chair last night and quickly slipped it on. She picked up the towel, soap and washcloth on the desk, grabbed her little overnight bag and headed towards the shower room. Memories of her time in the orphanage came rushing back to her as she pulled the cloth shower curtains closed and turned on the water. How refreshing it felt to be back in the only place that felt like home to her. She could have lingered there longer, but she remembered they were to search for clues to her past, for papers that might be hidden in the deep basement. She knew Sister would have already had breakfast and done her vespers, so Myra hurried and dried herself off. She put on her clean undergarments and quickly washed the ones she had worn the day before. She hung them on a hanger she had found in the shower room and carried all her belongings back to her room. She had no sooner finished dressing in her black sweater and skirt than Sister Bernie knocked on the door. The usual good-mornings and how-did-you-sleeps were exchanged. The breakfast plate of scrambled eggs and bacon with toast was delicious and Myra would have asked for seconds, but knew better. The budget for the home was always slim and Myra's presence would be a drain on the food that rightfully should be for the children living there.

At last, dishes rinsed off and put away, Myra and Sister Bernadette headed towards the deep basement, beneath the one where the kitchen was located. The light bulb above the doorway flickered some then glowed brightly as they descended the narrow, dusty stairs. The smell of musk, dust, and rot filled the air and Myra had a sneezing spell.

"This place needs to be cleaned out, but we seldom come down here. So, it has not been thought about too much. Such a pity too," said Sister. "It must hide lots of things we could use."

Sister Bernie pulled the chain of another bulb hanging at the bottom of the stairwell. Gray and dark walls stacked with boxes, broken furniture, books, and bits of ancient appliances, stretched throughout the long rooms of the basement.

"My goodness, Myra, where do we start?" Sister

asked.

"If things were put down here and never touched again, they would be in order of the time they arrived. If we can find something relating to the year I arrived, we might not have to tear everything apart."

"I have no idea what was put where, but that's a start. Let's dig in," Sister said, pulling a broken chair off some boxes.

So they began. Every time Sister thought they could use something upstairs, she set it next to the stairwell and explained to Myra what it was and how it could be used now. It was a tedious job and took up all of their morning. Sister was ready to stop the search for the day, but Myra was determined to continue looking for anything that might help her understand her lost past. Sister said that many people cannot recall their life before the age of five or six, but Myra knew differently. She had heard others recall being younger than five and the memories that stayed with them. She was determined to look alone, if Sister Bernie didn't want to continue. After lunch, Myra continued searching while Sister took a nap. The children had had their lunch earlier and a playtime outside, before resting on their beds for an hour, whether they slept or not. It was quiet in the dungeon, as Myra thought of the dark rooms she rummaged through, but she continued to pull out boxes and other articles Sister Bernie would have taken the time to examine and explain. By late afternoon, she had only covered a tiny part of the whole mess. She would have continued if Sister Bernie had not called down for her to come up immediately. Her voice sounded more authoritarian than usual, so Myra brushed her hands together, pulled the light switch off and came up to the bright, sunny hallway.

"What is it Sister?" she asked, but Sister merely stood there for a moment with her hands on her hips as though she troubled by something concerning Myra.

"I have just had the strangest phone call, dear," she said, motioning Myra towards the kitchen area. "Do you know an Eric Dawson? I think that was name," she said, looking at a piece of paper in her hand.

A surprised Myra answered: "Yes. I met him last night on the streetcar. Well, actually, he was waiting for the streetcar as I was and we struck up a conversation. He sat by me on the way here, but that is all. I hardly know him. Why? Did he call here?"

"No, not him, his Aunt, Mrs. Rogers." Sister opened the kitchen door where Sister Theresa was stirring a boiling pot on the stove. "Sister Theresa took the call and couldn't find you, so she woke me knowing I could locate you. However, as I took the phone, the lady said she would also like to talk to me." Sister sat down and poured some tea into a cup sitting on the table. She motioned for Myra to sit too, but Myra refused the tea she offered.

"Did you know he is in the Army?"

"Yes, he told me. He said his aunt, a widow, lives here and that he came to visit her before he reports for duty in Little Rock, Arkansas, on January 3rd. He also invited us to have Christmas dinner with them, but I thought he was only talking."

"Us?" Sister Bernadette asked. "He meant me too?"

"Yes, I had told him how you invited me to come here for my first Christmas on my own," Myra answered. "But I refused, knowing that you would never accept, and that I would never go alone, even if I wanted to."

"Well, young lady, after his aunt, Mrs. Rogers explained his plight and his desire to have a lovely Christmas dinner to remember over there, she added that he had told her of meeting you, and how nice it would be to have us as guests."

Myra put her hand over her mouth and giggled a little. "I can't believe it. How brazen an act to have his aunt call you. Of course you refused, didn't you?"

"No," Sister Bernie said. "I thought it was very nice of her so I accepted. Her nephew will pick us up right after church, and drive us to her home. I couldn't thank her enough. What a sweet lady. Why did you think I would not go?"

Myra shook her shoulders sheepishly. "I didn't think you could leave here on Christmas Day. You were

"Well, there are other sisters here, and I do have seniority since I have been here as long as I have been. I welcome the chance to get away at times." Sister took a big gulp of her tea, "She was kind enough to say they were not Catholic but hoped that would not make a difference. I told her we are all God's children and I know nothing in the Bible that says we can't break bread together."

"I guess I had better have some of your tea then, Sister Bernie. I can't believe Eric really meant what he said when we parted."

"What was that?"

"He said he would see me again. I thought it was all just his way of try to make an impression on me."

"Were you impressed, Myra?" Sister smiled at her.

"To tell the truth, I was a little impressed and I did think about him last night after I was in bed. However, Sister, and please don't start teasing me, I knew he was just another person flying by who would flutter in and out of my life."

Sister Theresa turned to them and said: "You two are like two peas in the pod. Look how you get on so well after all these years. Enough talk now; help me get the tables ready for dinner."

With that request, both women started carrying

"Did you find anything of interest, Myra?' Sister Bernie asked.

"No, but I won't stop until I search it all, even if I have to come down on weekends to do so.

Chapter Five

There was little time for Myra to go down to the sub-basement on her second day at the orphanage due to the Christmas decorating that needed to be done in and around the building and the large Christmas tree some kind people had brought for the orphans. The children were delighted even though it was snowing hard outside, which meant no outside playtime today. The older girls helped the younger ones place ornaments higher than they could reach. They gave an imaginary tale for each piece they hung, and everyone laughed although the tale might or might not have been funny. Myra helped Sister Theresa in the kitchen and licked the bowls clean of their raw cookie dough only after Sister Theresa had used most of it to make trees, gingerbread men and crosses. It felt so good to be back in the folds of the orphanage. It had been a happy place, and although Myra was sure God didn't hear her when she begged Him to help her remember her past, Sister Bernie had consoled her and made her believe in a better future. Often, Myra had stood below the large statue of Jesus in the chapel, studying his features, and seeing only a man. Myra felt that if he was the Son of God, then she was also a daughter of God. A God who let this man die on the cross and let her earliest memories be erased. Yet, she felt in her heart that maybe

God had a reason. After all, Jesus became an icon of religious belief at the time when pagan gods showed little compassion for humans. Only kings and noblemen counted then in a society devoted to greed, war, and building monuments to themselves. But did God rescue the poor by allowing Jesus to be crucified? Did he really rise from the dead? How Sister Bernadette scolded her for the blasphemy of such doubts when Myra told her how she felt. But, after Sister scolded her, she took Myra in her arms, trying to discover what it was about this child that brought out her pity. Sister Bernadette never revealed to the other sisters or to Mother Superior what Myra said, and she advised Myra never to speak of her questions to them. Sister was sure they would pack Myra off to a lunatic hospital when all the child needed was love.

After lunch had been served and Myra and the sisters were cleaning up the kitchen, Mother Superior sent for Myra. There in her office sitting in her high-backed, cushioned chair, Mother Superior seemed to have shrunk in the years since Myra came there. Her tiny face peeked out from her wimple as though she were a child trying to be an adult. Her eyes were like round, black dots on her face and seemed out of place with the rest of her features. Her quiet, squeaky voice seemed weaker to Myra, who had heard that Mother Superior had suffered a small stroke but had bounced back like the dark angel she portrayed.

"I understand, Myra, that you and Sister Bernadette have been invited to a Christmas dinner. Is that correct?" She motioned for Myra to sit before her across the large desk.

"Yes, Mother. It is an invitation from a family who lives near here," Myra said as she settled in the wooden chair.

"I understand you met the young soldier of the family on the streetcar."

"Yes, Mother, I did and I refused his invitation. It was his aunt, Mrs. Rogers, who called Sister Bernadette. It was very nice of her."

"Yes, my dear, but I understand they are not Catholic. It is hardly a proper way to celebrate Christmas."

"Mother Superior, I appreciate your generosity in offering me a room here for the holidays, but I am not under the rules of the house any more. Sister Bernadette has been loyal to you and the church for more years than I can count. Why would one Christmas dinner with people who are not of our faith be so evil? It is wartime, Mother. Cannot the church make this concession for the war effort? The young man is off to war and this could be his last Christmas ever, God forbid. Can we not bestow on him what may be his last request?"

The old nun looked down at the rosary beads she had stopped counting when Myra entered the room. She had to think before she answered this girl whom Sister Bernadette always defended. She was turning into a beautiful woman and from Mother Superior's knowledge of her, Myra was also a scholar who gave pride and good standing to the community. After a long silence, she raised her head and looked Myra in the eyes.

"Well, my dear child, I guess there would not be any harm for in having dinner in the home of a non-Catholic. It would be a pity to let the young man go off to war thinking we Catholics have no feelings for people of other faiths. I think Sister Bernadette will enjoy herself and she can keep an eye on you."

Myra felt some compassion for this old woman whose life had always been cloistered in a faith from which Myra felt she was moving away. "Thank you, Mother. I am sure Sister Bernadette will enjoy herself. I do hope you have a very nice and holy Christmas."

A nod from the old nun meant their meeting was over and Myra felt relieved.

It was much later, after the older children had wrapped some of the gifts sent to the orphanage by charitable organizations, that Myra was able once again to go to the sub-basement. Sister Bernie had a few sick children to nurse, knowing candy canes and chocolate balls were most likely the cause.

It was a little spooky to be roaming alone down there, but Myra kept her fear in check as she continued to poke around and pull things off of piles of junk. She uncovered an old photo of a group of nuns poised on the front steps of the orphanage. Examining it closer, Myra was able to pick out Sister Bernie, a tall and smiling nun whose face showed a beauty Myra had never before realized she had. She dusted it off and set it by the stairs. If it was put down here, supposedly no one wanted it, but she did. She had never seen Sister Bernie as a young woman. How old was this photo, Myra wondered, turning it around. On the back were the names in order: front row, second row and so forth. A Mother Superior was positioned at the top, but it was not the nun Myra knew as Mother Superior, the nun who was now the head of the orphanage. There was a date on the back, but it was blurry, and Myra would have to get a better view of it in brighter light later.

Myra had just returned to her search when she heard her name being called. It must be Sister Bernie, Myra thought, and yelled up: "I am down here."

No one answered.

"Sister Bernie," Myra yelled up again, "is that you?"

No answer again, but suddenly a box fell in the darkest part of the room, scattering its books across the floor. Myra quickly went to that area, straightened the box out, and began putting the books back in. As she reached for books on the floor her hand touched something soft and furry. She yelled and jumped back. If it was a mouse or animal it didn't move. Controlling her fear, Myra bent down to see it better. A small, brown furry arm was all that was visible. Myra touched it to see if it moved. When it did not move, Myra pulled it out and there was a little teddy bear, a child's toy. A feeling of calmness came over her. This was the teddy bear Gerta often gave her when she cried or was sick. Myra hadn't seen it for years. The Carpenters never let her have any of her belongings when she went to live with them. She remembered watching them thrust a piece of luggage at the official who had came to pick her up, saying it belonged to the wicked girl. In the trauma of the events that surrounded Myra at that time, there was no room for luggage or her past belongings in her thoughts. She picked up the teddy bear and hugged it close to her chest. "Oh, my little bear, where have you been?"

"What have you there, Myra? And why are you back there in the darkness?" It was Sister Bernie standing under the stairwell light.

"Oh Sister, look! I have found my old teddy bear. I haven't seen it for years. Oh Sister, I am getting closer. I just know it. My little bear." Myra walked towards her and held out the bear for her to see. "I always called it Teddy, but she called it just Mr. Bear."

"Who called it Mr. Bear, dear?" Sister asked.

Myra frowned as she looked at the toy bear. "I don't know." Then Myra remembered her name being called. "Were you calling me a few minutes ago?"

"No," Sister answered. "It would have disturbed the sisters this late at night."

Sister took the bear and flicked it on the railing of the stairs. Dust particles flew out of its body. "It is very dirty, dear. Maybe we should try to wash it."

"No, I will clean it. If we wash it, it may fall apart and it is very old."

Sister Bernie gave the bear back to her and motioned for Myra to head up the stairs. "It is time for bed now, Myra. You have been very busy today and tomorrow will be more of the same with Christmas Eve coming tomorrow night and the Mass at St. Catherine's."

Myra knew what Sister Bernie meant. They would prepare for Christmas Eve and the children would nap before they all lined up to walk the few blocks down Federal Boulevard to St. Catherine's Church for midnight mass. It was a tradition of the orphanage and nothing would ever change it. Father Lou at St. Catherine's always gave a lovely mass. Although Myra questioned her faith, Father Lou made the celebration enjoyable with treats for the orphans and his jolly laugh like Santa as they left to walk back to the orphanage, most of the time in very cold weather. Sister Bennie would sing Christmas carols and insist everyone join in. It made the cold walk bearable for the children. When they arrived back at the orphanage, hot chocolate and cookies would be waiting. All the gifts had name-tags and they were always stacked in separate piles to be opened in the morning. Everyone thought Santa Claus had come while they were at mass, all but Myra. She never believed in a Santa Claus as a child, because she was afraid that if he were real, he too would abandon her as everyone else had done.

Myra picked up the picture Sister Bernie did not notice and they climbed up to the warm hallway outside the kitchen door. Good nights were said and Myra climbed the lower steps up to the front hallway and up more stairs to the room they have given her. She felt tired but more than that excited by the finding of her old teddy bear. She laid him on her pillow and looked him over. "What secrets will you unlock for me, Mr. Bear?"

A shiver shook her body. She called him Mr. Bear again. Sister asked her who had called him Mr. Bear earlier. Myra didn't know, but someone had. She would think about it in the morning, for she was very tired. That night she dreamed of the woman again. This time the woman had Teddy and held it out for Myra to take, but just as Myra reached out for the bear, the woman took it back to her breast and said, "Remember me, Myra."

The dream jolted Myra out of her sleep and she sat up and looked around. The dream was so real. Only the sounds of a car or two driving through the snow outside her window sliced through the silence. She got up and walked to the window. It was snowing lightly and the street below glistened from the streetlight's reflections. She closed her eyes for a minute then looked out again to see a wide highway with sleek cars traveling dizzyingly fast. Three lanes of the road went west, and a barrier stood between it and another three-lane highway with cars speeding east. Myra stared at the sight as though she were in a movie theater. She looked back at the bed and the surroundings.   Nothing had changed, but as she glanced outside again, the huge highway was gone and the street looked as it did before.

She must have been sleepwalking. What other explanation could there be? The cold penetrated her body and she hurried back to the bed. She wondered if she was going crazy. Maybe the Carpenters had been right. She was a wicked person who made up lies about what had happened to her. Then she looked at the teddy bear lying next to her. A flash of understanding came to her. "You are not a liar," she reminded herself.

Chapter Six

A winter sun filtered through sheer drapes of the long windows in the parlor of the Queen Of Heaven Orphanage. Earlier, excited children had opened their Christmas gifts and sung Christmas carols and examined each other's gifts. Later, they cleaned up the wrapping paper from the gifts and marched into the dining room for a large breakfast. Then it was free time. Some of the orphans who had been taken to private homes for the holiday started to return. Myra always thought this was an unfair policy for the orphanage to participate in. Did they not realize how the children not picked felt? She had been to three homes during her seven years there, but she also knew how it felt to be left behind. If ever one wanted to crawl into self-pity that was the start. It should be all or no children included on the holidays. She knew drawing names out Father Lou's hat made the choices random but it still didn't seem fair.

Myra sat on a sofa near the side windows looking out at the street that had suddenly become a highway last night. She was sure it was just another dream but it was confusing. She remembered getting out of bed and walking to the window. Federal Boulevard was a main street in front of the orphanage and during the day, had a lot of traffic. So, why was this quiet side street turned into a six-lane highway Myra had never seen before? The neat Victorian houses and cottages across the street were like a painting from a famous artist. She felt her dreams were drawing her back to her beginnings, waking her lost memory. So how did that image last night figure into her life?

"Here you are Myra. All dressed and ready to go, are you?" Sister Bernie quipped as she entered the room, obviously as anxious as Myra.

Myra had put on the red sweater Sister Bernie had knitted for her Christmas gift. It looked rather nice over her black skirt and she found her inexpensive locket on a fake gold chain at the bottom of her overnight bag, which enhanced her attire.

"I just love this sweater Sister. I can't thank you enough. You are such an expert with the knitting needles." Myra smiled up at her.

"And I want to thank you for the religious brooch. Does it not look elegant on this drab black robe?" Sister looked around the room before she continued. "I know I should not say that, but I must confess I have longed to wear what most women wear at times."

"You look great and you always do."

"Myra, I was thinking about the silver brooch someone sent you. Wasn't there a return address? If they are real diamonds, surely no one in their right mind would mail something so expensive without insuring it, which would mean a return address?"

"Yes," Myra answered. "There was a return address. It was from a Yvette Levine in New York City. I did write back, but the letter was returned to me marked, 'Moved. Forward address not known.' It was strange too, because it looked as though it had been opened and it was not a stamped message but a hand written one on the envelope. The hand writing was not the same as the note with the brooch."

Sister shook her head, "How strange. But it could be that a different person lives there now and opened it by mistake. That person could have resealed it and mailed it back to you."

"If that is true Sister, Yvette had to move fast. I wrote the next day and my letter came back two days before I came here. I will do some more checking on it after the holidays, but it is very curious."

The loud gong of a doorbell rang in the front hall. Myra stood up and started towards the entrance but Sister Theresa was already opening the door. There was Eric dressed in civilian clothes looking so handsome. Before he saw Myra he was telling Sister Theresa that he was here to pick up Myra and Sister Bernadette. Then he spotted Myra coming into the hallway entrance and smiled at her.

"Ah, here is one of my passengers now," he said. "Merry Christmas, Myra."

Myra smiled back and nodded to him, "We've had a lovely Christmas so far."

Sister Bernadette had followed Myra and held out her hand to Eric. "How do you do? I am Sister Bernadette and how kind of your aunt to invite us for dinner."

Eric smiled at her and shook her hand. "It is a pleasure to meet you Sister. It is my aunt and I who feel honored to have such lovely dinner guests."

"This is Sister Theresa, Eric. She is the main cook here and very good one at that," Myra said as she motioned to the nun besides her. Sister Theresa blushed and bowed her head. "Myra has always given me such nice comments but I do like to cook. That reminds me, it is time for our dinner hour too and the children will be hungry. We had a large lunch hour, so it is only snacks for tonight." With that said, Sister Theresa turned to Myra and Sister Bernie and told then to have a nice time. The she walked to the hallway leading to the stairs.

Eric clapped his hands together and asked, "Are you two ready? It is a bit chilly out. Can I get your coats?"

"Thank you, my dear boy. They are in the closet over there," Sister Bernie said as she pointed to double doors on the side wall. Eric helped them both with their coats and opened the large entrance doors. The chill of the evening air was a reminder that the sun had just set and old man winter was present. Eric helped Sister Bernie into the back seat of the 1939 Nash and then opened the front passenger seat for Myra. The ride was not too far a distance from the orphanage. Up 38th Avenue to Tennyson, then right for three blocks to 35th where Eric parked in front of a lovely house sitting on the corner with a view of the valley and Sloan's Lake below. A Christmas tree showed through the front window and a Christmas wreath was on the front door. It looked like a painting, so cozy and comfortable.

The door was opened before they reached it. A nicely attired lady met them as they entered. She wore pearls around her neck with matching earrings. Her dress was green velvet, which complimented her stylishly short silver hair. She was a delicate woman with small hands and a dimpled smile.

"You must be Myra," she said as helped her with her coat. "And you must be Sister Bernadette?" she said, giving Myra's coat to Eric as she helped Sister out of hers.

"Now how could you tell us apart?" laughed Sister Bernie. "We are twins, you know," she said with a wink, which sent all of them laughing.

"I know I am going to enjoy your guardian, Myra. What a delightful lady," Eric's aunt exclaimed as she led them into the front parlor where the Christmas tree stood.

"I can see that Eric is tongue-tied by you Myra, so

let me introduce myself. I am Edna Rogers, Eric's aunt. His mother and I were sisters. When she died I rather took over the mother part for Eric and his sister Elizabeth. It was a long distance mothering, but we made the most of it, didn't we dear?"

"Oh, I am sorry Aunt Eddie, but you never gave me the chance to get started. So now that is over, shall we all have a seat?" Eric smiled as he motioned the women to sit on the long sofa against the wall. There was fire burning in the fireplace next to the Christmas tree, and behind the tree, a chair with a man's legs visible.

Eric bent around the tree and said, "I would like to introduce another guest, if he can peek around the tree."

An older man poked his head out of the space between the chair and the tree.

"This is Sam Hirsch, my aunt's lawyer and friend for more years than I can remember." Eric said.

The man stood up and reached out to shake their hands as Eric introduced them. He was a stately gentlemen with hair streaked in gray and properly dressed for a dinner out on the town. Myra thought he must have been very handsome as a youth for he had a debonair air about him. He also had an accent in his speech, which only made him more attractive.

Mrs. Rogers had disappeared into the kitchen but returned with a young woman and a small boy. "Here are some more of our guests; Eric, you must introduce. Sofia will be out as soon as she checks the turkey which is driving Annie crazy."

The young woman, Stella, was a distant cousin of Eric's and the little boy was Todd, her six-year-old son. It turned out Sofia was Stella's widowed mother. Stella's husband was in the Air Force and in training in Oxnard, California, where she and Todd would move after the holidays. Sofia entered the room and was properly introduced, but the contrast between mother and daughter was very noticeable. Stella was tall and thin and had nice features; whereas Sofia was short and seemed to have a permanent scowl on her round face. Her lips turned downward and she scrutinized Myra as though she disliked her on sight, but Sister Bernadette received a much warmer reception.

The dining room was behind closed glass doors which Mrs. Rogers opened with glee. "It is time for the feast of the year. Everyone has a place card, so find your place and we will be served by my adorable Annie who does wonders with the menu."

Annie, Myra found later, was a live-in helper for Mrs. Rogers and had been since Mr. Roger died. She hustled bringing in dishes of delicious odor, dishes looking like they belonged on the cover of *Life* magazine. The food was as good as Mrs. Rogers said it would be, and guests praised Annie every time she entered the room with another tray of food or took away dirty dishes. Myra thought Annie must have been in her fifties because she wore her gray-blonde hair in a bun brushed back in a sleek style, making her face look plump and rounded, like a washer woman of the old days. Annie was built round and short but Myra was sure she could hold her own if ever she got mad or had to defend herself.

Eric kept Myra busy with conversations about school and about subjects that had no meaning to either of them. They both knew that fact, but with the guests around them, anything personal would seem inappropriate. So, they made the best of the situation until the dinner was over and they all returned to the parlor. Eric settled himself on the sofa next to Myra as Sister Bernadette had an audience who found joy in her adventures with the orphans. Little Todd hung on to every word and settled at Sister's feet, which pleased her to no end.

When after-dinner drinks were being served with Eric's help, Myra shared the end table next to the sofa with Sam Hirsch. She studied him for a minute and then asked, "I hope you won't think I have overstepped my boundaries, but are you Jewish?"

His face showed no emotion as he stared at her. "Would it make a difference if I were?"

"Not at all. In fact, I had hoped you were," Myra answered.

"Why? Why would a young Catholic girl want me to be Jewish?" he asked.

"I don't think I was born a Catholic," Myra told him. "It is a long story and although I hardly know you, I would like some day to get your opinion."

He looked puzzled and rubbed his chin. "Are you saying you think you might be Jewish?"

"I don't know. Someone sent me a silver Star of David brooch with a note saying it was mine, but I know nothing about the Jewish religion."

"Why don't you ask the sender?" he mumbled, looking down at his drink

"I tried but my letter of inquiry was returned to me with a note that the person had moved and left no forwarding address. You see, I have no memory before the age of five and half. I was raised by a Catholic couple and eventually was put in the Queen of Heaven Orphanage when they could no longer care for me."

Now he looked interested in what he was hearing. "Why not ask them since you are an adult now?"

"I was ten when I last saw them. I know the man died and I was told Gerta, the woman, died too. It was Gerta who said she would tell me of my past when I got older, but I never got older with them."

"Other than the religious brooch why would you think you might be Jewish?"

Myra

"The sender of the brooch was a Yvette Levine. I thought that was a Jewish name." Myra circled her finger around her drink while noticing the reaction from Sam. He looked surprised and drew in a deep breath as though struck by a blow.

"Did I say some thing wrong?" Myra asked him

"Of course not. I smoke too much and just had a reaction," he said, squashing the cigarette out in the nearby ashtray.

The conversation ended there with the interruption of Eric.

"Are you flirting with this lovely lady, Sam?" Eric laughed as he sat on the other side of Myra. "I have been watching you two."

The subject was dropped and small talk took up the space of conversation.

When it was time to leave, Stella and Sofia were the first to leave. Little Todd wanted to take Sister Bernadette home with him, which made Sister plump up like a ripe tomato. As Sam put on his heavy overcoat, he reached into his pocket and brought out a small white card. He handed it to Myra and said, "It was nice meeting you, Myra. We should talk again soon."

Mrs. Rogers refused any help in cleaning up, saying Annie would not let anyone in her kitchen, as she knows where everything goes. She helped them with their coats and kissed them both goodbye.

"Now, you must not be strangers. Do come back soon. We enjoyed your company so much. Sister Bernadette, you are a jewel. I have never seen Todd take to a person like he did with you. No wonder you take care of children. What an inner beauty you have."

Sister Bernie smiled as though a saint had blessed her and promised she would keep in touch, although she and Myra knew that would be almost impossible considering Mother Superior's beliefs.

On the way home Eric asked Myra if she knew how to ice skate. "A little, but I haven't been able to partake in many sports in my life," she answered.

"I hear the ice up at Evergreen Lake is solid and great for skating. Can you make it tomorrow? It will be fun, I promise."

Myra looked at him for a minute. How was she going to get out of this and resume her search? "I am sorry Eric. I have to do something very important at the orphanage and I only have a few days left before I must get back to Boulder. I am sorry."

Sister Bernie spoke up. "Nonsense, Myra. I know what it is you have to do and I certainly can do that for you. Go with Eric. Have some fun for once in your life."

Eric smiled at her before Sister Bernie concluded, "She works so hard, Eric. She needs to get away from all her duties. You need no permission from anyone anymore, Myra." Sister reminded her.

Myra really would like to go up to the hamlet of Evergreen. She had once been there in the summer time on a field trip with the orphans group. Also, she felt she wanted to know Eric better and the feeling seemed to be mutual.

"Well, Sister Bernie if you promise you will do that for me, I guess I could go. No, I mean, I would love to go but I have no ice skates."

"Don't worry about that. We can rent them up there."

"And I still have those wool pants of yours hanging in my closet," Sister Bernie contributed, signaling again her agreement with Eric. "We can find a good warm jacket for you too in the donated clothing, so you are set, Myra."

For the first time ever in her life, Myra felt what true happiness was all about. She had been happy sometimes during her childhood, but not so deeply as she felt now.

Someone really cared to be with her. Her conversation with Sam Hirsch encouraged her to think he might be able to help her in some way. At least, he gave her his calling card and Eric had said on the way back to the orphanage, Sam didn't take to strangers very often. Myra really must have made an impression on him. When Myra asked about Sam's accent, Eric told her he was born in Hungary and came over as a young man after the first World War. He had met Donald Rogers at the University of Denver where both men were studying law, and they later became partners in their own law firm, Hirsch, Rogers, and Smith; the Smith later left the firm. Sam had a secret life, Eric said. He remembered his uncle telling him Sam had said he was married once, but never spoke of a wife or children. It was a conversation one always avoided with Sam.

That night Myra dreamt again of the woman with the dark hair. This time there was no running to catch her. They were in a sitting in a white room drinking tea. The lady had on a black dress with the Silver Star of David pinned on her shoulder. She touched it gently and said, "These are real diamonds, you know." Suddenly a man appeared by her side and undid the brooch. The lady screamed at him to give it back, it was hers, but his features were hidden in a shadow. He struck her outstretched arms and walked out of the room. It was the running scene again, down a long hallway and a large staircase into an entrance hall with huge white marble statues. The woman running in front of Myra opened the huge door of the hall and ran outside. In the distance the shadow of the man was walking towards the woods but the cold stopped Myra in her tracks. The woman turned again toward her and once again said, "Remember me Myra." It was always the signal to wake up, which she did, and found her bedding on the floor and her body shivering from the cold.

Chapter Seven

In the spring of 1942, Myra was as happy as she had ever been although the war was raging in Europe and with Japan. She felt as though an emotional harness had been lifted from her soul. She was in love and she was loved. Eric wrote her almost daily from his post in Little Rock, and called her at least every three weeks or whenever he could get to a phone. He was working for a leave when he could come to Colorado some time this summer. His father and sister were planning a visit with Aunt Edna and it was thought a good time for Myra to meet them.

Myra's studies kept her pretty busy. She was concentrating on journalism with maybe a teaching degree too. Life was as exciting as it had never been for Myra. Her nightmares became less frequent. Sister Bernadette had found her old suitcase but it revealed nothing of importance for Myra. School papers from her time with Gerta and Carl and few old outgrown dresses. Sister Bernie suggested Myra look over the papers before throwing them out. There was a pile of them and maybe in her childhood writings, there could be a clue. Sister put them away for her, but there was not much time to get them, let alone read them.

Myra

Spring break found Myra working in restaurant called The Sink. Fresh baked chocolate cake with ice cream was the favorite of its customers. She had arranged to stay in her dorm room for the holiday, and she could eat free at The Sink. On Easter Sunday, she attended Mass at the nearest Catholic Church, a service she rarely attended since moving out of the orphanage. At first, she had felt guilty about not going to church. After all, the Catholics had taken care of her for seven years. It was the statues of Christ that bothered her. Since the arrival of the Star of David brooch, she felt a slight betrayal of her soul when she knelt down to pray to him. She reasoned that if she didn't go to Mass she would not have to feel so ungrateful or guilty after her childhood of adoring him. This feeling rumbled around inside her brain like an idea waiting to be born. She vowed one day she would know why.

The first week after spring break, the housemother called Myra to the phone. To her great surprise, it was Sam Hirsch.

"Myra?" he asked, as though he wasn't sure of her voice.

"Yes."

"Do you remember me?" he asked. Her pause told him she wasn't sure. "This Sam Hirsch. We met at Edna Roger's home at Christmas time."

Myra felt her breath exhale. "Oh course. What a

surprise. It is nice to hear from you."

He laughed a little, "I had hoped you would call me. Then I thought maybe you lost my card."

Myra had not lost it and kept it in her wallet thinking about calling him but not knowing what or how to ask what she wanted to know. "I am sorry. I do have your card but I was afraid I would be a bother."

"Nonsense. You would never be a bother. I have thought about your view about your possibly being born a Jew. I really would like to discuss this with you if I could."

Myra couldn't believe her ears. "Oh yes, I would love to hear what you thought about my situation. No one has ever seemed curious about my heritage before."

"Good. Can we have lunch? I know for a fact that the luncheon menu at the Boulderado Hotel is superb. Could we meet there this coming Sunday?"

The Boulderado Hotel was known to be upper class in the society of Boulder. Denver's elite drove up to the Hotel to have an excellent experience with both food and ambiance. Myra had never been there but Diana's parents stayed there when she first came to Boulder. The other girls mentioned its elegant decor and envied Diana.

"I would love that, but I really have nothing dressy to wear there. My housemates tell me it is very elegant.

They might not let me in," she laughed softly.

"Nonsense again, my dear girl. You would look good in anything you have to wear. Should I pick you up or would like to meet me there?"

How would Myra explain Sam to the girls who watched everything and everyone coming and going? "I will meet you there as it is not too far from our house."

"Would twelve thirty be alright? At that time, the church crowds would have been there and gone and we could linger over our conversation. That is if you have no other plans?"

"No. That would be perfect. It will be nice to see you again."

"Oh, one more thing. Could you bring the Star of David? I would like to see it"

"Of course. I would love to show it to you."

"Until then my dear girl, Shalom." And the phone went dead.

Myra hung up the receiver and stood there for a while. What on earth can he tell me? Maybe I can borrow a dress from Diana or Betty? Is my search for my true identity beginning?

Diana was more than pleased to lend Myra a sheer

printed dress with a white lace collar and trim on the short sleeves. The material was heavenly to touch, so soft and delicate. At first, Myra felt it too good for her to wear, but Diana, always a kind girl, insisted Myra looked better in it than she did.

It was a sunny beautiful day on that Sunday. Myra felt good about herself and what might be ahead of her. The Flat Irons, a rock formation way above the campus, glowed with blossoms of spring colors. What an appropriate name for this formation, Myra thought. What furious shifting of earth it must have been when they were thrust upward like praying hands. Myra walked down Broadway from the campus, and the main street for the city of Boulder. She passed the railroad station next to the Boulder Creek and walked on through the downtown area. Stores were closed tight on Sunday and there was hardly any traffic on the streets. At last, the Boulderado was in sight. Myra took one last look at her image in a store window and moved on.

The doorman opened the doors for her as though she were someone important, or so she thought. Inside, a gentleman in a black suit and tie greeted her with a smile and inquired how many were to be seated. Before Myra could think what to answer, Sam Hirsch was behind the man explaining that this was his luncheon guest.

Sam pointed out a table near a far window and Myra followed him to their seats. It was a lovely large room with crystal chandeliers and shining table settings. Snow-white linens covered the tables adorned with small vases of three or four bright red roses. The elegance and the ambiance almost left Myra speechless for a minute.

She could hardly hear Sam explaining the menu set in front of her, but it didn't matter. She would eat anything they would set on her large china plate.

"Do you like shrimp, Myra? They have a wonderful shrimp cocktail to start off the meal."

She was honest with Sam and told him she had no idea what to order but would like what ever he ordered. After all, in the orphanage they were not given a choice. If they didn't eat what was placed on the table, they just didn't eat.

Myra's palate had never tasted such wonderful food. She had never been exposed to such delicate seasonings, or the sweet dessert trays she could choose from. If she died now she was sure she would be in heaven.

Their conversation was about her studies and world events. Afterward, when they were having tea and sweet miniature rolls, Sam asked to see the Star of David. Myra took it from her purse and handed the box to Sam. He opened it slowly and the look on his face revealed some emotion Myra could not place. Was it shock? Had he seen it before? It was something, she was sure. If Sam's face had not changed Myra would not have noticed, as Sam had shown very little emotion at Christmas time or during their lunch. Yet, his eyes widened and his mouth pursed together like he might whistle.

"May I read the note?" he asked

"Of course," Myra said. "There is another short line written on the back side."

The luncheon crowd had thinned and the silence of the room while Sam read the note was like waiting for a verdict.

Sam picked up the brooch and held it in his hand. His eyes seemed to tear up, Myra thought, but it could have been the soft lights of the room. He turned it over, examining the back. "Have you had a jeweler look at it and perhaps appraise it?"

"No. To be honest with you, I don't have the money to have that done."

Sam shook his head. "I could have it done for you, Myra. I think it might unlock some your lost memory, that is if you would let me?"

"I don't know Sam. For years I have wondered about my memory. I have had strange dreams too. I think I am afraid of finding out what happened to me because my dreams are like nightmares. Maybe I would be opening a Pandora's box."

Sam tapped his fingers on his wine glass. "What is the first memory you do remember, if I am not getting too personal?"

The question shocked Myra at first, for after all she and Sam were still in a sense strangers. Myra wasn't sure she really remembered.

"I am not sure," she told Sam, "but I think my first memory was waking up in a hospital room. Everything was white, the walls, the bed, and the light. Oh yes, the light. It was so bright I wouldn't open my eyes all the way but they kept calling my name."

"Who was calling your name?" Sam asked.

"The adults, I think. It was a woman and a man in white. I could hear whispering somewhere. I think it came from the hallway beyond the door of the room I was in. I started to cry. Then Gerta was there and she was holding me and kissing me. I remember hugging her so tight because she was the only one I knew."

"Gerta was the lady that you lived with until when?"

"Gerta and Carl her husband. They took me home, but it wasn't familiar to me. It was a ranch house outside of Salida. I remember asking if I was to go to school and Gerta asked if I remembered my old school? I couldn't. So my life started at that time. They had me baptized by the priest in the Catholic Church in Salida, so I thought I was a Catholic. I got the First Communion and all the teaching, but I could not accept it. It made Gerta and Carl unhappy if I questioned dealing with the church. I learned early not to ask, so I didn't."

"Did you ever ask them or did they tell you where you born or anything about your birth parents?" Sam asked.

Myra fiddled with her coffee spoon "I always knew they weren't my parents. I knew they had grown children and they were only taking care of me. Once Gerta told me when I was older she would explain why I was with them, but she felt I was too young to understand. I was eight years old. I felt I should know and threw a temper tantrum. It was the only time Carl ever spanked me, but I knew I could never ask them about that again."

"What happened to them?" Sam asked.

"Carl got sick. The doctors said he had a stroke, but he couldn't walk any more. His face was out of shape and he could barely talk. Their son came from California to see them, and he thought I was too much for Gerta to care for. I remembered hearing them talk about moving Gerta and Carl back to California. Gerta cried. She asked if I could move with them, but the son had children of his own and could not afford me."

Sam shook his head in disbelief, "That is how you ended up at the Queen of Heaven Orphanage?"

"Not exactly," she said. Now it was getting too personal and Myra didn't want to go there. "A friend of

Greta's knew a family looking for a girl my age to adopt. They had an only child who they thought needed a companion. She was really a brat who needed a psychologist, I think, looking back on it. Anyway, it didn't work out and they canceled the adoption, thank God. It wasn't a happy place for me so I was lucky. By then, Carl had died and Gerta was in California. I didn't have an address for the son and Gerta had no idea where I had been sent. She may not have known I wasn't adopted, for all I know."

"Have you tried to find her for the answers to your questions?" Sam asked.

"No. I was rather traumatized by the adoption experience, and," Myra started to cry, "I am sorry but I can't go into that. I found love and peace at the orphanage and Sister Bernadette was there for me. I have tried to move on. I think Gerta would be dead by now too."

Sam reached over and patted her arm. "I think I have overstepped my position, Myra. I am sorry. Please forgive me and we should change the subject now. Okay?"

Myra shook her head and smiled over at Sam. "Yes."

"I know that you and Eric are in love." Sam went on, "You are all he writes about, according to Edna. In fact, I am also here on an errand for him, but before we get into that, how does he feel about this brooch?"

"Oh Sam, I have not told Eric, and I hope you won't either." Myra said.

Sam looked startled, "Why not, dear girl? Have you told him anything about your lost memory or your nightmares?"

"Oh yes. He knows I cannot remember anything before I was five but I have not told him about the dreams or the brooch. I know I love Eric and I just don't want him or his family to reject me because all my life I have been rejected. If he thought I could be Jewish--and I am not saying this would happen, because you are like part of his family--he might wonder about getting serious." Myra paused for a second. "Oh Sam, I have never been so happy in my life; I like being important to Eric."

Sam smiled and put the brooch back in the box before handing it back to Myra.

Myra reached out for it and said, "I said something very funny about this brooch too, when I first got it. One of my housemates was reading the note about the diamonds being replaced. She said I told her I thought they were glass because someone had told me that. When she asked who had told me, I didn't remember saying anything." Myra looked for Sam's reaction. "Maybe I am nuts."

"Far from it, dear. Lost memories have a way of returning in a flash, not staying long enough for someone to figure them out. You most likely did own this as a small child."

Sam leaned over and reached into the breast pocket of his suit and took something out.

"Well, this is part of my errand. Eric is not a Catholic; his family is Lutheran. How would you justify the mixing of religions in that case?"

"We have talked about it, Sam. The Lutheran faith is an offshoot of the Catholic religion and Eric has said there would not be a conflict there." She paused, then continued softly. "However, if I were born a Jew, it might make a difference to Eric and his family."

"Why would you want to cut off what you were led to believe as a child?" Sam asked.

Myra looked down at the table because she was afraid of the reaction Sam might have to her answer. "I have a horrible thought every time I look at the statue of Jesus on the Cross. I feel he was a mortal man, although I know it is against all that I have been taught." Myra then looked Sam in the eyes. "I have prayed to God that whatever is in my soul making me think of Jesus this way be explained. I approach his statue and stare up at him and hear the words, 'He is mortal like you. He is the Son of God and you are the Daughter of God.' And I feel at peace with my thoughts. However, Sister Bernadette is not. She prays for my soul every day, she once told me."

There was silence from Sam and Myra felt she

might have said too much. She had never talked like that to anyone before, and only Sister Bernie suspected her feelings about Jesus. What now, she wondered.

"Well," Sam cleared his throat, "To change the subject again, I do have good news, I hope, for you." He leaned forward and put a small black box in her hand.

"This is from Eric and I have never played John Alden before." Sam smiled, "but I was asked by Eric to ask you if you would be his wife. If the answer is yes, Eric and Edna felt there would be time to arrange your wedding for August, when his father and sister are to visit here."

Myra opened the box and saw the diamond ring snuggled into the satin cover. She could only look at it for words had left her. She felt tears of happiness fill her eyes. Sam took the ring out for her and said, "If that is yes, let's see if it fits."

"Oh Sam, I am speechless. Of course I will marry Eric, but will you be my friend too?" she asked as Sam slipped the ring on her finger.

"Look, a perfect fit." Sam took her hand, "My dear I decided to be your friend when you told me about your concerns over your birth. I would never betray your secrets to anyone, I promise you, Myra." Another pause. "But if I can trigger your past memory, shall I keep that a secret too--should it be detrimental to your happiness?"

"I can't think that far ahead, Sam. Who knows what is to happen with the war and Eric being in it? Let us take one day at time. I give you permission to explore my past if you can find a beginning. I can't, you know. Not even a birth certificate, with only Gerta and Carl celebrating my birthdays on July 16th.

"Let me ask you one question. Does Hungary mean anything to you, Myra?"

"Only that is your birth country. Is it supposed to mean something?"

"No, not necessarily, but you mentioned a Yvette Levine as the sender. I knew a Levine family as a child. I am sure there are dozens of Jews with that name, but it might be a start."

Myra looked at the large clock one could see in the entrance of the hotel. "My goodness, Sam, we have been here for almost three hours. I think they would like us to leave."

Sam drove her to the freshman house and helped her out of the car. She didn't care what the girls would think, for now she had a diamond ring given at her love's request by his dearest friend. After all, the saying was now "There Is a War On," which meant nobody cared about proper ways to get engaged.

Myra had just walked into the front door when the phone rang. Being the closest to it, Myra picked up. It was Eric, and the dream of their future began.

Chapter Eight

Myra and Eric were married on August 6th, 1942. It was a small wedding with a reception at Edna Rogers' home. The wedding took place at St. Augustine Lutheran Church in North Denver, a decision Myra had agreed to, as Eric and Edna wanted a Lutheran ceremony, and Myra was unwilling to insist that he promise to raise their children as Catholics.

It was very hard for Sister Bernadette, but she loved Myra so much that she was happy for her. Eric was such nice lad with a family for Myra to have at last. Sister Bernie and Sister Theresa were allowed to attend the event. They had pleaded with Mother Superior that due to Eric's being a soldier with a horrible war in store for him, God would surely forgive and bless this young couple. Their attending a Lutheran wedding would ordinarily have been forbidden by Mother Superior, but then again, the world was changing and Myra had always been a good child. If anything should happen to the young man, Mother Superior thought, she would have to pray to God to forgive her error in judgment.

Edna Rogers took over the planning of the wedding from the start with Myra's blessing. She brought her own wedding gown out of storage. It was made of pale ivory satin with tiny seed pearls embroidered at the waist and neckline. The veil's crown with a long train of white netting and lace gave Myra the look of an angel. Sister Bernadette crossed herself when she saw Myra before the ceremony. "You could be an a Holy Angel, you are so beautiful," she told her with tears in her eyes and love in her heart. "I only want you to be happy, my darling."

Myra put her arms around Sister and said, "I am the happiest I have ever been, Sister. This is not the end of our relationship. I still need you and your prayers. I always will, you know?"

The guests were some of Myra's house sisters and the housemother from Boulder. Edna had invited old friends of the family in small groups that hardly filled the church pews. Sam gave the bride away because, as Myra explained to everyone, he had given her the engagement ring in Eric's absence. Besides, Sam and Myra had strengthened their friendship since their luncheon date in Boulder. He became a father figure for her as Sister Bernie had become like a mother to her. Two of Myra's favorite little orphan girls were the flower girls and Todd had come from California with his mother to be the ring bearer. Diana was happy to be Myra's maid of honor and she brought her present boyfriend. Having met Eric's sister, Elizabeth for the first time, Edna thought she should be a bridesmaid and it worked out perfectly. The reception at Edna's home was beautiful. Diana and her friend had a sense of humor that had everyone laughing. Even Sam cracked a smile as he toasted the bride and groom.

Myra had never seen a wedding cake so large and decorated so beautifully. She did feel guilty about not have the finances to pay for her own wedding, but everyone said that in wartime, what difference did it make? As long as Eric had his bride before he had to face his future, and God willing, came back safe and sound. Money didn't matter.

Mr. John Dawson, Eric's father was as delightful as his son. He was almost bald and had a pudgy figure, but also a dignity about him that was elegant and sincere. He embraced Myra on their first meeting like he had known her forever. Elizabeth was a tall willowy blonde with Eric's smile and personality. She laughed easily and seemed comfortable in her looks and surroundings. She told Myra she had always wanted a sister and Eric had excellent taste. It was a wonderful introduction into the Dawson family.

Edna and her late husband owned a cozy cabin just outside Estes Park and insisted the happy couple use it for their short honeymoon.

Myra was so happy she hardly noticed the landscape of snow-topped peaks rising up around the village of Estes Park until much later in their stay. They were to have four wonderful days alone before Eric had to report for duty. The little cabin was beyond the village off the highway that would have taken them over the Trail Ridge dirt road, supposedly the highest roadway in the United States.

"Some day, they will pave that road and then it will be a breeze to drive down into Grand Lake from here." Eric told her.

"How far does it go up the mountain now?" Myra asked him

"Uncle Dan and I took it to the top once but is a rough drive. One could get all the way over it, but the drop-offs are scary when your car stalls. Once we had to walk to the summit then back to turn the car around. It was touch and go for a while. A little space to the front and a little space back here: I was sure I was going to lose my Uncle, but we managed it."

"Are we going to attempt it?" Myra asked.

"No, my sweet wife. I would not put you in any danger of falling over a cliff. You're my life now and always will be," he said as he leaned over and kissed her.

Their wedding night was an experience that Myra never expected. She knew about sex from girl talks and books, but she always blocked out the endings because of her memories of Mr. Carpenter, which shut the door on any happiness in sex. She pondered whether or not to tell Eric about that part of her childhood, but what would he think? She loved him so much, how could she hurt him now? Eric sensed her tense up as he took her in his arms but that would be her virginity, he reasoned. It was a surprise that she was so timid in showing her naked body, but he also reasoned that too was a first time reaction. He was as gentle as he could be; yet he felt Myra's body stiffen as he entered her body. The pleasure he felt urged him on until he reached his peak and his body collapsed on top of her. Myra stared at the ceiling without blinking an eye. She could hear Eric's heavy breathing and feel his sweaty face on her breasts. Was that it, she wondered? It had hurt her like a stinging sensation, but as Eric continued, there was no feeling of euphoria as mentioned in conversations or the books she had read. What was she suppose to feel?

"I am sorry darling. Did I hurt you?" Eric asked

"A little, but it was alright." Myra answered, wiping some his facial sweat from him. She would never tell him how she felt because she loved him so much. If this was what she had to do to please him, she would fake it before hurting him.

"It is rather rough at first. darling. I just got carried away. It will get better, I promise you that." Eric smiled down at her and kissed her forehead. "Now, you are really mine, now and forever."

He rolled off her and stood up. His body was shiny from his ordeal of pleasure. His muscles were out lined in his arms and legs. He reminded Myra of the statue of the naked Greek God Mercury she had seen at the public library. Perfect in every way.

When he went to the bathroom for his pajamas, Myra slipped out of bed and quickly put on her nightgown and jumped back into the bed pulling up the covers. When Eric returned to their bed, he cuddled close to her circling his arms around her. In his arms Myra felt safe again. It is going to be OK, she thought as she drifted off to sleep.

That night she did dream but not her usual one. She was standing on hill above a wide paved highway. All around her were high snowy peaks and majestic views. She felt she was on top of the world. Starlings flew by begging for the crumbs she held in her hand. She tossed the crumbs into the air and laughed as the birds snatched the pieces in flight. She turned and headed down the hill towards a man calling her name. He was standing by a signpost with the words "Trail Ridge Road." He was not familiar to Myra and she wondered why he called her. As she approached him, he held out his arms to her and kissed her cheek. He was dressed in a white gown like doctors wore and around his neck was a stethoscope. He helped her into a large black car with an emblem like a shield on its hood. She had never seen a car like it before. She sat on the soft velvet seats and looked around while the man got in the driver's seat.

"Where is Eric?" she asked. The man smiled at her for a minute then answered, "I am here now."

Myra opened her eyes. Where was she? Where is Eric? Then she remembered but Eric was not besides her. She smelled the odor of bacon cooking somewhere in the cabin. Then Eric stuck his head in the doorway and said,

They stood on the sidewalk in front of the Union Depot in downtown Denver, Myra, Eric, John Dawson, Elizabeth and Edna Rogers, while Sam snapped their picture. It was time for Eric to leave and his train would be pulling out in a few minutes. Sam wanted to take pictures for a scrapbook he was putting together. "This will be the going off to war and the next one will be coming home from the war."

The words hit Myra like a sword cutting through her heart. The dream she had had in the cabin only added to her fear of losing Eric. The past two weeks had been like fairy tale. Getting ready for the wedding with all the excitement of being a bride and best of all was being with Eric again a few days before the wedding. Now it was to end for a time and Myra would need Sister Bernie's prayers more than ever. She could not have communion again in the Catholic Church, but she could be in touch with Sister Bernie and seek some comfort from her. For now, Myra was to travel to California for a week with Elizabeth and her father-in-law John, before returning to Edna's home to gather up her belongings Edna so gracefully insisted she store there. Diana and Myra had found a small apartment just off the campus and would split the cost of rent. With Eric's help, Myra would be able to afford that expense but she planned to continue working at the Sink.

The noise of the trains and the crowds of people brought Myra back to the present. Eric circled his arms around her waist and started towards the double doors of the station. The waiting room was a large area with benches in rows and full of those departing or waiting. Myra had never been in the building before and was amazed at the size of it. Eric directed all of them to a hallway sloped downward to a lower area where corridors for different tracks had numbers above the entrances. They found Eric's train track number and went up a series of stairs to the track where the train stood belching its steam. Eric swung his duffle bag over his shoulder and reached for his father's hand.

"I'll be fine Dad, don't you worry. Just take care of my wife."

"You know I will son, but take care of yourself too. Don't take chances and watch your back," John said, wiping a tear from his eyes. The he leaned over and hugged Eric tight.

Elizabeth was crying as she kissed her brother she but could not talk without sobbing. She shook her head and hugged him and moved back so Edna could say her farewell. Then it was Sam's turn.

"Remember our hunting and fishing trips, Eric. You may need the skills we tried to teach you," he said holding Eric's hand as he reached over for Myra's hand. "Myra and I have a special bond now and I will watch over her like a

Eric looked down at Myra, "I know you will Sam, and I appreciate the gesture for I know she will be in good hands. I love this girl so much I don't think she even realizes it"

"I do Eric. I love you with every part of my being. You have given me a new life and a new beginning. Just come back to me. Please! Please!" Her tears started as Eric kissed her long and hard.

"I will, I promise. I will. I love you," and he boarded the train steps and waved at all of them as the train started puffing and moving out. Myra waved until she could no longer see Eric on the steps. She felt so empty, so alone now. Another abandonment in her life, she thought, but this time, he would come back. She would carry that thought with her forever.

———————

California was a wonderland of dreams for Myra. She never thought she would travel there in her lifetime. The train ride was a great adventure for her too. She knew her life was turning around and when Eric came home they most likely would live near his family in California. She sent post cards to Sister Bernie and Diana, who had already settled into their apartment. Myra was sure every glamorous girl or handsome man was a movie star. Once she thought she saw Shirley Temple but she couldn't be sure. The beach was breathtaking for her as she gathered seashells from the sand then ran just as the waves came rushing in. The Dawsons did everything to make her stay as nice as they could. There were other family members and friends to meet with luncheons at wonderful cafes along the large boulevards. Elizabeth took her under care as though she was a fragile doll, and introduced her as the "newest member of our family."

When it was time to leave, John and Elizabeth saw her to a first class compartment and loaded her down with gifts for Edna and California souvenirs.

Edna met her at the train station and was full of questions about how things went for her with the Dawsons. It was too late for Myra to travel on to Boulder by the time she got to Denver, so she spent the night at Edna's. The next morning Edna insisted on driving her up to CU. Myra did not have much to pack as she put her baggage in the car. Myra put Mr. Teddy Bear on her lap and laughed when Edna supposedly talked to him as though he could talk to her. "Well, at least you have something from your past," she said as she patted Teddy Bear's almost bald head.

The apartment was cozy and Diana had had it decorated like a professional decorator. The front room was a blend of browns and tans on the sofa and curtains. Even the lampshades and side tables besides the sofa were blended into the color scheme. The bedroom where their two twin beds with their colorful flowered bedspreads were as charming as any Myra had seen. The Dawson's guest's room for her was glamorous too but she had expected that. Now she was unsure how she would be able to pay for her share of the furniture and extras. When she approached the subject Diana simply shrugged it off. "Myra, this is old throw away stuff my parents had shipped here last spring. I only bought inexpensive curtains and material for everything else. It is hardly worth a thing."

"But, Diana, it will be my place too and I want to share the cost," Myra begged her.

Diana ran her hand through her short blond hair. Her bright blue eyes locked on to Myra. "It is all part of your wedding gift from me, Myra. Please accept it as such. Besides, Eric gave me money for some of it, so no more talk about it, okay?"

That was a statement Myra had a hard time believing, so she was determined to pay her back somewhere or somehow in her future. Diana was becoming very dear and close to her. She didn't ask Myra questions about her past or the dreams that woke her up when they shared a room at the freshman house. Diana took one day at a time. She was very athletic and participated in every sport available to her. She tried to get Myra involved too, but there was always a test or studies that Myra came up with. Diana did know Myra was living on a shoestring money situation so she never pressed too hard. Myra would never let her pay for the ski tows, or the bus up to Winter Park or Loveland Ski areas or the lunches they would eat there. The only bothersome thing about Diana was her taste in boy friends. In Myra's opinion they never fit into Diana's lifestyle, at least not the style portrayed by her parents with their wealth and prestigious background.

Myra

It was almost as though Diana was pulling in the direction opposite the one her parents wanted for her. So far, her boyfriends seem to take advantage of her letting her pay for their date activities, which Diana didn't seem to mind. She was small in body structure with perfectly formed limbs and rosy skin tones. Her Swedish heritage was evident in her personality always challenging and trying new ventures. Her boundless energy wore Myra down at times, but living with Diana was a pleasure she enjoyed immensely.

So life for Myra was studying and writing letters to Eric. She watched for his V-mails, and calls to Sister Bernie and Aunt Edna kept her spirits high. She prayed constantly to a God she knew existed asking for the safe return of her beloved husband Eric. She attended Mass sometimes but she also checked out a book on Judaism from the university library, though she had little time to read it or understand it before she had to return it. She was as happy as she had ever been and the future looked so full of promises one day at a time.

Chapter Nine

The Shakespeare class had always been Myra's favorite. The last assignment was to write a paper on the first two chapters for the new term. Myra had worked diligently on it and was prepared as she shoved her brief case under her seat. Lunch had been a bowl of noodle soup, a glass of milk and an apple she had eaten at the Sink before classes. Now, her stomach roared a little, but a good belch would be a relief if she could do it quietly. Instead she vomited all over herself and then fainted dead away. She was only out for a minute and was aware that everyone was around her helping her to her feet.

"My God, dear girl." the professor said. "You are as white as a sheet."

She allowed herself to be helped to the clinic in the Old Mackey building and gladly gave in to be examined. Her main concern was to clean up her mess back in the classroom, but she was told it would be taken care of by the janitor. She was given a glass of water, which tasted so good going down calming her rumbling stomach. The nurse took her temperature, which was normal, and her blood pressure too. When everything checked out, they decided that Myra had eaten some bad food and she was sent home to rest for the day.

On Myra's walk home, her legs felt like rubber and a weakness she had never experienced before took over her whole body. The apartment was cool and quiet, Diana still in classes, so Myra lay on her bed and was soon asleep. It was dark when Myra awoke at the sound of Diana coming into the room.

"What happened? I saw Betty on campus a few minutes ago and she heard you fainted from someone in your class. Are you all right?" Diana asked, as she switched on the lamp next to the bed.

"They think it was something I ate for lunch. I threw up and I am so embarrassed, Diana. How can I go back there tomorrow?" she asked, sitting up. This movement only made her feel worse.

Diana felt her forehead. "You don't have a fever and that is good. The darn flu is going around again, so maybe you have caught it."

Myra began to stand up but her body caved in and she fell back on the bed. "Oh my God, what is happening to me Diana?"

"You stay in bed Myra. I will make you some hot tea but tomorrow, you are going to see a doctor. If you have the flu, you will need lots of rest." With that said, a determined Diana went into the kitchen and Myra did as

The campus doctor was a middle aged bespectacled man who looked as though he wished he were somewhere else, not in his office with several patients waiting. His nurse took Myra into one of the little white rooms and told her to undress. She hated to do that but she still felt weak and her stomach couldn't keep a thing she ate or drank down. Diana had come with her disregarding any classes she might miss, and waited in the office area. The doctor examined Myra completely even touching and looking up her private parts, which made her uncomfortable. Only Eric had made her forget the fear she suffered in her childhood concerning her body. This doctor, strangely enough, reminded her of Mr. Carpenter. It was not his looks but his attitude, making her feel like a piece of meat for his own pleasure.

"Did you say your name was Mrs. Dawson?" he asked her looking down at the chart on his tray.

"Yes, I am a newlywed. My husband is in Europe somewhere. Is there a serious problem with me?" Myra asked him, trying to keep her fear at bay.

"No, not a problem, my girl. You seem to be pregnant, that is all." He closed the chart and sat down at the little table in the room. "You are having what they call morning sickness. I will write out a prescription for you that should help you feel a little better but soda crackers can help too if you feel woozy."

A stunned Myra could only stare at the ceiling. She had to be dreaming again but the sweat on her face was real and she knew her world was changing.

"You can get dressed now and please stop by the nurse's desk for this prescription. Congratulations are in order, so good luck." He checked his watch and left the room. All Myra could do was lay there in thought until the nurse came in to see if she needed help. Diana had a worried look on her face as the nurse led Myra back into the waiting room.

"What is the verdict? The flu, huh?"

Myra sat on the nearest chair and started to cry. "No Diana, I am pregnant. I am going to have a baby."

"I knew it. I felt it was more than the flu." Laughing, Diana hugged Myra for joy. There was a little laughter from other patients with an older lady telling Myra it would be a wonderful experience. She had six children and every one of them was a blessing. Her youngest child, a freshman, was with the doctor now for a sprained ankle.

It took Myra a week before she called Sam with the news and for advice on how to handle the news with Aunt Edna and of course, her beloved Eric. She had already informed Sister Bernadette who was overjoyed. At first Sam was silent which led Myra to think he wasn't pleased. As their conversation continued, though, Sam was most concerned about her health. He admitted he was worried about her work schedule. He wondered if she should continue with college, but Myra assured him that after the morning sickness passed, as every one said it would, she would be just fine doing what she had been doing.

She did as Sam suggested by calling Edna for a weekend visit. This was the first visit she would make since classes had started. Edna was delighted and also excited to see her again. Sam picked her up early Saturday morning in his car. He was his usual demure self on the ride to Denver except for his worry about her health. He was advising her on her diet, her exercise, and letting Eric know as soon as possible. Edna had fixed a brunch of fruit, cereal, hot muffins, and delicious spiced tea. She and Annie had canned three bushels of apples, so there was applesauce and apple cider as well if they wanted it. She had also taken three large jars of applesauce to Sister Bernadette at the orphanage during the week.

Sam and Myra looked at each other. They knew the secret was out, as Sister Bernie could never keep that kind of news.

"Oh my darling, I promised not to say anything, but I am so happy for you."

Later Edna called John and Elizabeth in California and Myra could hear them laughing as they were pleased that soon they would be Grandpa and Aunt. It was a relief for Myra and Sam threw a wink her way. Now, as Edna put it, the Red Cross would have to be notified in order to get the news to Eric, whereever he was. She had some connection because of the years she had volunteered for various agencies, so she would get at it on Monday morning. The three of them drove to the orphanage to see Sister Bernadette. Myra's spirits were pitched high and she felt the nausea cease a little. "Maybe it was mind over matter," she said to herself. "Or the pills from the doctor."

Sister Bernadette was flushed and a little upset. "Oh Myra. Such wonderful news and at a time like this. You will never guess what has just happened."

Edna took Sister's arm for she was afraid the poor nun was having trouble breathing. "Are you not feeling well, Sister?" Edna asked her as Myra took Sister's other arm.

"I am fine but Mother Superior isn't. We just found her on the floor of her office clutching the cross in her hand. She isn't responding to us at all. We have called for an ambulance."

No sooner said when the sirens blared outside and within minutes the running feet of the ambulance crew. Sister directed them to the right door then motioned for the three of them to come to the parlor. The four of them sat down listening to the scurrying around and other sisters trying to keep order with the children who by now had gathered in the hallway and staircase. It seemed to take a while before a white coated ambulance person came into the room to inform them that Mother Superior must have had a massive heart attack and was now dead.

Sister Bernadette turned to Myra and said, "One life passing and another coming. Isn't that a circle of life events?"

Confronting Father Lou was a surprise, for he had not blessed her marriage when Myra asked. However, he now took Myra aside and said," Myra, you have to do what is in your heart, and may you have a wonderful life." He put his hand on her head and blessed her with the sign of the cross.

Eric had been notified and was able to send a telegram to Myra. It had to be short but it was full of love for her and their baby. The morning sickness had passed by Christmas, which Myra and Sister Bernadette enjoyed together at Edna's home. By then, Sam was trying to get Myra's memory back with interesting questions. She had told him about her dreams of the dark haired lady who ran from her but always turned to remind Myra not to forget her. Sam thought it may have been her mother and the separation for some unknown reason had left her so traumatized that she had closed that time of her life out of her memory. That sounded reasonable to Myra, but how could or would she ever solve the puzzle? By then, Diana too, knew all the facts of Myra's life, even the Carpenter saga that she didn't tell to Sam. Suddenly Myra didn't feel that empty feeling in the pit of her stomach, the one she felt almost habitually when she was growing up. She was now a part of a circle of relatives and friends who really cared about her. The baby would be part of her for life. Maybe God did have a plan for her, but which God? Was it Jesus and the Holy Spirit or the Hebrew God who entered her mind when confronted with her faith?

Myra

The letters from Eric were always a comfort to Myra. He could not reveal his position but Myra knew him to be in eastern Europe from the Red Cross's help in getting him the news about their pregnancy. In most letters, black ink blocked out sentences where Eric might have revealed something the censors thought too secret to write about. However, in one such letter, nothing was blocked out. The contents told of Eric and others invading a cave where art works and other precious items had been placed for protection. One of his companions recognized some of the paintings as done by major artists like the Austrian Hans Makart. What really threw Eric for a loop, though, he wrote, was finding a huge portrait painting of Myra. Eric was so stunned his commanding officer thought he had uncovered a Nazi hiding in the shadows. Then the officer thought Eric was having hallucinations in seeing his wife, so Eric said, in the portrait. The officer told Eric it most likely was stolen from or hidden by a Jewish family. Nevertheless, Eric was stunned at seeing an image of his love, and puzzled by the mystery of its existence. The cave had to be blocked by rocks and dirt until after the war, he wrote, but he would always remember its location.

Myra called Sam immediately on receiving the letter. "Sam, listen to this." And she read the letter to Sam. "Could there be a connection? Do you think I really am Jewish? Of course, it could be a portrait by a painter who was not Jewish, and the same for the girl in portrait."

"It could very well be an important piece of art put there for protection by the Nazi's or by a family of Jews.

Let us hope and pray that Eric comes out of this war safe. Then when we win, and I mean we will win, we can travel back there and see what we can find out about.

"Didn't you once say you knew a family named Levine when you were a child?"

"Yes, but that was in Szeged, Hungary. We have no idea if that is where Eric is now." He was quietly trying to piece his thoughts together. He had not mentioned it to Myra but he had seen a likeness of her before, but where and when? Was it a painting or picture from his past? Was it in Europe? It had bothered him frequently since he first met Myra. What was it about this beautiful young girl that caused him to relive his past in Europe? Of course he remembered the Levine family. He had married into that family, but it was an arranged marriage by a Jewish matchmaker. He didn't love the girl called Sarah, and her family was impossible to be around. He was just nineteen and America was his dream. So, he left, being disowned by family and friends, and he managed to seek out his fortune without any regrets. His European childhood came back to haunt him when he met Myra. He searched for answers in his quest to remember people and places and events he had tried to erase. In that area he was just as lost as Myra. He had tried to forget what he left behind. Sometimes guilt flared up inside him like a volcanic eruption. He wondered often if his parents ever forgave him. He had left and refused to look back, but he had also felt he had no right to marry again, or to have a family of his own. That was his penance for disgracing

Chapter Ten

On May 5th, 1943, Mathew Samuel Dawson was born to Myra and Eric Dawson at Fitzsimons Hospital in Denver, Colorado. He arrived with dark curly hair and blue eyes that would eventually turn dark brown His first contact with his mother was the feel of her fingers holding his tiny hand and looking him over like a precious jewel. He blinked his eyes open then closed and opened them again to see this beautiful lady smiling at him. Although it did not register at this time on such a tiny human, her smile would live with him for always.

Myra had returned to school and just taken her final exam the day before her labor pains started. Her due date for the birth was a few weeks off, so she thought. She had planned to move in with Edna to await the birth, but this baby was not going to wait. It was a long labor during which Myra was sure her body would split in half, yet she did as she was told. Push! Push! She knew that the doctor could give her a general anesthetic and make her unconscious, but he said it was safer for the baby if she stayed awake and helped by pushing. At last when this miniature person arrived and it was announced that the baby was a boy, Myra knew what his name would be. She had discussed the name with Sam months before. Myra knew nothing more about her heritage, but if it was ever discovered she was born a Jew, she wanted her children to have Jewish biblical names. She had written Eric about honoring Sam in the naming and he agreed. Therefore, when picking names, whether it would be a boy or a girl, she had asked Sam for nice Jewish names of both sexes. Sam was surprised when she chose Samuel and Yvette. Sam had thrown the name in for her to think about along with many others, including Eric, Jr. The girl's name would have honored the person who sent her the Star of David. In his letters, Eric only said he wanted her and the baby to be safe. The name wasn't important. He would be with her in spirit, he wrote, and God would return him safely to her arms.

It was Diana who had bundled Myra into the car after frantically phoning Edna that they were on the way to the hospital. Edna phoned Sam and Sister Bernadette to alert them that the birth was starting. All were worried that the baby would not wait for the thirty to fifty mile drive to the east side of Denver. However, Mathew wasn't willing to leave the womb where he was warm and growing, so he just made his pending arrival known.

In the waiting room, Sister Bernadette was fingering her beads, saying the rosary. Sam was beginning to realize what a real father had to go through. Edna played the perfect grandmother, stopping nurses and white-coated interns to inquire about her 'daughter'. Diana flipped through magazines and smoked one cigarette after another. At last the doctor came in and told them a perfect little boy was born, mother and child doing fine.

John and Elizabeth were delighted with the news. They had planned to be in Denver for the event, but now they would have to fast forward their plans and come as soon as they could. They wanted Myra to recuperate at their home in California. Myra wasn't sure what to do. She didn't want to leave Denver, yet she knew she could not impose on Edna too much. Sam had suggested she could return to college in the fall. With the addition of another dependent, Eric's paycheck would go up. There was good nursery care in college towns now due to the fact that many wives of the service men had to watch out for each other and their children if they were attending college. Myra's scholarship would continue and if she found good childcare, she could continue to work at the Sink. At times, Myra felt motherhood and baby care were going to be too hard. Yet, when she looked at her tiny son, she saw herself as an infant. Who would ever give up such an innocent baby-- as some one had given up on her? She vowed that would never happen to her son. He would always know who he was and he would always have a real family.

So, as soon as Mathew gained a few pounds, Myra returned to California in the company of a proud grandfather and aunt. Sam seemed a little upset as did Sister Bernadette, but she promised them she would keep in touch and she would be back in the fall. Sam had put the Star of David brooch in his safety box at his bank. Myra went with him to do so and her name was listed along with Sam's to enter the vault any time she felt the need to do so. What Sam did not tell Myra was that he had had his last will and testament redone in Myra's favor too.

Having no children or family links anymore, Myra was the perfect candidate. Sam was sure she was born a Jew and if it took him the rest of his life, he was going to prove it. He had accumulated some wealth in his life, and he felt the need for payback to his heritage.

Eric's letters to Myra were full of love and plans for their future. He had received the pictures of Mathew with Myra, which pleased him so much. He wrote personal letters to Mathew, some not to be opened until he held his son in his arms. Myra knew they most likely were written just in case he didn't make it home. She honored his request with the hope they would never have to be opened.

It was at this time that Sam received a letter from Eric. He repeated to Sam what he'd said about the painting in which he had seen the image of Myra. He had not told Myra all of what he had seen and he wanted Sam to know about it. Although Myra could have been the model, it was obviously an old painting by the looks of it. The strangest thing about the portrait was that the woman had a brooch on her shoulder that looked like the emblem of the Jews, the Star of David. Eric was wondering, since Myra had no memory of her early life, could she have been a Jew? Not that it mattered to Eric, he wrote, as he was more concerned about Myra knowing it.

Sam wrote Eric that it could be possible and he would try to uncover some of Myra's past, if Eric wanted him to do so. However, Sam asked Eric, would it make a difference in their future if Eric's hunches were correct? It was a relief when Eric's V-mail assured Sam that after seeing and hearing of the suffering of Jews in Europe, his love for Myra, if she was proven a Jew, would never falter. Both men decided not to mention their correspondence to Myra. However, Eric's concerns about the portrait awoke a distant memory in Sam. He was sure now that he too had seen that painting, but he could not remember where. It had to have been in Hungary, in the past which he had tried to erase from his memory. Was that the reason seeing the brooch had brought tears to his eyes when Myra showed it to him? What secret did it hold? The diamonds were real, as a jeweler had appraised it with Myra present. The value stunned Myra, which was the reason she gladly had Sam put it in his bank's vault. She trusted Sam as she would a father.

Summer sped by with horrible news of the wars being fought in the Pacific and in Europe. If it were not for Mathew being in her life, Myra was sure she would not have survived her fears. John doted on his grandson. He was the one who got up in the night to feed Mathew and change his diapers, and although Myra nursed him, Mathew adapted to bottles too. John had told Myra that was his job in the absence of his son. It was wonderful be surrounded by family with the only worry being Eric's safety. Fall was arriving too soon, and Myra was a little anxious to get back to familiar surroundings. She missed Sister Bernadette too. Diana had visited her in July while on vacation with yet a new man in her life. It wasn't the happy-go-lucky roommate Myra knew so well. She was quieter and seemed to be under the control of her new boyfriend, jumping up to fulfill his requests or glancing to see if he approved of what she said. Diana had always been in control, but on this visit she seemed aloof and afraid. She told Myra she had reserved a room for them at a private home near Chappaqua Park, a short walk to the campus, but big enough for the baby. The landlady loved children so there was no problem there. There was also a nursery day care nearby which would fit in with Myra's schedule. It was at the mention of their living quarters that Myra noticed the boyfriend's disgusted look at Diana. She wanted so much to ask Diana what was going on between them, but it wasn't the time or place, so Myra said nothing.

The apartment was just as Diana had described it. The landlady, Norma Moore, was as nice a person as Diana had claimed. She giggled often and smiled all the time. She was short and thin, and on the move constantly. She took to Mathew like a lost grandson and had put a baby bed in the bedroom Myra would have. Diana didn't show up for the first week before classes started. Myra had been busy establishing the care of her baby and signing up for her classes. The night before classes were to begin, Myra was happy to see Diana, but shocked to see the boyfriend too, with his luggage in his hands. That wasn't part of the deal-- to include him their living quarters. Diana told Myra that they would be a couple and not to worry about a thing. Diana was paying the extra rent and the baby would not bother them at all. The first month was a nightmare for Myra. Diana wasn't the same person she thought she knew. She hardly went to classes, and the boyfriend, who called himself Clancy, didn't work and lived off Diana's allowance from her parents. He was classified as a 4F because of some disability Myra couldn't recognize. Diana's athletic programs ceased, and Myra worried that Diana might be sick or mentally unable to handle her life any more. It took one visit from Edna and Sam on a lovely Sunday afternoon to evaluate the living situation for Myra and the baby. Sam took over and with Myra's permission found a suitable apartment for them near the campus. The move was hard for Myra as she didn't want to alienate Diana, but for her son's sake, she could not tolerate the smoking, drinking, and loud arguments.

A week after her move, Norma Moore came in to see Myra at the Sink. She was nervous and Myra could hardly make sense of what she said. She had had to call the police to move Diana and Clancy out of her house as they had damaged furniture and torn holes in the walls. Clancy had even threatened Norma and she could no longer feel at ease with them in her house. What she really wanted Myra to know was about Diana's health. She detected Diana throwing up constantly and her coloring was so pale. She was afraid that Clancy was beating her, but unless Diana filed charges against him the police could not do a thing. Mrs. Moore had tried to contact Diana's parents but was referred to their lawyer who in turn said Diana was no longer in the parents' good graces. Whatever happened to her now was not their business. In other words, they had disinherited Diana. No wonder Mrs. Moore was upset. Her rented apartment was in shambles and who was to pay for the damage? Myra was glad she had moved out when she did. All she could do now was tell the distraught woman that she was sorry.

Mathew's first Christmas was spent at his Great Aunt Edna's home as the past two years had been for Sister Bernadette and Myra. His Grandpa John and Aunt Elizabeth traveled from California to be with him too but this time they had brought another person. His name was Timothy Barns, a young man who presented Elizabeth with an engagement ring for Christmas. Myra liked Timothy on first sight. He was a handsome Navy officer, one who could have been featured on a recruitment poster.. He was blond and very tall and very much in love with Elizabeth. He blended in with the family and friends who dropped by with the ease of a professional greeter. Of course the ever-present Sam brought the wine on Christmas Eve and the holiday was a lively affair for all of them.

It was Sister Bernadette who worried Myra. She was losing weight and her coloring had lost the pink glow her face always had in Myra's memories of her. She was too quiet for a woman who loved to talk all the time. When Myra questioned her, Sister Bernie said it was true. Her appetite was not as active as it was at a younger age, but after all, was it not true that one gets less hungry with age? Other than that, she assured Myra, she was fine. Her greatest joy was holding and playing with Matt, as Sister Bernie called him. Strange too, was the way Mathew held out his arms to Sister when she walked in the room. Six months old and he knew who he wanted to hold him.

Myra and Mathew returned to Boulder before the New Year, as she was to help out with holiday parties that would be held at the Sink. She had only been back one day and Mathew was already asleep in his crib when there was a knock on her apartment door. It was after ten o'clock at night, which caused Myra to hesitate in opening the door.

"Myra." A voice called out to her. "Please Myra let me in. It's Diana."

Shocked to hear Diana's voice after not hearing from her since Mrs. Moore had evicted her and Clancy, Myra opened the door. Diana was alone dressed in a shabby coat and holding a piece of luggage. Her hair was a mess; the lovely blond strands so dirty one would never guess she was a blond.

"My God, Diana. What has happened to you?" Myra asked as she helped her into the room.

"Close the door before they see me," Diana said. "I have been trying to reach you but your landlords wouldn't let me in. They said you were not home and slammed the door in my face."

Myra shut the door and had Diana sit down on the sofa. "What in God's name has happened to you?"

"You really don't want to know, do you? But I am

going to tell you anyway," Diana said. She brushed her face with her hand. "My parents disowned me and Clancy was killed."

Myra gasped and put her hand over her mouth. "How horrible. When did this happen?"

"I am so thirsty. Myra. Do you have anything to drink?"

"I have no alcohol here if that is what you mean." Myra told her, "But I could give you some water. Would that be OK?"

"Oh, yes. Water is what I meant. I am not drinking any more. Not ever," Diana said shaking her head. "It is a long story and I need a place to get my head together. Can I stay here for a few days? I promise I won't be a problem."

Myra thought of her son and wasn't sure Diana's presence was the best for him. Myra would be working for two nights in a row and had a baby sitter lined up for Mathew. How would she explain Diana to her landlords? Mr. & Mrs. Smith were very nice to her and at times even offered to baby-sit Mathew, though Myra always declined. She had the daughter of one of managers at the Sink always available and Mathew was comfortable with the sixteen-year-old high school girl. She was at a loss for words as she went into the kitchen area and poured some water into a glass. She handed Diana the glass and sat beside

"Oh God, thanks," Diana said as she gulped it down. "I know what your thinking, Myra. You are thinking about your baby with me around. But I am thinking of my baby too."

It was then that Myra noticed Diana's stomach. She couldn't be too pregnant Myra thought, as Diana always had a flat stomach. This was a tiny bulge pulling her coat apart. "Yes, my dear Myra, I am going to be mother, but don't worry. It is months off. Around June, I think. I haven't seen a doctor yet."

Before Diana could go on, Myra helped her remove her coat and showed her the bathroom. Before she closed the door, Myra gave her a washcloth and towel. "Wash up some Diana and I will fix you something to eat. Then we will talk."

The cheese sandwich and hot tea seemed to calm Diana who ate the food like she had not eaten for awhile. Then she began her story.

After Mrs. Moore had them arrested in October, they had spent five days in jail. Diana had called her parents for help but was told by the housekeeper they were no longer taking her calls. Then Diana called their family lawyer and he confirmed the housekeeper's words. He told Diana they had heard about her unacceptable behavior and even her arrest from friends who also had a daughter going to CU. They had disowned her completely, and she was not to bother them ever again. Although she was their only child, they would leave everything to her half sister, a daughter from her father's earlier marriage. Diana and Clancy then hitchhiked to Denver and panhandled on the streets of the downtown area. Diana was not going to turn to dust in her parent's eyes, so after a few days she called the lawyer again in tears and desperation. She must have touched his heart because he informed her that she did have a trust fund that her parents had no control over. It was left to her by her maternal grandmother, and since she had just turned twenty-one, it was hers. However, she would have to come to Boston and sign the legal papers. It was a generous fund and being paid on a monthly basis would free Diana from the poverty she had thought she would face.

They had enough bus money to get to Kansas City, Missouri, but from there they had hitched rides all the way to Boston. Diana told Myra that was when she was so sick and vomiting. She was sure she was pregnant but Clancy didn't believe her.

They went immediately to the law office of Kent, Dunkin and Falter, Steve Kent being the family lawyer for years. He hadn't expected her for a few weeks and had nothing ready for the signing. He did call her parents while she and Clancy sat in his big leather chairs eating from a dish of nuts. He explained to her mother Diana's purpose for being there, and they could hear her voice cracking over the phone. Steve Kent told her mother that legally she had no control over the trust fund even if it was her own mother's doings. He had tried to make peace between Diana and her mother, but when he handed the phone to Diana, the line was dead. Diana told Steve Kent they had no money to stay around for a few weeks and she thought she might be pregnant. This was a girl he had watched grow up and achieve greatness as an athlete. Kent surmised that the uncouth man with her was responsible for Diana's fall from grace. He could not let her beg on the streets of Boston. Sailors and other service men had taken over the town at night behaving in ways they would never had thought about in their home towns.

He made a few calls to hotels in the center of town and near the Commons. If the couple would agree to find work until he could get the paperwork done he would put them up for that time in a small hotel. They agreed, and Steve Kent loaned them three hundred dollars to start them out. When they left they went straight to the hotel. It was a clean establishment and Diana made Clancy promise to stop his drinking and keep everything under control. Diana got a job as a salesperson in a department store and Clancy found work on the dock in Boston Bay. Life was easier for a time, but her parents were seeking a way to stop or delay the disbursement of the trust fund. When it was judged in Diana's favor, the papers were signed, but her allowance would not start for three months. It was another legal move from her parents.

Any alcohol now made Diana sick so she didn't join Clancy in his drunken sprees. She had an appointment with a gynecologist for the first week in December, but it never happened. Clancy was drinking heavily and insulting her and hitting her on almost a daily basis. It threw Diana into a state of despair, believing she was no good to anyone. She began to wonder what it was in Clancy that made her think she loved him. He was a bum. He had very little respect for anyone and he could get into fights over nothing at all. She had canceled her doctor's appointment due to a black eye Clancy gave her and, despite the morning sickness, started to drink away her sorrows. She knew it was wrong but it was the only way she knew how to cope. Clancy had said he was an orphan with no family he could remember. This had endeared him to Diana because of her respect for the orphaned Myra. She decided that he just needed someone to believe in him; she was sure she could change him.

One night Diana went out looking for Clancy, as he hadn't come home from his job. That was when she discovered he had been fired a week before for fighting. Later she found him in a bar on the waterfront talking to a group of drunken sailors. When he saw Diana, he started berating her and shoving her around. A sailor came to her rescue but not before Clancy hit her so hard she fell to the floor. She felt blood in her mouth and her head was spinning. She was aware there was scuffle going on; then the sound of a gun roared through the room. She must have passed out then because when she came around she riding in an ambulance with an oxygen mask over her face. Two days later she was told that Clancy had been shot and killed by someone in the crowd. He had made nothing of his life but had chosen to let his temper guide him.

Now his seed was growing in her and she wasn't fit to be a mother. She had no idea how many days she had lain in that Boston hotel room, but then she thought of Myra. Self-pity was not the way to go and because of the baby, she knew she had to get her last paycheck from her work and get back to Colorado, which she did. However, her money had run out before she got to Boulder, but she was sure Myra would help her until her trust fund disbursements started. It was Christmas break when she entered the Sink to ask about Myra's new address, which they gladly gave her. She had not bathed for a few days and her hair was a mess because dried blood still seeped from her head wound after she was released from the hospital. The landlords looked at her as if she was figure from hell and had turned her away every time she tried to contact Myra. Tonight it was different. She had sat in the bus depot for hours before she walked up to Myra's apartment house. She saw the lights in an apartment that had not been lit before. It had to be Myra. The end of Diana's story filled Myra with pity and love for this dear person who had taken a wrong turn in her life. She didn't deserve to be ignored by her parents or strangers on the street.

"Of course you can stay here, Diana. We can share my bed and from the looks of you sleep will be welcomed," Myra said as she directed her to the bedroom. "However, you must be very quiet as Mathew is right over there," she said, pointing to the crib in the corner. Diana softly walked over to the crib and blew the sleeping baby a kiss. Myra's pajamas were soft and comfortable, a feeling Diana had almost forgotten about. She was almost asleep as she pulled up the covers.

Chapter Eleven

By the time classes started on the campus, Diana had seen a doctor for the seeping scalp wound. He had shaved her hair over the rugged tear in her scalp and put stitches in to heal it evenly. Sam wasn't too pleased to know Myra had Diana staying with her. Myra explained to him that Diana would soon have her own money and would find a place of her own. The last of March, Diana's first payment arrived. It just so happened that on that day an apartment in their building was vacated, so Diana immediately asked to rent it. The landlords by now had accepted her as a good friend of Myra's and had no qualms about her living there. It turned out to be a blessing for Myra because Diana became the nanny for Mathew. After all, she had told Myra, she had had a nanny and knew exactly what to do. Also, Diana would not accept any pay. She felt more like Mathew's aunt than a friend of his mother.

V-mails from Eric always lifted Myra's spirits, and she glided through her studies that semester. Because Diana was there to take Mathew when she needed to study, her classes were easy. She had won an honor in a short story contest her professor had encouraged her to enter. That event gave Myra the direction she wanted to go in life. The dreams that had haunted her for years seemed to disappear with the happiness she was now feeling. She thought the dreams must have been caused by her lack of family; now the fears of the past did not seem important since her future was to be as bright as the sunshine the in the sky.

It was a different story with Sam. In his research on Myra's brooch and background, he had uncovered the name of a Hungarian artist. Although Matyas Vargas was a designer for stage settings, he had been known to also paint portraits. This artist might know something about a large, nineteenth century portrait of a woman wearing a diamond-studded Star of David--even if the location of its cave was not known. It was safe for now, Sam hoped. It was frustrating not to be able to contact the artist, who according to his research was working in Budapest. However, with the city still under the control of the Germans, there was no way Sam could go farther in that direction. In books, Sam had found a little information on Jewish religious symbols. It was amazing that he had forgotten so much of his childhood heritage; but when he decided to leave Hungary and his family, he had erased much that was worth remembering. With each lead in his search for Myra's past, he was beginning to feel more like a Jew again.

The year-end exams were over and Diana was getting uncomfortable in her pregnancy. Mathew had celebrated his first birthday at Aunt Edna's house where he was showered with all kinds of gifts. The Dawsons could not be there as Elizabeth and Tim were to be married the middle of June. Myra, Edna, and Sam were to travel to California for the big event. In fact, Myra was to be a matron of honor. She sent her measurements to Elizabeth and her gown was to be fitted when she got there. Myra was worried about Diana's condition but Diana told her Betty had offered to help her if she needed help. So, with reservations, Myra and Mathew left for California. The ride on the train delighted Mathew who was spoiled by all the attention he got from passengers and conductors. If only Eric could have been there, Myra thought, all would be perfect. On June 5th, a week before the wedding, Myra got a call from Betty. Diana had delivered a healthy little girl. Although Betty sounded a little hesitant when Myra asked about Diana, she assured Myra that while Diana had had a hard time of it, the doctors thought she would be just fine.

The wedding was the most beautiful ceremony Myra had ever seen. Of course, she had not ever attended a formal ceremony the likes of this one, but it was an eye opener on how the other half lived. She had to giggle some to herself, as she too was now part of the 'other half.' It amazed her that in two years she had advanced socially from struggling college coed to mother with wonderful family ties. One more year to go and then a degree in journalism would be hers, and Eric would be home.

Nothing lasts forever, as Myra soon learned. On returning to her apartment, she found a note to call Betty immediately. It was Diana, Betty told her. She was back in the hospital hemorrhaging again. Betty had the baby whom Diana had named Lilly Ann. Diana was asking for Myra to come to the Boulder hospital as soon as possible. A very frightened Myra called the baby sitter she had used before Diana took over. The girl came straightaway.

The hospital room was stark white and Myra had to control her thinking again as the white room stimulated her childhood flashbacks. Diana was as pale as the sheets that covered her, but her eyes brightened when she saw Myra.

"Thank God you are here." Diana said in almost a whisper. "I needed you so much."

"Hush, Diana, I am here now. You must rest. We will talk later when you get stronger."

"No, Myra, I have to tell you now." She tried to sit up. Myra put some pillows under her head. "I have contacted Steve Kent, the lawyer, remember?"

Myra shook her head yes. "He sent me some legal papers which I have signed and sent back. It was notarized too." She stopped as she took a deep breath. " I have made you Lilly's guardian in every sense of the word. Any money or inheritance she gets will be under your control until she is of age"

"Diana, stop this. You sound as though you..." Myra couldn't say it.

"I am not going to make it, Myra. I am dying."

"No! You are not. It is just the effect of the birth. You can't die, Diana. Not you. You have always been the strong one. NO! I won't let you," Myra cried out.

"Stop it Myra and listen to me. I don't ever want my parents to have Lilly. Do you hear me? Never. They have never been there for me and they will never have Lilly to shame for her birth."

By now Myra was crying and could hardly talk. "Please, Diana, don't give up. You have so much to live for now."

"Don't you think I know that? But I have to think of Lilly now. I have been blaming myself knowing Clancy was a bad choice, but it was a choice I made and I will not let my innocent child suffer for my mistakes." Diana was now crying too, but went on. "Please Myra, you are the most decent person I know. The only one I would trust my little girl to, to love and keep safe. You are a survivor Myra. You would be strong for your children." A hush and then, "I am dying Myra. The doctors have told me that much. It isn't just the hemorrhaging. Clancy infected me but thank God the baby is OK. They examined her completely and she is very healthy. What I have wasn't transferred to her in the womb." Diana smiled up at her. "It is going to be fine, Myra. Eric won't mind. He is a pretty decent person too. You really lucked out with him."

131

Myra

Myra was realizing that her perfect world was crumbling. It wasn't just herself now that would have to survive. It would be Mathew and Lilly and Eric in the face of their future. What could Diana's parents try to do to take Lilly against the legal papers Diana had just initiated?

"There are other papers too, Myra. Betty took some pictures of Lilly Ann and me so she can know her true mother. I do want her to know that much. They buried Clancy in a pauper's graveyard somewhere in Boston. I didn't even know his last name or where he was raised, but if Lilly ever wants to know that is about all the information I have about her father. He never told me why he was classified as 4F and could not be drafted, but I had no idea he was sharing his illness with me."

The oxygen tank which kept Diana breathing was pumping in rhythm with Myra's heart. How could she lose Diana now? The only real friend of her age that understood all Myra had revealed, things not even her beloved husband knew. The load of responsibility sat heavy on Myra, but she knew she had to be strong for Diana's sake.

"I love you, Diana. I will never let Lilly forget you. Never."

"Just like your dreams, huh?" Diana smiled up at her. "If there is life after death, I too will haunt Lilly in her dreams. Look how strong they made you? It will be different with Lilly because she will know her mother's background."

How Myra wished for that strength now. "I would promise your daughter the world if I could, you know that. I can tell you now that I will love her as my own, and you will always live in her heart."

"Just never let her be given to my parents. Promise me that Myra? She will have to know about them when she is older, but let her be the judge whether or not to contact them. How you picture them to her will be up to you, but by then with your influence she will make the right choices. She is my gift to you and to the world."

A week later, Diana died. She had arranged her burial site and services when she knew the truth about her condition. Nevertheless, it was very painful for Myra. She had been with Diana for her last breath and felt so bad about the parents not being notified, but it was as Diana wished. How can these things happen to people who are related to each other? Is that what had happened to her as a baby? Did she fall through the cracks between caring people now lost forever? She vowed that Lilly Ann never would be lost or left behind under any circumstances. She had written to Eric about the events but he would not have received her letter by then.

She felt sure he would accept Lilly Ann too, so she was not going to worry about that.

Chapter Twelve

Eric's family and Sam did not immediately take to the idea of Myra adopting Lilly Ann, but she eventually made them understand by describing her own life as an orphan. They did see the comparison and came to hope that Eric would approve. Sam helped her with the adoption papers. Although Eric's name would not be on these papers, Myra would legally be Lilly's mother. Sam explained to Myra that Eric could initiate his own part of the adoption when he returned.

Lilly was a good baby, sleeping most of the night at two months. Mathew took to her like his own special toy and often patted her gently when Myra was watching him. A whimper from the baby, however, would send Myra dashing to the rescue of Lilly, as Mathew's patting got too enthusiastic. Steve Kent contacted Myra and said he had transferred Diana's account to a law firm in Denver, a firm Diana had requested. That was how Myra discovered that Sam's law firm would be administering the estate. Sam was not informed until Myra called him, but he was happy about the transfer. Steve Kent also had written that Diana's monthly trust fund payments would be sent to Myra for Lilly Ann's care, another matter Diana had taken care of when she knew she was dying. Diana's parents had been notified about Diana's death and the birth of Lilly Ann, but refused to deal with anyone connected to their disowned daughter.

It was Sam who later told Myra that Diana had also inherited real estate from her grandmother, Lady Gloria Preston, and Lady Preston's husband. It seems Diana hadn't known about it either. Her grandmother's will had bypassed her parents, Sam said, probably because of some unpleasantness which had developed between the English and the American branches of the family. Lord Henry Preston was Gloria's third husband and Diana had spent some summer vacations with the Prestons as a child. Having no heirs on his side of the family, Lord Preston had left most of his estate to Diana.

Myra moved to a house farther up the canyon near Chappaqua Park She could now hire a real nanny for the children and also an automobile for herself. Sam helped her pick out a slightly used Ford and taught her how to drive. She never attempted to drive with the children in the car until she felt she could trust her driving skills.

The V-mails from Eric were a little disappointing. He did not immediately approve of the adoption but said they would talk about it when the war, which seemed to be coming to a victorious end, was over. He could hardly wait to hold her in his arms again and smell her sweetness. His pictures of Mathew gave him bragging rights, he said, and he passed them around the barracks when he got them and hung them above his bunk, when he had a

On the California front, Elizabeth was expecting a baby, and her pregnancy diverted attention from the adoption debate. Sister Theresa had contacted Myra too. Sister Bernie was not doing well. She was crippled with arthritis and they were considering putting her in the nursing home for nuns near Loretta Heights in southwest Denver.

Myra went to visit Sister Bernadette before they moved her and was distressed that this once jolly woman was half the size she had been. They talked of old times and about Myra's choice of religion for the two children. Sister was the only person who praised Myra instantly and unconditionally for adopting Lilly Ann. Just as Myra was leaving, Sister called her back and told her that Sister Theresa had some papers she had found in the suitcase Myra had arrived with all those years ago. She explained there were some drawings Myra had evidently done as a small child. Maybe they would help her if she were still trying to remember her past. Myra bent over and kissed the old nun who had been a mother to her. If love would last forever, she would always love Sister Bernadette.

That was last time Myra saw Sister, who died three weeks later in the nursing home and was buried at Mount Olivet, a Catholic cemetery which served several Denver parishes. The day of Sister's burial, rain and sleet mixed with snow. Sam accompanied Myra to the cemetery; he had enjoyed Sister Bernadette's humor and presence. Myra stood by his side under his umbrella and cried softly. She felt abandoned again, and also a little guilty because she had not attended Sister Bernie's funeral Mass, or even the Rosary the night before. If Sam did not feel like a stranger at Mount Olivet, Myra did. She had closed the door to her Catholic life, and now that Sister Bernie was gone, there would be no turning back. Sam reached for her hand and she gladly took hold tightly, as though the ground underneath her might open up and she might fall in. Diana's funeral had been rough, and now Sister Bernie was gone too. A chill shook her body as words from somewhere in her past said, "Death always comes in threes."

She sunk against Sam's shoulders, feeling faint and weak in her legs.

"Myra what is it? Are you all right?" Sam asked

"Oh Sam, is it true that death comes in threes?"

"Where did you hear that?"

"I don't know. It just came to me as a memory from somewhere. Someone must have said that to me," Myra said, as she gained control of her body. "I am so afraid. If I lose another loved one, I don't think I could handle it."

"If you are thinking of Eric, you must have faith. The war is almost over, and he will be home safe and sound. He has lasted this long. Do you think he would not survive after all he has been through?" Sam asked

Myra composed herself and said, "I am sorry, Sam. Of course he will be fine." She paused and looked around. "We don't belong here, do we?"

Sam nodded and they turned to walk to his car. Resist as she might, Myra felt the rain beating on the window of the car was her tears for Sister Bernadette and Diana. "Please God, if ever you have heard me, hear me now. Bring Eric home safely."

That night the dreams returned. Myra was again running, not to catch the lady with black hair, but away from her. The land in front of her was flat with trees standing along a dirt road in straight rows like columns on ancient Roman buildings. The road on which she was running seemed endless. Only the trees like silent soldiers were peripherally visible. She could hear the footsteps of the woman behind her but Myra's legs would not move any faster. A figure appeared to be standing in the middle of the road, waiting for her. It was a man in a long dark coat with a long beard protruding from his chin. He wore a black hat with a wide brim and a small braid of his hair hung down one side of his face. He held out his arms and called to her, "Come home Myra, come home." Just as she was about to reach him, the woman with black hair caught up with them. Myra jumped to the side and the woman struck the man with such force his face was scratched from her nails. "I will kill you if you take her from me. I will kill you." Then she started beating the man with a tree branch until he fell to the ground holding his hands up-

Myra

"Stop it!" Myra screamed and woke up in a sweat. It took her a minute to realize she was in her bed and could hear the rain beating on the windows, not the branch hitting the man. She was breathing hard as though she had been running, but her bedding and nightclothes were dry and warm. She listened for a while. Had she awakened the babies? She got up softly and walked to their room. Both of them were sleeping like angels. Whatever innocence showed in their little faces Myra vowed they would keep. She checked their blankets and left the room.

She went downstairs to the kitchen and boiled some water for tea. She found a teacup and some cookies in the cupboard and set them on the table. As she did so, the vanilla envelope Sister Theresa had given her fell to the floor and its contents scattered around. She had forgotten where she had put them when she returned home after her last visit with Sister Bernie. She bent over and collected them in a pile and set them on the table. The water boiled and while the tea simmered in the cup, Myra looked at the collection of childish writings and drawings. She was almost through with her tea when she turned a page of the papers and got a shock. There was a stick figure of a person in a black coat with a pointed beard and braid shooting out of his big black hat. On the back of the paper were Jewish symbols similar to Chinese writings. They were telling about the drawing, Myra thought. Sam would be able to read it and she would call him the first thing in the morning. The next page had drawings of more stick figures. One was a woman with curly lines falling from the head indicating curly hair. Then there was a small stick drawing that seem to be a baby crying as tears were drawn flowing from the figure's closed eyes.

Myra didn't sleep the rest of the night, and when the nanny came in to the kitchen she found her dazed and sitting like a statue staring out the window. Helen Cotter was an English nanny who had worked for an English professor and his family at CU. When the family returned to England before the war, Helen stayed behind and had been a nanny for other University professors. She had perfect posture and manners and refused to call Myra by her first name. Helen wore her hair in an upsweep on the top of her head. She had a lovely and gentle voice and didn't require more money than Myra could pay. She kept her room next to the nursery in a very neat condition. Her way with Mathew was remarkable; she read to him often, and changed Lilly's diapers as soon as they got damp.

"You poor thing," Nanny Helen said, noticing the teacup and untouched cookie package. "I know how dear your little nun was to you, but she would want you to go on, wouldn't she?"

Myra blinked and looked up at her, "Oh, good morning Helen. Yes, Sister Bernie would not want me to grieve forever. It is just—" she stopped at that point. No, she wasn't about to talk about her dream. "I just couldn't sleep." She started to rise from her chair and clear the table.

Myra

"Oh no, Mum, I will do that. The babies are awake and I will bring them down here while you try to get some shut-eye." Helen's accent was proper and English. "The little master loves to watch me fix his food and the baby has such a good nature."

So, Myra started for the stairs but paused to say, "Thank you Helen, but I don't have a class until noon. So if I should go back to sleep, will you remember to wake me?"

Then she heard Helen picking up the papers and went back into the kitchen to retrieve them, "I will put these in my room," she told the nanny. Myra took the papers and continued upstairs.

She would call Sam later in the day, but first she went into the nursery and kissed each baby. Mathew was standing up in his crib and held his arms out to her. He had a shock of black curly hair sticking up from his head and it was the color of Myra's. She picked him up and he snuggled next to her breast as if he was still nursing. "No, no, my darling. You are big a boy now." She laid him on the changing table and opened a drawer underneath it to pick out a diaper. She had just pinned it on him when Nanny Helen came in and took over. Lilly gurgled in her crib, content to watch the activity of the morning. Myra retreated to her room and barely laid her head on the pillows before she was again asleep.

She woke hearing a knock on her bedroom door. The day was dreary and snowing again and she was uncertain of the time. Nanny Helen softly opened the door and stuck her head in. "I am sorry to wake you Mum, but you have phone call."

"What time is it?" Myra asked.

"One o'clock, Mum. A Miss Betty called earlier to inform you that classes would be cancelled today due to the weather. I thought it best not to disturb you at that time. This is a call from a Mr. Sam Hirsch. He said it was important."

Myra reached for her robe and slipped into her slippers. "Thank you, Helen. I will take it. I need to talk to him, too."

"Sam, I was going to call you." Myra said. "I have discovered something very important for you to read."

"Myra, I have to talk to you too. Can I come up tonight?"

Myra glanced out the kitchen window. "It is snowing so hard and Betty evidently called and told Helen classes have been canceled for the day due to the weather, so would it not be dangerous to drive in this?"

"I'll take the train and get a hotel room for the night. I think we have a decision to make and it can't be made over the phone."

"But Sam, how will you get up the hill if everything

is at a standstill?" Myra asked.

"I know the snow plows are working. I am sure the taxis are running. Besides, we are not snowbound down here."

"Then," said Myra, "Do not stay in a hotel. I have an extra room here on the main floor. Stay here with us; then we won't have to worry about the weather."

"I will try to be there about six, if that is okay with you."

"Great. Don't eat; I had planned to cook an adult meal tonight for Helen and myself. She deserves a good meal once in a while. I shopped yesterday."

Chapter Thirteen

It had stopped snowing by the time Sam arrived. He was able to find a taxi for the ride up to Myra's. The table was set with lovely china Myra had bought on sale and a beautiful white linen tablecloth some one had given Eric and her for a wedding gift. Large candles were lit on both sides of the table. Nanny Helen let Sam in and took his coat and overnight bag to the hall closet. Sam could hear the children in the kitchen and Myra's soft voice talking to them. He walked into the kitchen to see the baby Lilly open her mouth for a spoonful of food. Mathew spotted him right away and held out his arms, food smeared all over his mouth. Myra turned around and smiled at Sam. "These babies like to bathe in their food."

Half an hour later, the babies washed and tucked into their cribs, Myra, Sam and Nanny Helen, sat down for a dinner of prime rib, small baked red potatoes with asparagus, and a salad with chestnuts and apples and a light dressing. Myra had bought a Challah loaf, a traditional Jewish bread, for Sam; and Nanny Helen had made a chocolate caramel walnut tart. Also Myra had splurged on a red wine the clerk at the wine merchant's store had told her was perfect for a meal containing red meat.

"I am not the best cook, but it was fun putting all this together. I hope you like it," Myra said.

Sam lifted his wine glass to her and said, "It was wonderful. Congratulations and a toast for your very marvelous meal, Myra, and to you Nanny Helen." The three clicked their wine glasses as Sam gave a Hungarian salute: "Egeszegedre"

Nanny Helen said, "Cheers and Happiness also."

Later, after the clean-up and Nanny Helen retiring to her bedroom, Myra and Sam went to the little room off the hall that Myra thought of as her office. This night it would be Sam's sleeping quarters. A sofa bed had been part of the rental furnishings and it was to be used to-night for the first time.

Sam fetched his luggage from the hall closet and opened his bag and brought out a folder of papers. He laid them on the desk and pulled out a few pages.

"These," he told Myra, "are queries about Lilly's adoption. Diana had a half sister by the name of Trudy Potts, and she is requesting the right to adopt Lilly. She knows Diana did legally give Lilly to you, but I think she also knows that: Lilly has a small fortune, and that could be her motive."

"Oh Sam, I will never let that happen. Is there any law to protect Diana's wish?'

"Luckily there is, but I have to work fast. You will have to sign this petition as her guardian and designated adoption mother. It asks for a delay before any of this woman's request goes to a court judgment. Lilly will legally be your child in three weeks, exactly six months after Diana signed her request for you to adopt her. This woman seems to be a troublemaker. Her petition will not reach anyone in charge of the adoption grant within those three weeks. But I have to get this filed, just in case she has another legal move of which I am not aware."

Myra was a little dazed. "How could this happen? Who is this woman, and why now? I don't think I ever heard Diana mentioning she had a sister."

"It seems she is the daughter of Diana's father by an earlier marriage. I am having her investigated and I will let you know what I find out about her. But for now, let's just take this legal step. Lilly will be yours before this hits the courts."

Myra shook her head, "I just can't believe this is happening. It could be my story too, you know. I think I fell through the cracks of the law, but it is different now, isn't it Sam? Why does life always throw me curves?"

"Don't fret about it, Myra. We have all the papers in order and I think everything is going to be fine." Sam pulled out some more papers, "However, talking about your past, I have a little more information that might jar your memory."

Myra

Myra was wide eyed as she watched Sam place the papers in front of her.

"You do remember Eric mentioning a painting that looked so much like you?"

Myra nodded and pulled the papers closer to her side of the desk trying to make sense of all that Sam was telling her.

"I did some research about immigrants from Europe and found an old Hungarian man from Budapest. He came over here after the last World War. Before that time, he was an art teacher in a small college outside of Budapest. An art teacher, I thought might know of such a painting. I was able to find him in New Jersey from old records in the public library so I called him. At first, he had no idea what I was asking about, but his daughter took over the phone and interpreted for me. He remembered a painting like the one Eric told you about. Its size, its beautiful lady, the Star of David brooch, and the 1870s costumes and colors in it seemed right. I sent him a picture of you, and he confirmed the likeness. The painting had, in his time, been in the Budapest Museum. A student he once taught knew more about it since the artist had worked in the student's home area. He thinks it was in the south of Hungary, but wasn't sure. He gave me the name of the former student, who, he believes, became an artist himself. But he thought that he would probably be fighting in the war."

Myra was amazed that Sam had been able to find

out so much. "Would the artist the old man mentioned know who the model for the portrait was?"

"That is what I am hoping, Myra. The artist's name is Matyas Varga, but I have no information on him. Hungary is locked to the outside world and the Russians are moving into the country." Sam picked up the papers Myra was to sign and handed her a pen he had found on her desk.

As Myra signed her name she began to shake and tears formed in her eyes. "Oh Sam, do you think I am ever going to find out about my heritage?"

"Yes, Myra, I do, and we must never give up your search. Look what is being uncovered now. A painting so much like you that it could be an ancestor. The diamond brooch is surely a clue, and the person who had it and the one who sent it must have a connection. You are almost twenty-two, with years ahead of you to live and discover. Even if I am not around, one day you will know the truth of your past. Just promise me you will never give up."

Myra wiped her eyes and kissed Sam's hand as he reached for the papers. "I promise, Sam, and you will be around to celebrate finding the lost girl."

Then it came to Myra that she had not showed Sam the childhood drawings Sister Bernie had saved for her. "Sam, I forgot. Sister Bernie did find a few more clues in my old suitcase. She forgot about them at the time because of the events that followed my marriage and Matt's birth, Diana's death and Lilly given to me. They are stick figures that may tell you something because on the back of the drawings are Hebrew letters, I think."

Myra went to fetch the papers she had taken up to her bedroom thinking she would also tell Sam of her dream last night. Sam had lit his cigar and was comfortably seated in the leather back chair by the windows. "Do you mind if I smoke? It is like a dessert after a great dinner."

Myra did mind but she would never tell Sam. She did however; keep the ashtray in a drawer in a small hall table. She fetched it and sat down on the floor beside him.

She gave him the first sheet and he could hardly believe what he was seeing. "The figure of the man. It might indicate a Rabbi with his beard and tall hat. The braids from his head indicate him to be an orthodox Jew." Sam studied the drawings a while before Myra reminded him to look on the back of the sheet. "Yes," he said. " It is Hebrew!"

"What does it say, Sam?" Myra anxiously asked him

He read it with his lips moving silently pronouncing the words. He turned the paper around again back to the other side. He shook his head in disbelief and looked at Myra and patted her head.

"This is a Jewish curse which I think is directed towards the man figure. The woman seems to hate him very much and the child, a baby, I think, is frightened by all of it. The woman has a stick and wants to beat the man as she has the stick in her hand ready to strike, but the crying baby seems to prevent it."

"Oh Sam, you will never believe me, but that is what I dreamt last night. I didn't notice this paper until after the dream. I had put the papers in the cupboard meaning to take them to my office, but forgot them with Sister's death, until they fell out when I reached in for a package of cookies. Do you think I am the baby in the drawings? Do you think I drew these figures?"

"I think you could be the baby, Myra, but I don't think you drew these." He said putting his cigar out in the ashtray. "Exactly how old where you when you realized you had no memory?"

"My guardians said I was almost six. Why?"

"Do you like to draw or paint?"

"I can't draw a straight line although I love looking at good art. Why?"

"This was drawn by an adult, I think, because the lines are too straight for a child six or under. It is rather like a drawing an adult would do to explain something to a child. Stick figures would make it easier for a child of three or four to understand what the adult would be trying to tell her or him. Also, the Hebrew writing would definitely not be that of a child."

"In my dream, Sam, I was running away from the lady with the black hair. I was on a dirt road with trees along the side. They were in rows like soldiers standing at attention, but they were trees. I only got a glance at them before I saw a man in the middle of the road. He had the high black hat on and a pointed beard from his chin. I noticed the braids from his hair hanging on the sides of his face.

He held his arms out to me and I thought I heard him say, 'Come home, Myra. Come home,' but the lady behind me was saying she would kill him first, and she started to hit him with a branch. He held his hands up to protect his face, but she kept hitting him. I woke up screaming for her to stop."

Sam took her hand and softly said, "I believe you Myra. I think your early memories are imbedded in your subconscious part of your brain. It seems they want to come out but some traumatic event is preventing it. I mentioned some time ago that maybe hypnosis might reveal what you can't remember. You didn't want to do it then. How do you feel about it now?"

"I don't know, Sam. I think I am afraid of the truth because of the horrible dreams I have had. Something terrible had to have happened for me to retain the dreams I have."

"I want you to think about it Myra. They have

made great headway in that area of mental health."

Myra promised she would think about it, but for now, the adoption of Lilly had to come first. They talked on for an hour before Sam suggested they call it a night. Myra helped him make up the sleep sofa and kissed his cheek as she bade him goodnight.

Sleep would not come for a long time as Myra thought over the evening events. She was sure now that she was most likely born a Jew. Was that the reason she looked at statues of Jesus with critical eyes and thoughts? Did someone tell her about the Jewish faith before she lost her memory? Maybe Sam was right. She should consider hypnosis. Maybe the dreams would stop for good and she and Eric could live happily ever after. Eric, she thought. How I love him. Then she prayed to the God she believed had brought her this far in life. "Please protect my husband."

Chapter Fourteen

April 1945 — Ohrdruf, Germany

By April, 1945, the war was going well for the Allied Forces. Operations Plunder and Varsity had brought American soldiers into the heart of Germany. On April 4, the 89th Division took and liberated the first Nazi concentration camp, at Ohrdruf, near Gotha. The camp was nearly empty, except for the corpses. Among those who saw stacks of emaciated bodies was Eric Dawson. That night he dreamed: Myra stood looking at him, her eyes brimming. She was wearing the antique black dress and the Star of David brooch he'd seen in that portrait two years earlier. She fingered the brooch now and said to him, softly, "It's mine; this curse is mine; these are my people. I love you, Eric." Then she turned, and vanished. He woke, filled with a sense of dread natural to anyone who had seen Ohrdruf, and with another, peculiar sense of foreboding.

The 89th marched on, toward Friedrichsroda. Resistance was relatively light, though rumor said that Hitler had a stronghold there in the wooded valley, and a factory designing weapons. Eric mused as he walked: how could humans treat other humans like that? Like so much cordwood? Cold. He thought of Myra, of little Matthew, of the strange baby named Lilly whose father had caused so much careless pain before he died. He would, he decided, love that baby; he would never allow her or Matthew to come to harm. But what had Myra meant when she said "this curse is mine"? And why had her figure vanished from his dream?

He didn't see the shell coming; he simply heard the whine and felt the fire burn through his legs, then lost consciousness.

And back in Boulder, several hours later, Myra woke from a troubled sleep to answer a knocking at her door. The Western Union messenger looked almost embarrassed, tentative; as he held the message out to her, he rubbed his forehead and squinted. "I'm sorry, Mrs. Dawson," he said. She took the paper from him and read:

Dear Mrs. Dawson, we regret to inform you that your husband, Sgt. Eric Dawson, has been injured in combat. His condition is grave. He has lost one leg and may lose the other. He remains unconscious. He has been transported by air to Portsmouth, England for evaluation. He will be repatriated as soon as possible.

Myra managed one scream, for Nanny Helen, before she fainted.

The first week after Eric's arrival at Fitzsimmons General Hospital Myra drove to see him every afternoon.

She had morning classes and was able to keep up. Graduation was two weeks away and by then Myra was hopeful that Eric would be out of his coma and aware that he was back in Denver. She was sure he knew she was there as he moved his fingers every time she took his hand. There would be more surgery, Dr. Collins had told her, but first the doctor wanted the open wounds to heal.

On May 8th as Myra sat with Eric, people in the halls of the hospital began cheering and running back and forth. Myra went to the doorway and a doctor she did not know picked her up and swung her around. Surprised by that, Myra pushed him away. She was about to close Eric's room door, when the doctor pushed it open.

"I am sorry but I was not flirting with you. The war is over. Do you hear? The war in Germany is over. It is time to kiss everyone."

"The war is over?" Myra repeated.

"Yes, it just came over the radio. It is finally over. Please excuse my enthusiasm but I lost a brother over there and I didn't want anyone else to go through what my family has gone through."

"Oh, I am sorry. Are you sure the news is correct?" Myra asked as she opened the door all the way.

"As sure as Harry Truman is President," he said as he dashed on down the hall to join the crowds of nurses

Myra

Myra returned to Eric's side. "Oh my darling, the war is over. We won the battle." Then she looked at his right leg. "You won, my dearest. You will get better too. We can have our dream again."

"Myra—" a whisper called to her.

She looked up to Eric's face and his eyes were open. He was looking at her.

"Oh Eric, you are awake. You know me, don't you? Did you hear the news? The war is over and we can get back to our dreams. Oh my darling, I love you so much." Eric blinked his eyes and tried to smile at her but his attempts to say anything more were useless. Doctor Collins came at that time and saw Eric awake.

"Good God, Mrs. Dawson, when did he open his eyes?"

Myra smiled up at the doctor, "When some doctor told me the war was over. He whispered my name."

The doctor took Eric's wrist and checked his heartbeat. He smiled down at Eric and said, "Well young man, you gave us a scare. We thought you were never going to wake up." A pause and then, "How do you feel Eric? Can you tell me?"

Eric twisted his mouth a little and whispered, "Like Hell."

Every day from that time on, Eric got stronger. His face was beginning to look like the old Eric's. His sentences became longer and he was aware of his situation. They moved him to another ward in the hospital where he had a roommate Myra tried to be there every day. John Dawson flew out, hating to leave Elizabeth in her last trimester of pregnancy. However, she had insisted, since Tim thought he would be able to be there with her.

John rented a car and drove from Edna's house everyday except the day when he, Sam and Edna attended Myra's graduation at the University of Colorado. She received her Bachelor's Degree in Journalism with a minor in Accounting. Matt and Lilly, now two and thirteen months old, also came with Nanny Helen and loved all the attention they got. Afterwards, Edna, who could not make it up to Boulder, had Annie do a buffet at her house. It was a joyous occasion topped off by Tim's call from California saying Elizabeth had had a boy. They were naming him John Peter Barns. He weighed a hefty eight pounds and 2 oz. John Dawson felt a happiness he hadn't felt for a long time and toasted both Myra and the new baby. It was then decided to drive to Fitzsimmons and share the good news with Eric. Sam agreed to drive Myra and the little ones, while Edna, John, and Nanny Helen came in the rented car. Myra was hoping she could get permission to bring the children into Eric's room.

It was a bright sunny day and the long ride to the other side of town tired out the little ones. When they got there, Matt woke up but Lilly still snoozed. Nanny Helen stayed in the car with her while the rest, Matt included, made their way into the hospital. The staff was very sympathetic to Myra's plea about Eric meeting his son for the first time and allowed her to bring Matt to his father. Sam had brought a camera for Myra's graduation photos but now he planned to use it on the father-son reunion.

Eric was sitting in a wheel chair beside the window. He had seen them arrive and was all smiles when they entered. Matt had seen a picture of his father almost every night; Myra had taught him to kiss it before he went to sleep. The minute he saw Eric, he ran to him and babbled "Dada, Dada."

It surprised everyone, especially Eric. He reached down to pick him up, but was unable to do so. Matt instead climbed on the wheels of the chair and planted a kiss on his father's cheek. The emotion was too much for Eric. He burst out crying, unable to say anything. Sam snapped away with the camera while Myra lifted Matt up to Eric's face. He reached out for Matt but was unable to hold him. He touched his hair and felt his little face. Matt touched Eric too in the same manner. It was a magic moment and there wasn't a dry face in the room. A few minutes later, Nanny Helen appeared in the doorway holding a sleepy Lilly. Myra took her from Nanny Helen and brought her to Eric's side. He looked her over and smiled.

"She is beautiful, Myra. When is she legally ours?" He spoke in a whisper since he still was not able to speak well or to control his body movements.

"Next week, Eric," said Sam. "I have all the papers ready to go. We only need your signature. I had planed to bring them on this visit, but this was Myra's day--and the birthday of a baby named John Peter Barns," Sam told him.

Eric looked at his father. "Elizabeth's?"

"Yes, son, and he is a big one. Tim called just before we came out here. I didn't ask the time of his birth because I was so excited about the baby, Myra and you getting well."

It was a happy family gathering that day, a day Myra would never forget. Eric was home; his son knew him, and Eric had approved of Lilly and the adoption. Her life was on "go" again. Her unknown past didn't matter any more. She had everything in life that she had ever wanted. But Myra had no idea what roads she would have to travel in the future. Someone might have cursed her bloodline and she would have to deal with it.

———

Myra moved from Boulder shortly after her graduation. She rented a house near Edna and near Sloan's Lake Nanny Helen was anxious to get back to England now that the war in Europe was over. Edna found Myra a dependable replacement from one of her many charitable organizations. She was a Jewish emigrant in need of a place to live until she could learn the American way of life. She spoke very good English and was willing to do anything Myra would have her do. Her name was Esther Steinberg. She was born and raised in Dresden, Germany, and had survived the Holocaust, although her family had not. Esther was 28 years old and had been studying to be a musician when the Nazis took the Jews of the city to concentration camps. Because she could play the piano, she was spared in small ways for entertaining the German officers who demanded music while they ate or celebrated another victory. She had been separated from her mother, a teacher, and father, a banker. A younger sister and brother had died in Auschwitz, she was told after her liberation. Esther was the first in a group of emigrants to be sent to America. A Jewish organization set up for that purpose had sponsored her and now she was to find her own way. She had short red hair and a prominent nose. Her face was oblong, set off by her large brown eyes. When Myra first me her, Esther seemed frightened and timid but she changed when Matthew and Lilly came in to meet her. There was a certain twinkle in her eyes and her smile changed her appearance completely. The children took to her at once. Myra knew she had found the perfect nanny for her children.

Eric would have more surgery before he could leave the hospital, but every week, he grew stronger. Sam had finalized the adoption of Lilly Anne, and Myra sighed with relief. Dr. Collins was worried about Eric's mental condition, though. He had bad days of depression, which was normal for a man with his kind of wounds. He would never walk again as his injuries had torn half of his hip off. No prosthesis could be attached to his missing bones. His manliness had been destroyed too, and he would never feel the glory of sex although his body yearned for it every time Myra walked into his room. Dr. Collins talked it over with Myra but had no idea how to help Eric emotionally.

Seeing him so sad, Myra decided that if Eric knew her story he might realize he wasn't alone in his painful recovery. Though he'd corresponded with Sam about her possible Jewish heritage, he didn't know about the brooch or her own sense that she was Jewish. He didn't know of her molestations in her childhood, or how she felt that Jesus had let her down. She did believe in God, but she questioned why her life was always full of disappointing curves. Eric didn't know of her dreams and he didn't know how close Sam was to the truth about her past.

So, with every visit, until Eric tired, Myra told him a little bit of her story. She was surprised when he said the painting of her look-a-like, which he had found in a cave in France on that secret reconnaissance trip, also had a diamond brooch on her black dress, shaped like the Star of David. That had never mattered to him, he told her. The fact that he had written Sam about it, and that Sam had not told her, made her feel uneasy.

Myra found a job at the *Rocky Mountain News* as a copywriter. It was a beginning and her hours were flexible enough for regular trips to the hospital. The war was still going on with Japan and there were lots of stories to write about. Ernie Pyle had also been a roving correspondent, and he was a great role model for Myra. His death in Japan on April 18th, 1945, had been a real blow to the Scripps Howard Newspaper Corporation. Reporters and staffers were still mourning his passing when Myra started working there. Nanny Esther settled in with the children as though she was born to the job. Myra often came home to the sound of music and laughter. Esther liked to dance and she would pick up one of the children and dance around the room with Matt or Lilly while they giggled and begged for more. Myra noticed how light Esther was on her feet and the radiance from her face as she danced like sunshine on a dreary day.

The Japanese surrendered on September 2nd after atom bombs destroyed Hiroshima and Nagasaki, killing and maiming so many Japanese citizens. It was a feeling of relief for the end of wars, but devastating to know the lives of so many innocent people had been destroyed. It was a victory in one sense and a horror in another. What would the world become with something so horrible and powerful as the atom bomb? It was frightening to think about.

This fear of the future for Eric and her children gave Myra the urge to write about how Americans and others regarded the war and the future. A war to end all wars, some said. Others felt the threat of the bomb would change the world. They speculated that the USA, and the American lifestyle they had always enjoyed would be teetering on a lopsided slide. Most people Myra interviewed on that subject felt all would be well. No other country would dare to start a war in the world. Myra wrote an article on that subject. The editor told her that she had captured the emotions of the people she interviewed. It was a heart-felt story and he felt it deserved to be on the front page of the News. That was the start of Myra's journalism career.

Eric came home for good on the 4th of December, 1945. Esther, being European and Jewish, had little knowledge about the American celebration of the birth of Christ. Eric, who now could talk much longer with a stronger voice, directed Esther how to decorate the house and explained the materialistic meanings that made Christmas such an important holiday. Deadlines bogged down Myra, as she spent her time shopping for gifts and keeping up on world news. Some days, she arrived home so exhausted she almost fell asleep at the dinner table. Esther was catching on fast. The supermarkets were beginning to take hold of grocery shopping, while Mom & Pop corner stores were struggling. An article about their struggle won Myra a News Writer Achievement Award and a small raise in pay. Although there was money always available to Myra's growing family, she only used what was essential. They lived on her salary and Eric's government payment. Only Esther's salary and house rent were taken from Lilly's available funds. In Myra's mind, the money would always be for Lilly when she became of age. For now, Lilly would grow up in a modest-income family and hopefully, would realize the importance of being kind, generous, and considerate of others as well as the value of money.

The only sadness in Myra's heart was Eric's growing depression. It didn't matter where she came from any more. Eric was her life and her love. On his bad days, he spoke of death being better than living. Sam was still Myra's confidant and recommended counseling and professional help, which did bring Eric back to life for a time. But after a few weeks, Eric seemed to sink into his morbid thoughts again. The children, however, brought the old Eric back to laughter and brought the glint back to his eyes. But the bedroom scenes with Myra's lovely slender body sent Eric back to the dark world of his thoughts. Myra could only hold him and kiss him, which wasn't always the right movement to make. He had said his sexual emotions were still alive and well. Seeing her naked tore him apart. There was no relief for him in that part of his body. He usually ended up crying and wishing he were dead. This action tore at Myra's heart like a dagger cutting her into pieces. It was an up and down life of hope and sadness for a year, but Myra never gave up believing that one day, someone or somewhere an invention would help Eric have a more normal life.

Myra's love for him sustained Eric during his dark days, but the guilt about the life he had once hoped to give her sent him sinking deeper into his misery. Frequent visits from his father and Elizabeth only showed how much his life had changed. He knew that one day he would have to end it although he thought Myra's love for him would most likely turn to hate. Yet, in his thinking, she would always have Mathew, a child of his loins.

The only thing that sometimes gave Eric courage to stay alive was watching Mathew grow into a strong and wonderful boy. Lilly, too, smiled and laughed her way into Eric's heart. Both children thought of 'Daddy' as the storyteller. He read their favorite books almost by heart because they demanded them over and over. If the weather was nice, Eric sat in his wheelchair on the back patio and threw balls back and forth to the children. At three, Lilly proved to have a stronger throw than Mathew who seemed to be more interested in butterflies and ant piles along the fence. From his vantage point, Eric looked towards the distant mountain skyline. Flashbacks of skiing, fishing and hiking in his youth scraped his stomach like a razor. The "Why me?" of his existence eventually passed. In the two summers after his return, Myra often drove the children, Esther and Eric up to Evergreen or Eldorado Springs, just south of Boulder. There was a swimming pool for the children and easy access to trails where Myra could push Eric's wheelchair. Life, for Myra, was Eric's happiness, and she tried to make him happy in any way she could.

Chapter Fifteen

1949

The summer of 1949 was as hot as any summer Myra could remember. Mathew and Lilly were five and four years old and full of energy. Matt would be a kindergarten in the fall and Myra promised Lilly she could go to a nursery school. Esther took over as housekeeper and also started teaching piano and dance lessons in the evenings. She rented a back room from a storekeeper in Tennyson Street's business district. She passed out flyers about her classes at the nearby public school and other businesses along the street. Every week, Esther's dance class grew, from two little sisters to a dozen pupils. Her piano class attracted three boys and one more girl. Her hours grew longer, but she never felt she couldn't handle her work.

That summer Sam flew to Europe. He had not given up on Myra's quest although she had put the subject on hold. Besides, he wanted to see if his childhood homeland was still recognizable. Myra's brooch was still in the bank, but he had taken pictures of it to carry with him on his journey.

Myra

Elizabeth had given birth to twins, a boy and a girl. She and Tim had settled in Hawaii where Tim was the head surgeon at a navy hospital. Edna and Anna still put up with each other, with Anna taking on more than just cooking. Edna's memory was failing and it made Anna more protective of her. Myra thought that this winter's Christmas celebration at Edna's home might be the last. She would have to start her own tradition. Meanwhile, she and Eric struggled with his depression, which had clouded their relationship for the past four years.

It didn't matter to Myra that their sex was not part of their marriage. She loved him, but try as she might, she could not reach the dark corners of his mind. Often she would wake at night to find him sitting alone in the dark front room, watching the night go by and listening to a far distant train chugging towards the mountains he loved. In the summers, John Dawson came out and together he and Myra tried to make Eric be what he used to be, if only in his wheelchair. They drove to the mountains and sat by bubbling streams watching Matt and Lilly learning how to fish from their grandfather. John loved being with them and each scream of delight at a caught minnow helped bring Eric into their joy. It was rare for Eric to smile and encourage the children. Sometimes, when the children and John walked down to the streams, Eric would reach out for Myra. He would softly kiss her and run his hand through her hair.

On one such occasion he told Myra where he had come across her look-alike painting. A little Hungarian town, but Eric could not recall the name. His unit was on a reconnaissance trip to discover where the Germans were waiting for the Allied forces. Certain resistance groups were to meet with them with information vital to the battle that was to take place. Eric's unit misunderstood the location of the meeting and instead found the cave full of artifacts, art, and gold and silver which local Jewish families had hidden before they were sent to concentration camps—or so he thought. They had found china, gold statues, coins of silver and gold, and family photograph journals full of smiling and happy people. It was when Myra's portrait was pulled from behind a stack of cardboard slats that Eric's commanding officer decided the Jews had hidden them there, not the Germans. The coins were the clue. Germans would have confiscated ready money. With that in mind, Eric's unit had dug deeper into the cave and hidden the treasures under big rocks and in the sandy soil. But Eric could not remember its exact location. He told Myra that he hoped, if any of the owners survived the holocaust, they would be able to find their belongings.

But he also wanted to know more about Myra's painting, as he thought of it. He knew from his first sight of her all those years ago, a wet soggy young girl forgetting her bag in the phone booth, that she was special. He loved her so much that the guilt of not being a husband to fill her sexual needs threw him into a deep depression. He often thought she and the children would be better off without him. He had produced an heir for his father's satisfaction. What else could he do in this torn and twisted body for the future of all of them? These thoughts haunted him daily. He knew suicide was against what he had been taught all his normal life, but now his life was not normal. He began to have dreams similar to Myra's. He was on the battleground again. He was hit again and it hurt like hell. Then, he always heard his name being called. He would turn toward the voice and there she was. His mother was holding out her hand to him. She was bathed is a white misty light and her smile touched off in him feelings he had not felt since he was child. He wanted so much to take her hand and follow to a place void of pain and full of peaceful moments.

So it was one September day, alone with his depression, the children in their respective schools, Myra working on a story for the *Rocky Mountain News*, that Eric Dawson swallowed enough pain pills to take him to that other world of his mother's reign and peaceful sleep. It was Esther who found him reclining in his wheelchair, asleep, she thought, until she touched his face. She called the ambulance and then called Myra to tell her what hospital they had taken him to. Esther picked up the children and waited by the phone for Myra's call. A few hours later Myra called home and said Eric had passed on, and funeral arrangements would have to be made. Myra's voice was like a hollow echo of a person who had no idea what to say next. Esther told her to come home before making any plans so that she could think about everything that had to be done. Myra agreed and said that as soon as she signed the paper for Eric to be taken to Olinger's Mortuary at 16th and Boulder Street in North Denver, she would come home.

Matt looked up at Esther and asked where his

daddy was, since his wheelchair sat empty by the front door. His blue eyes searched her face for an answer, but Esther could only say his mother would be home soon and would tell him what he wanted to know.

BUDAPEST, HUNGARY

Sam stood on the bank of the Danube River watching the dark waters flow past him swirling in circles and small waves as a few riverboats chugged up and down the river. It was eleven o'clock at night and Sam felt the need to be out and about in this city that was once so important to him and his family. It was under Communist control now with young Hungarian boys dressed in the dull green and gray uniforms of Russia. Where had their smiles gone, Sam wondered. Where was the laughter of his youth, the look of promise around every corner? Everything looked gray and dismal. Buildings needed to be renovated from the bombings and strafing of the war. Bridges had to be rebuilt after the Germans destroyed them to escape the Russian army. Four years now since the war's end and only one bridge was passable to the Pest side of the city. People scrounged in open markets that rationed every morsel of food. Heavy-set women with downcast mouths piled small amounts of meat, potatoes, and bread into mesh bags for the hungry people, as though the food supply were diamonds. People scrounged through the rubble of wood and bricks lying in lots after it had been swept from the streets. If there were items or junk that could be bought or exchanged for food, it was a good find. Small children were often among the scavengers, with the adults shifting in search of some small treasure. At one time the bridges across the Danube had been lit with lights strung through the iron cables and coils, but now only a car's light or some distant light from either side of the river's banks helped the walkers on the one bridge find their way. The famous chain link bridge was to be rebuilt as soon as the Hungarian government had the resources to do so. There was a lot of rebuilding to do, but under the Communist rule, Sam doubted the beloved city would ever be the city it had been.

Sam had taken a room on the Buda side of the city in the Hotel Gellert, which in old times had been famous for its luxurious baths and massages. His parents could afford such luxuries, and the family had spent many happy times there in its hallowed halls and dining rooms when they visited Budapest.

Sam over-stayed his time for venturing into the past. He had planned to be home by September but his search for the painting Eric had seen during the war had taken an unexpected turn. He had searched the museums and even the Paris Louvre, trying to find an artist who would know of such a painting. The art world was still in disarray. Some of the most famous European art had been taken to Germany, and people from all the free world were on a witch-hunt. The directors of the various museums had organized honest people to help to search for the lost treasures, but Sam drew a blank. Some of the directors were not sure of Sam's motives and gave him false leads and little help in figuring out where Eric had seen the painting and other pieces of art. It was true most directors told him, that some Jews did hide their treasures from the Nazis, but if they survived, which was unlikely at this point, they would have been sent abroad to Israel or to other nations that would take them in. Few Jews were returning to their old homes.

Sam scanned the maps of cities and towns, wishing Eric had given him a name or a location. Might it have been closer to the coast of Normandy? Now, Eric's memory seemed blank, or filled with his injuries and his struggle to adjust to his deformity. Sam was worried about Eric. He thought Myra's love for him and the tender care she gave him would bring to him the reality that life would go on. He had a son to be proud of, which was more than Sam could say of his childless life. Even little Lilly seem to capture Eric's heart with her constant smile and the hugs she always bestowed on her "Daddy." However, Sam's venture back to his past was for Eric and Myra too. Eric had agreed that if Sam could uncover anything concerning Myra's forgotten days it would be wonderful. But, try as he might, Eric could no longer pinpoint the cave where Myra's portrait was hidden. He barely could recall events leading up to its discovery since his injuries seem to have wiped out that memory. He told Sam that when he looked back at this time in his life, all the landscape seems to blend together. Some hills, villages off in the distance, hiding from enemy patrols, and finally connecting with an underground group in a gully somewhere. Was it along the coast of Normandy? He wasn't sure. How many days or far the distance between

Sam had met an old man in Paris sweeping up the dust outside of the Louvre steps. He had fought in the First World War, and life had not been kind to him. He hobbled on curved legs and bent slightly from his waist. Yet, he had a job, and that meant he would survive a little longer. At first when Sam asked for directions, he ignored him. As Sam started to walk away, the old man called him back. "Are you an American?" he asked

Sam shook his head yes, and the old man motioned for him to sit on the concrete wall while he tried to remember the best way to give directions. His English had a strong accent, but Sam understood him. Their conversation went to information about each other. When Sam told him that he was looking for some artwork, the old man said his name was Pierre Durant, most recently from the village of Sainte-Mere-Eglise near the coast of Normandy. He said it was the first village to be liberated by the Allied troops. Pierre spoke about how the war had affected the village and the people. Their Jewish friends were rounded up and sent off to the death camps. Pierre had hidden a family of Jews for a time but someone with a grudge against him turned them in. Pierre was sent off to a detention center for a time, until a distant relative was able to obtain his freedom by convincing the Nazis that Pierre could add to the manpower they needed for building defenses. He had suffered enough, they were told. When he came home there was no home for him. Citizens and friends were shot on the town square as a lesson to the other citizens about what would happen if they did not obey the rules of the new regime. Pierre

With this little bit of information, Sam pressed on in finding out what treasures Pierre knew about from the war years. Pierre said there were several places near the village that could be hidden from the Germans. The high cliffs along the beaches were dotted with caves and many ancient battles were won there because the entrances seemed to be always hidden from the enemy. Germans knew nothing of the history of their land and many citizens escaped capture and death because of their knowledge of the caves. Pierre then remembered something which had happened when he was a young man getting ready for the First World War. Dignitaries from the Louvre came with several horse carts loaded full of precious artwork and treasures from their most famous museum, to hide safely from the enemy. The location was a secure secret from the citizens and Pierre never knew what had happened to the lode. As a young man after the war, he stayed in Paris for several years before returning to his home in Sainte-Mere-Eglise. In fact, he told Sam, this was the first time he remembered any of it. If the French museums ever collected that material after the Great War, he had no idea. There had never been talk about it for as long as he could remember, until now. He never saw any of the artwork or treasures, so he would not have a memory of what was hidden.

It was only a nibble, but Sam thought he should follow that lead and go to the village of Sainte-Mere-Eglise. The train system was the first system the French had gotten back to normal. Therefore, Sam was able to leave in the morning and be in the village before noon. The village had taken a beating from the war. Beautiful churches from ancient times still lay in ruins. A few hotels were open for business and Sam checked into the one nearest the train depot. He spent a week walking the streets of the village and out on the land surrounding the area. He found several cave-like hiding places, but they would have been obvious to anyone looking for hidden treasures. On what he decided would be his last day, he walked farther afield from the village. The hills were higher than ones he had explored toward the west of town. He climbed to the top of one and discovered a crude stone arrangement like steps. They ended a few feet down as though they had disappeared. Sam descended to that spot and started to shuffle a foot to clear the dirt. Nothing appeared, so he bent over and started to dig with his hands.

"You won't find anything there, mister." A woman's voice from the other side of the hill stopped him.

He looked down at her and wondered where in hell she had come from. She wasn't there a minute ago, he would swear. "What did you say?" Sam asked

"I said if you are looking for an entrance to this hill, you won't find it, and if you do, there is nothing in the cave below." She put her hands on her hips and shifted her weight in a provocative motion. She had short blonde hair parted in the middle like a schoolgirl from a Catholic school--except she was not a schoolgirl. Sam thought she would be somewhere in her twenties, and he was surprised at her excellent English.

178

When Sam collected himself after finding this girl on the scene, he asked her, "How do you know what I am looking for?"

"There was once a group of American GI's who found something under that circle where you are digging. It has been gone for a long time." She sat on the ground and stuck a long blade of grass in her mouth. "I met one of the GI's looking for whatever it was. He never would tell me, but I suppose some poor soul had put their life's work there. He was handsome and I thought very rich. A farmer, he was, from Kansas. All farmers in France are wealthy, I thought, so those in Kansas must be even richer. How naive and mistaken I was."

"What happened?" Sam asked.

"We fell in love and we married. The old priest told us we had found our treasure in each other. Well," she said spitting out the blade of grass, "He was so wrong. We dug for my lover's treasure and broke open that circle of iron. If there had ever been a treasure there, it was gone. We did find a few stones in the rubble, but we didn't know they were real diamonds until we got to America. Can you imagine leaving this beautiful green place and living in small town in Kansas? Not a blade of grass. Tornadoes, and crops drying on the vine?" She took a deep a breath and went on to say, "Two years later, I sold the diamonds to pay for my trip home. I was much wiser and better in English than I had been learning it here."

Myra

"What happened to your marriage?" Sam asked, wondering how many similar stories could be told, in France, in Poland, in Austria, in Hungary—and wondering if he was crazy to even wonder whether this stranger's diamonds could have any connection to Myra.

"I got a divorce here and the husband would never come here to protest it. Not with my three brothers and cousins to beat him if he showed up."

"So," Sam said, standing up, "You are telling me there is nothing here now."

"No, not a thing. I heard a few other former GI's came over looking for something, so the town's people scooped the trash out, making sure there was nothing of importance there, and then filled it with sand then sealed that iron circle. I was surprised to see you up here digging like a miner. I could tell you weren't young enough to be a former GI."

He left the next morning for Budapest. Now leaning over a rusty railing looking at the Danube rippling by, he wondered if he would ever be able to uncover Myra's past, if indeed she was from Hungary. He knew tomorrow he would call Eric to see if his memory had returned as to the location of the cave.

Chapter Sixteen

That night in his room at the Gellert Hotel in Buda, Sam, who rarely dreamed, did dream.

He was in a dark room with black curtains on the windows. The mirrors were covered with white sheets and the smell of flowers was overwhelming. He heard someone weeping in front him before two large candles. As he approached the figure he was shocked to see it was Myra crying as she cradled her head in her hands.

"Myra?" he softly said.

Myra stopped crying and looked up to Sam with a tear-stained face. 'Oh Sam. Where are you? I need you." And she pointed to large wooden box under the draped windows.

Sam walked over to it and there lay Eric as though finally at peace. His face reflected the little boy Sam remembered when they spent their summers together. Then Eric opened his eyes and smiled up at Sam. "Take care of Myra for me, Sam. I couldn't hold on any longer. The painting is back where it belongs. Find it and you will find Myra's heritage."

Sam said, "Give me a clue, Eric. Where can I find it? Tell me, tell me." And he bent over and shook Eric's body. Eric was breaking apart like rag doll and suddenly Sam was aware that he was shaking his pillow.

In the distance a church bell gonged three times. The sweat pouring down Sam's face was like the tears he had not shed for years. He reached over to the end table where the telephone sat and dialed the Hotel operator. It would be daytime in Denver, and he had to talk to Myra. What was his dream telling him? He listened to his breathing while the connection went through. The phone was ringing and Esther answered. When she heard his voice, she called Myra to the phone.

"Hello. Sam, is that you?" she asked in a voice that was almost whispering.

"Yes, Myra. Are you all right? I just had a terrible dream or premonition about Eric. Is he OK?" Sam suddenly was afraid of Myra's next words.

"No, Sam. Eric died yesterday." Silence and then, "We think he took his own life. His sleeping pills bottle was empty and I had just got it refilled on the week-end." A sob, "Oh Sam, why did he do that?"

"Oh my God, Myra. I just dreamt that he had died. It is around three o'clock here and I had to call to make sure I was not having a nightmare. But I wasn't, was I?" He noticed his cigars next to the lamp on the end table

"Oh Sam, maybe it would be best to remember him as he was or used to be," Myra said.

"Impossible, Myra. I have his estate papers and will in my office. I need to be there. Have you called John and Elizabeth?"

"Yes, and they are on the way. John will stay with Edna. Elizabeth is coming alone. The trip from Hawaii is too far for her to bring her children; with the twins it would be impossible. John is very emotional, Sam. I guess you are right. We do need you here. I need you here."

"Hold on, dear. I know it looks pretty grim now, but think of the children. I should get there early tomorrow morning. Just hold on."

Eric looked exactly as Sam had seen him in his dream. Finally he was at peace. No more suffering or looking back to what life could have been for him. John Dawson was devastated but Elizabeth was holding up well. Myra was like a zombie. By the time of the funeral, her tears had dried up and she seemed to move with the tide of events that she had no part in, as though watching a play. Esther took over the children and the other chores. When the long ride back from the Ft. Logan Military Cemetery was over, Esther had the house ready for the visitors who would come by to pay their respects. Plates of food from neighbors and friends filled the dining room table and card tables Esther had set up. Matt and Lily knew their "Daddy" was now with the angels, but they didn't understand why everyone was so sad. When John first arrived he picked up Matt and cried, which confused Matt. Then he told Matt he would have to be the man of the house now and take care of his mother and Lilly.

Myra was shocked and said, "He is only a little boy. He is not responsible for our future. Why make him a man before he can realize his daddy's gone? We can take care of ourselves."

Myra had never spoken that way before to John, who took it as rude and as if he were a stranger to this boy and not his grandfather.

"I am his grandfather. I think I can say to him what I want."

"I am sorry, John. I just want to make it easier for the children. They are too young to understand what Eric's passing will mean to them and their future."

"Well, then, we disagree on that subject. Mathew lost his father and I lost my son. What did you lose? A crippled husband who could not truly be the husband you wanted?"

Myra gasped, "I can't believe you said that. I loved Eric for who he was and not for what he could or could not do. How dare you assume anything else?"

"I dare to speak my mind and don't give me any crap about your love for Eric. You only had a short life with him. I had him from the crib to his coffin."

Elizabeth touched her father's shoulder. "Dad, do you know what you are saying. Stop it this minute. You're being very rude."

"Rude? You don't know the half of it. Leave me alone." John's Dawson's grief poured out of him like spilt blood as he walked out of the room.

After this break-down he became remorseful but more distant towards Myra. The morning after the funeral, he left without calling Myra to talk to her about the future or even to say good-bye. Elizabeth had stayed with Myra and knew what her father had done. She tried to be the peacemaker, as she knew what Myra had been trying to tell John. She certainly would not want any of her children to feel obligated if one of their parents died. Myra felt guilty about her rudeness to John and became despondent until Sam told her she had been right. What five year old would know how to take care of his mother? Sam was sure John was just grieving and that Myra could call him later and make peace. Elizabeth agreed and stayed on for another week to help Myra however she could.

Myra did call John but he said more hurtful things to her and asked her not to call him again. Sam was appalled and Elizabeth felt helpless in urging her father not to cut off Myra and his grandson. John's grief was too deep at that time to even consider what his actions and words would mean for the future of all of them. To Myra, all the doors that had opened when she met Eric were closing on her now. Sam consoled her by saying John would come around, that he hadn't meant all that he had said. This was of little comfort to Myra, but her children gave her strength.

Life went on, with Sam always offering moral support. Myra would get a government pension as long as she didn't marry again. The children would have benefits and a small pension until they reached the age of twenty-one. The days flew by. To confront her loss, Myra started writing a book about her love for Eric, and her deep fear of being alone. Christmas was a miserable time for Myra. Edna was now in a nursing home as Anna was not able to care for her properly. Edna's failing memory and growing dementia had her running off at times, once completely naked.

Sam had handled Edna's affairs since her husband had died. He negotiated the sale of Edna's lovely home. Edna was given enough money to buy a small cottage in Arvada, a suburb of Denver, and bonds that would enable her to be free of money worries for life. Eric and Elizabeth were included in Edna's will; Myra would inherit Eric's portion. Myra and Sam visited Edna as often as their time permitted. Myra's work and her writings kept her mind clear. The children thrived under Esther's excellent care. Matt would be a first grader and Lilly would be in half days in kindergarten. That summer, Edna caught a terrible cold and died a few weeks later. Esther met a nice Jewish immigrant from Poland who, like her, had survived the death camps. They were married that autumn in the Colfax Synagogue and moved to a terrace apartment off West Colfax. But Esther would not abandon Myra. She insisted on taking the children to school, picking up Lilly from her morning class and Matt after school. She would bring them home and have dinner ready when Myra arrived. Myra hired a cleaning lady to help with the house chores, and Sam was always available to lean on.

Sam enticed Myra to operas and concerts and to the Cheeseman Park operettas during the summer months of 1950. All the while, Myra continued to work on her book. Once she had finished it she gave it to Sam for proofreading. It took him three weeks to hand it back to her with tears in his eyes. "It is beautiful, Myra. I could feel your emotions."

Myra mailed the book to publishers, but it was rejected by most. A few offered comments and corrections, but following them, she thought, would have made her story less true. Matt was taught to write to his grandfather, but he received no answers. Elizabeth kept in touch, though, and told Myra that John was to be with them at Christmas time.

As a Christmas treat, Sam bought two tickets for a musical to be performed at the Denver Auditorium. It would be the last Christmas event there. Old and outdated buildings were being torn down and new and exciting structures were taking over. There was even talk about new highways. The Platte valley was to have a north and south freeway. Even a major cross-country highway was planned to intersect Denver's northwest area very near the closed Queen Of Heaven Orphanage that Myra had called home. Things were changing and Myra welcomed change if it meant her children would be part of a new and wonderful generation.

The old auditorium was brilliant in its finale. During intermission, a tall and handsome man approached Sam and Myra. Sam was delighted to see him and introduced Myra to Michael Lieberman, the doctor Sam had been seeing for his arthritis and blood pressure. Myra had no idea Sam had such ailments and could hardly comprehend that he might be vulnerable.

Michael took Myra's hand and smiled down at her. "You didn't tell me you had a daughter, Sam. She must take after her mother."

"Oh, no you don't. Flattery will get you no points with Myra. She is more or less my adopted daughter, though."

Myra opened her mouth in disbelief. What was going on here with Sam and this man? "I am Myra Dawson, and if Sam has adopted me, he forgot to tell me," she laughed.

From that moment on, Michael Lieberman knew this was a special woman. Their relationship began with phone calls at first, but Myra was hesitant to enter a serious relationship. After all, she had given her heart and soul to Eric, and she was sure there was no one else who could make her feel so secure and loved as Eric had. By springtime, however, Myra's feelings for this dynamic doctor had begun to change, but not without a little help from Sam. Michael came to Mathew's seventh birthday party and the children were enthralled with him. Myra felt something too. Could she love this man as she had Eric? Sam assured she could because the heart had many channels.

After Mathew's birthday party, Myra started to dream again. This time it was not of the black haired woman, but of Eric back in the time of their honeymoon.

They were standing on the top of a mountain with the Trail Ridge Road below them. "Look," Eric said and pointed to the highway. "They have built another road and it is paved."

Myra tried to circle her arm around his waist, but he moved away from her. Feeling dejected, she asked, "What is it Eric? Did I hurt you?"

Eric looked down at her and motioned for her to go back down to the road.

"No, but your life has to go on. He is waiting for you there. See?"

Myra looked down where Eric was pointing. Dr. Michael Lieberman was waving up at her. She descended slowly, once looking up at Eric. He waved to her and as she approached Michael, she looked back up. Eric had gone, and

Myra

> *Michael answered, "He is gone, Myra. It is only me now."*

Myra woke up to discover she was in her bed and Eric had truly gone. Was he trying to give her a message? Then she remembered a dream she had had on her honeymoon years ago, a dream almost identical to the one she just had. She was looking for Eric and a doctor on the mountain told her Eric was gone. It was Michael who had reached out to her. Then like a light bulb going off in her head, Myra knew why Michael had looked so familiar when she first met him at the opera. It was a spooky idea; but did things like this really happen to people, she wondered. Was someone's spirit, someone she didn't know, guiding her life? Unlike her childhood, where dark shadows and hurtful adults haunted her days, her adult life so far had been mostly full of happiness and love. Maybe there was a reason for Eric's death. It was not an event anyone would wish on a loved one, but perhaps it had been a stepping-stone giving her courage to go forward with life. Looking back and wishing would never bring Eric back, so since Eric had planted his seed in Mathew, she could go on.

From that time on, Michael Lieberman was more and more important to her.

Chapter Seventeen

Myra had had little idea how hard it would be to get her book published. Sam thought it would be a best seller, but Myra felt he was biased because he was so close to her. She had written her book about her love for Eric, the pain of seeing him suffering when he came home from the war, and the feelings she had felt when the perfect life she had yearned for and had found with Eric started to unravel. She wrote of deep emotions though she left out her childhood molestations. She did write about her memory gap; and she described some of her dreams and gave them meanings. In was a book that she thought would appeal to any person growing up lonely, and finding and losing happiness. Writing her book was also a healing process, as her words seem to flow out of her.

In the meantime, the doctor, Michael Lieberman, continued calling her, arranging for dinners and weekend excursions to the mountains. He enjoyed the children, especially since Lilly, on her first sight of him, asked if he would be their new daddy. In fact, Michael seemed to love being with the children. Myra learned he had been married at one time, but that it hadn't worked out. They had not been compatible, he said, she being a Jewish princess and unwilling to work for their future together.

Myra laughed at the thought of a Jewish princess, a phrase she had never heard before.

That summer, Michael became a fixture at Myra's home. They talked of many things, though Myra avoided her childhood. One evening after a dinner she had cooked for just the two of them, Michael asked right out what it was like growing up in an orphanage. Myra was shocked as she had only told him of living in Salida with guardians who had died. She had let him believe that she was an adult.

"How did you know about the orphanage?" she asked.

"Sam filled me in some about your childhood. He thinks you are Jewish. Did you know that?"

"What else did Sam tell you?"

"I am feeling guilty now. I guess I should have asked you before, but you always seem to avoid your childhood. I asked Sam because I am beginning to care very much for you."

Myra felt her heart leap into a happiness she had not known since Eric had proposed to her.

"I mean, Myra, that you intrigue me more and more. I don't read books too much. I am more interested in current affairs and medical journals. When Sam said I should read your book and explained why, I was surprised. You are so natural and down to earth in what we have talked about; I had no idea you sprouted from such a past."

"Have you read my book Michael?"

"Only the first page, but I plan to read the rest as soon as possible, that is, if you want to tell me about it first. As I said, I am beginning to care for you very much and I hope you might feel the same way about me."

Myra had no idea how to answer Michael. She had given her heart and soul to Eric. How could she allow herself to feel love again? "I don't know how to answer, Michael. I know I must move forward for the children's sake, but I have only known one true love. I felt a love I had no idea could exist for me." She sighed, "You asked me about growing up in an orphanage. Well, I don't think any of us ever felt much loved. I was lucky in having one nun, Sister Bernadette, who loved me as her own and gave me a little more attention than other children. Nevertheless, not knowing where I came from did cause Sister some concern. You see, I could never believe that Jesus loved me as the song says. I felt he never answered my prayers, and if he was the Son of God, why couldn't he love me?"

Michael took her hand. "My poor darling Myra. Is that the reason Sam thinks you might be Jewish?"

"Oh no. It was the diamond brooch sent to me when I was a freshman at CU. I had never seen it before, but the sender wrote that it was mine. I didn't know the sender and I could not find any information about her, except for her name on the letter. Another coed asked me if I was Jewish when she looked at it. I had no idea it was a Jewish symbol. The Star of David."

"Now I am intrigued. Sam knows of this?"

"Yes. I met Sam when Eric asked Sister Bernadette and me to his Aunt's Christmas party. I had only met Eric a few days before while I was waiting for a streetcar in downtown Denver. He was waiting for the same car. We talked until I got off the streetcar at Federal Boulevard."

"So Sam was another guest?" Michael asked.

"Yes. He wasn't very friendly until I asked him if he was Jewish. Then he warmed up to me and I told him about the brooch. After that, he called me and we had lunch and the rest is history. He is like the father I never knew or had, I guess."

Michael brushed a strand of curly hair from Myra's forehead. "So my darling, is that the reason Sam went to Europe last fall? Was he searching for your past?"

"Yes, I think so, but he is from Szeged, Hungary, and I think he wanted to see the place of his birth and childhood. He left there after his arranged marriage didn't work out. I think his family disowned him, though I have never questioned him about that. I have wondered whether he thought his family died in the death camps.

Maybe he wanted to know that too."

Michael smiled at her and took her in his arms. "Oh my darling. Haven't we played pretend long enough? I think you know how I feel towards you, and I get a reaction from you that says I might be important to you too."

Myra could not restrain herself. She put her arms around his neck and snuggled against him. "I do feel attached to you Michael, but I am scared."

"Scared of what?"

"I never thought I would love again as I did with Eric. I think if I loved you and lost you as I did Eric, I could not survive. I have lost so much from the beginning of my life." Myra backed off and sat down. "I don't ever want to be alone again."

"Oh my Myra, I know what you're feeling. Remember each love is a different story. What you felt for Eric will always remain with you. Our relationship will be on another course of life. You will have a father for your children and my undying love for all of you. Eric never got that chance and that, Myra, makes our love different."

"And if it turns out that I was born a Jew, my heritage would even strengthen our love?"

"Religion has nothing to do with it, darling. I would love you no matter what race or religion you turned out to be."

Myra smiled at Michael. "That makes me feel wonderful. You have that quality about you Michael. You make me feel important."

"You are important to me Myra. I should get down on my knees because I am going to ask you to marry me." He did so. "I think I fell in love with you the first time I spotted you with Sam." Michael stood up, then pulled Myra up to him. He took her in his arms and kissed her passionately. They had kissed before, but nothing as meaningful as this kiss.

Myra leaned into his body as though she belonged there. Her reaction startled her, as it was not normal for her to give in so utterly to her emotions. She looked up at Michael, studying his face, and at that moment she knew she loved him deeply. He was right about each love being different. Eric would always remain in her life through Matthew, as Lilly would always represent Diana. They were the people who, along with Sister Bernadette and Edna and Sam, Myra considered her family. Now Michael would fill those empty spaces with the love they felt for each other. God hadn't closed the doors to happiness as Myra had thought.

Myra soon began studying with Rabbi Meyer at the synagogue Michael attended in East Denver. It was in October that she considered converting to Judaism. For some reason she felt more comfortable in the synagogue than she had ever felt in a Catholic church. She knew she would not be considered an Orthodox Jew because her parentage was unknown. But it didn't matter to Michael. They were married on December 4, 1951 in a traditional Jewish wedding. Sam orchestrated the whole thing, Myra being so new to the traditions had no idea where to begin. Michael's family consisted of a father and stepmother, a sister and a half brother. The parents and his brother flew in from Boston. The sister, Rose, was married with three teen-age children in school, and could not attend. The brother, Joshua, was in his last year at Harvard Law School, but could not pass up a chance to try out the ski areas of Colorado on his Christmas break.

They were gracious to Myra, Mathew, and Lilly, and enthralled by Esther and her husband. It was a small gathering with a family reception at the Brown Palace Hotel in downtown Denver.

Esther took charge of the children while the honey-mooners were gone. Michael was eight and Lilly was seven; both were happy that Michael was now their daddy. Myra and Michael flew to Hawaii for a week. The view of Diamond Head from their hotel room enthralled Myra. She had seen pictures of it but never dreamed she would see it in person.

Michael was a tender lover. He sensed Myra's fear of betraying Eric and worked his manliness slowly with kisses and body rubs until he felt Myra relaxed and ready for him. It was a different feeling from Eric's young body anxious to enter hers. Michael was like an opera, soft and moving slowly to the faster track. Eric was like a fire engine racing to meet the fire again and again until his young exhausted body lay in a sweat.

That night Myra's dreaded dreams returned.

The woman with the black hair was looking down at her and smiling. "You are safe now, Myra."

Myra felt warmth surge through her whole body. This lady loved her, she could tell. Myra felt safe with her. Then a door opened behind the lady. A familiar face appeared. His blood-shot eyes tore through her soul, and he held a large kitchen knife. The lady turned towards him and screamed as he plunged the knife into her chest. The lady fell on top of Myra and the man's breath, smelling of whiskey and smoke, almost choked her. Myra screamed and the man began to shake her; but as she opened her eyes, it was Michael holding on to her.

"What is it darling? What happened?"

Myra clung to him for moment. "I don't know. I think I was dreaming." She looked up at Michael's gentle face. "Oh Michael my dreams are starting again."

She had told Michael about her dreams before they were married and he felt it was a carry-over from her childhood and some of the difficulties she had faced as an adult. Michael was sure the newness of a way of life had triggered her dreams again.

Myra was shaking with sobs and Michael cradled

her in his arms and vowed to himself he would always be there for her. He would also try to find the cause and confront Myra's fears.

Chapter Eighteen

Sam noticed something different in Myra when he came for dinner a few weeks after the wedding. She was pale and losing weight. Michael was jovial and seemed to be as happy as a groom could be. While Myra was busy in the kitchen and Sam and Michael were enjoying their drinks, Sam asked Michael if Myra was well.

"She said she feels fine." Michael set his drink on the coffee table. "But she is having dreams. She told me about the ones she had as a child, but she didn't put the horror of them in her book. I take it she has told you about them?"

Sam nodded. "Yes. It has to do with her lost memory. What has she told you about them?"

"Just after she began them again--it was on our honeymoon--she woke up in a cold sweat. I asked her if she had ever tried to be hypnotized by an expert. She wouldn't even consider it. What do you make of it Sam?"

Sam also set his drink down. "I know something very bad happened to her when her memories were start-ing to take hold. I think she fell through the cracks somehow and her Catholic guardians had to abandon her to a horrible family and told the system a different story than hers. Social Services moved her to a Catholic orphanage."

Michael frowned. "So that was the story she didn't tell me. Was she molested?"

"I think so but I don't think she would ever admit it. As close as we have been since I first met her, she has never revealed anything like that. I have watched her actions with Eric and listened to some of her questions. I have seen young girls who have been molested. The fear in their eyes was like what I saw in Myra's when I asked about her past. Myra has always changed the subject when I get close to asking her any personal questions."

"I heard you two. What are you saying about me?" It was Myra with a platter of food in her hands.

Michael smiled up at her. "Nothing, darling, that you can't hear. Sam is worried about you. He thinks you're getting too skinny."

"Nonsense. I am just a busy mother and wife. I have deadlines to meet too. I will just have to adjust to all the activity I am whirling in now." She put the platter on the table. "I only have the salad to bring in, so you two gossiping gentlemen can come to the table."

Before she left the room, she said to Michael, "Darling would you check with the children? They ate

The children were delighted to see Sam. They were full of conversation, but Sam told them that if they went back to their room, he would be up to read to them after dinner. Squealing in delight, they ran upstairs to find their favorite books.

As Sam and Myra finished dessert, a chocolate cake with vanilla frosting, Michael cleared his throat and said, "Well, Sam. We asked you for two purposes. To have a home cooked meal and to tell you about my promotion, or offer of one."

Sam was surprised. He looked at Myra and noticed she was circling her fork around her plate. It was obvious she wasn't as thrilled as Michael. "A promotion? That is great Michael. Tell me about it."

"It involves moving back east and I think Myra isn't that happy about it."

"Of course, I am Michael. It's just that I don't know how it will affect my career as a writer for newspapers and magazines. Also to have the children moved so far away from the only place they have friends and memories."

"Darling that will all work out. You most likely would have more of a chance in your writing career back there. The Scripps Howard network has newspapers there. In fact, the Scripps family lives there. The children will adjust. At their age, their roots have yet to take hold."

Sam knocked on the table to get attention. "Just where is this place you will be moving to?"

"To Cincinnati, Ohio, Sam," Michael answered. "It is a beautiful city; the Ohio River divides the state of Ohio from Kentucky. I spent a summer there once and the life-style is a good one. It is very much a sophisticated and promising city."

Sam clasped his hands together. His face reflected his displeasure at losing Myra and her family but he couldn't say anything to that effect. After all these years, Sam felt Myra could have been his daughter and he thought she felt that way too. He would be lonely again as he was before she came into his life.

Myra took his hands into hers as if she knew his thoughts. "Sam, no matter where we go, you will always be my family. In some odd way, I felt from the beginning of our friendship, that you would lead me to where I belonged." She kissed his hands, "I think you knew that we came from the same ancient roots. You have always been there for me when I needed you."

Sam shook his head, "But Cincinnati isn't across town."

"It is a flight away Sam," Michael interrupted. "You will always be the grandpa to Matt and Lilly. I understand there is a strong Jewish organization there too, so we will still be in an area where we belong."

Sam smiled and said, "Well, I am very happy for you and Myra. I think I always wanted her to be happy." He cleared his throat and went on to say, "Let me digest this for a few days. I hadn't expected such news." Silence, "I had better get upstairs and read to 'my grandchildren.'" Sam forced his laugh, got up, and left the room.

"Oh Michael, my heart is breaking. I can't leave him. He means too much to me and I think he feels that way too."

Michael sighed, "Now you two are making me out as a devil. I am very fond of Sam too, but we have to think of our future. All the schooling I took for surgery and all the new medicines coming out. I would be the head of a department in one of the best hospitals in the country. How can we turn our back on that opportunity?"

"I know, Michael. It would be foolish to turn it down. But it is going to be hard to move so far away. I have never lived anywhere but here in Colorado."

"You don't know that Myra. You have no memory of any place else because something happened to you that you have blocked out of your memory."

Myra stood up and started to clear the table. "What do you want me to do, Michael? I have suffered with dreams that are nightmares and flashes of what could be past experiences. How can I recall something that was so horrible to me as young child that I could only survive by

"You could deal with it, Myra. You could discover what happened to you and overcome whatever it was that hurt you so much."

"How would I do that, Michael?"

"At least give it a try. Hypnosis might bring out what haunts you. Then you work from there. You have to go back, Myra, before you can go forward. Find out who caused your nightmares and go from there."

Sam entered the room again. "The children couldn't wait. Both are sleeping."

Michael asked him, "Did you hear our conversation, Sam?"

"I did, and I think you are entirely right. But I never wanted to push Myra that far." He picked up his dessert dish to help Myra carry things into the kitchen. "Maybe I was being selfish. I didn't want to lose her either, and I was afraid hypnosis would reveal a past where I had no place."

"Sam," Myra said. "That would never happen. If I should ever discover my past, no matter how it turned out, horrible or happy, you would never be less to me."

"Then, it is up to you Myra," said Michael.. "Hypnosis is one direction you could take. I think Sam would agree with me on that subject." Michael nodded to Sam who in turn nodded back.

"OK. You guys win. I will do as you two believe I should, but I am warning you. I might not be the same person you both claim to love and cherish standing here before you."

Myra turned and walked into the kitchen with Sam and Michael following.

"It is settled then," Michael said. "I will research the specialists, and no matter what, I will always love you. I am sure Sam, too, would never stop loving and admiring you."

Sam put his plate in the sink. "When do you leave, Michael?"

"I have to fly back there next month, but only to get acquainted with the staff and the duties I will inherit. I will look around the area too for suitable neighborhoods and good schools. Myra will not move there until the children are out of school. It was one concession I made her."

"Will you start your hypnosis back there or here, Myra?" Sam asked.

Before she could answer, Michael interrupted. "That would depend on my research. If I find a good doctor here, I think she should do it now before we move.

Myra

It was a sad night for Sam. He wasn't a young man any more, and his disappointment at the news made him feel as though an elephant was sitting on his back. As he drove back to his apartment, he felt a loneliness he hadn't felt for years. Myra had brought him back to the living reality of a world he had avoided. He was too old to cope with disappointment anymore, he thought. How was he going to live with emptiness again?

That night Myra dreamed.

She was seated at a dining room table. The dishes were all as white as the linen tablecloth. Wine glasses in two different sizes were set at each place setting. The silverware beside the plates sparkled under the light of the chandelier. Silver candlesticks with white long candles lined the middle of the large table. Myra was alone. Where were the people? She looked around the room. It was beautiful with large paintings hanging on the walls. Suddenly she heard laughter and the double white doors opened at one end of the room. Two maidservants entered laughing at something they had found funny. They each went to one end of the long table and started to light the candles. They didn't seem to notice Myra sitting on one side of the table. They spoke softly to each other in whispers but Myra could hear them. The problem was that they spoke in a foreign language so Myra had no idea what they were saying. One of the girls put her finger to her mouth warning the other girl that some one was coming. The doors opened and in walked a group of men, most of them wearing tall hats with braids down the sides of their faces. They too spoke in a language that Myra did not understand. Behind them women entered with white shawls over their heads and singing softly. The song was familiar to Myra. Where had she heard it before? The men sat opposite Myra's position, and the women found seats alongside of her. It seemed to her strange that no one tried to sit in her place. The maids disappeared through a side door Myra had noticed before. The oldest gentleman of the group, who seemed to be in charge, sat at the head of the table while an older woman sat at the other end. Men-servants in dark suits and snow-white shirts entered the room with a cart of wine bottles. As the group took their seats around the table, the servants started to pour wine in one of the glasses at each table setting. Then the maidservants came back carrying water pitchers and filling the water glasses. As all the servants left, the older man at the top of the table picked up a book. Myra noticed there was one at each place setting. He began to read in the strange language and heads moved slightly forward and back as though agreeing with him, following along with their books. Soon green parsley was placed in four spots on the table, and besides it a bowl of water. Each person picked up a sprig of parsley, dipped it into the water and ate it. This went on for a while. As the reader paused for a minute the servants brought in four more bowls resembling crushed berries and nuts, along with two platters full of a flat wrinkled cracker, or so Myra thought. Four other bowls held a white mixture like a mesh of crumbled roots. Everyone dug into the last item with a piece of the flat bread after a short read from the book. Some of the women made faces when they tasted it.

"How bitter the horseradish gets every year," whispered a woman sitting next to Myra.

"Oh yes, but how sweet the fruit and nuts taste after-

wards," another woman answered.

A third woman shook her head and said, "Well, blame Moses and his forty years through the desert. You forget the religious meaning of this food."

"Women, be silent or leave the table," the leader shouted at the women, and they bowed their heads in shame.

It bothered Myra seeing the ritual, until she re-membered what she had learned about the Seder when she studied Jewish traditions. She reached for a Matzo to taste the bitter root and the sweet fruit, but the man across from her gripped her hand. "This is not for you. You are a Catholic"

A woman seated down from Myra stood up and screamed at the man. 'She was born of my body and that makes her Jewish."

Myra looked down at the woman and saw a younger version of the lady with the black curly hair. A servant was told to remove Myra from the room, but she struggled against him and ran to her mother's side. "Mama, help me, Mama!" she screamed and woke up in Michael's arms clutching him tightly around his neck.

"It is all right, darling. I am here," Michael said brushing her hair off her face.

"Oh Michael, I need help."

"I know darling. We'll talk about it in the morning.

Go back to sleep."

And she did, snuggled close to Michael's body.

Chapter Nineteen

Michael had no luck in finding a hypnotist he trusted in Denver so Myra decided to wait until they'd settled in Cincinnati. Myra's house sold just in time for the scheduled move in June 1952.

It was sad to say good-bye to the Old North Denver area that had been a happy place for Myra since she had met and married Eric Dawson. Esther didn't take it well either, although she had recently discovered that she was pregnant. That softened her sadness at losing Myra and the children; still, they would always be dear to her.

It was different for Sam. He became moody and sometimes lost control of his feelings. Myra saw tears in his eyes as he was explaining to Mathew that they would be living far apart. Yet, he knew this was the right move for the family. He was considering retirement again since before he had had no need for change. He was a little past the usual retirement age, but keeping busy was his lifeline. Now, with Myra and the children moving away he would have time to research in depth the mystery of her brooch and family line. He would go back to Europe, back to the places where he felt he belonged in his advanced age. This plan enabled him to cope with the coming loneliness. He would no longer stay in Denver where memories would always confront him. He too would take flight, but he would not reveal this to Michael or Myra until he was ready to make the move.

Michael had been working in Cincinnati since March. He had had time to look for a home in a nice neighborhood. His new salary would allow him to find a comfortable home for the family. Co-workers and other doctors at the Jewish Hospital Evendale Medical Center had told him about an area called Indian Hills, a pricey but safe area, they told him. Michael was shocked when he saw the massive homes with acres of land surrounding them. He wasn't a millionaire as most of the population there seemed to be, but he loved the green lawns and the privacy which the many trees gave the homeowners. It reminded him of the Boston neighborhoods where he had grown up. He didn't realize how much he had missed the wooded areas of the eastern states. It took a while, but the last of April Michael found the perfect place. It was smaller than most of the homes in the neighborhood, but it looked like a painting of a European cottage set in a green forest. Inside was larger than it seemed from outside. Here were five bedrooms, one having been a maid's room before live-in maids became obsolete. Each bedroom had its own bathroom and there were two kitchens, one large with an eating area and a smaller one for light meals set in a nook whose windows looked out on a wide green lawn. A three-car garage was almost unheard of in Denver, and this "cottage" had an attached mudroom just next to the larger kitchen. Four of the bedrooms were on the northern part of the house accessible by a front stair-

214

case and a back one from the kitchen. The servant's bedroom was off the southern part of the small kitchen. A perfect apartment, Michael thought when he saw it, thinking of Sam. He knew how depressed Sam would feel when they left Colorado. He hoped that one day Sam would join them here in Ohio since he realized how much Myra meant to Sam.

The summer of 1952 was hot all over the nation, but Ohio seemed like the hottest spot on earth to Myra. She loved the new home and the wide-open space for the children to play. It was at night when the heat bothered her more. In Colorado there had always been a slight breeze no matter how hot the day, but here, next to the Ohio River, only the muggy heat was filling the night air. Window fans cooled the bedrooms but the constant whirling movement sometimes made sleep impossible. Myra never complained to Michael. He loved his new position and was so happy with their move and new home; she could not dash his joy. She would make herself like it here too, even if she felt pangs of homesickness for Sam, Esther, and the mountains.

As the family settled in and Myra unpacked box after box, everything was fitting into place. Neighbors dropped by with gifts of food and maps of the city. Best restaurants and shopping areas were pointed out to Myra. She was invited to afternoon teas and concerts in Hebrew. Mathew seemed distant from both churches and Myra suspected it was his Grandfather John's influences in the letters he now wrote to Mathew every week. At least, Myra

Myra

After the children were settled into their school, Myra went to downtown Cincinnati and applied for a job at the *Cincinnati Post*, a newspaper owned by Scripps Howard & Associates. The main headquarters were in New York City, but the Scripps family lived in Cincinnati. It looked very promising, she later told Michael, and for the first time since their move, she felt comfortable with her life again. A month after applying, Myra was hired as a part time feature writer. They bought a second car for her and she managed to get the children off to school before she drove down to her job. The Ohio River flowed in ripples as she watched out of her office window. The River Front Stadium was just two blocks down the side street from the building where Myra worked. Some days she took her lunch and walked to the river's edge. Sitting on a patch of grass watching the river's flow seemed to calm her. There were no more dreams since their move. She was hoping Michael would forget the hypnosis treatments because she was sure what she had forgotten in her young life would be too traumatic to cope with, as her dreams had been.

She wrote to Sam faithfully and hoped he would join them for the Jewish holiday Hanukkah. He wrote he would think about it but he seemed to have a lot of paperwork that kept him busy. It was never his style to avoid her questions, so Myra was wondering what he was planning. She would not press him for more information. Just keeping touch with him, was her goal for now.

Myra had been a reporter for almost a month when she suddenly became ill. She couldn't keep her food down and she felt weak and tired most days. When Michael heard her throwing up in their bathroom, he insisted she check it out. As if God had planned it, Myra was again pregnant. How could she not be happy? Michael was delighted. Myra was scared. It had been a traumatic time when she gave birth to Mathew, but she consoled herself by remembering the circumstances, the war, and Eric unavailable overseas. Myra had wanted Michael's children, but the timing was off for her career as a reporter. "Why now?" she asked herself, but "Why?" was the question of her life. Why could she not remember her life before the age of six? Why had she lost Eric when she felt no other disaster could happen? Sister Bernadette and Diana had left her too just when she needed them, so what could she expect from the fates that had always seemed to shape her life? She was twenty-nine years old and some days she felt much older. Of course, she concluded, she was now young and energetic enough for babies. In fact, Myra sailed through her pregnancy, and in April 1953 she gave birth to Morgan Michael Lieberman. The Jewish tradition and religious rites frightened her at first when Morgan was circumcised, and his cry hurt her to the very soul. However, he healed fast under the special care of his father, Michael, and all was well again. Two years later, on almost the same day, Rebecca Rose was born and the family seemed to be complete.

Sam was unable to attend any of the ceremonies for the new babies but he sent gifts to all the children. Myra was sad that Sam had moved back to the Communist country of Hungary, but in a way, she did understand. He had not told her or Michael he was relocating to his home country until he had found a suitable flat in Szeged and settled up his affairs in Colorado. He came for a visit the next year for the Seder celebration; Morgan was barely two years old and Rebecca Rose was a newborn baby. Then he left for good. It was a sad parting for Myra, but she knew this was something he had to do. What Myra or Michael didn't know was that Sam was searching for Myra's roots.

Myra had gone to a hypnosis clinic in Cincinnati, but her mind seem to resist remembering her life before age six. Once, she almost made it, but that ended when she woke up screaming for Bertha, a name she had no conscious recollection of. The doctor then believed whatever had happened to Myra was so terrifying it might be dangerous to go on with further treatments. The dreams were now sometimes repeating scenes still meaning nothing to her, but Myra began to put them where they belonged--in the past and not in her future. Life was rolling along with Michael's promotions and workload. The family returned to Colorado for short vacations and it was like a homecoming reunion with Esther and her growing family of three children, and with the old friends Michael had made when living there. Matthew and Lilly enjoyed the returns. For Myra, it was difficult to erase the sadness the old neighborhoods brought to her. Morgan and Rebecca were a handful too on the trips, and Myra was always happy to get home to Ohio

For Sam in Hungary, it was a different story. He was under surveillance constantly. His background as a lawyer concerned the Communist government. Was he a spy, they wondered? Why was he allowed to return to Hungary? Sam felt himself confined in researching Myra's past. There was an uneasiness among the people he interviewed. The questions he asked about old works of art and Jewish families who no longer existed, made the authorities nervous. The Russian police had long ago taken over his childhood home, and his little flat was so small he felt like a sardine in a can. He often walked by the house in his old neighborhood. The backyard no longer had the pond or the round shaded patio where he and his family had enjoyed the summers. Instead, the yard had been cut short, and an apartment house blocked the views of his childhood. Sometimes he remembered his gentile friends, but if he thought he recognized one he was shocked. They were too old, and too frightened to acknowledge him. He told himself that they had had to join the communist party in order to survive in this world.

His only lead in his search was an encounter with the artist Matyas Vargas, in the only museum open in Szeged. The name immediately struck a memory. This was the name of an artist someone had mentioned to him years ago. Vargas was a handsome man, tall and muscular. His dark wavy hair brushed up neatly and past his forehead. Sam was sure he wasn't a communist in spirit, as he seemed to be quite interested in what was happening in America. That was an opening for Sam to ask about a painting, probably done in the 1860s, of a beautiful lady with a large diamond-studded Star of David brooch on her dress. It took Vargas by surprise. His expression startled Sam for a moment, but then he realized he had a clue at

"What is it, man? What do you know about the painting?" Sam asked, holding his arms out to him.

Vargas stepped back as though getting a second breath after a shock. He looked around the room to see if anyone was watching them or close enough to hear them.

"Who are you?" Matyas asked him

"I am an American searching for a past life to connect a friend to her roots." Sam also looked around to see if there was anyone in the room. "I was born here, but I left as a young man"

"What has the portrait to do with your search?" Matyas asked.

Sam whispered that they might be watched and asked if Matyas would meet him at a bar down the street. Sam's Hungarian was clear. Matyas agreed and left the room immediately. Sam slowly walked around the room as if studying more of the paintings. When he was sure his presence did not seem unusual, he left the room and the building. It was a dark and chilly evening but still reasonably early. He crossed the street and slowly looked into the buildings that might have had an arts display, though such displays were scarce. The Russian government had taken what they wanted and rationed out enough food for the people of Szeged. Even the synagogue, robbed of its golden glory, sat with piles of rubble by the front door and broken windows. A few Jews had come back and were trying to put their lives together again. The Russians made sure any money the returning Jews had was confiscated with only enough left to them to survive. Sam was considered a wealthy American Jew, but the people of his faith were afraid to approach him. It was thought he was a spy and any connection to him might have dire consequences for them.

A half an hour later, Sam reached the only place open to non-Russian foreigners, wishing for an alcoholic drink. Matyas was sitting in a booth at the end of the counter. Sam sat on a stool next to the booth and ordered a drink. He looked over at Matyas and shook his head. He then asked, "Weren't you the man in the Museum who told me about some of the art pieces?" He made sure the bartender heard him as the city reeked of treacherous people who would go to the authorities to garner Russian favor.

"Yes, I am that man. Did you enjoy the exhibit?" Matyas asked, letting Sam know he was playing along. "If you are interested in the art world, we are getting back more of our confiscated art works. Tomorrow, there is one exhibit you might find interesting."

"Really! Yes, I would like to see it," Sam said, a little disappointed that he would have to wait another day.

"It is near the river Tiza on the north side along the river's edge. The building would have to be shown to a stranger unless you are familiar with our city."

"I am afraid much has changed since I grew up here as a boy. Would you be so kind as to accompany me there tomorrow?"

Matyas smiled a little and made sure he was sure he was heard. "Of course, I would be happy to show you there. I have a few art works in the exhibition too. I have studied and performed art designs for the stages of theatre in Budapest. Shakespeare is making a comeback after the war. I have been able to design for some superb operas as well as for classic theaters. You may like what you see tomorrow."

"You are an artist?"

"I started drawing maps for the Hungarian Army; then the Germans enlisted me to do that too. I was lucky in that sense not to have been in the combat."

Sam was surprised and happy that he had made a friend. He was sure Matyas was not a political radical in one section or the other. Art has its own agenda and politics have no artistic agenda for most artists or musicians. He could wait one more day.

Chapter Twenty

October 21st 1956 was a cloudy day with the feel of fall in the air. Sam was packing a small suitcase and his journals that he had kept while researching the painting. He was tired of the scrutiny and very tired of the small space of his flat. He would go to Vienna tomorrow unless Matyas Vargas came up with a new clue. His grandparents were from Vienna and he wondered how their home and synagogue had fared through the war. From Vienna he would go to Paris and search the museums again. Maybe he had missed something the last time he was there.

He put his luggage inside the small closet behind the ragged blanket the landlord had given him when he paid his monthly rent. He was never sure whether someone had gone through his things when he left his rooms. So he had, from the beginning of his month's stay, hidden his papers. The thin string he had used to tie around the suitcase was sometimes broken, but his papers were never touched because of Sam's clever method of hiding them. Tomorrow his rent was up, so that would be the day he would leave. This time, he carried the briefcase with him as he left the apartment building and headed to the place Matyas was to meet him. It was to be

on the south side of the Old Chain Bridge, the main highway bridge for the road that wound around the downtown
square and passed Sam's childhood home on the way to
the Yugoslavia border.

There were not many people on the streets as Sam
walked along.   However, there were small crowds of
people gathered in doorways and between buildings. As
Sam passed, some of the huddled groups looked at him as
though they had something to hide. One old man approached him and told him to mind his own business, although Sam had no idea what he meant. He hurried
along. There was a sudden rush of feet running towards
him. It was a group of young people with banners in their
hands, shouting Hungarian slogans. Sam walked faster to
the bridge where Matyas stood like a soldier on duty.
When he saw Sam approach he hurried to him.

"Thank God you are here. Have you not noticed
the crowds of dissenters? It is the revolt against the Communist government. The symbol of the Revolt, Nagy Im-
relmre, must have given the order. It was only a matter
of time."

Sam was flabbergasted. "Why?   What is happening?"

"Bloodshed, my friend, when the Russian armies
get the command. There has been secret talk about a revolution for months and now it is happening. The leader
in Budapest has had enough of the Communists and evidently the time is here. Something must have happened. A

weakness within the Communist party or a useless bloodshed from outside Hungary."

Sam watched Matyas's eyes glisten and his chin rise high. Matyas could have been a model for the grand statues Sam had seen in Budapest and Szeged. His profile was perfect, like a Roman god's. He lit a cigarette and sucked the smoke deep into his lungs before exhaling.

"Are you one of them, Matyas?" Sam asked.

"No, I am afraid not. I am not a political activist, only an artist. I do fear for the safety of my friends and neighbors who will be involved."

Sam turned to see more people running past and felt the sway of their weight on the bridge.

"What should I do, Matyas? Do you think I will be in danger?"

"You are a Jew, American or not. You have roots here. There would be no reason for the Communists not to use you in some political plot against anything America could interfere with. I think you had best leave too. I can get you to Budapest but you will have to cross the border on your own. This rumbling might last for a few days, but you'd better leave tonight. Have you any Hungarian money on you?"

Sam reached inside his suit pocket. "Yes, enough to

"Then go now back to your flat and stay inside. I know where you are staying. I followed you last night. The landlord would not go against the government, but he might use you in a political way. He is shrewd, and you may have to pay him off. Hide whatever you have in that briefcase on the clothing that you are wearing, and take very few clothes. You have to travel light."

Sam could not believe his ears. How in hell did he get into this mess? It was 1956. The war was over, but now he realized that, though it was over for him and America, it had not ended for his beloved city and country.

"But I only want to know about the portrait. It resembles this young lady in America who cannot remember her past. She was raised a Catholic but when she was eighteen, something happened to her making her believe she was born a Jew. I have adopted her so to speak, and I search for her identity to stop her horrible dreams."

"That is your journey here?" Matyas asked. "Describe the portrait."

Sam went into detail about the portrait with the lady and the large five-pointed diamond brooch. He showed Matas a photograph of Myra.

"I believe I have seen that portrait you describe. This woman's face looks remarkably like the one in the painting titled "The Lady in Black." Before the war it was hanging in a museum in Budapest. At that time it was on loan to the museum from the family that owned it," Matyas said, dragging smoke from his cigarette. "I can't remember the family's name."

"My God, Matyas, that is what I want to know. Myra might be cured of her nightmares and live a normal life. Can you not help me?"

"I can only help you get away from here now. I will try to remember later, on our trip to Budapest. Dress warmly. The nights are getting chilly and you will need space to hide your research papers if that is what you have."

Luckily for Sam the landlord and his family had left the building. No doubt they feared being targeted by the young revolutionaries. It was going to be a bright day for October. Shouts from the street below were at times loud and furious. Other times, the crowd of young people was driven back by the police. But as Sam watched from his window, he could see brutality and hatred from both sides of the conflict. Yes, he thought to himself, if I were the landlord and his family, I too would hide. At nine p.m. Matyas drove up in a narrow coupe. It had a rumble seat opened for luggage and Sam swung his suitcase over into it. He wondered whether the car belonged to Matyas or was borrowed from a friend. Matyas seemed to understand his concern and said it was his car, the only material thing he was able to own outright. "Some artists are regarded highly in the communist party, and it seems they favored my ability."

"Will you get in trouble by helping me get to Budapest?" Sam asked.

"Not at all, my friend. I was scheduled for stage design for the Hungarian Ballet to be held next month. They knew I was to go and they think I am loyal."

"What about me if they stop us?" Sam asked.

"You will have to be an American artist trying to learn from my experiences. They won't question that with your passport and money, if you have some to give out. Just be calm and show no expression. The young communists don't smile much, nor are they very friendly in dealing with you. Just follow my example, though, and you will be fine. From Budapest, you may be able as a foreigner to get a train to Vienna. It all depends on the revolt up there."

There was a full October moon and Sam was able to look at the landscape he remembered so well. The trees of the forest were all in line like soldiers waiting for orders. One could look down a column and see almost to the end of the tree line. Suddenly, like a light bulb going off in his head, he remembered that Myra had dreamed of such a scene. Trees like soldiers along a narrow road.

It was Matyas' voice breaking the silence. "Good God in Heaven. What have we here?" From Sam's seat he could make out a man in the middle of the road trying to flag them down. He was a Jew with his high black hat and braids swinging from the sides of his head as he shook violently

"Help me, please."

Matyas and Sam looked at each other as Matyas put his foot on the brake of the car. As they stopped, Sam saw a woman clothed in black run out from the trees and up to the man. She started to beat the man with a large pole and suddenly she drew a knife out of her bodice and stabbed him. She swore in Hebrew, adding a life-long curse. Then Sam saw her turn towards the car and scream, "He stole my child."

Matyas was out of the car in a flash and ran to the man lying on the road as Sam sat frozen; it seemed that ghosts were repeating an act he had heard about, a ghost from Myra's dreams. The woman vanished into the woods as fast as she had appeared. Matyas yelled for Sam to help him carry the man to the car. As Sam did so, he looked back on the road they had traveled. He thought he saw a little girl standing there in an eerie light crying, "Daddy!"

"Myra, Myra, is that you?" he called. Then the light and the little girl disappeared.

"Who are you talking to, Sam? Come here and give me a hand with this fellow. He has fainted. I don't know what frightened him."

"Did you see her? Did you see the little girl stand-

"I saw nothing but a crazy man acting like someone was after him. Look; there is no blood on him. He seems to have passed out. Help me get him into the back with the luggage."

With his heart beating madly, Sam helped Matyas lift the man. He was indeed Jewish and there seemed to be no mortal wound on him though his face was beardless and pale as death. He was breathing but he was not responding to their questions.

"What should we do with him, Matyas?" Sam asked.

"We will take him with us to Budapest. He may need a hospital." Matyas shook his head, "I have never seen anything like this. I thought I saw a shadow. A figure in black, but it never materialized. Yet he was screaming. I wonder why."

Sam covered the young Jew with the ragged blanket he had taken from his room at the last moment. "I don't know. But I seem to have shared his hallucination. I thought I saw a woman in black attacking a young Jewish man just now, but if my seeing had any reality, it must have happened years ago. It's one of Myra's dreams."

They got back into their seats and Matyas started up the car. He looked at Sam and asked what he was talking about.

"It is a long story and I will tell you now as we ride." Sam told his story to Matyas from the beginning, from meeting Myra as a young, troubled, coed to knowing her as the present wife in a happy second marriage with four children. He described the nightmares she had told him about, especially the one about the woman attacking the young man, the one he had just "seen" on the road. "You see, Matyas, she still has her nightmares, and what she cannot remember clouds her heritage for her children. When her first husband saw the painting for which I am searching, he thought it was a reflection of his beloved wife. He was badly wounded and later died without explaining where he had seen the art works hidden by Jewish families. He did describe the large diamond-studded Star of David brooch in the painting, and it was, I believe, the same one that had been sent to Myra back in 1941. There has to be a connection."

A groan from the back had Sam looking around to see how the young man was doing. He had been listening to Sam's story of Myra and he could not take his eyes off Sam. "The woman is a myth," he said. "But she affects the mind."

Sam was taken by surprise. "What do you know of her? If she is only a myth, how can she affect the mind?"

The boy sat up, his expression clouded. "She has been a myth since I was born. She did exist once, but not anymore. Her name was Miriam. It is her spirit that haunts us. It was her dream of life that you saw when you came upon me."

Sam turned completely around and stared at the

boy. "What are you talking about? Myra does live. I know her. Who is this 'Miriam'?"

Matyas could not understand their conversation and asked Sam what the Jew was talking about.

"He says the woman Myra described did exist but now is only a myth or spirit to frighten him and others. I have no idea what he is talking about. I have told him so, and look at him now. He is scared to death."

"It was the spirit of Miriam that you witnessed when you rescued me," the boy said in Hungarian. "She was the reason the families were torn apart."

"What families are you talking about?" Sam asked as he reached for the boy's collar. "The woman who told me of this awful scene lives in America and has been my friend for years. What do you know of her background?"

Before Sam got an answer, Matyas nudged him. "There are the lights of Budapest, my friend. We will soon be able to rest and find a place for your young Jew."

A strange foreboding came over Sam. He was on the verge of discovering the truth, he thought, from this young person. He would not let this chance pass him by.

"I have to question him, Matyas. He could have information about the painting and the brooch."

"I know of the painting," the young man said. "The

brooch is Miriam's strength. It has mystical powers."

They were approaching the city limits and although it was in the middle of the night, sounds of shouts and yells could be heard.

"I must get off here in Pest," the young Jew said. "The synagogue is on this side of the river Danube. They will help me."

Matyas stopped the car a few blocks from the lighted bridge. Sam jumped out of his seat and grabbed the boy before he could run off.

"Tell me boy. What do you know of the painting and the brooch?"

Sam held the boy tight against the car and raised his hand up as though to punch him if he didn't answer.

"There is a curse on the brooch, put on by my ancestor who made it for his wife, Miriam Singer. It belonged in the family of Furst. The man's name was Sandor. He cursed the brooch he had made especially for her. He said that if she were ever unfaithful to him, her descendents would suffer."

Sam put his hand down and asked," What you are saying? The lady in the portrait is Miriam Furst?"

"Yes, his beautiful wife who fell in love with a gentile and ran off with him. Sandor put a curse on all his

own children born of Miriam. I am of that family. The
curse has befallen me as it has others down through the
years."

The young man tore loose from Sam and started to
run down the street. Sam chased after him while Matyas
put the car in gear and followed the runners. The young
man tripped and fell as Sam came up behind him. They
struggled for a time, until Sam yelled. "Your name. I only
want to know your name. I do not mean to hurt you."

The boy stood up and hesitated for a minute. "My
name is Moshe. I am a descendant of Sandor and Miriam
Furst, four generations removed. Now let me go, old
man."

The shock of the information left Sam bewildered
and confused. The boy broke away and ran while Sam
stood there looking at the pavement beneath his feet.
Matyas was sitting in the car and yelled at Sam to get in
before any more events happened this night.

"You had best come to my apartment for the night.
I doubt you could catch a train at this hour," Matyas said
as he turned the car around and headed to the main highway. They crossed a lighted bridge. The paved road
climbed up a steep incline and circled around the Buda
Castle wall nestled into the hillside. They exited on a
wide boulevard and encountered a group of people holding signs like they had seen in Szeged. This crowd was of
older people with determined faces. Matyas slowly drove
through the crowd and a few threw curses at them. They

passed through and then turned into a side street which also sloped upwards, and headed into a district of homes and large apartment buildings. Matyas stopped the car beside one of the buildings. Across the street was a block-long playground with one arch light in the middle. "This is it my friend," Matyas said as he opened the car door and went to the back of the car. Sam got out and both men took luggage from the back of the car. Sam followed Matyas into the building and up four flights of stairs to a wooden door. Matyas unlocked the door and held it open for Sam. Following Sam into the apartment, Matyas snapped on a light hanging from the ceiling. The light bulb was dull and it took Sam a while to adjust his sight. It was a room larger than his last residence, but it was a combination of a living room and kitchen. On the right side of the room were bedroom and bath. A long brown couch sat along the wall of the larger room, and there was a closed door next to it.

Matyas noticed Sam's survey of the rooms. "That door opens to my studio. It is full of my work but it has a view of the Danube and below which gives me all the light I need for my work."

Matyas walked to the small icebox near a kitchen window. "I have to get some ice here, but I think I do have a few beers, if you don't mind warm beer."

"I got used to warm beer in London. I would be happy to share your beer," Sam said, feeling very weary. His legs felt like rubber so he dropped his case besides the couch and sat down. "I feel so tired. I do need a good night's sleep."

Matyas opened the beer can and found a glass for Sam. The warm beer felt refreshing to Sam and when he finished, he laid his head on the seat and fell asleep.

Chapter Twenty-one

Sam opened his eyes in a strange room. For a few minutes he had no idea where he was. Then he remembered. He was on Matyas's couch with a blanket covering him. His shoes had been removed and were lying on the floor by his feet. He sat up but a sharp pain raced through his body and he lay down again. He could hardly breathe for a minute. The window at the end of the room was open and shouts could be heard in the streets below. What was happening to him? He had never felt like this before. His head was spinning and he broke out in a cold sweat. The sounds of shots being fired further frightened him. How long he had been there he had no idea: there was no clock in the room. Suddenly he heard footsteps on the stairs outside the room; then Matyas and another young man entered.

"You are awake now?" Matyas asked him as he walked over to Sam and felt his forehead. He turned to the young man and said, "He is burning up. All night long he has been moaning and sweating. I did not know what to do. He is an American and we must help him."

The young man took Sam's hand and looked into his face. "Have you ever had a heart problem?"

"Who are you?" Sam asked, near despair because he was not in control of his body.

"I am Dr. Edmond Herschkovitz. Matyas said you were Jewish and feared that no Hungarian doctor would attend to you. Luckily, he is a friend and found me dodging bullets on the way to my clinic."

Sam looked up at Matyas and asked, "Why did you think I needed a doctor, my friend?"

"Sam, you have a fever and you seemed to be unaware of me and anything that has been happening to you. When you became delirious I had to get you help. The Revolt has started. I could not find a doctor at the regular clinics. They are either scared or trying to help the wounded. There is shooting and confusion. People are dying in the streets. Dr. Herschkovitz was trying to help, but he was unable to move out until I saw him. We crouched and ran, and got out of the lines of fire. I told him about you. He came with me. Let him examine you."

The doctor took Sam's wrist and felt his pulse. He brought out his stethoscope and listened to Sam's heart. Then he reached inside his little black bag and brought out a small bottle of pills. "These are from America, my good man. I think they are good for your heart. They are called Aspirin. They have worked before on some of my patients. Take two of them," he said as he poured two pills into Sam's hand.

Matyas went to the sink and filled a glass with

water. Sam's tongue felt like cotton and his vision felt blurred from the light at the window. He swallowed the pills and lay back again on the couch. He could hear the doctor and Matyas deciding what could be done for him.

"He cannot leave in his condition. He must rest," the doctor said.

"But I will not be here very long. I have two days to set up my art for the Ballet."

"Do you honestly think they will have the ballet? Everything has closed down. Trains no longer run, the borders have been reinforced with Russian Communist troops. You will be lucky to drive back to Szeged." The doctor checked Sam's forehead again.

Sam sank back into conscious sleep. He could hear the two men talking, but he was drifting in and out, only aware that he was not where he belonged.

"Herschkovitz?" The name ran through Sam's mind like a bolt of lightning, opening doors he had closed years ago. That was his birth name. Who could this young man be? He tried to wake up fully, but all he could do was stay half asleep, half awake. He could not open his eyes or speak. Yet, he heard some of their conversation.

"Matyas, I have known you from treating the dancers and actors you have worked with. You are not

"No, Edmond, but this man is searching for an important piece of art on behalf of another American Jew. I thought I could help him, but now, as our situation grows worse, he should leave. There is no way I can help him now under the government rulings we have. Are you a Communist?"

"No, I am not a politician. I lost my mother and two sisters in the death camps. How I managed to survive had to be the hand of God. He has plans for me and being a doctor is as close as I can get to helping as a Jew in this country."

"Why did you return, Edmond?" Matyas asked him

Edmond closed his bag and said, "Where could I go? My father and brother survived. We had no sponsors from another country. My father wanted to come back and I was able to study at the medical school through connections he had before the war. Nice people and old friends my father had when he ran his banking business. All the money and our house no longer exist. Why not come back and help build a better society?"

"You are a dreamer, Edmond. If anything, our government has not moved forward. Look at our rationing, the rules we must follow. How are we a better society?"

"We have to crawl before we walk, Matyas. If you had been in the concentration camps, you would think you were in heaven now, although I hope heaven to be better, if I make it." Edmond laughed. "For now, we must survive and do what we can to help our people."

Dr. Hirschkovitz grabbed his black bag and headed towards the door.

"You are not going now, are you?" Matyas asked in a worried tone.

"I have to go, dear friend. There are others in worse shape than your American friend here. His heartbeat is a little fast and he may have had a slight heart attack, but the aspirins should calm him down. He should just rest. I will try to find something better for him, but that is about all I can do for now. I will try to get back tonight, God willing. Just keep him warm. Hot tea and bread if he is hungry. When he gets out of Hungary, he should go directly to a cardiologist in Vienna. But it would not be safe for him in his condition to try to leave with all that is happening here."

Sam was aware of what was said and he heard Matyas mummer something to the doctor about his age. "I do not know. I would judge him to be near or in his seventies."

The apartment door opened and closed and all was quiet as Sam sunk into a deep sleep.

———

Myra woke up with a start. The grandfather clock

in the downstairs hall sounded two gongs. Two o'clock in the morning. What was it that woke her? Why was she thinking of Sam? Was he calling her name? Something was wrong and she knew it. Where was Sam now?   In his last letter he was in Hungary. What had she heard about Hungary lately?

She slipped out of bed and put on her robe. She didn't want to wake Michael, so she quietly opened the bedroom door and went downstairs. She had put Sam's letters in a drawer in her desk in the study. She had to know what part of Hungary Sam was going to visit. If she remembered correctly, he was going to the place of his birth but Myra had forgotten the name of the city. She picked up the small pack of letters from Sam and went to the kitchen. She put on a fresh kettle of water and took a cup and saucer out of the cupboard and a tea bag from a canister. She began to sort through the letters before she found the last of his letters. He was in Szeged, Hungary, where he was born. Maybe her imagination was getting the best of her, but why was she afraid for him in the middle of night?

The kettle whistled and Myra jumped up to shut off the gas under it. She poured the boiling water into her cup with the tea bag and put the cup on the table. She stirred the water to absorb the tea and added a spoon of sugar.   While the mixture cooled a little, she began rereading Sam's letter. He told her what his childhood home looked like now and complained that it was turned into a Communist gathering place with an officer and his family encamped in it. He could see through the wooden arch gates that opened onto the street that their pond, garden, and fruit trees, except for a lone cherry tree, were gone. Half of the family's land had been confiscated and an ugly six-story apartment house loomed in back of a wooden fence. He had just arrived and was disappointed with the state of his former home and the city of his happy childhood memories. How sad and yet how glad he was that his parents had most likely been dead when all this took place. He had found a small flat where he would stay for about month, still searching for the past.

Myra knew what Sam was doing. He was searching for the portrait Eric had seen a dozen years earlier in a cave during the war. She had put that in the back of her mind although she did sometimes still have dreams. They seemed to follow a pattern now. An event or an unknown fear for a loved one seemed to trigger them. They almost always involved the lady with long black hair, though occasionally a different person appeared. Her sessions with a hypnosis specialist had frightened her, and she refused to go through more of them.

Myra sipped the hot tea slowly, enjoying the warmth it sent through her body. It was like the warmth she felt when Sister Bernadette nursed her from a cold or one of the childhood diseases and hugged her close. How she missed Sister Bernadette.

"What are you doing at this time of the night?" It was Michael standing in the doorway rubbing his eyes.

"I didn't mean to wake you, darling," said Myra.

Myra

"Just had a dream about Sam and I think he was calling for me. I thought I had better read over his letters and find out where he is now."

"Did you figure out where he is?" Michael asked, getting his own cup and saucer from the cupboard.

"Yes. He is in Hungary." Michael dropped his cup, which crashed on the floor, and looked at Myra.

"My God, Myra. You know there is a revolution going on there now." He motioned to her not to bother with the pieces of the cup. "If he is there, he may very well be in trouble."

Myra paused and looked up at Michael. "You are scaring me Michael. Do you think he may be in the middle of it?" She finished picking up the broken pottery and put the pieces in the wastebasket inside the pantry. She retrieved another cup and saucer from the cupboard, put her used tea bag into it, and poured the hot water in for Michael. She noticed her hands were shaking.

"Michael, I am so scared for him. Is there some way we can find out?"

"I am not sure, but I don't think the Communist ambassadors in Washington, D.C. would be of help. The Hungarians are revolting against the government, as they have been doing in Poland. There would be no help from those quarters."

"There has to be a way. Have they closed the borders to people of other nations?"

"I know what you're thinking, Myra, and there is no way in hell I would let you travel there. Do you realize how stupid that would be? You have children to think about, and me. Do you realize what you might be risking? It would affect us all, not just you."

"I know Michael, but Sam is there because of me. I know that. He is searching for my past and it is becoming a dangerous search."

"You don't know that for sure. He retired and there was nothing to keep him in Denver. I think he felt he had to return to the land of his roots just out of curiosity about what the war did to the place."

"Well, you think what you must, but in my heart, I know I am right."

Michael put his arms around her and kissed her neck. "Darling, I love you more than anything in this world other than the children. Let us go back to bed and maybe by morning we will hear something."

Myra did dream that night. She was standing in the road looking for her mother and calling for her. Why couldn't she see her face? Instead, she saw Sam and another man lift an injured person into a funny looking car and drive off.

Chapter Twenty-two

Sam opened his eyes trying to hear what was being whispered somewhere in the room. The bright light above him was blinding so that he could only try to open his eyes fully. Where was he, he wondered? What had happened to him? Then he remembered. He was in Budapest trying to get out of the country and into Austria. Something had happened though for now he could not put it all together. He tried to move his left arm but a pain shot though his body like a lightening strike. His movement brought some attention to his pain.

"Do you feel some pain, old man?" A young woman in a white uniform was leaning over him and speaking in Hungarian. She checked some of the wiring protruding from his upper body and adjusted the fluid bottle that was connected to his arm by a spidery web of more wires. He could not talk for his voice seem to have failed him. He tried to look around but only saw the peeling paint of the wall next to him before he closed his eyes and drifted into sleep again.

Matyas Vargas entered the room. The young woman turned to him and said, "He woke up but only groaned in pain. I had to adjust his medicine because the volume was down too low."

"Did he say anything?" Matyas asked,

"No, but I think he tried. He moved his arm but I think it hurt him to do so. Should I call the doctor?"

Matyas looked at the uniformed man standing besides the nurse. "Who are you?" he asked.

"I am from the Russian Command Headquarters. I was sent here to investigate this American. Who are you?"

"I am Matyas Vargas of the Budapest opera and theatre organization. I am their top artist for stage and scenery. Why are you investigating this man?"

"We were informed he was a Jew with an American passport. We have to know if he is a spy for the United States. We have checked on his identity; he was born in this country, according to his passport. He could be here on false pretenses."

"He is not, I assure you. He is only a visitor who journeyed back to his roots. I would not have been involved in such piracy, my dear comrade. I am a true citizen with no involvement against the government."

"Then, my comrade, tell me--why are you involved with him at all?" the young man smirked.

"I was on my way here from Szeged when the Revolt started up. He approached me to ask about getting out of the country and to Vienna. I thought the decent thing to do was offer a ride since I had a job here . . . if the revolution has not stopped it. On the way, he explained to me about his quest. He wondered if any of his family's belongings remained. He felt guilty about leaving the family decades ago, and he wanted to atone for his youthful mistake."

"If that is true, and he found some family treasure, he would not be able to take it. It is now part of our Communist domain. Did he find anything of value?"

"No, he did not. He became ill as we entered Budapest. I could not leave him to die on the streets. I brought him here."

"What is going on here?" It was Dr. Hirschkovitz entering the room.

The young Communist looked shocked. "Is this your patient, Doctor?" he asked, looking guilty about something, or so Matyas thought.

"Yes, he is now. Is there something wrong with his papers?"

"No, Comrade. I was sent here to make sure he was not a spy for the United States. I, that is, we had no idea you were treating him. Please accept my apology and I will immediately report that he is in your hands if you can vouch for his visit."

Edmond looked at Matyas before he turned his attention to the young soldier. "I met him two days ago when this comrade sent for me. I could see that he was very ill and he needed heart treatment. When his condition worsened we brought him here. Tests later proved me right, so we operated last night. He is no enemy, my brother. He is truly an American visitor." Edmond pointed to Sam's briefcase lying on the table next to the bed. "Look for yourself."

The young man walked to the table and picked up Sam's case. He took out a pile of papers in which Sam had written about his experience and the fruitless search for his family's belongings. His last entry was about leaving Hungary and getting back to the states and Myra's family.

"Who is this Myra?" he asked as he placed the papers in his own briefcase, which meant he intended to take them to his commanders.

"A young girl he adopted, I think." Matyas said, relieved to know that Sam had not had time to write about him or the boy Moshe. "I think he would want the papers back when he wakes up. There is nothing of a criminal intent against the government in them."

"How do you know, artist?" the soldier asked him

"We got to know each other a little on the ride to

Budapest. He is just a retired lawyer from America curious about the family he left behind all those years ago."

"Come, young comrade," Edmond said, patting the young man's back. "That is exactly what I thought after reading his papers too. Just leave them and if he doesn't survive, I will make sure you get them if you still feel they would be of importance to your leaders."

"I know you, Dr. Hirschkovitz. You saved a member of my family and the commander's too. He thinks very highly of you, so I will trust you." He returned the papers to Sam's briefcase, saluted Edmond, and left the room.

Matyas started to say something, but Edmond put his fingers to his lips. The nurse had her back turned from them and was checking Sam's pulse.

"No, nurse. I think he just needs to rest. I see by his chart everything is stable for now. If he begins to fail, then be sure you call me. I most likely will be here most of the day."

The nurse turned and left the room.

"What a break," Matyas said. "I was sure Mr. Hirsch was writing everything down. I cannot read English handwriting, but I thought he recorded what was happening."

"He did, Matyas, but I was able to read some of his

papers and removed them while they were getting him ready for the operation. They are in my secret drawer in my office here. I thought they might check his background so I left what he wrote about his family and what he thought they might have left behind when they were sent to the death camps."

"He did mention that subject, thank God."

Matyas felt a sense of relief and smiled at the doctor.

"Who is this adopted daughter he talks about? Myra, I think he said," Edmond asked.

"She seems to be the reason he is here. It is a long story I will tell you about later. I did find an address for her in his address book and I think if it is possible we should write her about his surgery. I don't think this revolt is going to last much longer. The Russians seem to be crushing the dissidents and Freedom Fighters. The streets are still dangerous; there are bullet holes everywhere, but few new bullets. I hear there are to be executions of the leaders soon. Poor Nagy and his ideas."

"I have heard that Sandor Petofi has repeated the National Poem and Imre Nagy is trying to calm the situation. This could start up all over again." Edmond said checking Sam's pulse. "I wish this would let up, and when it is safe, we should inform the girl of this man's condition."

"It will not end soon, my friend," Matyas said as he searched Sam's address book. "I think we should try to get him out of here now."

"Impossible. He could never make the journey until he is stabilized. Moving him could cause his death."

"Why would you care, Doctor? Is it because he is Jewish as you are? He is not of our country now. He left Szeged as a young man, he told me, and left a wife he had been matched with by a matchmaker. He didn't love her, he said, and his parents disowned him."

"Then that is the reason to save him," Edmond said. "He has atoned for his youthful error. Maybe his soul needs to find peace."

"Is that a Jewish tradition?"

"No, it is a moral tradition. How many years must he live with his guilt? Maybe he just wants to quiet the turmoil he has felt and find his own peace." Edmond looked down on Sam. "Besides, and you may think this to be unbelievable, he does remind me of my own family."

Matyas laughed a little, "Well he is a Hirsch. Maybe he is related to you?"

Edmond felt his brain turn on like a light bulb in a dark room. His father did have a brother who went to America, leaving the family to wonder about him, but that was years ago, before the war and way before Edmond was born. Edmond always thought of it as an old wives tale designed to teach a lesson about their Jewish traditions and tell children to always be true Jews.

"I doubt he is any relation of mine." Edmond said, smiling at Matyas, "Unless he cut half of his real name off. But I have heard that Ellis Island officials do change names if they find the spelling difficult."

Matyas nodded towards the door, "Then shall we let him rest and hopefully get through this surgery? I have never heard of repairing the heart as you did in this operation. Has it been done before?"

"Yes, but it is still in the testing stage. I have done it twice before, and both men lived. I have also heard of others in Sweden who have been successfully operated on with very few problems. It is not a chance most doctors will take unless there is no other way to save the person. In this case, I had to go in replace those arteries with some from his leg. If they take hold, he will be just fine."

The two men walked out into the hospital hall where narrow cots were lining the hallways and wounded civilians lay. Edmond immediately began to check some of the patients as Matyas continued down the hall leading to the front door.

———

"Myra. Help me!" Myra sat up straight in the bed. Michael was sound asleep next to her. She rubbed her eyes and looked around the room, and then she slipped silently out of bed and quietly went down the stairs to the library. She closed the door and turned on the lamp next to the sofa. She picked up yesterday's newspaper and began to reread the articles about the Hungarian Revolution.

"Sam is there and he needs me," she said to herself, remembering her dream of the previous night. She closed her eyes and searched her mind as to what she should do. "I know it was Sam's voice. He reached for me and I have no way to get to him."

She stood up and picked up a heavy volume on Europe from a shelf. She found a chapter on the history of Hungary with maps of the cities. She thought about Sam's last letter. Then she paged through the book until she found the city map of Budapest. That was the place he had mentioned while explaining his small flat and the rude landlords. She scoured south from Budapest since she remembered Sam had said he was heading toward the southern part of the country. She found the city of Szeged. Her finger would not relax from its position, as though it had a mind of its own. That was the city he was in now, she thought. She closed her eyes and visualized trees standing like soldiers in a straight row and a dirt road cutting between them. She took a deep breath as the picture in her mind became real to her. The woman with the black hair was again running, but this time it was Sam who was trying to get away from her. Myra could hear his heavy breathing and the see the sweat run down the sides of his face. His breathing could hardly keep up with his running.

"Run Sam. Run!" she screamed before she realized she wasn't dreaming this time.

"What in God's name are you doing, Myra?"

It was Michael standing in the doorway. "Are you dreaming again?"

"Oh Michael, Sam called my name and awakened me. He needs me."

"How do you know that? You have had these dreams most of your life. We really should talk about it, Myra. You have to get help."

"Michael you have known about my dreams all these years. Can't you believe that I have no control over them? Isn't there a mystic group of Jews who go beyond the normal in sensing what's really happening? I have talked to Rabbi Goldstein about my nightmares. He told me he read of similar stories from the history of the Jews. Very sensitive people like me. How was Moses able to talk to and hear God? Why are so many Jews able to rank high in professional jobs in the corporate world? So many talented people, like actors, singers, and high achievers, are from a Jewish heritage. We are called the 'Chosen People'. Where did that come from if not from some-where in our genes? Maybe we were formed to be on a higher level than the non Jews."

"You are talking nonsense, Myra. Come to bed. You are sensitive, I have to admit, on affairs that you have no knowledge about, and on people you think of as friends. But you also worry about useless things. Yes, there's a revolution going on in Hungary. But I've been thinking: Sam is an American. Even if he is in the middle of that revolution, he will not be harmed."

"Michael, you don't fully understand my connection to Sam. I was raised a Catholic and now I am a Jew. I never knew what a Star of David was until I was sent that brooch, and I never met a Jew as an adult until Sam came along. I am beginning to understand why I lost my memory. My guardians kept a dreadful secret from me to protect me, but it was the worse thing they could have done to the adult I am now. Sam sensed that. He was taken aback when I showed him the brooch, as though he had seen it before."

"You think Sam recognized the brooch? He would have told me if that were true. He said nothing about that, only that he suspects you might be from a Jewish family."

"My heart tells me I am Jewish, Michael. Sam was right. The dreams are my past. The woman with the black hair has to be related to me. The man with blood-shot eyes and smelly breath was someone who hurt me. I feel like I was pulled away from my heritage by some un-thinkable event. I think Sam knows it too. That is why he is there in Hungary."

"Myra, you are not being rational. You must come

back to the reality of life. So you fell through the cracks during some dysfunctional event. That is not what you are today. Why can't you just let it be and enjoy the life you have now?"

"Oh Michael, I do enjoy our life, more than you will ever know. But this shadow of my unknown past keeps preventing me from feeling whole. And I am worried about Sam."

Michael turned to leave the room, "I won't argue with you now. We will talk about it in the morning. Come back to bed."

Myra closed the map and the book. She stood up to replace the book in its rightful place. Suddenly she heard it again. "Myra! Help me. I need you." She fainted and fell to the floor. Michael rushed back into the room and picked her up. He carried her upstairs and put her on the bed. He checked her pulse and opened her eyes to see if they were dilated. Neither was abnormal. She slowly moaned and opened her eyes.

"What happened, Michael? Did I fall?"

"You fainted Myra. I am going to give you something to make you sleep for now. Tomorrow, we are going to get to the bottom of this nonsense."

"Did you hear him? Did you hear Sam, Michael?" she asked.

"I was halfway up the stairs and I heard you fall. I heard nothing else."

Michael went into the bathroom and got a bottle of pills from the medicine cabinet. He poured some water into one of the paper cups they kept in a drawer and went back to the bedroom. Myra was sound asleep. Her breathing was normal and her forehead showed no sign of a fever. Michael put the cup and the pill on the nightstand on his side of the bed. Outside the wind was beginning to blow hard and then a strike of lightening lit up the room. Looking out the window, Michael saw the rain beginning. Another strike of lightening and Michael thought he saw a person under the large oak tree by the circular driveway. He waited for another lightening strike, but the light from the sky showed no one was there. He left the window and sat on the bed.

"I must be dreaming like Myra," he said to himself. "I was sure Sam was standing by the tree." He pulled the covers over himself and Myra, then pulled her close.

"My poor darling," he thought as he closed his eyes and drifted off to sleep.

Chapter Twenty-three

Sam felt the rain on his face. *He wondered how long he had been out in the rain. He had been standing next to the big oak tree in Myra's circle driveway, trying to get her attention. There was light in the lower level, but no one heard his calls.*

"Wake up old man. I can't dry you off if you don't help me." It was a woman's voice speaking in Hungarian. He didn't know his eyes were closed, but he did as he was told and found himself in a tin bathtub full of water and a young nurse pulling at his arms trying to get him to stand up. He pulled back and looked at the nurse.

"Who are you? Where am I?" He spoke in a weak voice.

"I have had it with you, old man. You come around and ask the same question every day. I cannot lift you from the tub. I will need help." The nurse left him and called for help from the doorway.

A big well-rounded man with a bald head appeared at the doorway. "What is it, Kati?"

"I need help getting the old one over there out of the tub. Dr. Herschkovitz said he needed a bath since his wires were removed two days ago and his heart was healing nicely. The orderlies put him in the tub but they left for their lunch and now I have to get him out."

The big man walked over to Sam's tub and smiled down at him. "Saba, my man. It is good to see you fully awake. I will be very gentle and help you to your feet, so give me your arms."

Sam looked at the nurse. "Not in front of her."

"She is Kati, your nurse, and has seen everything you've got in the ten days you have been here. There will be no surprises, so give me your arms."

Sam reluctantly did as he was told and as soon as he was out of the water, the nurse draped a huge white towel over his body. He felt weak and began getting dizzy.

"The doctor thinks you should try your legs out since they have been inactive for a while. Take one step at a time and I will be by your side to hold you up if you need help."

Sam looked up at the big man and wondered why he was here. Ten days, the man had said. What had happened to him? Why couldn't he remember?

They slowly moved out of the room, Sam taking

one small step at a time. The big body next to his held him tightly around the waist as they shuffled along the narrow corridor of the hospital. Sam felt like his legs were putty with no bone structure or muscle. At last they came to a doorway into which the big man directed Sam. A small single bed made up with white sheets awaited him. He was let down gently by the big man and immediately put his head on the small pillow. He still gazed at the big body and at the nurse called Kati.

"Thank you Jonas. That should give him a bit of an appetite now," she said as she covered Sam with another white sheet.

"Tell me, young lady, what has happened to me?"

She adjusted his pillow to be directly under his head. "You have no memory, Sam?"

"I would not have asked if I did. Have I been sick?"

"You suffered a heart attack. Your friend called on Dr. Herschkovitz. The nice doctor operated on your heart. You are very lucky, you know? Dr.Herschkovitz has only done three surgeries such as yours and all have survived. The World Medical Association wants him to write a paper about it, but he won't."

Why not?"

"Because he is Jewish and who would believe him?

At least that is what he believes-- and then what good would it do for the poor heart patient? He is a very intelligent man but a very private person who does not like publicity. Most likely after what he and his family have been through, one can't blame him, can one?"

"What has he been through?"

"Oh you know. The holocaust and the death camps. He managed to survive and save his brother and father, but he lost his mother and sisters. He is a very courageous person but he does not like to talk about how he was able to survive. I think it was his medical ability although he was not a licensed doctor at the time, just a teenager."

Sam relaxed his body, feeling all the aches and pains of his muscles. He looked towards the window where a little beam of sunlight was slipping through a space between the closed wooden shutters. Below the window Sam noticed the peeling paint on the wall and his memory returned to that moment when he first saw it. He felt so sick at that time, yet he remembered the peeling paint. Why?

"I must go now and get some soup for you and other patients. We will get your nightshirt on you when I come back. Just stayed covered," Nurse Kati said as she left the room.

Sam shivered. He thought of what the nurse had just told him. His birth name was Herschkovitz. Would this young doctor be related to him? He had journeyed here to find the painting resembling Myra and now was he finding instead, his own family? Impossible. He had two younger brothers and an older sister when he left for America years ago. He had not deliberately disconnected them from his life, but the family he had shamed when he left the wife he didn't love—that family had disconnected from him.

Later, after the hot but watery soup, he was given a pill to help him heal. Kati was happy to see that he had been able to stay awake for several hours. There were still sounds of a battle on the nearby streets and heavy machines were passing by the hospital in the streets below Sam's room. The noise reminded Sam he was still in the middle of the Hungarian Revolution. Yes, he thought, he was lucky to have met with Matyas Vargas. He lay down again and the pill took effect as he drifted into a sound sleep.

"Samuel, Samuel, wake up." Sam could hear his father calling him. Papa always emphasized the 'U' in his name.   I am dreaming again like when I thought I was standing in the rain by Myra's big oak tree, he thought. "Samuel, Samuel. Do you hear me?"

Sam turned his head in the direction of the voice and slowly opened his eyes. It was night now and a dangling light bulb lit the room. A Jew sat beside his bed with a white beard and the scull cap on his head. He looks like Papa, thought Sam, so this must be a dream, like Myra dreams. Back to the past, he thought. But then the Jew asked him a question.

"Samuel, do you know me?"

Sam raised his head a little and then realized he was not dreaming. It was his father. "Papa, you are still alive? How is that possible? You would have to be over a hundred years old?"

"No, Samuel, I am your brother Joshua. Do you not remember me? I do resemble our father."

Sam blinked his eyes and stared at this man who resembled his father.

"Yes, I had a younger brother by that name, but I was told my family was all dead."

"No, Samuel. I am not dead, nor are two of my sons, Dr. Herschkovitz and Benjamin the lawyer. We survived, my brother, but we thought you were lost."

Sam opened his mouth but nothing came out. He looked at the man sitting next to his bed. He does look just like Papa, Sam thought to himself. Then his voice returned and he asked, "How could this be? What are you telling me?"

"I am telling you that my son Edmond told me about this American lawyer and that he bore a resemblance to me. When he said your name was Hirsch, I had to see you. I knew immediately who you were. I have come here several times while you were not conscious. Today, the nurse told Edmond you were fully awake and I had to come to see you."

Joshua? You are little Joshua?" Sam could hardly contain this information.

"Yes, brother Samuel. I am he and you are my lost older brother."

Then the tears started rolling down Sam's cheeks. When Joshua started crying too, the brothers reached out to each other and embraced a long time with sobs of joy.

At last, Sam let his brother go and lay back to examine him. "I can't believe my eyes. I came here on a mission but I had no idea that some of my family survived those horrible death camps."

"It was a horrible time, Samuel. We try to lock it away from our memories and face the future. But you! What has happened in your life? You got to America ... ."

"It is a long story, Joshua, and one I will tell you about when we both can talk of our past. Now, I must heal, thanks to my nephew, Edmond. I had no idea who he was. In fact, if I heard his name, it didn't register until recently."

Joshua patted Sam's arm. "You are fine for now. When you are well enough to come home, it will be with us. I live with Benjamin and Anna, his wife and their small son. My Benny was lucky to survive, and so was Anna, but those are stories too long for now."

Joshua got up as if to leave, but Sam grabbed his hand. "Joshua, I can't tell you how finding you has made me feel. I have been a loner all my time in the States, and now I feel the light at the end of the tunnel is getting brighter."

Joshua gripped Sam's hand tighter and said, "Edmond said you had adopted a daughter. You must have been married?"

"No, I never married again. The perfect woman was never found for me. Edmond most likely has found my identity card mentioning Myra. I didn't adopt her but I am as close to her as if she were my own. We met about fifteen years ago when she was eighteen and like me all alone in this world. We grew close to each other through her marriage to a young friend of mine, and her widowing. Her children call me Grandpa. It is for her that I came here. But it is a long story and one I will tell you about later. You will be fascinated."

"I will wait patiently, big brother. Now you must rest, and I will rejoice before God that the prodigal son has returned."

After Joshua left the room, Sam felt a strange peace come over him. A little brother he chased after and helped to bathe and dress—a little brother had survived and now Sam knew he was with family again. It was wise to come here, he thought. I must send Myra a cable telling her about my family.

———

Four days later, Myra answered the door to a Western Union deliveryman who handed her an envelope and had her sign on the bottom line. She closed the door slowly as she studied the envelope. There was a nice fire glowing in the sitting room and she found the chair by the fireplace warm and cozy. It had been raining for weeks, she thought, and now snow. At times she wished to be back in Colorado where the snow melted on the streets faster than one could blink, the minute the sun came out.

She lifted the envelope's top sealer and withdrew a telegram from Sam. It must have been very expensive as it was a long letter. She read it fast and then re-read it.

He is safe, my Sam. How wonderful that he has discovered some of his missing family. However, she shivered over the words that told of his heart attack and the dream he had had, of standing in the rain outside her house by the oak tree. She remembered that night and her certainty that he was calling her. Michael had been wrong. It wasn't a dream but a transformation of identities in a time of severe need. She believed that an unknown factor could cause that to happen. After all, weren't her dreams the same thing? The older she grew the more she believed that someone or something out there in the world had been trying to contact her. Black

Myra

Magic? Maybe, and maybe not. She knew she was sensitive to certain people and certain ideas that came up in her dreams. The connections were in her soul, and some day she would discover her birth parents and her roots. She called Michael to tell him the great news.

Chapter Twenty-four

The sunset was a beautiful ending to a beautiful day, Myra thought. She was in her upstairs reading room which doubled as an office for her and Michael. All the bills were paid here, and all the expenses discussed. Michael had at last agreed to make the trip to Vienna and Budapest. It was the spring of 1959, three and a half years after Sam had recovered his family. Sam was now living in Vienna. Myra had wanted to visit him for a long time. Morgan and Rebecca had been too young for a trip to Europe, though, and Matt and Lily had been involved in the sports of the various seasons. Now, Morgan was six, Rebecca four. Matt was a strapping sixteen years old. He was a blue-eyed athlete too popular with the girls, Myra thought, but a loveable and sensitive son to her. Lily was a teenaged copy of her mother, Diana, full of energy with the athletic body and shapely legs Myra had admired on Diana. Lily had stayed platinum, but Matt had taken on the look of the Dawsons. Peace had been made years ago, and every summer, Matt and Lily now made a trek to California to be with their Grandpa John. Lily knew she had been adopted, and she knew her dying mother Diana had requested she be adopted by Myra. Lily believed that her birth was meant to be and with Myra's help and understanding, Lily had grown into a normal and happy individual, not haunted by the question, "What if my mother had lived?" As for Lily's father, Myra tried to paint Clancy as an artist who died before his time. Lily never asked about his past life or childhood, and for that Myra was glad. She would have had to lie to Lily because she would never tell the girl what she really thought of the scoundrel.

Sam wrote often and told her of his convalescence and his newly discovered family. He moved to Vienna as soon as his health allowed it. His nephew Benjamin, also a lawyer, could not leave Hungary, since the borders were closed to Hungarian citizens. However, Benjamin knew lawyers in Vienna and recommended Sam. In Vienna, Sam found the peace and beauty of life again, although the city had been thought to be wiped more completely clean of its Jewish population than any other city in Europe. He found the apartment building where his grandparents had lived when he was a child, but it was too run down for Sam to consider a proper place to live. He found an apartment near one of the many Vienna parks and leased it out every year he stayed there. The building had once been a mansion of a wealthy Jewish merchant, one whose fate had been sealed from the beginning of the war. The rooms were large and spacious; bas relief engravings enhanced their décor. There were ten apart-ments in all, some much larger than Sam's. His apartment had a large foyer with a floor of black and white marble tiles. The dining area was near the large windows facing the park, and the kitchen--smaller than most American kitchens--was behind a swinging door on the left. There was a study adjoining his large bedroom and bath, which delighted Sam. He could almost hear the ghosts at night if he let his imagination go full throttle. The Jewish hymns and the candlelight of Seder rushed back to his memory like a broken dam. It felt good to be back in Vienna, partly because Budapest was only a drive away, if he ever were allowed to go back. He had begged Myra and Michael to come over. He knew of several pensions where they could stay in a style he thought they would like. He had missed Myra and he wanted to see the children badly. Now, Myra had written they would be coming over in June.

Myra had the packing almost done. Matt and Lily would have to do their own packing, as they alone knew what they liked to wear. She sat down at her desk and started a list for the caretaker they had hired to watch their house, water and cut their lawn, and be sure newspapers and mail were not delivered by mistake.

The phone on the desk rang and Myra sighed. There was always an interruption when she would like to concentrate on an important list. It was that way when she wrote her newspaper columns every Friday; but this was Tuesday, so there was no excuse not to answer the telephone.

"Hello!" she barked and immediately felt a little foolish.

"Myra? This is Elizabeth"

"Oh Elizabeth, I am so sorry. I thought it was an-

"It is OK. I understand. I have bad news. Daddy died this morning. I knew you would want to know first before you told the children."

"Oh my God." Myra felt the shiver go through her body and she couldn't think of a thing to say.

"Are you there, Myra?"

"Oh Elizabeth, I am in shock. John always seemed the picture of health. Was he sick?" she asked.

"Not that we know about. We were with him for Easter and he seemed fine. Since we moved to San Francisco, we have been able to spend a lot of time with him. Tim always checked him out when he visited and there was nothing suspicious in Dad's checkups."

"What was the cause of his death?" Myra asked.

"Would you believe it? They think it was a massive heart attack, since there were no warning signs that he was in pain. His live-in housekeeper and her husband were asleep in their downstairs rooms when they heard a loud bump. They both rushed upstairs and Daddy was lying there on the floor. He was already dead but the coroner thought he had gotten out of bed before he died. The lamp on his nightstand was on and he had scribbled Eric's name on his note pad. Not once but twice. Isn't that weird?" Elizabeth started to cry. "Can you and the kids come out? You are the only real family I have left.

You know what I mean? I need you here." Her crying became uncontrollable.

Myra didn't have to think twice. "Of course, Elizabeth. We will be there as soon as we get every one gathered."

She hung up and put her head down on the desk. She could feel her tears slide down onto the cherry wood. "Why, God?" She mourned not only John's death but the grief of losing his support and all the happiness he'd been part of before Eric died. For time had not lessened the love she had for Eric, or the memory of finding and being included in their family. The dreams were still ongoing. At times, Eric appeared in them and she felt a peace inside her soul, knowing that she was and is someone to be loved. She wondered if Eric had come to his father to help him in passing on. She would not be surprised if that was the case. After all, she knew Sam had come to her when he was very sick. Lately she had been studying some Jewish myths and mystic beliefs. Maybe they were true. After all, they were still believed by some of the orthodox Jews. If the accounts of supernatural happenings were not true, why were the Jewish suicides or criminals always buried away from the rest in Jewish cemeteries, near the boundaries? Were the Jews afraid of haunting?

Her thoughts circled for a minute. John Dawson had written Eric's name twice. Did Eric appear to him?

She tried to call Michael, but he was in surgery. She wondered how to tell Matt and Lily. "I can't do it. I just can't."

"You can't do what, Myra?"

It was Michael standing in the doorway of the room.

She ran to him and embraced him tightly around his waist. He in turn wrapped her in his arms and kissed her forehead. "Oh Michael, I tried to call you but they said you were not available."

"It turned out be less of an operation than we expected. What is it? What has happened?"

Myra pushed Michael to the chair and had him sit. She then told him about John and her fear of telling the children. She sat on his lap and nestled her head on his shoulder and cried.

It was Michael who told Matt and Lily of their grandfather's death. There were the usual tears and memories that poured out them, but it was Matt who made the decision to stay in California for the summer after the funeral. The hired help would remain until John's estate was settled, so Matt would not be alone. He wanted nothing to do with the European trip. The funeral and the planned trip would coincide, so Myra knew her dream of seeing Sam again had to be put on hold for a while. She understood Matt's feelings. It would be a grieving process and then a healing time. How could she not be in the States if he needed her? For Lily, it was a different story. She too was glad to cancel the trip because now she could participate in all the summer sports her friends were partaking in. Morgan and Rebecca didn't know Grandpa John well; for them a trip to California was not that different from a trip to Europe.

When Myra called Sam to tell him the news, it was a sad conversation. He had not been that close to John but liked him as a person. Now, he faced his own immortality, thinking of all the old times in Denver and how the Dawsons had made him feel at home. He was of that generation, and now he was the only one left. It was disturbing for him to know that Myra and Michael would not be coming over this year, for after the news about John, how long did Myra think he would be around? Myra solemnly swore she would come over as soon as things settled down, with or without the rest of the family.

That is what exactly happened. The exception was Rebecca Rose who was only in a pre-school program three days a week. Myra would take her four-year-old daughter, and Michael would stay home with Morgan and Lily, a solution Michael was happy to accept. The whole family flew to California for John Dawson's funeral, and their presence comforted Elizabeth. Morgan, Lily, and Michael then flew back to Cincinnati while Myra and Rebecca began their flight to Europe after making sure Mathew was settled into John's home, and that Elizabeth and Tim would keep an eye on him.

Rebecca was the image of her mother, with long black curly hair and large brown eyes set in a perfectly shaped face. She was curious about everything and knew no strangers, a trait that worried Myra and Michael. Though they warned her to beware of some strangers, they also tried not to change hr personality. Rebecca was often the shining light in a crowded room of friends and children. She was always directing her pre-school mates about what they should do and not do. The teacher adored her and tried to teach her through child's play. Rebecca had already acquired some writing skills and her artwork took on the reality of her thoughts. The people she drew had arms, legs, and faces, with mountains in their backgrounds and clouds in the sky. It was remarkable for one so young.

The flight from California went non-stop to New York and a bigger plane then flew them directly to Vienna. Flying into the city, Myra noticed construction on the edge of the city. The war had left its scar on the city and what Myra was seeing was actually some of the reconstruction. The airport was crowded with travelers but Sam had written she should be met near the luggage pick-up area. True to his word, he was there leaning on a post next to the baggage platform where the bags were landing. He smiled and rushed to hug Myra tightly. He felt so thin that Myra wondered if he had been sick again.

Sam looked down at Rebecca and smiled at her. "My God, Myra, she looks just like you." Then he bent over and lifted the girl in his arms and kissed her cheek.

"Are you my Grandpa?" Rebecca asked.

"I am the next best man to that. Are you disappointed?" he said, smiling at her.

Rebecca put her arms around his neck and Myra saw tears fill his eyes.

As Sam controlled his tears, he put Rebecca down and helped Myra find their luggage. As they approached the front of the airport, Sam told Myra he had booked rooms for them at the Park Hotel Schonbrunn. It was across the street from the Schonbrunner Tiergarten, a large park leading to the palace built in 1696 for the Empress Maria Theresa. It had been a prime sight-seeing area of Vienna since 1752.

They hired a taxi instead of taking an underground train because Sam wanted Myra to see this once-beautiful city. Myra was in awe of the many lovely parks and broad boulevards. They had arrived mid morning, and the lunch crowd was enjoying the sunshine in sidewalk cafes and eating picnic lunches on the soft and well-kept lawns. The taxi driver crossed bridges and back again and it confused Myra. Sam explained that he had asked the driver to take a scenic drive so the Americans could see some of the city.

At last, the hotel was in sight. It was a block long with five or six floors and painted a bright yellow. Balconies hung out on the second floor apartments and a small roof covered the large entrance to the hotel. Sam had explained to Myra that his one- bedroom living quarters were much too small for them, so he had picked a hotel near the zoo and park. He thought Rebecca would enjoy the area until they left for Hungary.

The elevator was small and narrow so their luggage came up later with a bell captain Sam tipped generously. The room had one large bed and a dresser with chairs near the windows. The bathroom was off to the right of the door and had ample room for extra clothes and necessities. Washcloths were not available, and the soap was a thin slippery disc that disappeared with one use. The view was lovely.

That night, Myra dreamed again. This time it was a warm and fuzzy feeling, like she had come home. People she had never dreamed about before were welcoming her back and dancing in the streets of a small village. Then the lullaby began and Myra hummed along with it.

"Teule baba, teute itt van mar az." Then in English she sang, "Sleep little baby sleep. The night is here."

Chapter Twenty-five

Sam arrived early the next day to meet Myra and Rebecca for a tour of Vienna. They met in the lobby and had a buffet breakfast in the bright dining room at one end of the hotel. Rebecca thought it was wonderful that she could pick and chose her fruit and cereal. The food didn't look like the breakfasts she had at home, but she was eager and hungry enough to eat everything her mother pointed out to her. Over coffee, Myra brought Sam up to date about her family, and Sam sketched his family more fully for her. While Sam paid the breakfast bill, Myra and Rebecca waited outside by the entrance. The sun was bright and a slight breeze rustled through the trees across the street. How familiar that felt to Myra. She wondered if she had been here before since she had a lovely feeling of being where she belonged.

They walked though wide paths of the park, visited the zoo, and stopped a vendor for a sweet snack. The museums fascinated Rebecca but the most interesting to Myra was the Belvedere castle. Sam had told her most of the paintings were confiscated from the loot the Germans had stolen from Jewish homes during the war. The artist Gustav Klimt, an Austrian icon, had painted a lovely lady, an oil and gold-encrusted portrait titled "Adele Bloch-Bauer 1" in 1907. Myra wondered if the painter might have painted the portrait Eric had seen in the cave, the lady with the Silver Star of David on her dress. Eric had thought it was a painting of Myra. There were other paintings by Klimt. "The Apple Tree," " Beech Forest," and "Houses in Unterach on Attersee Lake" all amazed her. But the portrait of "Adele" stayed in Myra's imagination.

Three days later, Sam, Myra and Rebecca were on their way to Budapest, Hungary, on the train. They had left in the morning right after Myra had called Michael to report on the sights they had seen. Vienna was full of music, she told Michael. They had gone to the opera one night and Rebecca sat enthralled by all the glitter and colors along with the music. Myra told Michael that Mozart's spirit seemed alive at every café and public music hall. How wonderful to be remembered so long--although she was hearing crazy stories about Mozart's life.

They passed through the checkpoint at the Austrian/ Hungarian border where stern young men in green Russian uniforms eyed them suspiciously as they check their passports and luggage. One young soldier did almost smile when Rebecca said hello to him.

The train bounced along through a landscape of farmhouses and barns with plow horses munching in the distance. It was a fertile agricultural lowland but not as flat as the Great Plain south of Budapest. Rebecca was becoming a wonderful traveling companion. She questioned everything she saw and lapped up what Sam could tell her. Myra studied Sam as he pointed out certain objects to Rebecca. He was thin and his once round features seemed to have shrunk. When she hugged him on their first day together, Myra could almost feel his ribs. He seemed pale and weaker than she had remembered him. Soon the Cathedrals of Budapest appeared on the horizon. The Danube River flowed between the cities like a snake. The song was wrong, Myra thought; the Danube wasn't blue but brown and dirty. A lot of Europe still needed to be cleaned and rebuilt even though the war had been over for almost fifteen years.

The train station was bleak and full of smoke. People were crowded everywhere catching a train or arriving from one. Sam pointed to a bench and told Myra to wait there while he collected their luggage.

A small child stopped in front of Rebecca and stared at her American clothes. Rebecca said hello to the little boy, but the child said nothing. It was not as long as Myra felt it was, but suddenly an old woman appeared to scold the child.

"I have told you to wait for me over there, child. Why do you not obey your poor grandma?" The old woman shook her finger at the child.

"I don't want to go, Grandma. I want my Mama. Why are we leaving?" The language was Hungarian but Myra understood them clearly.

"Then the grandma said something that stunned Myra. "You will be fine my darling. I promise I will send for you as soon as it is possible. Just always remember me, my love, for I shall never forget you."

Suddenly Myra was seeing another old woman, and she became the child pleading with the woman not leave her. "No, don't leave me. We will never find each other again. Please Grandma, please!"

Rebecca was shaking her and Myra looked around at her surroundings. There was no little girl or an old woman.

"Mama. What is wrong? You are talking in words I don't understand."

Sam appeared before them and looked puzzled. "What is wrong?" he asked

"It is Mama. She was speaking in words I don't know. She didn't see me when I talked to her. Is she sick, grandpa?"

Myra shook her head and looked up at Sam. "I don't know what happened. A little girl stopped in front of us and would not answer Rebecca when she said hello." She took a deep breath and continued. "Oh Sam. I think I was dreaming again, only this time while awake."

"No Mama. A little girl did stop here and she said hello and went that way with her mother." Rebecca pointed to the metal gates leading to departing trains.

"I think I was talking in Hungarian, and I don't remember if I have ever known that language," Myra explained to Sam. "I was so frightened, as though I was being abandoned again."

Sam gave her his arm and helped her to stand. He looked down at Rebecca and said, "Don't be frightened, little one. It may be that your mother spoke in Hungarian, the language of the people who live here. I know she has studied the language; how wonderful she remembered it."

Then, a tall handsome young man raised his arm and called to Sam.

"Oh here is my nephew Edmond," Sam said as he waved back.

"I thought maybe I had the wrong time for your train." Edmond looked at Myra and offered his hand. She shook it and introduced Rebecca. Edmond bent over to the child's level and presented her with colorful box.

"I know little girls like souvenirs of the places they visited so I took it upon myself to buy you a little gift." He handed the gift to Rebecca who politely thanked him and smiled as wide as she could.

Sam made the introductions and they were off to the front of the depot. Edmond glanced frequently at Myra and smiled when Sam looked his way.

Myra

"This woman is very beautiful, Uncle," he whispered to Sam as they loaded the trunk of the car. "I can see why you want to help her."

Myra was still shaking from what she thought was a flashback. She didn't notice the scenery passing. Some of the war-damaged bridges across the Danube had been repaired, and the traffic flowed across them in smooth symmetric lines, indicating that life does go on in spite of the atrocities that had changed the world.

Edmond had pointed out sights as he slowly moved in and out of traffic. He pulled into the circle driveway of the Hotel Gellert. It was an impressive hotel with a staff of well-dressed but unsmiling people. The clerks seem to have been trained to simply do their job, filling out the forms that told the government who was in the country Sam took care of the registration while Myra watched the young bellboys carry their luggage from Edmond's car. At last they were told to follow the luggage cart up to their rooms. It was a larger elevator than in most of the places Myra and Rebecca had stayed. Their rooms on the fifth floor were clean and well decorated, with white linens and curtains. The windows looked out on the traffic circle and on some of the bridges across the Danube River to Pest, the hotel being located on the Buda side of the river. This hotel was famous for its baths and for the pools in its sub-basement. There was also an outdoor pool behind the hotel. Sam had suggested they take in the pool so Rebecca could enjoy splashing around and Myra and Sam could unwind. They rented suits and met up at the entrance to a long tunnel leading to the pool. There were windows like portholes where the walkers could see swimmers from under the water. They fascinated Rebecca and Myra had to pull her along every time she stopped to watch. Sam was already in the pool, as Edmond had returned to the hospital where he practiced.

The water was warm and soft on their bodies. Rebecca had met up with another child around her age and was frolicking and kicking as she had been taught in her Cincinnati swimming class.

Sam delighted in their company. "You know Myra, if some one had told me I would be back here at a place that I knew as a child with you when we first met all those years ago, I would have called them a liar. But here we are."

"Sam, how old is this hotel?"

"I don't know much about its history but I remember my parents and grandparents saying they enjoyed being here as children. Why do you ask?"

Myra looked around the large pool area and shook her head. "It was the walk down the hall to the pool. It was the portholes on the sides where one can see the legs of the swimmers. Rebecca was surprised and happy to watch them." Myra treaded water and went on. "It seemed to open a door for me. It was like I had been here once, but yet it wasn't that familiar either. Do you think I might have been here before my memory was lost?"

"I don't know, Myra. I do think you are connected some way here in Hungary, but not in Budapest."

"Then where, Sam? Did you find more information on the painting?"

"I am not sure, but I think it came out of Szeged or Gulya. That is why we are going there in a few days. Maybe something will awaken your memories like the hallway to the pool might have. That is why I am so happy you are here; I think the key to unlock your memory may be there."

Rebecca was calling to her mother to watch her jump into the pool, so the conversation with Sam was over. It left Myra wondering. Did she spring from this old land? Was her beginning mixed with the Jewish laws of their times? Why was she abandoned if that were true? She felt a thrill trickle through her body. Maybe she was going to discover who she really was.

The next day Edmond picked up the three Americans and drove them to his brother's home. It faced the street but Edmond opened a large double door shaped in the wall. They drove through the narrow space into a lovely backyard with flowers and fruit trees surrounding a small pond.

"This is typical of what our house was like in Szeged," Sam said. "Benjamin planted it for his father Joshua, my younger brother."

A door at the back of the building opened and out ran a small boy screaming, "Uncle Eddie, Uncle Eddie. We have been waiting for you."

Edmond shut off the motor of the car and emerged to pick up his nephew. "This is Jocko, my nephew and Benjamin's oldest son."

He put the child down and said, "Jocko, this is Rebecca, a little American girl for you to play with."

Rebecca leaned against Myra and shyly looked the boy over. Jocko held out his hand, which Rebecca refused to take. Myra smiled at the boy and asked him how old he was. He held up three fingers and turned away when his father came out the door.

Benjamin had to be the picture of a young Sam; the resemblance was uncanny. He held out his hand to Myra and said, "We are so happy to meet you, Myra. Uncle has told us so much about you"

He stepped back and motioned for the group to enter the house. "Goldie, my wife, has made us wonderful Hungarian dinner. Come, my Goldie, our guests are here."

Goldie lived up to her name. She had golden hair and blue eyes along with a very slim body tied with a colorful apron, Hungarian flowers embroidered into the cloth. In her arms she held a smiling baby.

"Welcome," she said in Hungarian, and Myra answered in the same language. Rebecca shook her mother's hand and said, "Mommy, you are talking strange again, like you did with that boy."

That statement sent Myra shivering, and looking at Sam she shook her head. "Did I?"

Sam shook his head yes, but explained to his sister-in-law that Myra had studied the language knowing that oneday she would be in Hungary.

Myra knew that was not true. She had picked up a few of the words, but other than that, she had never studied a foreign language. Now she was frightened. How did she come to understand these people and talk to them in their language? This was unreal to her. One does not just pick up a language in another country so quickly unless, and this sent her shivering again, she was taught it as a child and it lay dormant in her. Suddenly a memory entered her mind. It was Greta waving her pointed finger at her saying she must always speak English. How had she forgotten that?

"Are you OK?" It was Sam holding her arm and looking worried.

Myra smiled at him and assured everyone she was fine. Her Hungarian greeting had surprised her, though. She had no idea how she remembered that greeting.

Edmond explained to his brother and his wife what

Myra had said, and they laughed and motioned everyone into the dining room where a lovely table awaited them. The dishes were porcelain with bright and colorful flowers similar to those on Goldie's apron. The kitchen just beyond the dining room sent delicious aromas floating into the whole house.

From a side door an older man entered. He eyes lit up at the sight of Myra and Rebecca and he held out his hand to them. Myra was stunned to see the resemblance once more to Sam. Yes, Sam was truly with his family. However, Sam had said his brother Joshua was much younger than he was, but this gentleman looked older. Then Myra remembered the concentration camps and realized that living through it all would have aged people.

Joshua kissed Myra on both cheeks and was saying in Hungarian how happy he was to meet her. Myra did not dare answer in his language but nodded her head as though she understood his meaning. The evening went on enjoyably. She felt she was where she belonged. Maybe Sam was right and she did come from this part of the world; but how did she get to the United States and Salida and from there to Denver? The Grangers should have told her how they came to be her guardians. Yes, they were good to her and they thought they were protecting her, but when Carl died and Gerta relinquished her to be adopted, why didn't she tell her or leave an explanation for her to read when she was older? They knew her memory of her past life had been erased by something horrible. They could have told. Now the love she had thought she had for her early protectors disappeared like a wisp of smoke.

The next few days were sightseeing trips to museums and palaces opened to the public for the first time in Hungarian history. The Danube flowed through the city like a silent testimony to the horrors of its past, not only of the Second World War, but of many wars and conquests. Now the city of Budapest was a mixture of races and languages. The Jewish Synagogue on the Pest side of the river had once been one of the largest synagogues in Europe, and now it still stood tall and grand, but the building showed its scars. Yet, it was a special place to Sam's family, a holy place where the Jews who had returned could once again worship without fear. "Next year, Jerusalem!" was a phrase most of the Jews Myra met said at parting.

"It is only a wish or dream meant give courage to their Jewish brothers," Sam had told Myra. "It doesn't mean they're emmigrating, although many would leave if they could."

Sam had told Myra about Matyas Vargas and she was anxious to meet him. It was a lovely sunny morning when they departed from Budapest for Szeged. Edmond had a meeting in Szeged and offered to drive them down south in his car. Edmond had guessed that Myra could understand Hungarian and often talked with her when Rebecca was not around. They were becoming very good friends, which made Myra feel more comfortable in this strange country where perhaps she had been born.

The landscape after they left Budapest became as flat as a table. The great Hungarian plains were as flat as Sam had told her they'd be. One could toss a ball forward and it could roll to the other side of the border. Myra giggled at the thought. Sam smiled at her, thinking she was delighted to be in Hungary. Off in the distance one could see small farmhouses surrounded by acres of flat land being cultivated. Soon there were trees. Funny trees, Myra thought. They stood in neat rows for what seemed like miles. Not one tree out of place, more like soldiers standing at attention. The sentence went over and over in Myra's mind. The trees in a row were in a dream once. The car slowed as they approached the outskirts of Szeged. As they crossed over a dirt road next to a forest, a man stood in the road with his arms opened to her and a woman in torn clothes with blood red stains running down her dress stood by a tree as they passed and blew a kiss to Myra.

Myra grabbed Sam's hand. "Sam, did you see that. Look! Look!"

Sam looked in that direction but only saw the forest as they passed by.

"I saw nothing Myra. What did you see?"

"A man standing in the road holding his arms out to me. He had a black fedora and a full beard. A woman appeared out of the trees and blew me a kiss. She was all bloody and had torn clothes."

"Wasn't that part of a dream you had a few times? You told me about it years ago," Sam said. He checked on Rebecca who was napping, curled up in Myra's arms.

"Oh Sam, he was holding his arms out to me and beckoned with his hands. What am I getting into?"

"I think in this day and age, the old system of Jewish Chabad-Lubavitch is starting a come back in the belief that if they follow the Torah and Jewish tradition the real Messiah would appear sooner. The Jews have been waiting for him for centuries, you know. This sect of Jewish religion started in Russia in the village of Lubavitch in the late 1700s. In this century a very religious Rebbe by the name of Menachem Mendel Schneerson came to America in 1941 and began teachings small gatherings in Brooklyn. My new friends here have told me they hear from the rumors passed around that the Rebbe Schneerson has gathered much attention and many Jews are beginning to follow his view."

"What does that mean to me Sam?" Myra asked with tears glistening in her eyes.

"It means, my dear, that he teaches the souls of the dead never completely depart. Maybe you were a part of those phenomenal beliefs. Maybe you have an old soul searching for your place in this world, and your birth became a sin that had to be cleansed."

"I am not a believer in that tradition, Uncle," Edmond broke in. "I think one must live in the world of today and adjust to life as it is."

"Your have frightened me, Sam. I cannot accept your theory. You now believe that I had a Jewish mother? I know I have locked secrets in my memories, but I never felt that I was Jewish until I married Michael, and only because I became one in marriage."

"I don't mean to frighten you, Myra, but think about it. You have visions at times and, once in a while, something unusual happens, brought on by what you think you see. This is not a new religion, my dear. Jews believe if they live by the true sacraments of their faith, God will reward them by sending the Messiah to save them from the evil they have endured."

"Listen to you, Myra," Edmond said. "You have been talking to Sam and me in Hungarian. Uncle must have guessed right about your birth, and he only wants now to find out why you were abandoned."

Myra looked down at her sleeping daughter. "So do I Edmond. So do I."

Chapter Twenty-six

The Tisza River divided Szeged. The Danube River at Budapest flowed southwest and Edmond was traveling slightly to the southeast, towards Yugoslavia; Szeged was located near the southern border. Edmond drove over the highway bridge that spanned the Tiza and into the downtown area of the city. How different it was from the hustle and bustle of Vienna, and even Budapest was a little livelier. Here people seemed sadder. Life and chores seemed necessary and happiness was not apparent even in the crowds. Edmond explained they were lining up to buy sugar, butter, or meat. Getting rations was a chore, he explained, and not a pleasant one. Some days it took hours to get to the head of the line, and many times, after getting there, people found that the food they wanted and needed was sold out.

Poor people, Myra thought, as they drove by the lines of humble men and women, hardly looking up to see cars pass by. They were in a town square with a few stores open and meagre goods on display. As they crossed the square, Rebecca pointed out a store window with beautiful painted dolls in Hungarian dresses "Oh. Mommy, look at those dolls. Can I have one?"

It was Sam who answered her. "Of course, my dear Rebecca, but first we must check into our penzion."

"What is a penzion, Grandpa?" the child asked.

"It is where we will stay while we are here. Some of the people have been permitted to rent out rooms in their homes. It helps them to buy food, which helps the government to get money too."

"Uncle," Edmond stopped Sam. "It is best not to talk about the government to a child. She would have no idea what you are saying and she could repeat what was said. It is sad, but there are ears every where."

"I do not see ears. Do you Mommy?"

"See what I mean, Uncle?" Edmond nodded to Sam.

"It was only a way of talking," Myra told her daughter. "It is like a secret we use to keep from Lily and Mathew at birthday parties."

"Oh, I understand. We must not tell anyone we have a secret--right Mommy?"

The car stopped in front of a long brick building with the familiar arched opening into the courtyard. A fat little man emerged from a door a few steps up from the courtyard and greeted Edmond with a handshake.

"Welcome, my doctor. How good to see you again," he said as he started to help with Myra's luggage. "What have we here?" he said as he saw Rebecca step down from the car.

"This is a relative of my Uncle Samuel, here. This is his daughter Myra and her daughter Rebecca Lieberman, from America."

The little man stared at Rebecca in a way that gave chills to Myra. He seemed frozen until a woman emerged from the doorway and stepped down next to him.

"Joseph, why do you stand there? Pick up the luggage and bring our guests inside." She nudged the man with her elbow. She held out her hand to Myra and said in English, "I am sorry madam. We do not have Americans as guests very often, or not all, I mean. Joseph means well. He is not used to seeing people from so far away."

Myra smiled at her and held out her hand, "You speak English very well."

The lady took Myra's hand and smiled widely. "I was an English teacher at one time. But now my brother and I have this house, which helps us have a nice life." She looked at Rebecca, who was staring at her.

"Well, well, we also have a child. How wonderful. What is your name, little girl?"

"Rebecca!" Myra scolded her, "You do not answer a question with a question. Tell the lady what she asked you."

"My name is Rebecca Lieberman. Now what is yours?"

"I am Anna Vesolovsky and I love little girls. Welcome my child." Then she reached for Rebecca's hand and led her up the steps into the house. Joseph stopped staring at the newcomers and picked up the luggage with Edmond and Sam helping with smaller pieces. They entered a hallway with three opened doors and followed Anna down it past a small kitchen on one side and a dining room on the other. The last door was closed but Anna opened it to reveal a larger room with comfortable chairs and a long sofa and several lamps. Large windows looked out to a garden in full bloom. A glass door opened onto a brick veranda with steps leading down to the garden. Myra was surprised to see such beauty in a city that had seemed to lack color and beauty. On the far side of the room, a staircase led to the upper floor and Anna headed that way.

Upstairs were four bedrooms smelling like fresh flowers and as colorful as any that Myra had seen since arriving in Europe. "Would you like a room together for yourself and your daughter?" Anna asked Myra.

"Yes, if it is possible. We sleep very well together, don't we darling?"

"Then in that case, you shall have the larger room two doors down, with its own bath," Anna said as she led them down the hall to another bright room looking down at the garden.

"It is beautiful. Thank you so much," Myra said as she laid her purse on the large bed. "Was this your original home?"

"Yes, our father had a nice factory before the war. We are grateful the government has let us keep the house," Anna said.

She turned to Sam and said, "Your room will be the first room, if you don't mind. There is water closet at the end of the hall. Will that do, sir?"

"It will be just fine and thank you so much," Sam said as he gave Myra a glance meaning--Myra thought—that she should stop the personal talk. He had warned her about being too personal as, again, the ears were everywhere.

Later in the cool evening, Rebecca was busy trying to put together a puzzle, with Anna explaining the Hungarian word for each piece. Edmond had left for the evening. Myra and Sam were walking in the garden when Myra asked Sam how these people could have the luxury of such a beautiful garden when most of the city of Szeged looked so gloomy.

"They are from the family of Vesolovsky. Their ancestor was a famous opera singer, Janos Vesolovsky. He was born near here, and through him this area became prosperous with tourists and music lovers. Since his time, his descendents have always had a lot of respect. The Communist Party here is well aware of their place in society, even if it was back in the 1830's. They are afraid *not* to respect this family which had tried to bring peace between the peoples of Szeged, even if at one time the family was Jewish."

Myra was amazed. "How did that happen?

"Janos' s son was a cantor for the synagogues here and in Gyula but times were very hard for the Jews. Janos Vesolovsky was still remembered and popular, but the family most likely feared that their status would be reduced and their property confiscated because they were Jewish. Evidently, the family voted to become Christians"

"What was the name of his son?" Myra asked.

"In Hungary, the last names come first, so his would be Vesolovsky Guzstov; he married a Tereza Array. In researching the history of Hungarian Jews, I had to delve deeper into this opera singer, Vesolovsky. A cantor in the family tree struck a bell for me. Later, Edmond was able to find old documents hidden by distant family members during the persecution of the Jews. An old man he treated during the war told him about them. They represent a Jewish heritage he wanted the world to know

"He gave them to Edmond?" Myra asked.

"Not exactly. Edmond recalled the papers only after the man died, but he did remember the man telling where they were. He was afraid the Communists might wonder why he, a Jew, was in the Cathedral across from Cathedral Square. You see, the old man buried the papers in the Cathedral because that was the safest place." Sam motioned for Myra to join him on the stone bench along the path.

"You would never guess where he had hidden them."

Myra laughed as she remembered the sacred icons of the Catholic Church. "Was it on the statue of Jesus?"

Sam opened his eyes wide in astonishment, "How did you know?"

Myra shook her head in surprise as she had only been kidding when she said it. "I think it was just a lucky guess." But she was remembering a time when Jesus seemed to scorn her with his blazing red eyes.

"Yes, that is where the old guy thought them safest. He found an opening in the clothing where Jesus' drape overlapped his gown. Someone had made it deeper, apparently using a shard of pottery which he left on the windowsill next to the statue. He pushed the papers down as far as they could go, and put the pottery into the opening. Edmond somehow was able to find the papers and take

303

them to the synagogue. He has not seen them since he rescued them. When I was telling him about the family, he remembered them and was able to get me copies."

"Why were you suspicious about Vesolovsky?"

"If Eric had seen the portrait we now know exists, it would have to have been hidden by a wealthy family. I went back in time and looked up Jews with wealth, and the opera singer's name did sound Jewish. It was just a hunch that proved correct."

"Why would the Jews have to hide their history or identity back in those days?"

"It was a time of unrest. The Russians were burning Jewish villages and eliminating the Jewish population. With a famous celebrity as a grandfather or related to him, the family of Vesolovsky thought it would be better to become Christians. Many Jews at that time also converted, at least in public, for survival. Now, this generation of Vesolovsky' s is Christian.

It was getting dark and Myra checked her watch. "It is late. I had better fetch Rebecca. She has to be exhausted. I know I am."

"One more thing, Myra," Sam warned her, "I don't know what Anna or her brother think of their situation. They could be spies for the government since they have been able to keep their home and provide a personal income. They might be allowed to do so because they're spying, and the house could be wired. So please be careful what you say or ask. Especially with Rebecca."

"I understand Sam. I will be careful. Tomorrow you will give us a tour?"

Sam shook his head yes, and they entered the house.

Chapter Twenty-seven

That first night in Szeged, Myra dreamed she was walking down an unpaved street. *Horses were pulling large carts of hay and wheat the farmers were bringing to town to sell or barter. She questioned how she knew that, but her thoughts were interrupted by a voice yelling at her from one of the laden carts.*

"Miriam, how are you? Where have you been?"

Myra stared at the man in disbelief. She didn't know him so she kept on walking. "Why is he calling me Miriam?" she wondered. But the farmer caught up with her and walked his horse besides her.

"What? Are you too grand a lady now to know old friends? It is I, Hiram Szabo."

Myra looked up at him. His pointed beard had particles of dust mixed in it and his clothes hung on him, too large for his small frame.

"Sir," Myra said in an angry voice, "I don't know you and my name is not Miriam. You have mistaken me for someone else."

Myra

"God in Heaven, you who everyone thought so nice and poor and pure and religious, walking along like a princess. I never thought you of all the people in the village would turn her nose up at an old friend." *He kicked the horse to gain speed and passed her by, but he did turn around and yell at her, "May the curse of the Furst family always be with you and your children."*

Myra jerked awake and sat up in bed. The moon was high in the night sky and illuminated the room. Rebecca slept soundly next to Myra curled in fetal position, hugging the new teddy bear Sam had bought her in Vienna. Myra pulled the cover up around Rebecca and silently slid out of bed. She walked to the large windows and looked down at the garden. When she saw a figure dash out of the bushes, Myra moved back behind the sheer curtains to watch unnoticed.

A flicker of light below her window was a door opening and closing—and then Joseph was revealed walking toward the figure. They shook hands and spoke so quietly that Myra could not hear them. As they moved to the stone table and sat down, Myra could make out the man's face. He had gray hair and pleasant features, from what she could see. He wore a dark suit and Joseph was talking with his hands trying to express something. As Joseph got more emotional his words carried up to Myra.

"No, Janos. She has not seen it. I told you she would not. It is the little girl. She is the exact duplicate of her ancestors. She is beautiful--the mother--but I don't think she knows a thing. If the government found out, they would take action."

The man Janos spoke to mumbled and Myra could not understand what he said, but she knew they were talking about her and Rebecca. Then Joseph's voice got a little louder, "Janos, I can't be asking questions. They hear everything. I can't even warn the Americans if what you think might be true. I think that lawyer knows more than he lets on." Then there was mumbling again.

Myra stepped back from the windows and crawled into bed by her daughter. She put her arms around the child and knew she had to protect her if these people were talking about her. If Joseph thought Rebecca was a duplicate of her ancestors, then he would know of her own past. Was it possible she was born here? Why did she understand Hungarian but not Hebrew words? Was she at last to know who she really was?

The next morning at breakfast, Myra watched Joseph closely. Every few minutes he looked at Myra and finally he said in Hungarian to Anna, "She is watching me. Maybe she does not like her meal?"

"The food is fine, Joseph. I was just studying you. You have certain features in your face that interest me," Myra said in Hungarian.

"You speak Hungarian? I am sorry, my lady. I did not know you understood me." Joseph wiped his forehead with the hand towel he held.

It was Anna who broke the silence. "Are you Hungarian, my lady?"

"No, I really don't know. I was adopted as a baby. I took a language class in college and that is where I learned your language."

Sam had not yet joined the breakfast group, but Myra was afraid she had given fuel to whoever might be listening.

"Mr. Hirsch adopted you?" Anna spoke in Hungarian so Rebecca would not understand or repeat what she said.

"Yes, and what a wonderful father he has been," Myra said as she heard Sam's footsteps on the stairs leading to the basement kitchen. "I wish you would not say anything to him as he is very sensitive about our relationship."

Both Joseph and Anna nodded and continued with their duties.

Later Edmond picked them up in his car and drove to the Klauzal Square they had passed when they entered the city. He found a parking area near the square.

"This is where our little princess saw those beautiful dolls, in the corner window of that store." Edmond pointed out a storefront. The four of them crossed the street and entered. Rebecca raced to the front window.

"Here she is, Mommy. The doll I saw yesterday. Isn't she beautiful?"

"Yes, darling, but she might cost more than we should spend," Myra answered.

Sam coughed to get Myra's attention. "Now Mommy. I have been an absent grandfather. Let me make it up to my granddaughter. The cost would make up for the seasons I was not around. We should also find gifts for Mathew, Lily, and Morgan. Will you help me find gifts for them, Rebecca"?

It was agreed, and while Sam and Rebecca shopped, Edmond excused himself, saying he would be back shortly. Myra looked around the shop but there was nothing of interest to her so she also went outside to look at the shops down the street. She could understand how depressed the country was when she eyed the cheap clothes on exhibit in the windows. How dreary, she thought. But there was a china shop farther down the street with an amazing display of beautiful dish sets and glassware. Myra entered the shop and the salesgirl quickly approached her.

"May I help you madam?" she asked. She was a plain looking girl with a long braid wrapped around her head.

"Well, yes. Where do these lovely dishes come from?" Myra asked, speaking in Hungarian.

The girl picked up a dish and showed Myra the signature. It was a piece of Hollohaza from their factory north of Budapest. "Have you never seen their product before?"

Myra shook her head no, but then asked how much a dinner set for twelve would be. The girl's blue eyes widened.

"Twelve settings, Madam? I would not know. I would have to ask the owner. Would you wait please? There is a chair by the window."

Myra nodded and took the seat as the girl hurried up the staircase in the back of the store. Myra looked outside to watch the people in the square. It was an interesting sight. Then her eyes caught sight of an older man with curly gray hair entering a bookstore across the square. It was the man she had seen last night in the garden with Joseph. She jumped up and ran across to enter the bookstore with the smell of musty old books and cigars.

Her entrance had everyone look up from his or her books or conversations. It was as silent as a mortuary for a minute, then every one went back to doing whatever they were doing. The gray haired man was looking at her too, and she walked up to him.

"Pardon me sir, but could you help me?" Myra asked him.

"No English," he replied.

"Then how is Hungarian for you? I need to find an old book and this looks like the place to search." She stared at him as he stared at her. Their eyes locked in a silent conversation as though they both knew they were playing a game. Yet, Myra felt a sense of connection to this man.

"What kind of book, Madam?" he asked as he studied her face.

"One on art. Old art books that express the lifestyle and past happenings and places here in this country."

"Oh Madam, I am afraid you would not find such books here at all. We live in the present now and our lifestyle is completely different. We do not like to remember how things were before our present government took over. We are very happy now."

"I see," Myra said, looking straight into his eyes. The she leaned over so no one could hear her and whispered in his ear, "You do not fool me old man. You speak perfect English and you know something about me, and I want to know."

He backed away from her and his face turned as red as a beet. In Hungarian he said, "I do not understand your English, Madam. I am sorry but I cannot help you. I must go."

Myra

As he turned towards the door he ran smack into Edmond and behind him was the salesgirl from the china shop. The three of them collided in the doorway but the man pushed past them and hurried down the street.

"Edmond." She said in English, "He knows something, I know he does."

Edmond covered her mouth with a kiss. "My darling." In Hungarian this time, "I have been looking for you. Your child has made her selection and wishes to show you. Come, my darling."

But the salesgirl charged in front of Edmond. "My lady, if you are still interested I have a very good price."

Edmond told the salesgirl they would not be interested at this time. Maybe later. And with that he took Myra's arm and they left the shop.

"Do you know what you just did?" Before Myra could answer he told her. "He is a very important man with the government. He could report you to the secret agents. We would all be in trouble."

"But Edmond, I saw him last night in the garden talking to Joseph. They were talking about Rebecca and me. Why would they mention us if he didn't know something about me?"

"I don't know, Myra. We will have to talk to Sam about it. I hope you haven't caused all of us to be under suspicion as enemies of the regime."

Sam and Rebecca were walking down the street loaded with gifts. Rebecca ran to her mother as excited as a little girl could be.

"Mommy, look what Grandpa bought me. Isn't she beautiful?"

The child held up a beautifully dressed Hungarian doll with a red dress decorated in little beads of all colors. Her headset was like a crown also studded with tiny beads. Under her dress peeked snow-white petticoats, two that Myra could see. Her body was of sturdy white cotton and her legs had on boots the color of the dress.

"She is lovely, Rebecca. You will have to take good care of her."

Edmond shook his head and said to Sam, "You know they will not let goods leave the country, Sam. How are you going to get all the gifts to Vienna?"

Sam looked at the bulging knapsack the store had found for him and shook his head. "I have no idea. Do you?"

Edmond opened the car doors and unlocked the trunk of the car to place the gifts in. "I don't know, Sam. I would have to think about it. I am not involved in the black market and if ever they caught me trying to send things as innocent as these gifts, I could be jailed. But we will worry about that later. Right now we have to tell you something."

On the drive back to the penzion, Edmond and Myra told of what had happen. Sam was speechless for a time. Then he said to Myra in Hungarian, "See, we must be careful, my dear. I had my suspicions about Joseph and Anna, so maybe we should leave tonight."

"No." Edmond told him. "That would really make them think the worst. We should stay a few days and then leave. Remember, Uncle, I have a small practice here and I don't need any problems from officials of the state."

Sam agreed, and after delivering the gifts to their quarters, Edmond decided to show Myra the sights of Szeged. They drove down an avenue called Szentharomsag after leaving the Lajo area where their penzion was located. It was lined with homes all having arched entrances just wide enough for a small car to drive through. Of course they had been built a few hundred years before and the entrances by the wooden arch doors were for horses and carriages and protection. No one could get into the houses unless they came through the arches. Edmond slowed down and then stopped directly in front of an arch whose door was open.

"This, Myra, is where your Sam and my father were born and raised. Not many Jews lived in this area because there was a Catholic Church of Matyas with a Cath-

Myra looked down the narrow short alley to the back yard of Sam's old home. "Look; there is a cherry tree right in the middle of the yard."

"Yes, and an ugly apartment building the Communists built on our land after confiscating it during the war. There was once a pond and fruit trees all over. My mother used to make fruit wine every year for Purim and Seder. The flowerbeds have been dug up for some unknown reason."

Edmond drove slowly past as Sam was beginning to tear up.

"Edmond," said Myra, "could you stop at the church? I need to see it. I was raised a Catholic, you know, and some of their teachings are still fresh in my mind. Matthew and Lily had both Catholic and Jewish training, but Rebecca has never been in a Catholic Church. I want her to see the statues and icons."

Edmond agreed, but as he drove into the circle drive in front of the large white church with its cross perched high atop its arched roof, Rebecca was fast asleep.

"Oh well, I shall go in alone. Do you mind? I will only be a minute," Myra said.

The church was trimmed in gold with colorful paintings on the walls. A water line almost to the ceiling was evidence of a past flood. Myra knelt in one of the pews and looked up at the images of saints and of Jesus.

Was Jesus now smiling at her? Was he welcoming her because he knew she belonged here? No. It wasn't that, because she did not belong here in this church; she belonged in the synagogue Edmond drove by on the way to the square.

"I am Jewish just like you, Jesus, so bless me and help me find my way." She got up and walked out to the car, omitting the sign of the cross on her breast, the sign which she had made for years.

"Now where, Uncle?" Edmond asked.

"Why not run us through what used to be the Jewish sector? Myra's memory might be jolted to remember places and things, if she see that area."

"Is it not the Jewish sector any more?" Myra asked.

"A few Jews have trickled back but most of their houses remain empty and haunting to those who may have had guilty feelings. Every one was scared. No one was brave enough to help or hide the people they had grown up with, the people they had done business with. Instead those very people pillaged some of the homes. Art pieces, china dishes, porcelain figurines and vases ... "

"Art work?" Myra asked Edmond.

"Well yes, most of it. True friends of the Jews saved some very valued pieces; but that was not so dangerous or noble as hiding the people would have been.

Here we are." Edmond turned a corner. Ahead was a bedlam of junk sitting on the sidewalks. There were houses with broken windows and lace curtains floating in and out as if waiting for someone to come back. Edmond drove slowly past the ghosts of the past until they turned another corner and a few blocks ahead saw an old mansion.

"It looks like someone lives here," Myra said as they passed a few houses in better shape than the bedlam had been Clothes were on wash lines visible between the houses.

"Yes, the ones that returned do live here—as do those who sought a new place to live." Edmond turned another corner and stopped the car. "Do you want to walk some, Myra, and see if there is anything you might have known as a child?"

By then Rebecca was awake. "Yes," said Myra. "How about it, Sam? Shall we take Rebecca for a little walk after her nap?"

Edmond refused to walk with them as he had treated some of these people; if he were recognized, he would hear all kinds of requests for advice and lists of symptoms.

Sam and Myra walked on each side of Rebecca, who was skipping along trying to avoid the cracks in the sidewalks. They crossed the street and walked towards the mansion. "Was this owned by a Jew, Sam?" Myra asked. "It must have been a very grand place at one time."

"Yes, it had a high gate and an iron fence all around the property. The Germans tore it down and the Russians did the rest of the damage. All these houses along this avenue had fences and lovely gardens. What a shame such beauty is lost now."

As they walked up to it, Rebecca noticed that the door was open. "Look Mommy. Someone is home. Let's go in," she said as she ran up the walk and up the stairs and into the house.

Sam and Myra were fast on her heels trying to grab her before she got through the door, but she was in before they could. Rebecca was staring up at a fat lady with a scarf on her head and rugged features like a painting of a farmer's worker.

"I am so sorry madam," Myra told her. "She ran from us; we are sorry to have come into your home."

Sam also tried to apologize but the woman cut him short.

"Who do you Americans think you are? You burst in on my clean floors and not one invitation was given you to enter." She spoke in broken English.

Myra tried to apologize again and turned Rebecca around to leave. As she did so, she noticed the old pocket-style sliding doors to the dining room were open. In the room was a long table with a snow-white tablecloth and crystal glasses with lovely plates set for a dinner. Myra walked into the room and stood looking. The women followed nagging about them being here, but Myra wasn't hearing her. Myra walked down a few table settings, pulled out the chair and sat down.

"What is she doing? We are to have guests tonight and if you don't leave right now I will call the police."

Sam put his finger to his lips indicating she must be silent. Rebecca took the woman's hand and smiled up at her. "She won't hurt anything. She is trying to remember."

The woman wanted to know what she was trying to remember, but looking at Myra in a trance across the table, she hesitated. Then, as though a lightning bolt had roared through her brain, she raised her hand to her mouth and said, "No! I can not believe my eyes.""

Suddenly Myra reached for something in front of her, like a plate that was not there.

"I can too have a matzo cracker and don't you hit my hand again," she said. Her voice was like that of a child. Sam shook her to bring her back to what she was doing, and Rebecca was looking confused. The lady had run out of the room and in Hungarian called for someone to come quick.

Myra suddenly looked up at Sam. "Oh Sam. What

just happened? Did I do something awful?"

"No, dear. But we must leave now before she does call the police." Rebecca took her mommy's hand and kissed it as they started out of the room. The woman had returned with the gray haired man Myra had first seen with Joseph in the garden and had confronted at the bookshop.

For a minute they looked at each other until the man offered his hand to Sam and said, in Hungarian. "I am Janos Peto. You have entered my home and upset my housekeeper."

Myra was shocked. She could only stand there and listen to Sam explain why they had entered the house.

Janos Peto looked down at Rebecca and patted her head. "You like old houses, do you?"

"No sir, I am just looking. I did not mean to make trouble," she said as she tried to pull her mother towards the door.

"Sir, she is here again," the housekeeper said, pointing to Myra. "Like the Messiah the Jews wait for."

"Be quiet, Olga. It is not that way at all," Janos told her; and when she opened her mouth again to speak, he reprimanded her to be silent.

"I am sorry. My housekeeper is a dreamer and she

is protective of me. Is there anything more I can help you with?" Peto was looking directly at Myra.

"No and we do apologize for upsetting your house-keeper. Thank you for being so kind, and now we will leave," Sam said as he joined Rebecca and Myra by the front door.

As they walked towards the car, Sam tried to get Myra to tell him what she had just experienced, but she was silent. A few feet from the car, Myra stopped suddenly and looked at a two story house across from them. She ran across the street and up the wooden stairs. The front door opened easily and she was in before Sam or Edmond, seated in his car, could realize what had happened. Sam put Rebecca into the car and told her stay there while they went to get her mother.

Edmond was up the stairs in the house before Sam could settle Rebecca.

"No," yelled Myra, "don't shoot."

Edmond looked up to the top of the stairs and saw nothing but a dilapidated staircase. He looked at Myra who by now had fallen to the floor next to a kitchen door holding her head. Sam came in and for a minute he could not fathom what was going on. He knelt by Myra but she pushed him away.

"Run. He will kill you. My head is bleeding. See the blood? It runs into the cracks of the wooden floors."

She kept moaning until Sam took her into his arms and gently swayed her back and forth. Edmond picked her up, and the three of them left the house. As they emerged down the front steps, Janos Peto was there offering help.

"What happened?" he asked as he reached for Myra's unconscious body in Edmond's arms; but Edmond kept walking to the car, holding Myra close.

"We do not know, comrade," Edmond answered. "She is hallucinating something from her past, we think. She remembers nothing of her young years."

Edmond thought he heard Janos say very quietly, "Thank God," in Hebrew.

As Edmond tried to place her in the car, Myra opened her eyes and saw Janos. "You saved me, didn't you?" Then she closed her eyes again.

Edmond looked at Janos for a minute and believed there was a tear rolling down his cheek. Sam was busy comforting Rebecca, who thought her mother was sick.

"I want to go home, Grandpa. I want my daddy," Rebecca sobbed in his arms.

"Yes, my dear. We will go home. Mother is going to be fine. She is just tired," Sam consoled her. He glanced at Edmond and said, "We must leave tomorrow. Can you arrange it, Edmond?"

Before Edmond could answer, Janos did. "I can arrange it, Mr. Hirsch. Be at the train station tomorrow at noon, if Mrs. Lieberman is well enough. I will assist you and the good doctor here can drive his car back to Budapest."

Chapter Twenty-eight

1969 — Cincinnati

Myra watched the men from the moving vans carry out the furniture and boxes of their belongings and stack them neatly inside the trucks. Michael had said they would need two or three vans to move everything in the house although Myra had had a garage sale and sold quite a lot of goods. However, during their two decades in Cincinnati they had collected many things that could be eliminated. Their new home in Maryland, as described by the real-estate agent, Lydia Green, was a colonial style, and it was sold with most of its furniture as part of the bargain. The elderly couple that had built it back in the 1920s had died, and their children just wanted to get it sold. Michael bought it sight unseen except for a few photos sent by the agent. Michael's new job was the goal he had set for himself as a young doctor. How could she not be happy for him? He was to be Director of Medical Research in one of the most important hospitals in the nation. The Johns Hopkins Hospital in Baltimore had tried before to get Michael's attention, but the timing had been off and Michael hadn't felt ready. Now he was.

Matt was 26 years old and in his last year of law

school at the University of California, Berkley. He was engaged to a lovely girl, and Myra was very happy about his choice. The two sets of parents had met during the early summer. It was clear Mathew fit into their lifestyle like a born member of their large family. There would be no worry about Matt's future. He had always been a good student and she knew he would be a great husband. The wedding would be in San Francisco and would take place on Christmas Eve, so Myra would have to time to settle into their new home by then.

Lily had graduated from the University of Ohio, although she had eloped with a fellow student when she was a junior. She had had two children and a broken marriage before she fell in love with Linda, her soul mate, as she told Myra and Michael. She also had inherited her grandparents' estate, as they never indicated in their will that it should go to anyone but direct descendents, and Lily was the only direct descendent. Now as happy as she could ever be, she and Linda lived in a villa just outside Paris, sharing their children with their American ex-husbands on vacations and special occasions. At least Lily's ex was a good father, and often brought the children down from Akron, Ohio, to see their mother's parents. Lily was taking care of her children financially, giving them a healthy lifestyle, and they now had a wonderful stepmother.

Morgan was a husky athletic boy of sixteen. He was in every sport he could manage and keep his grades up. Then there was Rebecca. Mother and daughter never mentioned the incident of Myra's illness in Hungary. Rebecca was old enough to realize her mother's illness could reappear if she should ask Myra what caused her decline there in Szeged. Her father had told her some of the facts concerning Myra's past and the dreams that terrified her. So, that said, Rebecca never mentioned the experience although she did talk of the happy times in Vienna and the museums. Rebecca had emerged unscathed from all that she witnessed there.

Ten years had passed, and so much had changed, and yet nothing had changed except the loss of Sam. He had died five years ago with his family around him. Edmond had received permission to take Sam's body to Vienna and bury him next to his grandparents in the large Jewish cemetery there. Myra often wondered how Edmond had worked that deal out. She dreaded the memories of her zombie existence at that time. She was aware that the gray haired man called Janos Peto had met them at the train station and journeyed with them up to the border between Hungary and Austria. She knew Sam had wired Michael and he had flown to Vienna to meet them and take charge of them. That was a time when Myra felt she had no soul and she was an empty vessel, just a body she cared little about. Michael and Rebecca had kept Myra's thoughts relatively sane during the trip home, but once home Myra became a nonentity again, not knowing what or where to turn. She had lost her faith in the Catholic religion, and now her Jewish religion seemed almost the same as the Catholic.

The next years were a soft and warm memory. After her breakdown, Michael had found a clinic that housed mentally ill patients. Myra's diagnosis was more of confusion than illness, but her sessions with the doctors there seem to bring her back to reality. It was an expensive place but the surroundings were well worth the money. She lived for several months in a large brick building surrounded by a lush green lawn in the summer and soft white snow in the winter. The staff was a group of dedicated people who really cared for their charges. There, Myra learned to relax when she dreamed and to talk about what could have caused her to dream. She was taught to face her fears by confronting them with the knowledge that she was not really a part of the dreams but only a spectator. The time came when Myra felt she could handle a nightmare by pretending it was another movie, and although she was a part of it, she really was just an actress in a play. She came home for weekend visits, and within a year, both Myra and Michael knew she was ready to face life again. Sam flew over twice to see how she and the family were coping, the last visit just a year before he died. Myra had wanted to go to Vienna for Sam's funeral, but Michael and her counsellor thought it best for her not to be tested again in an area where she could have flashbacks. Therefore, the rabbi at their synagogue, who had met Sam on his visits, made a public homage to Sam on behalf of the family of Michael and Myra. It was another chapter in her life closing.

Then it had been years of a normal life for Myra as she watched the children grow. Her dreams still came and went, but she could cope with them. She believed that now they occurred for a purpose. It was like someone was controlling them, trying to tell Myra something. If she ever discovered the truth, she thought, a heavy curse or burden would be lifted from her and from others to follow. But what could it be? Rebecca would be next in line, she believed, because of what she remembered about Szeged and the moonlight in the garden and the meeting between two men. Sometimes, she dreamt of blood seeping through the cracks of a wood floor, or of the face of man with gray hair. Why was he so familiar to her?

All this she confessed to her counsellor, and to Michael, but they told her the nightmares had no predictive powers. Did she ever remember an event with blood? Did she know why the man seemed so familiar? The dreams had to be about something she had suppressed for years, they argued, and the danger was that knowing the truth might be a setback for her. Knowing the Hungarian language could be possible if she or her parents had been born there. It would have been her first language if it was the land of her roots. Her experience in Szeged hid a feeling of despair, and should it surface, there could be a caustic fear of falling down a large black hole. They didn't believe she needed to confront that.

Therefore, when Myra did think of Hungary and Szeged, she would close those thoughts by writing poems or articles on different subjects for the newspaper, where she had worked part time since her return to sanity, as she called it. She would hate to leave this beautiful city of Cincinnati as she had made true friends and had wonderful memories. Her charitable work and her work at the newspaper kept her busy enough to feel normal most of the time. Now, as their furniture was being sent to Maryland for storage, she, Michael, Morgan, and Rebecca were taking a trip to Colorado. The children could hardly remember their short trips there as toddlers. Esther and her family had moved to Arizona but still kept in touch with the family. Myra could not think of anyone in particular from her days there, but she did want to return to Salida, because, as she told Michael, she was as happy there as at any time in her life.

———

A week later they were at the Denver airport. Immediately, Myra could smell the fresh air of the area, not the musty sweats of moisture and heat that she often felt in the Ohio summers. They taxied downtown and registered at the Brown Palace Hotel, a historical hotel with the air of gentility and wealth. The children were fascinated by the views from their rooms and could hardly wait until the next day when they would tour Myra's old neighborhoods.

As they set out the next day in their rented car, however, Myra was thinking one could never go back home again. The district seem to have grown, and large buildings were being built higher than The Daniels and Fisher Towers, always the landmark building one could see when entering the flat area surrounding Denver. Their first stop was the General Rose Hospital where Michael had interned. There was no one left with whom he had worked and that was a disappointment for him. Like him, everyone had moved on. Then they followed Colfax, the longest street in the nation, from the plains clear through

Denver and into the western suburbs. At Federal Blvd, Michael turned north, heading for the Queen of Heaven Orphanage. Myra could feel her heart beating like a drum. They crossed a busy interstate highway next to where the orphanage had been. There was nothing left of the orphanage's building, as they approached the area. A fast food diner sat where the front steps had been. Myra gasped and stared as though she could not believe what she was seeing.

"Are you sure this is the correct place, Mom? Morgan asked

Myra could not believe it was the same neighborhood. "Stop Michael. Find a place to park. I want to get out for a while."

Michael turned the next corner and parked near the sidewalk. Myra got out and Rebecca started to follow her, but Michael held her back and shook his head no.

"Let your mother get her memories in line with what it is now."

Myra walked to the corner in front of the diner. She watched the traffic speed past under the bridge that was Federal. Then she remembered long ago when she once looked out the window from the parlor of the orphanage on a Christmas night. The Victorian homes across the street had disappeared, and what she was seeing now was what she saw then. A shiver went up her spine and a voice inside her told her to hold on and not panic. As she had come to realize in her counseling, there was a reason for this unique experience, and one day, she felt, she would understand.

When she returned to the car, she asked Michael if he would get back on Federal and drive south to the Catholic church of St. Catherine's. She wanted to see if it had changed although they had passed it before the I-70 highway. Michael parked in the driveway in back of the church, and again, alone, Myra walked around to the front of the church. The main doors had been replaced and in the vestibule a new basin with the holy water had replaced the larger gold-trimmed bowl she remembered. Myra hesitated for a moment. Should she dip her fingers and bless the lord? No, she was a Jew now. She walked down the main aisle of the church until she stood before the statue of Jesus hanging high above the altar. This was the Jesus that stared at her always, as though he was asking her what she was doing here. As a child, she had feared his eyes, as they seem to be looking at her in shame.

"Well, Jesus, I am back and you still look as though you know something about me. When will you reveal your thoughts to me? Why do you still hang on to my soul? I never loved you and you knew it. Set me free now."

"How would that be possible my dear?" a voice from the doorway next to the altar spoke. A priest appeared and walked down to meet her. "What troubles

Myra felt betrayed again, as she always did in this place. "Father Lou?" she asked.

"Father Lou? My goodness, no. He passed on years ago. Did you know him?"

"I was in the Queen of Heaven Orphanage as a child. I used to come here with the rest of children. Many years have passed, father, and my life has changed drastically."

"So it would seem. Are you happy? Has your life been fulfilling? Why has Jesus become your nemesis?"

"Yes, father, I am happy, but it was a rough road to get through. I discovered I was born a Jew, and although I didn't know my background, it seemed to me as a child that everyone I loved abandoned me or died. I guess I blamed Jesus, for who else was there? He seem to stare at me at mass, and I could almost hear his thoughts. I was sure he was saying I had sinned and my punishment was not loving him."

"Look, my dear lady. You could stand anywhere in this church, and Jesus would be looking at you. It is the genius of the artist, and we were fortunate to acquire this lovely symbol of our Lord Jesus Christ."

Myra knew he was right because no matter where she sat or stood, Jesus did look at her, and at all the children. Why had she felt he had singled her out? "Yes, of course, father, you are right. I guess I felt I didn't belong anywhere and his image in my childhood mind was reminding me every time I came here."

The priest offered his hand, and Myra gladly took it into hers.

"It is not a bad thing that you felt that way. Many orphans must have felt abandoned as you did. Just know through me, that Jesus loves you no matter what you believe today."

"Mom, are you all right?" It was Morgan and Rebecca coming down the aisle towards her.

"I am fine now, children. The priest has been very kind. Thank you, father, so very much."

The three of them headed towards the front door. Myra hesitated for minute, then dipped her fingers into the holy water and made the sign of the cross, as in the old days.

Chapter Twenty-nine

Myra and Michael sat in the front seat of the rental car with Morgan and Rebecca playing word games from their back seats. Once in a while they spotted a deer or mule elk eating between the trees and mountains. When they came to Kenosha Pass, Myra asked Michael to stop for pictures. There before them was a flat land spreading to the distant mountains that seem to be farther down the road. Myra had remembered this route which she often took with Carl and Gerta when they had to go to Denver on business, or to the yearly Denver rodeo to sell some of their animals.

"Mom," Rebecca asked, "Did you live this far in the mountains?"

"I did," Myra answered, and added, "Every time we came to this pass, I would think I was on the top of the world. You can almost see forever."

"Do you know what the mountains close to us are called?" Morgan asked trying to trip up his mother, as he loved to do.

"No, not all of them, but when we come to Buena

Vista, you will see a string of mountain peaks named after Universities from back east. They are called the Collegiate Peaks."

Myra raised her hand towards highway they would follow. "Look, over there. You can barely see it, but that mountain with a rounded gorge below the peak is called Silverheel's Mountain. She was a bar hostess in Fairplay during an epidemic back in the 1800's and when the miners or their families got sick, she took it upon herself to nurse them."

"Did she get sick?" Rebecca asked.

"I think towards the end she did get sick and died. The town of Fairplay was so taken by her ability to put everyone above her own sickness; they named that mountain after her. But wait until you see the mountain peaks as we drive from Buena Vista to Salida. They are called Mount Harvard, Mount Yale, and Mount Princeton."

When at last, they arrived in Salida, Michael checked them into a motel on Highway 50. Driving up Fifth Street, Myra wondered if there were old friends she remembered who might still live here. Myra was so nervous she could hardly eat dinner. The family drove around the town with Myra showing the kids where she went to church and school. Next they saw the park by the downtown area, and drove across the bridge where the Arkansas River flowed past the Rio Grande train station. Reluctantly, Michael drove up the winding road to the 'S' on the Sugar Loaf Mountain because Morgan bet he couldn't.   From there they could view the whole valley where distant lights of the farms on the outskirts of the town shown like lost stars in a dark pool of ink.

The next day, Myra directed Michael to the farm where she had once lived. The old house was still there, in poor condition and empty, but the acreage seem to be split in half with newer houses and roads that Myra hardly recognized.   Maybe it wasn't a good idea to return to the place where she thought she was the happiest. The truth from the Grainger's would have made her happy, she thought.   But everyone she trusted had said she might have an episode like she had when Gerta first brought her home. Now, looking back as an adult, she felt different. If she remembered one day of her six-year-old life, she could search that area of darkness and come to terms with the results and fight the fear of her dreams.

That night Myra dreamt again. *She was helping Carl dig a hole in which they were to plant a tree. A special tree with hardy roots and sure to grow six feet or more, Carl had told her.*

"Just think, girl, when you are grown this tree will be so large you won't believe it." Carl said, putting his foot on the big shovel.

"I will remember it Carl, and one day I will be back to see if that is true." Myra answered.

"Well," said Carl, "you're back now, and it took you long enough.   You came here for memories, but you failed to

notice this tree."

Myra gasped and remembered she had not noticed the tree. Maybe it wasn't there anymore either.

"I did not see it. Are you sure it is there?"

"God Damn sure. You get all these clues and what do you do? You get sick. You never look at the big picture, Myra. Your life is right there before you and it will never be clearer, but not you. No, not you. You come back here for what? Your life didn't start here, nor will it end here. Open your eyes Myra, and for once see the clues."

Myra woke and sat up saying, "No, no, it is not true."

Michael pulled himself up to sit besides her. "What? Another dream?"

"Oh yes, Michael. It was Carl this time telling me I don't see the clues in my life. Maybe he is right. I have not dreamt of Carl or Greta since I left them."

She stood up and walked to the window where Highway 50 was unusually quiet, as it was late at night or in the early morning. "I did hate them both when they gave me up for adoption. I told you about that time. I know I was still a child, but I wish they had told me my history then."

"They must have known you could not handle the

truth, if they knew the truth, at that age. After all, you erased something horrible you experienced as a young child. They probably feared for your sanity since you had had a spell when you arrived."

"Carl was a man of few words, Michael, so why am I dreaming about him now, and why are we planting a tree?"

Michael shook his head no. "Go back to sleep, Myra. We will talk about it tomorrow. I am too tired to think."

The next day before they drove out of town, they went to the cemetery and found Carl's gravesite. It was Michael's idea, thinking that might ease Myra's anxieties. Next to it was a large pine tree similar to the one in Myra's dream. "If this is the clue, Michael, why can't I see it? Here is the tree, as large as Carl said it would be. Why is it in the cemetery?"

Rebecca brushed off the stone to read its inscription. "Here lies Carl Grainger, born not in this country but loved it like a father. RIP. What does RIP mean mother?"

"Rest in peace." Myra told her.

Michael laid the floral arrangement they had bought from the only florist in town. "Here you go, old man. It is only a reminder that once you lived here and once you cared for my love, Myra."

Myra

Myra wiped her tears with her hand and silently said to the stone, "I forgive you Carl, again." She looked the tree over from top to bottom and remembered Sam telling her she had to be a branch from a family rooted like a tree. The clue was to find that family tree.

The family piled into the car and drove off towards Denver.

———

It was as though they had been thrust into a different and unknown world as they drove up the long driveway to their new home in Maryland. Rebecca crouched down in her seat, not willing to know where she was and still hurting about leaving her friends in Ohio. But Morgan whistled and rolled down the car window. "Boy, look at this, Becca. It is nice. Really, I think you will like it here." He realized Rebecca's sorrow at being pushed into a new life. He felt that way too, but he had also learned from his mother's recollection of her childhood what she might have felt, and she had had no family to lean on. He was mature enough to realize he would survive the move. It was going to be a new adventure for him and he wanted Rebecca to feel that way too.

The double front door was opened and a lady in nice business suit was waiting for them. "Hello! It is nice to meet you after all our exchange of letters and phone calls.""You must be Lydia Green?" Michael asked.

342

The greetings went on for a while. Rebecca left the group and walked up the front stairs. Inside the entrance hall were circular steps leading to the upper floors. Doors on each side of the hall were opened and Rebecca could see a piano and covered chairs in a row before it. On the left side of the large hall was a sitting room with large windows and heavy drapes pulled back to show snow-white sheer curtains. Every thing in the room looked like crystal and shone like diamonds. Rebecca was thinking, this is a museum, not a home. There were huge paintings hanging from the wall by the curved stairs, and some just as large in the rooms Rebecca could see.

When at last the group entered the house, Morgan again let out a loud whistle. "Boy, oh boy. This is a mansion, isn't it?"

"Well, yes, I guess you could call it that. Plenty of room for you teenagers," Lydia Green said as she motioned the family to a door farther down the hall. It was a study with built-in cherry bookshelves on two walls. In two large windows, light brown drapes were pulled back to bring in the sun. The study looked out on a garden of flowers and bushes, with a few marble statues of children playing or reading.

"This is beautiful, Mrs. Green. I wasn't sure about buying a house unseen, but I think I lucked out with this one, "Michael said. "The pictures you sent had no depth to them. I thought it to be much smaller."

"Why is all the furniture from the previous owners

still here?" Myra asked.

"Well their children were adopted, and according to them, they were servants to their parents. I was shocked, as was the whole village, that they hated the Olson's so much. They didn't want to keep reminders."

"Really?" Michael asked, in shock himself. "How could that be with this lovely home and all? Surely they had a life of education and leisure?"

"We all were amazed too, but Harry Olson said he never wanted to step in this house again. His sister, however, now Mrs. Connie Williams, did come and take the jewelry and some of the artwork that meant something to her. She said she would give some of it to her brother. You see, they were really brother and sister, two years apart."

"I should think she'd want some of the paintings we saw on the walls. Are they not ancestors?" Michael asked.

"Exactly what I asked Mrs. Williams. However, she bluntly told me they were not ancestors to her or her brother. So, she waved her arms around said, 'All this must go now. Lower the price if you must but get rid of it.' So, my friends, I did that, and you were the first to contact me." She motioned to Michael.

Myra looked at Michael. "I don't think it feels like a family home, dear. Maybe we should wait before we get our furniture out of storage." She had whispered her words, but Mrs. Green had heard her.

"Oh, my dear. Please don't make any judgment until you see the rest of the house." She smiled at Myra, but there was something Myra mistrusted in this woman. She seemed nice but not honest, as though she was playing a game with them. Her smile seems to be glued on, and her determination to show them the house was like play-acting. She held her long thin neck high and often touched a gold piece of jewelry pinned on her jacket, as though her nerves were urging the importance of this sale. There was something about her that didn't seem right to Myra.

Mrs. Green directed them to the side rooms, talking endlessly about the big parties they could give for friends. As they walked from one room to another, though, the dining room was Myra's stopping point.

"Michael, I can't live here. There are ghosts," she whispered, gripping his arm. "Can't you feel it? I get chills with every room we enter, but this one is the worst."

Rebecca was standing by her parents; she too could feel something about this house. "Daddy, this room is almost like the room in Szeged when mom got so sick."

"Rebecca you would not remember that. You were only four." Michael scolded her, but she was not going to back off.

"I do remember, Daddy. I was the one that ran into the house in the first place. It was my fault because when mom came to get me she saw the dining room and was as white as a sheet. Then the fat woman screamed and that old man came down from the upstairs and talked to Grandpa. Later Grandpa Sam took Mom by the arm and had her walking down the street. Grandpa Sam put me in the car with Edmond but mom had crossed the road and gone into another empty house. Both Grandpa and Edmond went in after her. All I know was that she fainted and then got very sick for a long time. It was my fault."

"No, Rebecca. Don't ever think that. I never meant for you to feel that way. I thought we had talked about your trip and you were OK with it," Michael said.

"We never really talked about it, Dad, because you thought I was too young to understand. But I do understand when she says there are ghosts here. I feel something too."

Lydia Green could see her commission check fly out into the afternoon air. "I have never heard of such a thing," she said in an angry voice directed at Rebecca. "There are no ghosts here. No one who has ever lived here has ever mentioned things like that."

Michael looked at Rebecca and then at Myra. Morgan stood in the doorway, his arms crossed and his face solemn. He had always been his mother's protector. "If she doesn't like it here, then let's get moving," he growled. Then, loudly, he questioned Mrs. Green: "Who exactly would not have complained, Mrs. Green, if the old people who built the house just died and, according to you, their children wanted to get rid of it right away? You said we were the first ones to contact you. So what people are you talking about?"

The poor woman turned every color of the rainbow and stuttered excuses. Michael led everyone out the door and into the car. They spent the night at the Hilton Hotel in the middle of Baltimore.

Chapter Thirty

June 1974 Rebecca graduated from her private girls' school. Myra could not believe how beautiful she was in her prom dress. Michael had become the protective father every time a new boy entered Rebecca's circle of friends. She was in the top ten of her class, and Smith College had formally announced her acceptance in April. Myra knew this was going to change her life again, with her last child gone and the nest empty. She had thought that she and Michael might move from the four-bedroom home in the lovely gated community they found after their experience with Mrs. Green. They might want something smaller now. She was fifty now, and Michael at fifty-nine was too young to retire. There was always the writing for Myra, and lately she had been studying Jewish history. She knew in her heart that she was Jewish and maybe the mystic beliefs of their religion were strong in her. Myra sometimes wondered why she had felt unknown presences in the mansion, but she had felt them, and so had Rebecca. The ghosts or spirits, she figured, were dead and trying to correct problems left behind. Her dreams were of the dead too, she felt, trying to align her life and truth. It did not matter to her any more. The dreams didn't bother her much, and maybe for a good reason. She wasn't a frightened little girl any more. She truly felt she was the happiest woman on the earth. She remembered the priest's words in St Catherine Church in Denver, and realized the present was more important. So, she moved on.

Matt and his wife had made her a grandma. He was now a lovely two-year-old called Joshua. As often as she could, Myra flew to California for visits with her grandson. It often occurred to her that Eric and his father would have been proud of that baby and of Matt. He was a successful lawyer with a loving family and a lovable extended family of in-laws. California was home to him and that is where he would stay.

Lily was the only child who worried Myra. Her relationship with Linda was over and Linda had flown back to her husband and kids. Lily sold their villa and moved to Rome for a while. Her letters were full of her adventures, including some events Myra would rather not know about. Lily sounded like a person trying to find her way. But wasn't everybody these days? Cults and chanters from Hari Krishnas to druggies and the likes of Charles Manson who killed innocent people just for the fun of it—these were signs of a sick society, she thought. And now Lily was part of a cult, or so Myra thought. The Hari Krishnas had invaded America, but Lily had found them in India. Her financial planner had written to Myra when Linda left that Lily's estate was safe because Lily had made sure it was. The financial advisor had to laugh when he called Myra later and said Lily had requested that half of her estate be given to the Hari Krishnas. That, said the advisor, was out of the question. Lily could have tried to fire him on the spot, but was prevented by the terms of her grandparents' will, which guarded the estate against any change of venue from his firm. Lily would die poor if she wasted her resources fighting the will's conditions.

So what was next for Myra? It was the diamond Star of David. She would really like to know about it. Who sent her this magnificent, expensive, piece of jewelry? Yvette Levine was probably not the name of the sender, she decided. If there were a New Yorker by that name, Sam would have found her. Sam had failed in unpacking some of her dreams, but his journey had connected him with his family again. Maybe the Star of David was magical. Maybe it was a good omen for a good Jew.

She missed Sam. He had been her father and strength at a time when she really needed someone. He was sure of her ancestry before she was, and he devoted the last part of his life to finding the portrait Eric had once seen. Was the woman in the portrait an ancestor? Maybe she would never know, but Sam's had been a valiant search. Maybe now she could go back to Vienna and visit his grave. She was feeling strong and certain of herself now. There would not be any more seizures or fainting spells because the fear she had had before was gone. "What was there to fear anyway," she often asked herself. It was a subject she would bring up to Michael next week during their vacation at the Greenbrier Hotel and Spa in West Virginia, a place where they had often enjoyed wonderful days of activity and relaxation during these past years. The seclusion of the place and its lovely scenery always brought peace to Myra. She had taken up golf for Michael's sake. The massages and wonderful formal dinners with the music of a harp playing soothed their souls. It was like a dream for Myra, living in a world she had not in her youth thought possible for her.

Yes, she would convince Michael that she had nothing to fear in Austria.

Greenbrier the next week was as refreshing as always. On their last afternoon, they finished a tennis match and returned to their suite for a shower and nap. Myra packed everything but the fine clothes they would wear to that evening's party, and their travel clothes for the next morning. Their dinner partners for that evening were a retired scientist and his very young and glamorous wife. For her birthday gift, the old man had given her a week of cooking classes offered by the hotel. "What else could I give this wonderful lady who has everything she wants and needs but does not know how to cook?" He laughed as his wife glared at him. It seemed she was more in love with his money than with him.

Later that night, Myra broached the subject of going to Vienna. Michael was tired and wanted to talk about it later, but Myra knew this was the right time. His defenses would be down after an active week. He might agree to anything just to be left to fall asleep. They discussed the pros and cons of the travel. He would not be able to go with her if she were to go this summer, but in the fall after the children were back at their colleges,

Then Myra threw a suggestion Michael could not ignore. She would take Rebecca with her again, and Morgan too, if he wanted to see some of Europe. It would be important to Rebecca to clear out the cobwebs of memory she experienced as a four year old. However, Morgan and a friend had traveled to Italy as freshmen in college and he truly loved the country. Now he had a summer job as a student intern working with mentally disabled children. He liked the work and would be graded on his job. Myra knew that, but she thought it would add to Michael's accepting the idea. Of course Michael immediately reminded Myra of Morgan's summer job and said it would not be proper to pull him away. He would be tied up until a few days before he had to go back to college. The question of Rebecca accompanying her mother would be a different story. Rebecca was eighteen now and could handle anything they might come up against if Myra should need help. Michael agreed to think about it after both of them talked it over with Rebecca. That was all Myra wanted from him, as she knew Rebecca would love to go back to Vienna and maybe to Hungary if they could get a permit to do so.

———

They flew to London on the 10th of June. The travel agent Myra had worked with to plan their trip placed them in an elegant hotel in the heart of London, an easy distance from all the places they wanted to see. For a week, they did the tourist sightseeing wonders. The Tower of London fascinated Rebecca, but Myra felt

Myra

"Imagine Anne Boleyn brought here to this place. It had to be cold and frightening, knowing she was to die if she could not plead successfully for her life. King Henry the Eighth used to love her and waited to wed her longer than any man in heat." Rebecca laughed.

As their group of tourists approached the room known as Anne Boleyn's room, Myra felt shivers run through her body. She could feel old souls in a cry unheard by the others in the group. She looked at Rebecca and knew immediately she too had heard the cry. Rebecca looked at her mother and nodded her head, agreeing to leave this area.

They departed silently walking to the hall from which they had entered. The stairs were on the other side of the open hall and they started in that direction. Suddenly they both heard the weeping of a woman. For a slight moment they both saw a shadowy female figure sitting at the bottom of the stairs. She was there and suddenly she wasn't. Rebecca grabbed her mother's hand and dashed down the stairs into a long hallway and out the door of the Tower. When they passed the large front gates, Rebecca stopped to catch her breath.

"Mother what is it about you and me? I once read some Jews have these mystical powers of seeing and hearing ghosts. Do we have that gene? I thought it was so silly, but then I remembered that mansion daddy was going to buy until you and I felt the spirits."

"Oh darling, one does not have to be Jewish to feel

those things. It happens to people from any race or religion, I think. Yes, we do seem to have a sixth sense, but why we have it, I do not know. It could be our souls are conscious of our feelings and warn us to be careful."

"I know what you mean. I never told you before, but that Lydia Green, the woman who was trying to sell that mansion? It was about four months later; I saw her obituary in the paper. She had been found dead at the foot of that curved stairway. I told Daddy, but he asked me not to tell you"

"I didn't know you read obituaries, Rebecca. Are you trying to be in bad situations?"

"No Mother. I was turning the paper trying to find the theatre section and that name popped out of a headline in the death notices. Police felt she had been murdered, but later decided she had tripped on something at the top of the stairs and fallen to her death. I think she was as scared as we were when we told her what we felt."

"So your father told you to say nothing about it to me? Did he think I would faint or go into a trance like a zombie? My darling girl, I am through with that part of my life. I don't know some of my past, but I know who I am today. Nothing is going to make me mentally sick again."

"I know mother, but Daddy didn't want to take a chance. So maybe since you feel so sure of yourself, we

Myra

Sirens from ambulances coming their way interrupted them. They watch an ambulance stop in front of them and moved out of the way. People were running in and out like a swift stream of water.

"What has happened?" Myra asked a woman who had been with them in the group.

"He fell down the stairs, he did? The guide. He was directing us to another section of the Tower, and suddenly he seem to slip toward the stairs and like someone had pushed him, he fell all the way down."

"Was he badly hurt?" asked Rebecca.

"He was dead by the time other guides reached him. There was blood coming out of his mouth and nose. He was totally dead," the woman told them. "He was looking for you two and asked the rest of us if we had seen you. He said 'the young girl who looks like her mother.' Then he said a few unkind words about you, then he slipped, and being so near to the stairs he went all the way, but to me it looked like he was pushed although there was no one near him."

"How weird," Myra said. "He only spoke to us when we gave him our tickets"

Rebecca looked at Myra and took her hand again. "Let us get out of here, Mother. We did nothing wrong but leave the group." Myra clasped her hand and they

"Mother, do you think *Shedims* are protecting us?"

"But *Shedims* are demons.   Where did you hear about that?'

"In our classes at the Temple years ago.   Do you think they really exist?"

Myra was shocked but said, "I don't know anything about spirits existing between the spiritual and the physical worlds. We will study about them later or consult the Talmud."

Both were feeling bad about the poor guide, but why would he be asking for them?   It was a large group, so why would he notice their presence?   It was weird but they promised each other they would not talk about it any more and they would say a Kaddish for him.   Tomorrow they would leave for Vienna and a new adventure.

Chapter Thirty-one

The night before they were to leave for Vienna, Myra had a dream different than any others she could remember. *She and Rebecca were walking along a dirt road. It wasn't familiar to her but it was scenic and enjoyable. Rebecca was humming a song Myra knew. What was it? A lullaby? A man was walking towards them. He was hatless and his gray blew slightly in the wind. As he drew near them, he waved to them.*

"Look mother. It is Grandpa Sam." Rebecca yelled as she ran towards his open arms. Sam smiled at her and asked where had his little granddaughter gone?

Myra felt so happy to see him and tried to run to him, but her legs would not move. She stood frozen on the spot and her yells to Sam and Rebecca were hollow and empty. They did not see or hear her, but she heard them.

"My little girl, I have solved the problem of the curse. You will be safe as will your mother when she finds the secret of the Star of David."

"What secret, Grandpa?"

"The curse that was put on it by a very vicious man of

your ancestry. Your mother has been the most haunted but that too will stop when she finds the large envelope in the secret place."

"My God, Sam. I am here. Tell me where to look." *Myra screamed, but it was Rebecca who shook her awake and stood over her. "What is it mother? Were you having another dream?"*

Myra looked around the room. The clock on the console said 3:00 A.M. The streetlights from outside gave an eerie light through the sheer curtains.

Myra sat up and patted Rebecca's cheek, "Oh my darling. I guess I was dreaming but it is OK now. Go back to your bed. I am fine." But Myra wasn't fine. A curse? She had never heard of that before. Oh Sam, why couldn't you be here to help me she thought? A curse? Why was The Star of David cursed? Then Myra wondered if some one could do that and have it last for generations?

It was a beautiful sunny day when they arrived in Vienna. The city had grown since their last trip years ago. The traffic was as crowded as any American city. New buildings were going up where empty lots or old house had been before. They had made reservations at the Hotel Kaiser-Schonbrunn where they had stayed before. It had been renovated since their stay and it was a pleasant surprise to see the nice suite in which they had been booked. It was lovely to shower and get in fresh clothes and have their first dinner in Vienna at the lovely dining room on the main floor. The elevator was still small in space, which Rebecca recalled with glee. She had remembered how crowded they had been with just Myra, Sam and herself, with a few pieces of luggage. Since she was a child, the hotel clerk had said they could all fit in it. Myra was always surprised how many of Rebecca's memories stayed with her. At least Rebecca could remember her young years where Myra's memory was and always would be a mystery. The next day they walked to the Imperial Palace for a tour. They took the underground train to St.Stephen's Cathedral. They found an outside café and had a wonderful lunch. The rest of the day they spent shopping. After a short nap, they had dinner in a lovely restaurant the hotel clerk had recommended. Every afternoon, in London and now in Vienna, Myra would call Michael and report all that they had seen and where they had eaten. He told Myra he was lonely, to hurry and find Sam's grave and get home.

At times, Myra felt her body quiver with excitement when Michael told her how much he loved her. How was she able to find such love and happiness after the childhood she would never forget? Why was she so lucky? Was she really part of the Jewish chosen ones? She looked at the sky and the people in this beautiful city because the feelings from within her seem to light up her spirits. Her prayers seem to reach her soul and she felt a true happiness in understanding that all that had been in the past was a doorway to the future, to the present she lived in now.

The next day, they took a taxi to the Rossauer Cemetery, the oldest Jewish cemetery in Europe, Myra thought. The tombstones were ancient and some had probably been smashed and toppled by the Nazi's, Rebecca told her. It was hard to translate to the caretaker just whose grave they searched for. Myra was about to give up and hire a translator for the next day. But Rebecca would not think of it. She cupped her hands near her mouth, and as loud as she could she yelled, "Does anyone here speak English?"

Myra was shocked and was about to tell Rebecca so, when a young man in his Jewish attire came around the corner of a tombstone and said, "Yes. I do."

He was a handsome young man with the red hair of his braid on the side of his head falling on his face. He brushed it back and adjusted his black hat and smiled at Rebecca.

"I am Julien Zelnick," he said, holding out his hand to Myra. "Can I help you?"

Rebecca was immediately star struck. She stood there with her mouth open but could not speak. In fact, the young man stood there looking at Rebecca as though he had lost his voice.

Myra sensed she needed to take over. "Yes, please. I am Myra Lieberman and this is my daughter Rebecca."

A weak hello came from Rebecca and from the young man too.

"We are looking for the grave our grandfather, Sam Hirsch. He was an American but was buried next to his grandparents. I am not sure if it was his mother's side or his father's. Could you ask the caretaker if there is a record? We have come this far to make sure his tombstone and grave is properly cared for."

"If he was your grandfather, did he not tell you his history?" Julien asked

"He adopted me when I was a college coed, and then had no family. He helped me to grow emotionally and intellectually. We, my family that is, were very close to him until he moved back here. I was unable to come to his funeral."

Julien smiled at her and nodded to Rebecca, "I will certainly do what I can. How would you spell that name?"

Myra looked at Rebecca before she could speak. "I think his Jewish name was different than his American spelling. We knew him as Hirsch. Sam Hirsch, but I think it might have been Hersch."

"It sounds like he may have shortened the name and maybe changed the spelling." Julien looked around and saw the caretaker coming towards them. "Here is the man who can help us. Let me ask him."

Julien walked towards the man and they engaged in a conversation. At first the caretaker shook his head no, but Julien kept talking, his hands flying in every direction. At last, the caretaker raised his shoulders and walked towards the women.

Julien introduced him as Homer Katz, and said he would try to help them. Homer motioned toward a little cottage by a large mausoleum with the huge Star of David of concrete embedded into a stone wall. The cottage held several files and papers were piled in every nook and cranny. He asked again the name of the relative she was seeking. "The little stinker," Myra said to Rebecca. "He spoke English all the time." Then Myra told him, he shook his again no.

"If he changed his name to Sam, he would have been Samuel, and Hirsch could have been the beginning of a long Hebrew name.

"That would have been Herschkovitz, wouldn't it mother?" Rebecca asked Myra.

Myra blinked as though she suddenly remembered. "Yes, it would be Herschkovitz. He was able to connect with his biological family in Hungary several years ago. I thought he might have used his American name."

The old caretaker opened one cabinet after another. "Can I help you Rabbi Katz?" Julien asked.

The old man looked at him and pointed to a group of cabinets across the rooms. Myra and Rebecca looked at each other and leaned on the desk. That movement knocked off some papers and folders. Afraid of upsetting the old man, Myra rushed around and started picking up the scattered papers. Rebecca bent over to help her and then suddenly looked at Myra, "Mother! Look at this!"

Myra took the piece of paper out of Myra's hand. It was an old photograph with torn corners and wrinkles across some of the surface. Myra opened her mouth but could not speak. She could only stare at the picture until Rebecca took it out of her hand and showed it to the caretaker.

"What is this?" she asked the man, and Julien looked over the man's shoulder.

"Oh, it was probably left in someone's pocket. We do go through their clothes after we disrobe them. They have no clothes in death or burial," he said causally.

"Mother, it is a portrait of you," Rebecca said, taking it from Myra.

Julien was shocked and almost stuttered. "My God, I thought I had seen you before," he said to Rebecca. "That is a miniature of a famous painting. I have seen it in art books. My grandfather showed it to me and said he viewed it in the Budapest Art Gallery as a child, years before the last war."

Myra stood up and felt a sharp pain in her chest. "Did he tell you anything else about it?"

Myra

"I can't remember; it was so long ago. I think I was fifteen then and Grandfather died a year later. He was a survivor of the Holocaust.

"He had sent most of his family to America when Hitler started his campaign against the Jews. He was a jeweler of high standards and quality. He had three stores, one each in Budapest, Vienna, and Paris. Many people would buy nothing but his designs. He was wealthy until the Nazis broke into his stores and took everything. They arrested him and made him a broken man. The fact that his family was safe kept him going. He was never able to get back all he lost, not even his health."

Myra brushed off the chair beside the desk and sat down. "Why do you at that age think you remember? Was it here or were you in America?"

"I was born in New York City. My father and his two sisters along with my grandmother, were the family grandfather sent to safety. After the war, my parents went often to Hungary to beg him to come to America, but he would not leave. Grandmother had died before the end of the war, and he felt at peace in a country where he and grandmother had been so happy. I was his only male heir, so I spent many summer vacations with him. I thought he was God until I went to Hebrew school in New York. As I grew older and more aware of who I was, then my grandfather's words meant more to me."

Rebecca asked, "Then why are you not in Budapest?"

Julien smiled at her and said, "After a few years, Grandfather felt he could not live in Budapest because the Communists had taken over. He settled here while he was still free to travel and tried to make jewelry again, but I know my father sent him living expenses. I moved here a few years ago to attend a wonderful Hebrew school, so that I too may become a Rabbi. I am here today to honor his tombstone, as I do every week." He held out some white stones he had taken from his pocket.

Myra looked at the picture again. "This is the painting my first husband saw in France during the war. We have been looking for it for years now. The gentleman whose grave we are trying to find was looking for it too."

"Mother, you never told me that. You could have posed for this painting. You are identical to the woman," Rebecca said as she looked at the woman again. "The Star of David. It is on her gown, mother. Is that your Star of David?"

Julien almost yelled at them, "You have that Star of David brooch?"

"It was sent to me when I was a freshman in college. The person who sent it was perhaps fictitious, but her letter said it belonged to me. My first husband saw the real painting in a cave, but he died of war injuries so disabling, he couldn't remember where he came upon it.

He was in shock at the time he saw it, as he too, thought it was a portrait of me."

"So, that is where the portrait went," Julien said. "The art world has been looking for it since the end of the war. Many Jews took precious objects when they fled. That was one of the items. It is titled the 'Lady in Black.'"

"Well, it is not there now; the man whose grave we seek searched before. He was told by a Hungarian artist that the portrait was safe but that he had no idea where it was," Myra told the young man.

"I think we should have a conversation," Julien said. "I think I might know some of the history of the painting and the brooch."

The old caretaker looked up from his stacks of paper. "I think I remember where the grave is. We do not get many Americans to bury here and I was walking by it the other day." He picked up his old bent cane and motioned for them to follow him.

Julien turned to Rebecca and said "Talk of miracles, that I should choose this day to come here when I usually make it much later in the week. I just felt I had to come today. No reason at all. Just a feeling." Julien said. "You look just like the portrait, my dear girl. I didn't realize your mother also resembled the painting until you mentioned it."

Chapter Thirty-two

Myra and Rebecca put the arrangements of flowers on Sam's grave. Then they placed white rocks on the tombstone. Julien had given them the rocks when they passed a metal bucket filled with them. Myra felt the tears run down her cheeks and Rebecca handed her a handkerchief.

"Let us pray, shall we? It is a blessing but it is in Hebrew. Do you mind?"Julien asked.

"That would be wonderful," Rebecca answered, and took her mother's hand as Julien also reached out for their hands. Julien had a soft and melodious voice, so understanding his words was not as important as feeling the healing comfort from his Yiddish. Or was it Hebrew? Rebecca could not tell the difference. Myra kissed her own hand and reached over to place the unseen kiss on Sam's tombstone. Rebecca followed her mother's lead but blew a kiss. The tree next to the grave shook its leaves like ornaments in the wind although there was no breeze.

"I promise you, my good ladies, I will visit his grave as often as I visit my grandfather's," Julien told them as they turned to leave.

Myra

Myra smiled and thanked him for his trouble. She told him she would send money for the upkeep of the grave if he didn't mind. The old caretaker had watched from a slight distance. He noticed the shaking of the tree, but said nothing. Being a former rabbi, he understood what might have happened. "The spirit of that man is still lingering there," he said to himself. "He must try to get through all that he was trying to do on earth in order to find his own peace." He believed these American women would find Samuel's peace for him.

Julien Zelnick was excited to have more time with them. As he had told them in the old office at the cemetery, he could give them more information about the painting, and maybe a little about the brooch. It had been an emotional afternoon for Myra and she wanted nothing more than a light dinner and a telephone call to Michael. Julien rode home on the underground railway to their hotel hoping to make a date for further conversation the next day.

Rebecca begged Myra to set a time for him, as she believed he was sincere about helping them. Myra relented and invited the young man into the hotel bar for dinner. They found a round table and a lovely young girl waited on them almost before they sat down. Rebecca and Julien ordered tea and sweet biscuits and a special Viennese plate of meats and vegetables. Myra, who never was much of a drinker, ordered a cocktail with a salad. She felt she would need the alcohol to help her sleep.

"You see," Julien started as soon as the drinks were

served, "in my family tree there were always jewelers. I do remember Grandfather mentioning the brooch on the Portrait of the Lady in Black."

Myra was suddenly interested in his conversation. "What are you trying to tell us? You know something about the Star of David Brooch?"

Julien started to stutter. "Well, I well, yes, if it is the piece of jewelry in the portrait."

Rebecca stared at him and said, "How old is the portrait? Mother's brooch could be a copy."

"What? You have the brooch or one like it?" Julien asked.

Rebecca nodded yes to his question and asked how they could tell if it was the original one in the painting.

"All makers of jewelry put their mark on expensive pieces they make," Julien told them, but now he feared he might have opened a Pandora's box. "I mean I was made to believe as a youngster that the brooch had been made by an ancestor of my family. That is why my grandfather loved the portrait so much. It could have been his pride in his family, or something to that effect."

Myra paled at Julien's information. Was this the brooch that was cursed? Could this young man give her the clues Sam mentioned in her dream?

Myra

"I can't think any more tonight," Myra said after eating half of the salad and drinking all of her cocktail. "I know it is not very late, but I do feel the need to go up to the room and sleep." She put some Austrian shillings and bills on the table, but Julien stopped her as she stood up. He counted the money and handed Myra some of the change she had put there.

"You overpaid, Mrs. Lieberman. There is enough for our drinks and tip, although we do very little of that here."

Rebecca covered her smiling face and to herself thought, 'Of course you would not tip. You are use to spending very little for many things.' She had noticed his worn coat with its tattered sleeves. Even his hat was in need of a good blocking.

Myra stood stunned for a while and thanked Julien. Then she asked Rebecca when she would be coming up.

"I will just as soon I finish these wonderful biscuits and my tea." The look on Myra's face was not a happy one. "Mother, I will be right up, I promise. Julien is a nice young man and I want to ask him some questions. Remember, we would not have found Sam if not for him, and I will not sleep if I don't ask him my questions."

Julien blushed beet red and opened his mouth in surprise. "I promise, Mrs. Lieberman, we will only talk for a short time since I have classes tomorrow and do not wish to detain you either. I would like to know if we could meet tomorrow after my classes. That would be about 3:30. I could come back here if you like, but I do think I may be able to help you in your research."

Myra gave in with a nod and warned Rebecca not to be much later.

By the time Myra had showered and called Michael about their day's adventure, Rebecca unlocked the hotel door, smiling and excited.

"If you're talking to Daddy, tell him to go to the bank's safety box and look closely at your brooch."

"Why would he have to do that?" Myra asked, holding the phone away from her ear.

"Because if there is a jeweler's mark on the back of the brooch we want to know what it is." She grabbed the phone out of Myra's hand and told Michael why they wanted to know. It took a while but by the time Myra had the phone again, Michael had agreed to check out the brooch.

The cool shower and the alcohol had done the trick to completely relax Myra and she drifted off to sleep like a baby.

A bell tower clock somewhere in this ancient city struck three o'clock and Myra awoke to the blackness of the night. She could barely make out Rebecca's form in the bed across from hers, but she could hear her softly breathing. She tossed and turned for a while then drifted into a feeling of being asleep but not really sleeping. *She felt a chill in the air, and she was sloshing along a wet pavement holding on to a lady with a bun in the back of her black hair. Traffic was zooming by and people were everywhere. "Where are we going Grandma?" she asked. But she could not understand the answer. The lady was carrying a small suitcase and she was carrying her Teddy Bear.*

"Hold on to your Teddy Bear, Myra, the lady said to her, "He is very important. You must never lose him. He is the clue." Myra sat up with a jerk. The clue? Didn't Sam also say that to her in a dream lately? My God, she thought, the Teddy Bear. She hadn't seen it for years. What is going on in my head again? Did she not cry for her grandmother once when Michael suggested she be hypnotized? It was so traumatic for her the doctor felt it would be better if she could not remember. For the rest of the night, Myra laid on her bed trying to remember and wondering what had happened to her beloved stuffed toy.

———

The morning sky lit up like a painting from God. It was a bright orange, pink and purple, with white soft clouds drifting over the city. Myra silently got up and went into the bathroom. After her morning shower, with her make-up in place, she entered the bedroom to find Rebecca still asleep. She shook Rebecca gently and whispered, "Get up you sleepyhead. We have another day of adventures."

Rebecca turned her face towards her mother; her hair was half covering her face. She smiled at Myra and raised her arms in a stretch.

"Oh what a beautiful Morning," she began to sing, and Myra pulled back the covers and started to tickle her. Laughing and happy, Rebecca headed for her turn in the bathroom.

Later, as they sat for breakfast in the hotel's small café, they recalled yesterday's happenings.

"I can't believe we found a copy of that painting. Do you think Grandpa Sam had it in his pocket?" Rebecca asked as she scooped up a spoon full of cereal.

"I think it could be possible." Myra paused, and then said," Do you remember that ragged old teddy bear you played with as a little girl?"

"Sure I do. I loved that squeaky old bear. Why?'

"I had it as a child, you know, and I dreamed about it last night. Why do you call it 'squeaky?"

"Because," Rebecca said as she bit off a piece of toast in her mouth, "if I gave it a hug it would squeal and crackle. You would never wash it, and I thought it was because inside his stuffing was a toy that squeaked when

"Do you know what happened to it?" Myra asked

"Gosh, mom, it has been so long ago." But Rebecca scratched her head. "Oh yeah. I remember now. On our last move, I saw Daddy put it in a shoebox and place it with the things the movers were taking. I asked him about it and he said I was too old for it, but because it had been yours as a child, he felt we should keep it."

So the bear with its clue was somewhere, somewhere, in Myra's big house—like a needle in a carefully tended haystack?

———

The matinee concert at one of Vienna's opera houses was delightful. It put Myra in a better mood to deal with whatever came her way. She was anxious to meet with Julien and learn more from him. Rebecca was so thrilled by the concert that she approached the master conductor and got his autograph.

After some delicious pastry from a sidewalk café and a few souvenirs bought for family and friends back at home, they strolled the large pathway of the park around the Schonbrunn Imperial Castle. The trees lined the paths like tall soldiers guarding the park. There were a few benches along the paths and Myra and Rebecca found one not too far from where they would exit the park for their hotel.

It was time, Myra felt, to tell Rebecca about the

Carpenters. She started where she could remember. Waking up in the hospital room with strange people looking down at her. She thought her heart would pop out of her chest she was so frightened. Then Gerta and Carl appeared and she felt safe again. She retold the story of her route to the orphanage. At last, Myra was able to tell her daughter how Mr. Carpenter had raped her and how his crime had been covered up, how she was made to look like a troublemaker and sent to the orphanage.

Rebecca could not believe her ears. She stared at her mother, then took Myra's hand in hers as if to console her. "Mom, I think we are going to discover the reasons for all those bad dreams that almost destroyed you."

Julien arrived right on the dot of 3:30. He was all scrubbed up and in a civilian suit with his red hair nicely combed and shining like a bright penny. He looked like an American tourist, Rebecca thought. He was so handsome Rebecca wanted to swoon. He was taller than Rebecca had thought since his old clothes of yesterday had hung on him like he was wearing the wrong size.

He smiled widely when he saw the women and advanced towards them quickly. He held out his hand to Rebecca and said, "Well, I am on time, right?"

Myra smiled at him and said, "You are very prompt, Mr. Zelnick. My, don't you look handsome."

Julien blushed again and said, "Thank you, Mrs. Lieberman. You both look very charming and ready for our research."

Rebecca didn't think that listening to him was a research project, but who knows? Maybe he could shed some light her mother's past.

Myra smiled at the two young people. It was clear they had an attraction for each other. Therefore, she asked them if they would like a drink in the hotel bar before starting out for dinner. Julien would accept, she was sure. They found a little round table beside a large window, which gave them the chance to watch the people passing by. They had just started their drinks, when a loud speaker in the room called for a Mrs. Myra Lieberman. Myra looked surprised, but only Michael knew where she was, so she thought it might be serious.

She walked up to the front desk and after saying her name, she was directed to a phone booth across the lobby. "Hello," she said.

"If I know you, you are thinking something might have happened." It was Michael's voice.

"Oh darling, did something happen?" she asked.

"Rebecca told me to get the brooch out of the bank vault and I did just that." He sounded so nonchalant "But I also took it to Bernie's Jewelry Store where we know people. I thought if it was a piece of jewelry from the past, we had to have people we trust."

"So?" Myra asked him, "What did you find out?"

"You won't believe it. Bernie himself called in a gem professional. He took it and examined it for a long time, I thought. Then he whistled and Bernie and I thought he was going to faint. Darling, your brooch is worth millions of dollars and should be on display in a museum. It is a famous piece of work a Jewish jeweler made for a special lady some time in the 1800's. It was thought to have been taken by the Nazis or lost during the war."

"Michael, I can't believe what you're telling me. Where is it now?"

"Bernie and this master jeweler had it registered by officials of the National Association of Precious Jewels and put in a very safe place. They called in a famous diamond cutter to examine it and he was amazed. The diamonds are so precisely cut he told us he never seen such a piece of jewelry. I went with them and watched it placed in a vault you would not believe. I had to sign some papers saying it is legally yours. It is under your name, but that is not all. The jeweler who made it did have his mark on it. I could not recognize anything but the Hebrew letter for 'Z.' Bernie knew exactly what his other markings meant."

"What does this mean? All these years we have kept it. I have even worn it on special occasions. You are telling me it is a masterpiece?" Myra questioned

"It is complicated and could be dangerous. If a master jewel thief should discover that it has survived, he might try to get to it. I was told by these experts it has to be kept a secret. The world of old jewelry is a tight knit one and we could be in danger if some one wanted to have it. So, mum is the word, dear. You had best get back as soon as you can."

When Myra hung up the phone she felt weak in the knees. She had read novels and seen movies about jewel thieves Did Sam know how important it was? He wanted to keep it safe for her too. Then she remembered Rebecca had told Julien about the brooch. How was she ever going to quiet him? Could he be a spy? She walked back slowly thinking of what to say.

Rebecca and Julien were laughing and enjoying each other's company. She took a deep breath and sat in her chair.

"What that Daddy, mom? Did he have any information for you about the brooch?"

Myra took Rebecca's hand and shook her head no but went on to say, "He did get it and took it to old Bernie. You know the man we buy all our jewels from? I am sorry dear, but there were no markings. Still, the diamonds are real. It is most likely worth $6,000.00 if not less."

She looked at Julien who was studying her face. She picked up her glass of wine and swallowed every drop. "I guess we had better get a cab and head for dinner?"

Chapter Thirty-three

It was a restaurant the concierge at the hotel had told them about. The exterior was lovely; inside, heavy red drapes lined the tall windows, with sheer white curtains under them. The waiters wore black and white suits with black ties, and each one had perfect posture as he explained the menu to his customers. Myra and Rebecca ordered beef and fish, but Julien chose only vegetables, keeping his diet as Kosher as he could. While the orders were being prepared, Myra asked Rebecca to follow her to the powder room. Once inside the enclosure, Myra stooped to make sure no one was in the several cubicles. Then whispering to Rebecca, she explained about the brooch and how they could be in danger if anyone from those secret societies trying to find precious jewels and artwork knew about it. She must not say anything more to Julien, she said. He might be a spy since his ancestor was the maker.

Rebecca's mouth flew open and a gasp of surprise came forth. "Is this for sure, mother?" she asked. Before Myra could answer, a few well-dressed ladies came into the room. Myra motioned for Rebecca to move out, which she did, though she was still in shock.

"You will not breath a word of this, Rebecca. Your father warned us, and we must go home tomorrow or as soon as we can get a flight."

"I won't mother, I promise. But Julien can't be a spy. He just can't. What do we tell him about leaving so soon? He would be suspicious if he is a spy."

Myra laughed as though they had told a joke when she noticed Julien looking at them as they entered the large room. "I will handle it, dear, so just back me up. For now we will have dinner. Then tonight we will make our plans."

The question of the night didn't come up until dessert. Then Julien dug into his crème brulee.

"So tell me Mrs. Lieberman, your husband didn't find any markings on the brooch?"

"I am sure if there was a marking the man we have trusted for years with our jewelry would have found it. I think my husband said he called in some professional who also could not find any marking except for a tiny cross, he thought. Would your ancestor make the sign of a cross?"

Julien gulped in disbelief. "Certainly not. He was Jewish from top to bottom. So some idiot made a copy of it."

"I am afraid so, Julien. It was given to me most likely by a Catholic who was making fun of my refusal to worship Jesus. I was raised in a Catholic orphanage but I never felt I belonged there. When I won a good scholarship, someone must have been envious."

"But you said they were real diamonds, Mrs. Lieberman." Julien told her.

Myra felt she had slipped somewhere, but her answer almost surprised her. "I gave it to the man whose grave we visited yesterday. The man we called grandfather. He said he had placed it in his strong box in a bank, but now that I think about it, he gave it back to me when I received my diploma. He must have had the fake jewels replaced by real ones as a gift for my graduation."

"That sounds like Grandpa, mother. He was always surprising us with gifts. We just didn't know the difference," Rebecca added.

They could not tell if Julien believed them or not, so Myra had another idea.

"Julien, you seem to know more about us than we do about you. What is your history?"

Julien sat silent for a time looking down at his empty dessert dish. Then he looked at Myra and began his story. He was an only son with two older sisters, taught at a young age that he was the last of a very religious Jewish family. His father was adamant about Julien becoming a rabbi while his mother, not brought up as an Orthodox Jew, was more flexible. It was his mother who always made him think hard and clear about his life's path. She wanted him to be a doctor or a lawyer because prestige was important to her. She was a Jewish mother who wanted to brag about her son, the celebrity. However, being with his grandfather on many summer vacations, he decided that he wanted to please this very dear man too. There was also a pressure to find a nice Jewish girl to marry, but the girls he knew and some he dated, were more like Jewish princesses. He would never be happy in a marriage if he had to cater to a spoiled wife. His cousin on his mother's side did just that by marrying "a nice Jewish girl." Julien knew his cousin Marvin was not faithful in his marriage and had even started to believe his own lies-- although at times he was confronted with the truth. No, he assured Myra and Rebecca, if he could not find a girl worthy of his way of life, he would not ever marry.

Rebecca looked down at the floor feeling very humble. She would not ever be able to marry someone like Julien, due to his strict religious lifestyle. Then she reminded herself this was just another person who interested her on this trip. Why should she care?

"So, Julien," Myra said, "we will be leaving tomorrow if we can get a flight out of Vienna. I just want you to know how wonderful it was to make your acquaintance. You have been very helpful in the cemetery and in giving us the history of a Star of David brooch."

Julien wiped his mouth with his napkin and placed it beside his dish. "I thought you were to remain another week, Mrs. Lieberman. There is so much more to the history of the original brooch."

"Oh, I am sorry Julien, but my husband has not been feeling well and he wants us to come home as soon as possible. We only came to check on our dear Sam's gravesite." She hated to lie as she felt there was something special about this young man, but Michael had warned her to be careful.

Well then," Julien began, "I had better get your address to report the upkeep of your grandfather's grave." He looked at Rebecca with sad eyes.

That threw Myra off completely. How could she avoid that request?

"Oh, yes. Well I don't have a pen with me, so if you give us your address   we can make arrangements by mail?"

The always prepared Julien produced a pen out of his pocket and snapped his fingers at a passing waiter to ask for a piece of paper.

The paper lay in front of her and the pen she held in her hand. "Let us see," she said smiling at Rebecca with a help-me-please look on her face. Both of them were at a loss for words. Any excuse they gave him would make him very curious. Just as Myra was putting the pen to paper with a fictional address, she looked up and saw Edmond Herschkovitz walking by their table with a very tall and muscular man walking behind him.

"Is that you Edmond? she asked

Edmond Herschkovitz was dressed in a black suit and just as handsome as she remembered him. He stopped immediately, looking completely surprised.

"Well, my goodness. Look who is here, Rebecca." Myra said, and then quickly added, "It is Edmond, Grandpa Sam's nephew. Dr. Edmond Herschkovitz. Do you remember him?"

"I know your name and I think I have seen your picture when Grandpa Sam visited us in Ohio. You were the doctor who helped Grandpa when he was so sick. It is nice to see you again," Rebecca said as she held out her hand to him.

Myra noticed that the stern looking man behind Edmond wasn't happy about the interruption.

Edmond seemed lost for words, so Myra introduced Julien to him to start a conversation.

"This is a new friend we met at the cemetery trying to find Sam's grave. Julien, this is an old friend and relative of the man whose tombstone you helped us find. Edmond, this Julien Zelnick."

Edmond's face turned solemn, and he eyed Julien

in a surprising manner. "Pleased to meet you Julien," Edmond said, turning around to show the man behind, "This is my friend Hugo who accompanied me to Vienna." Edmond looked down to Rebecca and said, "You two ladies would be the last people on earth I expected to meet here in Vienna and in this place."

"We came to visit Grandpa's grave. Mother was sick when he died and could not come. She has wanted to come for a long time."

Then Edmond turned back to Myra with his face hidden from Hugo. He moved his eyes in the direction of the front door of the restaurant. Not once but three times and Myra got the message that he wanted her to leave immediately. It was also a gesture that Julien could recognize, but it was Rebecca who looked scared when she saw Edmond's expression.

"My you have grown into a lovely lady, Rebecca, just like your mother," Edmond said. "But not to change the subject," he added, "We have brought a very important comrade here for surgery that could not be done in Budapest. I have been beside him all day, so Hugo and I were permitted to leave for some good Viennese food. Our two companions are watching him for a few hours; then they will be permitted to have a nice Viennese meal too."

Myra knew exactly what Edmond meant and took the hint.

"Oh dear, what timing. We have just finished our meal and really have to leave," Myra said as she stood up and held her hand to Edmond. "It is too bad we haven't more time. It has been a long time since we last met. We leave tomorrow for home as my husband isn't feeling well. We came to see Sam's grave, and that has been done, so we have no reason to stay longer."

"Yes, it is a shame, but maybe one day we can visit each other and catch up on all the family news," Edmond said, looking relieved that Myra got his meaning.

Rebecca and Julien stood up and Rebecca went to Edmond and gave him a hug. While in that position she noticed the man called Hugo had the shape of a gun in his pocket where he had put his hand. "I won't forget you the next time, cousin," she laughed. "Take care and tell the rest of the family hello for us."

He felt stiff to her hug but did kiss her on her cheek. "I will do that Rebecca, I will. Have a nice flight home." Then he turned to Julien and said, "I am sorry we do not have the time to get acquainted, Julien, but thank you for helping my relatives find the grave of my Uncle Samuel."

With that he turned and walked to the back of the room with Hugo following him closely.

Outside, before they hailed a taxi, Rebecca exclaimed, "He had a gun mother. That Hugo had a gun. Is

Myra could hardly understand what Rebecca was saying. "How do you know? Did you see one?"

Yes," Rebecca tried to lower her voice, "I did when I was hugging Edmond. I was looking over Edmond's shoulder and I saw it in his pocket and his hand was holding it."

"Oh my God!" Myra said. "Did we put him in danger?"

"No, Mother. He was giving signals to leave, and we did. I think he was allowed to come here and be sure the treatment was correct since the hospitals in Hungary have so little modern x-ray equipment."

Julien suddenly rubbed his neck and said, "I left my scarf back there. I shall only be a minute." And he dashed back into the restaurant to retrieve it.

"My God, Rebecca, what is he trying to do? He for sure will do some damage."

Rebecca started towards the door too, but Myra grabbed her shoulders. Do not make matters worse, Rebecca. We may have already doomed poor Edmond."

Rebecca started crying. "I don't know what Julien is trying to do. I didn't notice a scarf on him, did you?"

Myra took her hand and started walking up the street. "We must get out of here now. Let us try to flag down a cab."

"What about Julien? He may also be in trouble."

"He may be a courier for that Hugo or the group Hugo represents. He may have asked the concierge at the hotel to send us here. Forget him Rebecca. We have to leave now."

Myra raised her hand to a cab that was coming their way and it slowed down to a stop. Before they got in, Julien was running up the street yelling, "Stop. Stop, I have something to tell you."

Before the cab door was shut, Julien hopped in and gave the driver the hotel name and address. Then he sat back and said to them, "Your friend or relative will be all right. I was not seen but observed them studying the menu. They smiled at each other and seem to be very cordial."

"Thank you Julien, but you could have done more damage than help had they seen you. We only know that Hungary is still under Communist rule," Myra said, not hiding her distrust of the young man.

"I know that Madam, but for now, we must get you two out of the country."

Rebecca looked over at Julien sitting next to Myra, "How do you know that? Who are you?"

Julien put his finger to his mouth and nodded toward the cab driver, silently warning that he might hear them. There was not a glass between the driver and passengers, but the driver did seem to be concerned only with his driving.

As the cab pulled up to the hotel, Julien stepped out and looked around like a bodyguard. After Myra paid the driver, the three of them hurried into the hotel. Everything looked so normal in the lobby as they passed through. The three of them squeezed into the small elevator and pushed the floor number of their room.

The minute Myra got off the elevator she knew something was different. There was a breeze in the hallway. As they walked toward their room they saw that the door was wide open, and the breeze coming from their room was due to an open window. The room was in shambles, clothes scattered everywhere and makeup kits turned over, and their travel luggage opened, its lining cut up.

"What in God's name?" Myra exclaimed. "Just look at this room. Was nothing left intact?"

"Oh mother, what are we going to do?" Rebecca cried as she clung to Myra's shoulders.

Julien looked around and asked Myra if their passports were safe.

"I put them and travel checks in the hotel's safe. I

always do that when we travel. Rebecca, go down and check us out of the hotel. Here is the password, and the numbers you will need to get everything of ours in the safe. Our credit card is already on file, so there should not be a problem. Do not mention the break-in to anyone, and get back here fast."

"I agree," Julien said. "And get things together ready to pack. I will be right back," he continued. "There is a luggage store a block away. I will return with some luggage. Lock the door and be careful, Rebecca." He took out a small pistol and checked the bathroom and closets. He peered out the open window, left then right, and then shut it. He nodded to them. "It is all clear. I will be back as soon as possible."

Chapter Thirty-four

It had been two years and still Myra remembered the fear she and Rebecca had felt in Vienna. Julien Zelnick had rescued them from some unknown but immediate danger. Sometimes she dreamed about Julien holding a gun and ordering them to run. Other times he was a vision of tenderness and compassion who whispered, "I am not who you think I am." Those had actually been his words as he rode with them to the airport.

Rebecca saw him in a different light. From the time Julien stepped from behind a tombstone in that Vienna cemetery, she felt he was special. His handsome face and Orthodox garb told her heart an irresistible story. In the brief time they spent together, Rebecca knew he was the man she had always dreamed of as her shining knight. Neither the gun he revealed in their hotel room, nor the bravado he displayed making sure their travel plans would go forward, but the look on his face when they said good-bye—that was the image which would never leave her memory. College kept her busy, but she never let Julien's handsome face disappear when thinking of her future.

The Star of David brooch was put in the protective

hands of a government agency which researched precious art and jewelry taken from the Jews of Europe and the world. The future for the brooch would depend on Myra, who would relinquish it permanently as and when she saw fit. She knew that a museum or antiquity agency would pay more money than she ever dreamed she would have, back when she'd purchased that tiny metal crucifix for Sister Bernadette all those Christmasses ago. But the money was not important to her. It was the curse that accompanied the brooch that Myra wanted to understand, and exorcise. Who in her ancestry would have had the power to create a curse that had apparently lasted for a century? Why had she been the one to suffer from it?

The house was quiet and felt empty with Rebecca working as a summer camp councilor in the Pocono's. Morgan had graduated with all the pomp and circumstance a Harvard degree merited. Now, he and three of his close buddies were traveling throughout Europe, experiencing the world of his time.

Matt and his growing family had bought a new home along the Pacific coast of Malibu. They were into decorating and meeting new neighbors. Life was beautiful and wonderful for Matt. Myra thought of how proud Eric and his grandfather would be of his skills as a lawyer and of his family. There was now a boy of five and twins, Abigail and Adam, one year old this past June. Michael and Myra had flown to California to celebrate the twins' first birthday, but now things were settling down. Michael had suggested they might want to move to a smaller house now that the children were out on their own. It would be not belong before Rebecca too would be independent.

Myra sat on the bed she had just made up for the day. A cool breeze from the open window across the room seems to kiss her cheeks and she smiled. Maryland had yet to experience the heat of summer. Light rain had been falling for a week now, making the lawns green and trees burst with woody smells of fruits yet to appear.

She closed her eyes and imagined she was a little girl for a second. Then a strange thing happened. She was aware that she was sitting on a lady's lap. In front of her was a white box the size of a ladies compact. The lady lifted the lid and there was the Star of David brooch. Myra reached out and touched the shinning rocks. "What are these?"

The lady answered, "They look like diamonds, but they are only glass."

"Who owns this pin?"

"You do my dear, but only when you are grown."

"Why do I have to wait to grow up?"

"Because you must learn and experience many things before you can wear this piece of jewelry. It will belong to you when it is no longer a threat to you, or no longer cursed."

Myra

Myra opened her eyes. She had not been dreaming this time. She had actually felt a memory returning, a memory she had hidden deep within her, long ago.

Then, wide-eyed this time, Myra remembered that horrible Sunday afternoon, looking out at the campus of the University of Colorado. It had been December 7th, 1941, and a sunny day for the time of the year. She had received the brooch and the note accompanying it on the day Pearl Harbor was attacked. She remembered a voice asking her if any of the diamonds had been replaced. Who was it reading the note to her? and who had told her the diamonds were glass? She remembered a fellow student living in the house because the V-12 sailors had occupied the women's dorm. What was her name? Betty? But the other person telling her they were glass, not diamonds, who was she? The larger events of that day when Pearl Harbor was bombed by Japanese warplanes had erased that moment until now. Sam had put the brooch in his safety box at the bank after they became close friends, and she was with him when he did. He'd known the jewels weren't glass. The look on his face when he first saw the brooch had been a shock of recognition.

She had to call Michael. She had to know if ever the diamonds in the brooch had been replaced. A week later, Michael had investigated her question and reported that the each diamond had been examined separately and that there was no sign that the gold around the diamonds had been disturbed. They were rare diamonds from an African mine, a mine so dangerous to the miners it had been closed in the late 1700's or early 1800's. The color and hue of the diamonds were so rare, very few were sold, and those existing today were still on display in France, Rome, and Egypt in heavily guarded security rooms, safe through the two World Wars and flurries of smaller battles. That loyal curators managed to hide them safely away was a miracle. Even the location of the mine where they were discovered had disappeared in the desert sands of time, Michael reported.

Myra knew then that eventually she would surrender the brooch so that it could take its place in history. Rebecca would never have it, or the bad luck that could be passed down with it. "It stops with me," Myra silently said, "but not until I know the full truth about this unholy Jewish brooch."

The fall winds of November rumbled around outside the house, reminding Myra how quiet the house was with Rebecca and Morgan away at their universities. Morgan was in med school, wanting to be in his father's profession. Rebecca was working for a degree in teaching English as a second language, and triple-minoring also in history and English and journalism. Myra suspected she was in touch with Julien Zelnick because on her visits home she was full of stories about Vienna and the Jewish population being restored after the war. Julien was a nice young man, but there was something Myra could not put her finger on concerning him. If he was not what we thought he was, what is he? Was he a secret service person? Rebecca had looked up his family name in the New York phone book and had found a name that might have been his family. She was too embarrassed to call, though, to find out if she was right.

Lily was now living in southern England, near the city of Exeter in Devon. She was now with a man who had encouraged her to leave the Krishnas and start a craft shop near the city. On her calls to Myra, Lily sounded as English as a born English person. She seemed to be happy at last, and the gentleman who made her happy was named Cliff. He had put her on a very strict budget, trying to instill in her the belief that life could go on without much money. It seemed to work. Myra hoped Cliff wasn't another con artist, using a faked personality as a shield or weapon. Lily's children had visited them once and according to Lily, they loved it there. One day, when they got older, Lily hoped they would join her in Devon and maybe work with her in the business.

Myra had written small articles for the local newspaper, but now she wanted to find a different field of writing. She knew that they would move to a smaller house some time next year, so maybe she could start sorting and packing items to move and to give away to local charity shops. Why wait until the last minute, she asked herself, as she settled into the chore.

It was like remembering a lifetime, going through items that had become obsolete but held so many memories. A purse Matthew had sent her from Hawaii, a pair of evening shoes that no longer went with anything she owned, and some of Michael's suits that were out of style and too snug for him now--though he still had the figure of a well built man. She started with piles of clothes, packing them in empty boxes they had saved for some reason. The shoeboxes were piled high on their old out-of-date luggage, so she would need something to step up on. She found a foot stool and brought it over to the pile. As she reached up to pull out some of the shoeboxes, a group of them tumbled down on her. She lost her balance and sprawled on the cement floor of the storeroom, but she was not hurt. Lids had flown off some of the boxes and a few were upside down.

She got up and started to collect the mess of lids and boxes and shoes. But when she reached for an old upside down box, and lifted it to get the contents back into it, she found a surprise. This shoebox didn't contain shoes, but Mr. Teddy, the beloved stuffed bear of her childhood. Rebecca had once told her that Michael had put it into a box when they moved from Cincinnati, but she'd had little idea of where to look for that box. She picked him gently and brushed his ratted fur body.

He crackled. Of course, Rebecca had said he made noises. But Myra had forgotten her plan to search him out and see what caused the crackle. Now she pushed his stomach, and sure enough there was a sound like paper being crushed. She put everything on hold and took Teddy into the kitchen. She found a sharp steak knife and laid Teddy on the island counter. "I am sorry, my most loved toy, but you must have an operation. I promise I shall sew you up again after I clean you up."

The knife sliced the brittle threads of Teddy's stomach as though it were a sword. Balls of cotton had fused together like popcorn balls and clung to each other like glue. Myra took them out and placed them on the counter. Then as she felt around to bring more of the balls to light, a piece of paper hit her hand and crackled like a witch's laugh. She withdrew it from Teddy's body and discovered an old newspaper curled around like a ball and glued at each end, as though protecting what lay within it. Very carefully, Myra split open the glued edges until at last a document fell out. She straightened out the newspaper and picked up the official document, dislodging an envelope that fell on the counter top.

She could not believe what she read on the document. It was her birth certificate, announcing her name and those of her parents, with the date and year of her birth. Myra Steinman was born in Szeged, Hungary. Strange as it seemed, her father's name had been crossed through with a pencil. What was that supposed to mean? Maybe they had spelled it wrong? Or maybe he wasn't her biological father? Her birthday, she saw, was July 16, but the year was wrong. 1922. She was older than she thought. All these years she thought she knew how old she was, but now, as though a bolt of lightening had transformed her, she was older. She was fifty-six years old whereas she had celebrated her fifty- fourth birthday last July, two years too late.

Her head began to spin and dizziness overcame her. She sat on a kitchen chair as though in a trance. She didn't hear the front door open or Michael's voice calling her name. His appearance in the kitchen didn't startle her as she stared motionless, looking out the bay windows above the kitchen sink.

"Myra! My God, darling, what is wrong?" Michael knelt besides her and shook her gently.

She turned her face to him and a sudden recognition lit her features. Michael saw the teddy bear all torn apart and spread over the island counter, "What is it Myra? What have you done?"

"I am old Michael, I am older than we thought." She held up her birth certificate and Michael took it from her. He read it and shook his head.

"It is your birth certificate darling. You found your birth certificate."

Myra nodded yes and said, "All these years Teddy held it for me. Why, Michael did they tell me I was younger than I was?" She stood up next to him and pointed to the date of her birth. "And why is my father's name scratched through?"

Michael picked up the wrinkled newspapers. It was a 1930 copy of the *New York Times* and the headlines blasted the hardships of the Great Depression.

Chapter Thirty-five

Myra's mother was Mary Goldman, daughter of Jacob and Marta. The name of her father that had been scratched through was Abraham Steinman, but when Myra examined the certificate more closely, she saw two initials faintly printed over the word "father." Michael had seen them too, and together they made out the letters, JP.

As stunned as she was, Myra finally felt as though she had been set free from the world of uncertainty she had lived in most of her life. Her mother was Mary Goldman. . . . But was her father Abraham Steinman? There were still so much she didn't know about the Star of David brooch and the curse she had heard about, or perhaps dreamed about. She struggled to remember when she had first become aware of the curse. Was it in a dream about Sam? Had Julien mentioned a curse? Had he told Rebecca? No, she mused, her memory of the curse was not that recent; it was connected with her dreams. Her spirits rose to the highest level of her soul. Now she had a direction to follow.

"Michael, I have to go back to Szeged. I have to know more about my family."

"There are political changes in the works for that country, honey. I think you should wait and see which way the wind will blow for Hungary. Besides, you and Rebecca were in danger, according to that young man Rebecca always talks about."

Myra had almost forgotten the robbery and the danger which had made Julien say they must leave immediately. But how could she wait much longer? After all, she had added two years to her life in just one afternoon.

"I have waited so long and dreamed forever of identifying my family; it is cruel to ask me to wait longer."

"I think you should wait. Hungary is still under Communist rule. What if you return and cause trouble for Sam's family? You said Edmond was a Communist now. Do you want to put him and his family in danger?"

"I said he acted as a Communist that night, but he definitely gave us the signal to leave immediately. He could be part of a conspiracy to get rid of the Russians. If he were a true Communist, he would not have warned us, would he?"

Michael was throwing his hands in the air trying to make his point to Myra when he noticed the envelope that also lay in the pile of cotton.

"What is this? he asked as he leaned over Myra,

"Ah—that fell out of Teddy too. I almost forgot it. Open it, and let us see what more we can learn."

The envelope was yellow with time and brittle too. Michael carefully opened the top of the envelope and slid out a folded piece of what use to be white paper. He flattened it on the counter. Myra stood next to him and they both read it silently.

My Dearest Niece Myra,

I cry in writing this, as soon you must leave us. I do not write well in English, so my wish is for you to understand what I must say. I hope by this time you will be older to understand why we send you with Berta's girlfriend from Szeged. She is poor like us but her husband has agreed to keep you until Berta can come for you. You must forget that horrible Jacob Singer and what he did to you. If you read this in future, we want you to know you are loved and God will be kind to you. The curse of the brooch is over for you. It was stolen in Szeged when another very bad man, Mendel Levy, killed your mother and Abraham. He later was caught, but he denied he had stolen the brooch. He was hung in the town square for the killings, but the brooch was never found.

The Graingers have said they will give you this letter when you are old enough to understand, if Berta is unable to come for you for any reason not in her control. I am your Aunt Margaret and Berta my older sister, not your grandmother. When you witness the killings your mind went blank, and Berta became like a grandmother for you. A few years later, our Papa said you must leave and come to me in Amer-

ica. I am not a good Mama so Berta stayed on until that Jacob Singer appeared and he made it difficult to have around. He is many cousins removed from us, but Berta's heart is too kind and took him in.

Berta is to find a safe place for this letter. She wants you to know about your family and your heritage too. She promised me the Graingers would know where she has hid it. My darling little girl, I hope you remember me and Papa and Berta. We do this for you because we love you so much, and we hope the curse has been lifted from Sandor Furst's evilness that cursed our beautiful great-grandmother, Miriam Singer Furst, and her descendents and her brooch. When she left, everyone suffered, especially our Grandfather Lazlo, and the word spread of the curse. People are frightened of her name so much they run. Be courageous, our lovely little image of Miriam as too of your mother.

Shalom and God be with you.

Aunt Margaret

Myra looked at Michael. "I don't remember any of this." Then she did remember her treatment with a psychiatrist who put her in a trance but stopped it suddenly, fearing Myra would be better off not remembering what had happened to her.

"Michael, do you remember that hypnotist who put me under in Denver a long time ago? Or was it Cincinnati? Oh darling, I am getting confused."

"I do remember. Why?"

"Why did he stop the treatment?"

"Sam and I were there in the room with you. You became hysterical and screamed for your grandmother. The more he tried to veer you away from her memory, the more frantic you became. He said if he continued, that locked up memory could cause a complete breakdown."

Michael took Myra in his arms and kissed her cheek. "Oh my darling little love. We are getting there now. We have names and places and as soon as Europe, and particularly Hungary, are back to what they used to be, we will travel there and search out the rest of the truth from which these aunts wanted to protect you."

Myra dug her head into Michael's shoulders. She looked up at him and said, "Michael, I am not as young as we thought. How old will I have to be to find my family or anyone who knew what happened to my parents? I was a young child when I left, way before the war. Will anyone who knew about my family still be alive in two years, or ten years? How many Jews returned to Szeged? How old would they be now? And what about their memories? I don't know if I can wait any longer, Michael."

"Listen to me Myra. You are not that much older than you thought, but two years difference explains why you knew the Hungarian language when you were there. Something came back to you. Two dining rooms scared you, and you ran into an empty house because somewhere in your unconscious was a memory of that particular house. The blood on the wood floor could have meant you witnessed your parents' murder. Don't you see darling? We can retrace what happened from here until we can go there."

"So you want to me sit around forever, not really knowing what happened to me so horrible that I forgot everything as a child?"

"I promise you Myra, as soon as it safe for you, we will return."

Michael looked at the poor Teddy, his insides sprawled all over the counter top. "What are you going to do with Teddy?"

Myra smiled and started to scoop up the rotten cotton balls. "I am going to get fresh material for his insides and wash him up before I stuff every thing back in. Who knows? Perhaps Rebecca will have a child who needs a Hungarian Teddy Bear."

Michael folded the letter, put it back into the envelope, and handed it to Myra. "Well, we are starting to uncover the mystery of your nightmares, darling. Some unseen soul has been with you all these years, and now you have a little hint of why you were given to the Graingers. But their raising you as a Catholic was unforgivable since they knew your background."

"They were kind to me. I can't hold a grudge against them for trying to help in a religious way, and maybe they thought I needed some God in my life. Now I understand why the statue of Jesus always seemed so foreign to me, though. I must have had some Jewish training as a child. Now I know I was old enough to understand my religion before I was baptized and suddenly found Jesus looking down at me so strangely."

Michael helped her clean up the fluffy mess as Myra gently put Teddy Bear in a white towel and left him on a kitchen chair until tomorrow. They held hands as they shut off the lights and went to their bedroom. They didn't hear the sigh in the night, or see poor Teddy falling onto the floor, his slight smile still on his lips.

Chapter Thirty-six

Michael and Myra found a lovely patio home in another gated community and moved during the summer of 1976, soon after finding Teddy Bear and the letter he contained in his stomach. Myra had restored Teddy to his old beautiful self. He had clean fur, new crystal eyes, and stuffing inside of his body that felt comfortable to hold and squeeze. When Rebecca saw him, she wanted to take him to her university room, but after she read the letter he'd contained, she decided that her mother should keep him close until the next generation of Jewish children were born.

At that time, Rebecca was full of information about Julien Zelnick. He was returning from Hungary for the Passover, and if his plans reached fruition, he would not be returning to Hungary. He wanted to see her, and there were some things he had to tell her. Rebecca reminded her parents that he had said he was not what they thought, so he had secrets to tell her. On the other hand, Rebecca had been very much taken with another young Jew named Isaac Spellman whom she had met at the University. He was very attentive to her and was a great help with some of her difficult studies. He was a scholar with high standards, and although they spent many hours together, he never really expressed his feelings for her. He was quiet and had a tendency towards shyness. Still, he felt more comfortable talking to Rebecca than to anyone else. If they were with other couples for a Broadway play or an opera, he became silent but polite. It was a personality Rebecca didn't understand, but she felt he really liked her. Comparing Isaac to what she remembered of Julien was like comparing night and day. Yes, she was anxious to see Julien again.

When Myra received an invitation to attend Passover with Julien's parents in New York, she was shocked. Two years after Rebecca met their son, they wanted to meet her parents. Rebecca was thrilled and begged her parents to attend as she had already committed herself to be with the Zelnicks. So it came about that the Liebermans and the Zelnicks finally met at a Seder dinner which Mrs. Zelnick cooked for them all. They were a lovely family and well educated. Julien's sisters were married, and each had a son and a daughter. His maternal grandparents were in their 80's and getting fragile, but kept up on the events in the lives of their grandchildren. Morgan too, had been invited, but he was mired in his studies and asked to be excused.

It was a month or two later that Myra and Michael finally learned from their daughter that Julien was not studying to be a rabbi. He had been recruited right out of college to join a secret organization of Holocaust descendants dedicated to finding and recovering belongings taken from wealthy Jewish families. He had been sure he had his ancestor's famous brooch in sight when he met

Rebecca and Myra in Vienna. True, he did visit his own grandfather's grave every week, and it was a coincidence that he happened to be at the cemetery the day Rebecca and her mother were looking for Sam's grave. But he also knew that the Sam Hirsch they were looking for was somehow involved in the mystery of the brooch. And although he knew where Sam's grave was, he had pretended not to know in order to find out more about them. The organization to which he belonged suspected that one day someone would come to see Samuel Herschkovitz's grave, and that would be their clue.

Of course, Rebecca had unknowingly told him about the brooch her mother owned. But he had been honest with Rebecca when he told his story on the day they met. And, Myra now learned, in spite of her mother's instructions, Rebecca had told him that he was correct, that the initials on the back of the brooch were his ancestor's trademark. But Rebecca had also told him it was in a very safe place, and that no one could get to it unless they had her mother's consent.

Myra was stunned that Rebecca had disobeyed her, but she was assured that Julien's group would not do anything to endanger her family. Through all their secret ways of learning about the objects of their searches, the organization had independently come to know where the brooch was. But they also knew that the rightful party now had it. They believed that sooner or later the Star of David Brooch would be a world-famous piece of jewelry, like the Hope Diamond, sold or donated to a major museum and kept safely for posterity. But they trusted the

Jewish family which owned it to make those decisions. They too knew of the importance of secrecy for now.

Hearing that, Myra began to wonder how Julien had known they were in trouble when they ran into Edmond Herschkovitz at the restaurant. Julien declined to tell her in order to protect those still in the organization, as blowing their cover could mean death for them. He did however, have the group's permission to send Myra copies of a letter indicating his own ancestor's grief in learning that a curse had been put on the brooch he had made as a perfect piece of jewelry for a lady who was a perfect woman. The hundred-year-old letter was written in Hebrew, but someone had added an English translation between the lines of the old script.

The Zelnick letter fascinated Myra. It increased her respect for Julien's family and softened her attitude toward him as a suitor for Rebecca. But it was too old to contain any indication of where the brooch had been hidden during the war.

Reading and rereading the letter, Myra was spun back into her deeper personal questions. The jeweler had believed the curse to be real. But how do curses work? Had Sandor Furst's curse caused her to lose out on a normal childhood, and to lose her memory? Why had she been the one to suffer when, all those years ago, it had been another person who did something horrible? Was her mother Mary also a victim of the curse? Was that reason her father's name, Abraham, had been crossed through in Aunt Margaret's letter? The letter from Aunt

Margaret hadn't mention a curse, but it did say that Myra had witnessed the murder of her parents.

The haunting image of blood on the wood floor would, she thought, mean that she was reliving that horror through her dreams. Of course, and Michael agreed, that would have been one of the causes of her memory loss.

Further questions and speculations almost overwhelmed her. Miriam Singer Furst did indeed look like her as a college coed. Rebecca had tried to have Sam's small photo of "The Lady in Black" enlarged, but the process blurred the image. Where was the painting now? If Julien's group was searching for it, too, then Julien would have known immediately that she and Rebecca were descendants of the Furst Family. The family look of the females seemed uncannily exact from generation to generation. Did that mean that she and Rebecca were to be included in curse?

Michael reminded her that the brooch was safe, that no one was wearing it, or had worn it for a long time. He tried to reassure her that no crazy curse could follow it further.

By now, Myra knew why Miriam had fled her husband and children. Both she and Rebecca had been researching the history of the Furst family. They knew that Sandor Furst had been a devious man, one whose questionable financial dealings were so farflung as to have been reported in the American press. Old *New York Times* articles Rebecca and Myra had found on microfilm in the Smith College library confirmed his shady character. They had concluded that his personal life must have been equally self-centered. If he couldn't have Miriam, they decided, then he would make her and her children suffer. Myra had wondered if her lovely ancestor ever did find happiness, but they found nothing about her in the microfilmed 1870s *New York Times* articles they examined, neither in the society pages or the obituaries. What had happened to her, Myra wondered.

And, again, where had the brooch been all during the war, since it had been with her mother at the time of her murder? Could the murderer have lied about having taken the brooch? Had he had a chance to hide it before he was caught? There was so much Myra wanted to find out; but Michael was right. She would have to wait a little longer.

———

Two years later, at Rebecca's graduation, Myra and Michael met Isaac Spellman, their daughter's favorite studying partner, a very proper though quiet and shy young man. He'd come to the graduation ceremony in Northampton, Massachusetts, then tagged along for the train ride to New York City, where the family planned to celebrate at Delmonico's Restaurant.

Julien Zelnick was by now working on Wall Street at the Stock Exchanage, learning about buying and selling, and running around like an ant with the rest of the young

men in the trade. He hadn't attended the graduation ceremony but had promised to catch up with them for the
festivities at Delmonico's as soon as he could get free. He
hadn't counted on Isaac Spellman being part of the
crowd. The Zelnick family would also be there to celebrate Rebecca's happy occasion.

On the Lieberman side, Morgan, now a medical
intern in St. Louis, flew in with his love interest, wanting
his parents to meet her. She was a lovely girl with poise
and beauty, and sincere about meeting Morgan's family.
Her name was Sarah. In the ladies' restroom, Myra and
Rebecca wondered how they could gently excuse themselves from Isaac, as he seemed to be planning to stay
with them for the rest of the day. (Michael had only
shrugged when Myra pinched his side and asked him to
think of something.) What were they to do?

The Zelnicks were wondering too, who this strange
gentleman was, and why he was thinking he was included
in their dinner plans.

Rebecca approached him privately before they
caught a taxi at the train station and told him as nicely as
she could that this was only a family affair and that she
was not the planner of the dinner. She would have to say
good-bye now, and she would talk to him later.

His face turned red with anger and he mumbled a
few cuss words. "I had hoped to make this a memorable
evening for you Myra. My parents could not come but

"Your purpose?" asked Rebecca. "I don't know what you are talking about, Isaac. I am having a memorable time tonight."

Isaac pulled a small box out of his suit pocket and held it out to Rebecca. "I was going to ask you to marry me. You are educated now and it is time for you to settle down."

Rebecca put her hands over her mouth for a minute. She could not believe this was happening. "Oh, Isaac, I had no idea you felt that way about me. You have never shown any romantic feelings."

He held out the ring box again and opened it. Michael walked over to the couple to ask what was going on, but he was stopped in his tracks seeing the ring being offered to his daughter "What is this?" he asked.

"Sir, I am asking your daughter to marry me, but she is hesitating," Isaac said to Michael.

Rebecca looked at her father and said, "Daddy, I never encouraged him. I thought we were just good friends."

"Good friends?" Isaac yelled so that the rest of the families standing nearby heard his voice. "Is that what you thought all the times we were together? In our religion, you would not have spent so much time with me if you had no feelings for me. I thought you were a Jew from a good Jewish family, and yet you don't know a thing about the rules."

Myra walked over and took Rebecca's arm. The girl was shivering and pale.

"Mom, Isaac thought I was going to marry him because of the time we spent studying together. He has a ring for me." She took a deep breath and continued, "Isaac, you make me so sad, and I do like you, but I do not love you. I could never marry you. I love another."

Both Myra and Michael stood back in shock. This was news to them—that Rebecca was in love.

Isaac stood stunned and motionless. He looked around at the crowd of Zelnicks and Liebermans watching him. "You will regret this Rebecca. You will see." And he turned around and ran down the street.

Stunned and nervous, Rebecca clung to her mother and apologized to Julien's family. During the ride to Delmonico's, sitting between her parents, she rattled on about Isaac and his misunderstanding. They did attend the operas at times and school productions of plays, but he never tried to kiss her or hold her hand. Why was he under the impression that they would marry, or that she loved him in that way?

Julien met them when they drove up to the restaurant and could hardly wait for Rebecca to get out of the car. He was surprised to see that she was in distress.

She took his hand and they walked away from the family so that she could tell him about the encounter with Isaac. Myra could see him stop and wave his hands in menacing way, but Rebecca pulled him farther down the street.

Michael suggested they go into Delmonico's and get their table. The children would join them later as soon as Julien had heard what happened.

A short time later, Julien and Rebecca did join them, and both were smiling from ear to ear. It was hard to believe that Rebecca was crying and distressed a half hour ago.

"Look everybody, I did get engaged after all. To Julien." And she leaned over and kissed him.

Julien blushed a pink color and said, "That was what this night was all about, besides rejoicing at my Rebecca's graduating in the top ten of her class. I wanted both families to be here when I asked her to be my wife. However, it seems Mr. Spellman hurried things along faster than I had planned."

Every one laughed and congratulated the couple. No one noticed the pale face of Isaac Spellman outside the window, watching, his eyes blood red with anger.

Chapter Thirty-seven

Rebecca and Julien decided that as long as they had pledged themselves to be man and wife, they would delay the nuptials a year, though they would see each other easily now that Rebecca was moving to New York. It was Morgan who surprised every one during Hanukah, announcing that he and Sarah were to be married in June, a decision they made because of Sarah's mother's wishes. Her mother, Roselyn, feared that she might die before Sarah became a wife and maybe a mother. She and her husband Isador both had heart problems. Sarah was the youngest of three children in the Rosen household and her mother, in her own foolish way, wanted to see her children settled in marriage before the parents passed away. Besides a doctor was a good catch, after all.

Julien was still learning the stock market and had signed up for extra classes to help him reach a top position on the Exchange floor. Rebecca was teaching English in a public grade school and writing a few articles for local newspapers; and Julien was just a bus ride away.

The wedding in June was fabulous in Myra's eyes as she remembered her own two weddings, both so simple yet so wonderful. She and Eric had had a Lutheran ceremony with Aunt Edna, Sam, John and Elizabeth, Diana, and a few other friends. She and Michael had married in the temple with only a few relatives and friends. It had been a marriage from which love had continued to grow over the decades. Sometimes, when she and Michael were newlyweds, Myra did feel guilty about loving him so dearly when it had been Eric who had opened her eyes to love. She still relished her memories of Eric and the few short months they had actually been together during the war. But in her dreams, Eric was not so much a lover as a complainer, and his wheel chair was always there. How could that be--when she did love him from her very soul at that time? His incapacity did not change her love for him, though that was something she had not been able to convince him of. His death by overdose made her feel guilty for a time. But she had healed, as Sam had made her face life again. Sam was a philosopher, Myra thought, but now standing there next to Michael as Morgan and Sarah said their vows and stepped on the wine glass to the 'Mazeltoff' from the audience, Myra felt she had done her best for Eric.

She looked over at Eric's son, Mathew, who had flown with his family to Chicago for this special occasion. He gave his mother a wink and smiled just like his father. Chicago was Sarah's hometown and it was only fair to have her wedding blessed by a Rabbi she had known since childhood, and by her relatives, who would not have been able to travel to St. Louis, where Morgan and Sarah both worked. Sarah's mother, Roselyn, made sure her daughter's wedding was noticed in the community. The

The surprise was that Lily and her "mate," as she called Cliff, also showed up. Lily was as slender as her mother, but her hair had turned dark with patches of gray in it, the color of old Clancy's hair, Myra thought in silence. Cliff was indeed a gentleman in his manners and grace of his body—tall, with neatly cut hair and an elegant suit and tie. Lily had on a dress which Myra recognized, to her delight. Of course, it was Diana's. It was the dress Myra had borrowed and worn to the Boulderado hotel back in Boulder, Colorado, to her first lunch with Sam.

"My God," Myra thought. "It is still wearable."

Lily had told her earlier that she only wore trousers, the English word for pants, but Cliff would not let her today. He was conscious of his appearance and he differed from Lily on that subject. However, he once told Myra, "Opposites do attract, don't they?" He would not attend the wedding with Lily if she did not wear a dress. She found it in an old trunk Diana's parents had left for her, and it fit perfectly. So there she was, sitting proudly behind them, once in a while rubbing Myra's neck. It was nice to see all the children together again. It was like the icing on the cake. The reception was as grand as a reception could be. The Rosens had gone all out for their last child's wedding. Mr. Rosen owned a clothing store and evidently felt he could afford it.

The Jewish songs and dances roared through the air, while the men hauled Morgan up on their shoulders and twirled him around and around. Sarah, too, was lifted up on shoulders and bobbed up and down as the music got faster and faster. Then, suddenly, the sound of a gun flew through the crowd and everything stopped short. An unbelievable event was happening. Myra caught a glimpse of movement from the drapes next to the main door, and saw a figure dressed in black, a skullcap on his head. The shooter darted out the door and out of the hall.

The shocked crowd was immobile for a minute and then Morgan was kneeling over the person who had been shot, giving him first aid. Then a group of furious men ran out after the shooter. The victim was a young man dancing next to Julien. An ambulance was called and the men returned from the chase, not having caught the villain. Luckily the young man only suffered a flesh wound on his shoulder. Had the bullet been higher in range, it would have hit Julien in the head. The police came and questions were asked, reports taken, as the bride's mother grew hysterical. The bridal meal had been eaten before the dancing, so the police asked everyone to leave their names and addresses and exit the building. They would be contacted later as to what they might have seen.

Later, Myra and Michael gathered the family into their suite at the Ritz Carleton. The grandchildren old enough to know what had happened were wide-eyed and full of questions for their parents. No one had seen the gunman, but Myra had seen the outline of his body. He wore a skullcap but his face was in the shadows of the curtain. Michael could not tell the police who might be upset with Morgan or Sarah enough to hurt their wedding day.

It ruined the wedding festivities for Sarah and her mother, but Morgan took it in stride as evidence that there were crazies in the world. It was determined that Sarah or Morgan had no serious enemies to ruin their wedding. There was no sign or clue as to who could have done such a dastardly thing in a room with children present. It was believed that some thug off the street had problems with the Jewish religion and had committed an anti-Semetic hate crime. Three days later, Myra and Michael flew home. The parting of the family was sad since they seldom got together. Morgan and Sarah had left for their honeymoon in Italy. They were going to Verona for the operas as Sarah was an opera lover and the operas were to be performed in one of the oldest ancient arenas. Morgan reassured Sarah that everything was going to be all right.

Mathew hugged his mother and made her promise to call him if there was any more trouble like that. He had been told of Rebecca's problem with Isaac but thought Isaac unlikely to be the shooter since the wedding was in Chicago instead of New York, and Rebecca was nowhere near the dancer when the shot rang out. Lily and Cliff flew to Cleveland, rented a car, and visited her children. It had been over a year and their letters to her talked of their growth and achievements. She desperately wanted to see them. Rebecca decided to fly home to Maryland with her parents, while Julien headed back to New York to his classes. It was a sad parting for them but they had decided after the shooting that they would move into together when she returned.

It was a decision that Myra approved for the safety of both of them, but morally she felt it was not right. However, they were adults now--and who was she to tell them "living in sin" would not be right?

The Italian honeymoon and Morgan's closeness calmed Sarah. Meanwhile, the police in Chicago had no clue as to who the shooter could be, so they put the case on hold for further investigation.

———

Rebecca as a budding journalist had access to the archives of the *New York Times,* and even a small desk in the huge *Times* building. On her breaks from teaching and writing, she scoured through old papers, trying to discover more about her family. (It was more pleasant to use the archives in the newspaper's morgue than it had been to read her college's microfilmed copies.) She focused on the 1930 issues. What had happened to her mother before the age of six or eight, as she would have to have been at that time?

One snowy night in December, just a week before Chanukah, Rebecca was doing an article on early days in New York. She had to refer to old editions of the *Times,* so she made her usual trip to the paper's basement archives. As she reached up to pull a folder from the highest shelf of a bookcase, another folder fell from the second shelf. She looked around to see whether someone was playing a trick on her from the other side of the book-case, but she was alone. She picked up the folder and a few pages dropped back down to the floor. As she bent to get the loose pages, she spotted a 1932 obituary section face-up. Rebecca picked it up and put it on a little desk used by reporters doing research. She scanned the articles and then spotted a headline about a woman killed by a distant cousin.

Margaret Goldman, a sister of the deceased Mrs. Bertha Goldman, had alerted the police that the killer was Jacob Singer. Miss Goldman said that Mr. Singer was a distant cousin, and that he became angry with Bertha Goldman when she asked him to move out of her apart-ment. He had beaten her unmercifully until she was dead. Mrs. Goldman was 39 years old. Mr. Singer was picked up in a bar near the docks. If found guilty, he will be fa-cing execution.

Rebecca could not believe her eyes. It was now clear why her mother had been forgotten in the mountains of Colorado. Then she wondered why Aunt Margaret hadn't come for her niece. Working like one possessed, Rebecca turned to other obituary columns, scanning day after day, month after month: 1932, 1933. The answer came several hours and two thick folders later, in the 1934 obituaries archive. Margaret Goldman's death, like her sister's, had made headlines. She was found shot to death in the house of a gang lord, Mr. De Bellio. She was 27. Evidence of a gang crime was discovered when Mr. De Bellio' s body was found in his car next to the railroad tracks in a New Jersey hot spot. It was thought to be a war over territories, and De Bellio suspected his girl friend of several years, Miss Margaret Goldman, of being a spy for his enemies. An informer said De Bellio shot Miss Goldman and arranged a meeting with the Don of the encroaching gang, planning to do away with the boss. However, Mr. De Bellio' s own men turned on him. Seven bullet holes were found on Mr. De Bellio' s body. The article went on to say that both sisters had met with untimely deaths due to the people they knew. Both had immigrated to the United States from Hungary. Bertha's killer had been executed just a month before her sister was murdered. Neighbors of the two women told of a child who had come to New York with Mrs. Bertha Goldman. Investigators could find no trace of a child, and the case of the missing little girl was closed.

Rebecca wiped a tear from her eyes, trying to hold back her emotions. Now she had the answer for her mother. She noticed both sisters were buried in the Jewish Cemetery in the Bronx. She placed the papers back in the folder and marked it with her black pen with the words "Aunt" and "Grandmother." She forgot about her own article as she picked up her notebook and went up stairs to her desk where only a few reporters and cleaning people were moving about. She left a note on the desk for the features editor saying she had an emergency and had to leave without finishing her assigned piece. Deadline or no deadline, the story would have to wait.

Chapter Thirty-eight

Myra heard Rebecca's news with an uncertain disbelief, and then with an indescribable emotion. Realizing that she was the lost little girl nobody knew about made her angry with the Graingers for not telling her who she was and where she had come from. Why? What were they hiding from her? What had caused her amnesia? Had they told her that her grandma had been murdered? Was that the cause of her memory loss? Her anger lessened as she contemplated possible answers to such questions. She struggled to remember more. What was the first thing she remembered about Gerta and Carl? She had to remember, even if she had to go back and be hypnotized again. What had they told her years ago when the hypnotist stopped her treatment? That she had become hysterical and screamed for her grandmother? The doctor feared he would uncover something in her past that would sink her into a deeper unconsciousness? She remembered Sam telling her to be patient. It would all come out in the end. What end did he mean? Rebecca's information meant that Myra had a place in the world; no more an abandoned child, she was someone born in Hungary, to someone who had loved her.

Could the souls of her dead family help her with the nightmares? The lady with the black hair she

dreamed of for so many years and always tried to catch--
she might have been a sign. The familiar scenery in
Szeged, Hungary, was probably a memory trying to come
to light for her. Her confinement for a while in the mental institution had helped her to realize that the dreams
and voices were from the past; this had helped her to heal
and return to life in the present. The main question now
was why? She knew she would not rest until she understood everything. Her Mother was Mary Goldman. The
person she'd called "Grandma" was her aunt, Bertha Goldman, and she had known her Aunt Margaret, too, in New
York. Aunt Margaret's letter said she had witnessed her
parents' death. That would have been too much for a
small child to understand. How old was she when they
came to New York? Wouldn't she have been old enough
to remember what had happened in Szeged? What else
had happened there, to turn her mind blank? She decided
that Sam was right. Answers will come out in the end,
but again, what end? She was getting older. Her children
were adults now and Michael was determining to retire
next year. What is the end?

Her dreams returned after Rebecca sent a copy of
the articles she had found in the newspaper's morgue.
The dreams were different now; they'd aged as she had
aged. There was a room white as snow and doctors looking her over and shaking their heads. Someone's hand
patted her arm but when she turned her head in that direction it was dirty small man with blood shot eyes and a
terrible breathe. He smiled and two of his front teeth
were missing. Myra screamed and woke in Michael's
arms.

"What is darling? What is happening to you again?"

"The dreams, Michael. They are coming back. A memory I am sure, but a strange one. A white room with doctors and a horrible man with missing teeth and blood shot eyes."

"Your Aunt Margaret said you had witnessed the murder of your parents. Do you think that memory is coming back and you see the man who was the murderer?"

"I don't know." Myra looked at her husband and regretted that she had caused him so much trouble in their life together. But she knew she would have to discover the truth before she could be the wife she wanted to be.

"Maybe I should try to be hypnotized again?" she asked, wondering if he would let her.

"Of course, darling, if is what you want. I can ask around and find a reputable doctor who might be able to help you."

"Thank you darling. I am sorry I am such a pill for you," Myra said, kissing him on the cheek.

"Hey, if I didn't have you I would not feel like I'd had a full cup of happiness all these years. No one said life was going to be sunshine and roses forever, did they? We deal with what we have using the resources we are lucky enough to have. I love you, my darling. Now go back to sleep and dream of fields of clover and white clouds drifting in a clear blue sky."

The following weeks and months were all about Rebecca and her planned wedding to Julien. It was to be a grand affair, and Myra was happy to think of the family all together again. Even Lilly and Cliff planned on coming and bringing her children too. It was to seal Myra's victory over whatever traumas her life had held. Her dreams came and went, and her memories flashed here or there. She had learned a long time ago to ignore them most of the time. Besides, she knew what she needed to know for now: her aunts had sent her off with the Graingers to protect her. There were puzzles still, but their solution could wait. This was Rebecca's time. Still, the religious question sometimes nagged her. Why did the Graingers have her baptized Catholic? Surely that was not part of the care Gerta had promised her old friend, Berta.

In the meantime, the Star of David brooch was safely hidden while Myra tried to decide whether to sell it to a museum, or to give it to Rebecca. She did worry about passing the curse on to her daughter, though. Only foolish beliefs, Myra would tell herself, not wanting to think that a curse had ever affected her, or could harm the girl.

It was a beautiful summer day in June 1979. A perfect day for Rebecca and Julien's wedding. The shopping and arrangements were done. Many months of planning the food, the flowers, and the European honeymoon were finally winding down. Now only the main event was left.

Myra had never seen Michael so happy. He was so proud of his daughter and her choice of a husband. True to her word, Lily and Cliff and the children were in attendance, as were Mathew and his almost grown children. Myra could not think of a more perfect day where everything was going as planned. She felt happier than she had ever felt. If there were dark clouds in her memories, she had erased them from her thoughts. How lucky she had been. Her children and Michael had become her life completely. It didn't matter what had happened in the past. This was today and she was happy. Michael, too, noticed the radiance coming from his wife. How lucky he had found her, and what a wonderful life they have had. She was extraordinarily beautiful today with that shining light in her eyes and graceful walk of her body. She could be a bride again. Age had yet to find a place for wrinkles or aches and pains in her body. How could God grant him such a rich life with a beautiful wife and children? He would give a nice bonus to the Temple of Beth El Hebrew Congregation in Falls Church, Virginia after the ceremony. It was the oldest Jewish congregation in the area, the one they had attended since moving to Maryland. Michael had reserved hotel rooms at the Fairview Park Marriott for the out-of-town guests. Everything was ready for Rebecca and Julien. The hotel was also hosting their bridal dinner after the wedding, and what more could be done? Michael was checking his mental list, trying to insure he had done everything the father of a bride should do.

The Rabbi did a beautiful service and Rebecca was exquisite. Her long hair was pulled back and the ringlets hung down her back in soft curls caressing her gown. Her long white veil cascaded from the top of her head, flowing around her gown like sheer woven air. Her eyes sparkled as she kissed her mother and father after they walked her down the aisle. Julien looked at her as though he were dreaming. He smiled as the Rabbi took Rebecca's hand to help her up to his level. It felt magical to Myra and she knew Julien would take good care of her little girl. Then as the ceremony went on, Myra recalled a few weeks ago when Julien had asked to speak to her alone.

Michael had been at the hospital on an emergency call and Rebecca was not available working at the newspaper. It wasn't a long ride from New York, and Julien would return that afternoon. Myra had fixed a nice lunch for them on the patio that looked out on a lush green lawn that went down to their small lake.

Julien seemed to be nervous at first, but finally he told her things she had wanted to know for a long time. "I just wanted you to know that I have received word about your relative Edmond Herschkovitz."

It startled Myra for a minute. Then she asked Julien to go on. "There was a secret group of Freedom Fighters who infiltrated the Communist Party. They were bound to have freedom for Hungary. I was recruited out of college after I went to Vienna to visit with my grandfather. My father felt it was our duty to help where we could. I pretended to be studying to become a Rabbi, when all along I wanted to get into the world of finance. A man called Janos Peto formed the Freedom Fighters. He is not Jewish, but it is said that he once loved a Jewish girl who was already married. Your Samuel's relative was part of the outside circle, having never joined the Communist Party but serving them in medical cases. He was to report any suspicious activity against the Freedom Fighters in any of the homes he visited or among the people he nursed."

Myra could not understand exactly what Julien was getting at until he said, "Edmond Herschkovitz and his family escaped a few month ago to Vienna. His father had died a few years after his brother Samuel." Julien drank his lemonade and cleared his throat again. "Then somehow the Communists learned about the brooch and how valuable it had become. They wanted help in finding it, and they approached me. They knew my background as a descendent of its maker, so I was like a gift to them. They didn't threaten me but they did bribe me. The head of the Freedom Fighters told me to agree, so I did, and became a double agent."

Myra remembered Edmond's look when he saw them in the restaurant and motioned with his eyes for them to leave. "So, Edmond was warning us," she said.

"Yes, and I knew the signals since I had worked with him when I visited Budapest. I knew I had to get you and Rebecca away from there fast because the man with Edmond most likely had spies in the place before he would let Edmond enter. You see, Edmond was becoming unreliable to them. Although he was thought to be the best doctor in Hungary, he wasn't turning anyone in for unusual activities, which made the comrades suspicious. He had to make plans for escape with his family."

"It is wonderful that they made it to Vienna, Julien, but why are you telling me this now?"

"Rebecca wanted me to clear things up for you. I had told you when you left Vienna that I was not what I seemed to be. Now that we are to become family, I wanted you to know the truth. I am sure you must have thought after we had dinner together that I was a spy, or that since the Star of David brooch was made my ancestor, I wanted to get it back."

"I have to admit the look on your face when Rebecca told you about the brooch was very telling. It scared me to death. I had no idea of its value until then, nor that foreign countries might want it." She patted his hand and smiled at him, "I am so happy that you did tell me, as now I know you are perfect for our Rebecca."

Michael nudged Myra out of her thoughts and pointed to a pair of their grandchildren. They had the giggles and their parents were trying to hush them. It was Mathew's youngest two who were not familiar with Jewish ceremonies.

They made a lovely couple. Rebecca with her dark curly hair and Julien with curly red hair gave Myra hope that their children might be red heads. Then the nonsense about the curse of the Star of David would not enter into their lives.

The hotel dining room was decorated in Rebecca's colors of red and white , with roses of the same colors. The bridesmaids were in white silk dresses trimmed in red, with bouquets of red and white roses. Myra remembered a time when snow white tablecloths and sterling silverware would have given her a panic attack, but now she could only feel happiness. The Temple staff had been strict about seeing the invitations of every person attending the wedding, as Michael wanted to be sure there would be no incident like the one which marred Morgan and Sarah's wedding. He felt foolish arranging that with the Temple staff, but he knew Myra would be more comfortable if she felt secure for the wedding.

He had never seen her so happy and beautiful. Their road had at times been bumpy, but now at last he was looking forward to retirement next year, and every indication was that they were going to have wonderful life. They could go to all the operas and New York plays with lots of traveling to visit the kids scattered all over. There was so much of the world he wanted to see.

Myra was busy greeting the guests at each table and making sure all the food was to their liking. Cameras were snapping and the paid photographer was mingling in the crowd to take pictures for the newlyweds' scrapbook. Mathew' oldest son was snapping away with a small camera and bumped into Myra a few times. He always stopped to kiss her cheek and say, "Hi, Grandma. Having a good time?"

Myra

There were a few faces in the crowd that were familiar to Myra yet she couldn't place them. One old man with a head of gray hair seem to be alone. She asked Julien's mother if she knew him, but the groom's mother didn't. She did think he was a friend of Julien's, maybe from Europe as he did have lots of friends there. That caused Myra to think that Julien's mother had no idea what Julien had been doing over there besides studying to be a rabbi. Her name was Golda and she was a quiet little lady, but outside of her family, she did not have a clue about the world around her. In contrast, Julien's father was the encyclopedia of anything or anyone you would like to know about. He was aware that the world around him needed his attention. Julien's mother must have learned early in their life together how to shut out his worldly conversations by nodding yes or no without paying much attention to what he meant. One learned quickly not to engage him in a conversation, which he could turn into a lecture.

This was the epitome of happiness, Myra thought. Her children were beautiful and had had wonderful childhoods. They had the lives they chose and so far, they all seemed to be happily married. Maybe because Myra had an unusual childhood she had made sure her children would never feel abandoned or not loved. What she knew now about her childhood would be sufficient. She could stop searching. Once in a while, though, she looked over at the old gray haired man and felt she knew him. But where would that have been? He watched her too as though he knew her. Today was most likely the happiest day in her life, though, so Myra was not going into memories. She was looking to the future. Michael was retiring next year. They had plans to travel to Italy since Morgan and Sarah had been overjoyed about the operas they saw there on their honeymoon.

Then too, Myra wanted to visit the Vatican to understand what she had been taught about Catholicism. Part of her still hung on to Catholic beliefs. She would always remember the silence of the prayers at St. Catherine's and the stories of Jesus Christ. She now believed that he did live, and that because he dared to preach the teachings of God, they killed him. Not the Jews as stated in the bible, but the Romans who egged on the Jews, most likely with threats, to call for the bloody crucifixion. They could not have believed him to be the Son of God, she thought. He was a brave man, who brought God to the world, and for that he should be honored. Myra thought of herself as somehow like the Romans. She didn't listen to Jesus because she feared his statue as a child. The Romans didn't listen because they feared the end of the many gods they worshiped, and they feared a new way of living. Now, she could see very little difference between the Catholics and Jews. Cantors and priests both sang in the name of God. The holy wafer of communion tasted like the matzo bread of the Jews. No salt was in either product. So why, she asked herself, were they on different roads reaching out to God who created all humans? She'd ask the Pope himself, if she got the chance.

Michael grabbed her waist and whirled her around in a dance along with all the other guests who had decided to kick up their heels. The music floated through

Myra

Myra's body and she felt like a young girl might feel,
though she wasn't that young. She was just happy, and
she moved to the tunes, then reached up to kiss Michael.
His eyes were bright and happy. And then his face turned
to horror. His white shirt and tux was turning red as he
leaned towards Myra and fell at her feet. Michael had
been shot.

Chapter Thirty-nine

When did the screaming stop? Myra had knelt down and caressed Michael's head in her lap. It is a dream, isn't it? This could not be happening. The screams and the sound of feet rushing to her couldn't be real. ... But it was. Mathew knelt besides his mother and began telling Michael to hold on. An ambulance was being dispatched and the police were on the way. In the distance of the reception hall, they could hear a voice screaming out.

"I love you, Rebecca, and if I can't have you, no one can." Then the sound of broken glass and more screaming and shuffling feet, and someone saying, "Oh my God, he tried to kill Rebecca, and Michael danced in front of her."

Police arrived on the scene quickly and found Isaac Spellman standing in the entrance hall. A few witnesses yelled that he had killed the bride's father and tried to kill the bride. As Isaac raised his gun once again to aim at Rebecca, who stood facing him with wide eyes and an incredulous look, a policeman shot him. Isaac's body slumped to the floor, and some one grabbed one of the white tablecloths to shroud it until his body could be taken to the morgue.

Myra

Myra heard and saw no more as she slumped onto the floor besides Michael. When she next opened her eyes, she was in an ambulance and a nurse was administering an IV in her arm. "You were lucky, dear. The bullet only grazed your shoulder." It was then that the memory of Gerta and Carl came rushing back to her. A white room--and a nurse stood over her. She was shaking and frightened until the face of Gerta leaned over her and said, "It is all right my dear. We will take you home now." She closed her eyes again, feeling in a peaceful place with Gerta and Carl.

———

Myra was sitting surrounded by her children and grandchildren as Michael's coffin of white ivory, with the gold Star of David at its center, was lowered into the grave. She had fought the traditions of Jewish funeral rites and would not let Michael be buried in a wooden coffin, even though the Rabbi had explained, "Dust to dust my dear." She did permit holes to be drilled in the coffin so that Michael's body would be in contact with the earth. She didn't permit Michael's body to be surrounded by the six people called *shomerim* who customarily stayed with a corpse until it was buried. She wanted to wait for Michael's few relatives to arrive, so again, he was not buried as soon after death as the Torah recommended.

She was too numb with grief to think about the delusional Isaac. Why had this happened again? The man who loved her deeply and who protected her in all their years together was gone. Who was going to comfort her as Michael had done? Who would make sense of all the nonsense of her dreams? But then other thoughts took over. She was only thinking of herself when it was Michael who would not live to see his future. He was cut out of all the futures he and Myra had planned to enjoy. They thought they would grow old together and laugh about life's ups and downs. He wanted so much to be part of their life. "Oh God," she screamed in silence, "Why Michael? Why not me? Why again must I face the tragedy of loss and love? Why was Michael the one to lose his dreams and hopes?"

She looked over at Rebecca who was sobbing loudly in Julien's arms. "My poor darling," Myra thought. "She will never forgive herself for Isaac."

Rebecca was talking between bouts of crying and sniffling, "I only felt sorry for him. He was so alone and I thought he needed a friend. So I befriended him and he opened up his spirit." After a spell of shuddering, Rebecca continued: "He was deeply religious. He taught me more about being Jewish that I had ever known. But he was strict." She broke down again. "So, I just listened to him and hoped one day he would find a nice Jewish girl to marry." It was a few minutes before she could go on. "I never once gave him the idea that I would be the girl he wanted. I talked about Julien all the time, so he must have known I was in love." Her look was a plea for understanding. "We never held hands or touched each other in any way at the plays or operas we attended. It was just a friendship."

Myra

The Rabbi took a shovel from a cemetery worker and picked up some dirt from the hole Michael would now lie in. He shoveled the dirt on top of the casket and then handed the shovel to Myra. She stood up with the help of Morgan sitting besides her. She slowly took the shovel and scooped up more dirt and threw it on the casket. Then Morgan and the rest of the family did the same until the casket was no longer visible. Now the *shiv'ah* would begin and last for seven days. They were driven back to the home Myra and Michel had shared with love. All its mirrors were covered with black cloths. Pictures were taken down and curtains closed. Members of the Temple served the symbolic *se'udat havraa'ah*, a meal of condolence. It was a traditional meal of eggs and bread. The *shiv'ah* would last for seven days though Myra was not sure she would last that long. Morgan would perform the *avelut*, reciting the mourner's Kaddish every day for a year. He would also recite the mourner's prayer, ("May he remember ...") in a synagogue or at home at the end of the year. *Yahrzeit* candles would then be lit. It was going to be a year of sorrow for Myra and the children.

When the *shiv'ah* ended and visitors were allowed to comfort the family, many members of the Temple came to Myra. The children were now free to go back to their homes, and she felt they should. Life had to go on. Rebecca wanted to stay with her mother for a while. Julien didn't want to leave her, but he understood her reasons.

Myra really didn't know many of the members well but she accepted their condolences with grace. At the end of the week things quieted down and very few people came to pay their respects. One afternoon Myra and Rebecca, who was still blaming herself for being kind to Isaac, were having cool drinks and cookies by the large window looking out on the patio and the lake below. When the doorbell rang, Myra dreaded the intrusion. She was tired of greeting people she hardly knew. Tomorrow, she would contact the caretaker of the gated community and have him close the gates he had graciously left open for the mourners. Rebecca didn't move to answer the door, so Myra, knowing that her daughter was as tired of people as she was, got up and walked into the front hallway. She opened the double doors to the front patio, and there stood the old gray haired man she thought she had seen at the wedding and reception. While she was still trying to place him as he stood there with his hat in his hand, he spoke.

"I am sorry to bother you, my dear, but I have come to offer help if I can. May I come in?"

Myra stepped back and motioned for him to enter. She turned and walked to the sunroom, offering him a cool drink and some cookies. He said that would be fine if it wasn't a bother to her. Rebecca was still watching the ducks on the lake and sat as silently as she had been when Myra went to answer the door.

"This is my daughter Rebecca," Myra said as she pulled out a chair for him to sit on. "Rebecca turned her head a little and said, "Hello."

"What is your name?" Myra asked as she poured

lemonade into a glass. "I had no idea how many people at the Temple knew us because I knew very few of them."

"Oh, I am not from the Temple," the man said. "I am Janos Peto from Hungary."

Myra dropped the glass and it shattered on the floor. Rebecca turned in her chair and gasped. "Mother, it is the man Julien told us about. He is the founder of the Hungarian Freedom fighters."

Janos was surprised by what Rebecca said. He stood up and said, "I am sorry, my dear ladies. I didn't mean to frighten you." He looked at Rebecca and shook his head. "No, my darling little girl, I am not in that capacity any more, and Julien should never have said I was."

Myra stared at him, and then like a flash of lightning, she remembered him.

"You carried me out of the house, didn't you?"

Rebecca remembered him too, "Of course, you carried mother from the house where she became ill in Szeged. I remember you too."

"No, Rebecca. Not that time," Myra told her. "He picked me up from the bloody floor where my parents were murdered. I was only a child," she said to Janos, "and you told me to forget what I had just seen."

Janos bent over to pick up some of the broken glass but Myra stopped him. "No, leave it be. I will get to it later. Please sit and tell me what you know about me."

He did as he was told, though he looked as pale as his gray hair. "It is a long story, my dear. You might not like what I could tell you."

Rebecca spoke up, "Listen Mr. Peto, my mother has a lived most of her life in the darkness of her past. Why would you think she would not like to know?"

"Rebecca, please. Do not be cruel. I am sure Mr. Peto would not be here if he had not planned to tell me. Right?" Myra said, looking at him.

"I wasn't sure if I should open old wounds, my dear girl. It is so soon after your terrible loss," Janos replied. "But maybe it is time that I raise the quilted curtain of time and let you see the light you came from."

Chapter Forty

"I guess I should start at the beginning long before you were born, Myra." Janos began to tell Myra what he knew of her ancestors, beginning with a wealthy merchant from Szeged, Sandor Furst, who had witnessed the deaths of two wives and wanted a much younger wife this time.

"On a buying trip to Gyula, Hungary, Sandor saw a very beautiful young girl. She was Miriam Singer, daughter of a poor farmer's family. Her parents, Abraham and Rosza, had raised her to be a devout Jew. She was their only daughter though they had four older sons. They had hoped she would attract a rich husband and have a life different from their dreary existences. Miriam was only sixteen, with long black curly hair and skin as fair as an angel's. Sandor could not take his eyes off her. He sent a servant to inquire about the beautiful girl selling apples from a small cart connected to a skin-and-bones horse."

"How do you know such details?" Myra asked Janos

"Miriam had a brother, Simon, two years older than she, who became a famous writer. He and Miriam were very close. Whenever he could, he would accompany her to watch as she sold the products of the family's farm. As an adult, he wrote extensively about Miriam and her fate. And I found some of his early letters among some old records."

Then Janos started his tale again. "Lust for the girl led Sandor Furst to bargain with her parents for Miriam's hand in marriage. He would build them a stronger farmhouse and give them four more cows and two pigs and two goats. They only had two milk cows and one skinny horse along with ten chickens. The vegetables and fruit they grew barely kept them from starving.

"Miriam's mother did not like Sandor, but her father, looking at his fat belly and face, decided that Miriam would be a wealthy widow in a few years. It was hard on her parents to agree to the marriage, but Sandor eventually convinced them that Miriam Singer should marry him.

"Simon felt sad for his little sister as he heard her cry at night. She had told him that she loved Arpad Tibor; she said that to marry Sandor Furst would be the death of her. Arpad was as poor as the Singers. He knew Miriam would have a life of poverty if she chose him, but at least she would be happy. Still, parents' words were law to the girl. She married Sandor in Gyula on a wet, stormy day, though she whispered to her brother Simon, "See? The storm is God's warning that this marriage should not take place."

"Sandor insisted they leave right after the wedding as he longed for his comfortable bed in order to make love to this delicate little wife.

"Sandor was so pleased with his young wife that he had a jeweler named Katz, famous throughout Hungary for his beautiful designs, make a brooch for Miriam. Every aspect of the brooch had to be the best quality--the silver, the diamonds, even the clips which held it tight on Miriam's dresses. A few months after giving Miriam the brooch, Sandor insisted on hiring the best portrait artist in the region to paint his lovely wife. In Lazlo Mednyansky's masterpiece, "The Lady in Black," Miriam is wearing a black silk dress and her exquisite brooch." The portrait became well known. Museums in Budapest, Vienna, and even Paris borrowed it to show in their galleries.

"The years passed, and Miriam's father and mother died with Sandor still alive and getting angry more often. If Miriam even spoke with a man, even one of Sandor's relatives, he might hit her. She gave him three sons--Sandor Jr., Laszlo, and Jacob, the youngest. It was Laszlo that Miriam felt closest to, and proudest of. Young Sandor and Jacob were duplicates of their father. They were quick to anger, impulsive, and arrogant.

"The wars between European countries created difficulties for the Furst family, as it did for all Hungarian Jews. New borders were established and some Jewish lands were taken over. It seemed more important than ever to keep the Jewish community together.

"When Miriam was in her early forties, she decided she could no longer take the beatings and beratings of

Sandor. Their sons were grown, and Laszlo had married a lovely girl, Berta Gottlieb, from a good family. He was happy, which made Miriam feel free to leave her husband.

"She wrote her brother Simon a farewell letter, explaining how she had met Arpad Tibor one day at a market in Budapest. Arpad had never married and the bond between them was as strong as it had been twenty-five years ago. She was packing her bag and would be gone by the time he received the letter. She wrote that if there was truly an understanding and forgiving God, he would not punish her further, given the miserable life she had lived with Sandor. She signed it *"L'Chaim,* To Life." Miriam and Arpad were never seen again.

"Soon after Simon received that letter, he got another letter from Laszlo. His mother's leaving had devastated him, he said, but the one thing his brothers would never have was her Star of David brooch. Miriam had given it to him the last time he saw her. It was a few months later that Sandor swore in front the rabbi and congregation that he was cursing everything about Miriam. In front of the Lord in a very high angry voice, he solemnly swore that whosoever inherited the wonderful diamond brooch he'd given her would be especially cursed with bad luck, bad love and poverty. He did not know then that the brooch was with Lazlo, but according to Simon, it wouldn't have mattered. He cursed everything about Miriam, all of her descendents, which included his own sons as well as any children she and Arpad might have. Sandor swore in front of God so loud that surely his voice hit the heavens. His curse became legendary among the Jews of Hungary with some of them believing that God had granted him this cruelty because over the years Sandor had poured money into the temple's coffers."

Myra could not believe what Janos had just told her. Rebecca stared straight into the eyes of Janos and said, "Are you telling us that this is the curse we have heard about? My mother's dreams are related to a silly old Jew's curse?"

Myra stopped her. "So I'm a descendent of this Sandor person and cursed by him?"

Janos looked down at his hands and then with tears in his eyes he said, "This is your family, Myra. Sandor and Miriam are your ancestors. You are almost an identical vision of your great-grandmother."

Rebecca spoke up, "That is why Matt's dad was so shocked during the war to find that portrait. It was Miriam."

"I don't understand." Myra said, "How did I end up with the Star of David?"

"I sent it to you, my dear. The war in Europe was going to get worse. I knew a little of its worth; it would be a gold mine for anyone who would melt down the star and take out the jewels. I knew it belonged to you, and I thought if anyone could break its horrible curse, you could. You wouldn't know its history, and you might need money."

"You were Yvette Levy?" Myra asked, her eyes wide in disbelief.

"No, Yvette was part of our underground group in fighting for Hungary. She was an American and with her ability to travel between borders, she supplied us with money and arms and vital, unique information. She was with the movement from 1930 until she died."

Jonas paused, then said, "Yvette was caught by the Germans during the war, and although she was an American, they hung her. Because her grandparents were from Germany, she was considered a traitor as well as a spy."

Rebecca shook her head. "I don't understand. How did you get the brooch?"

"Myra?" Janos said, "Do you remember your parents, now that you seem to remember their murder?'

"I only remember my mother's face looking at me. The blood on the wooden floor was, I thought, a dream. Lately, I am beginning to remember more. Your face was often in my dreams, and I thought you were familiar when I saw you in Szeged."

"Ah yes, I remember how shocked I was, and everyone in the room, when you spoke broken Hungarian. If your husband had not come to fetch you, you might have blown my cover."

Myra shook her head. "It wasn't my husband that day. It was Dr. Edmond Herschkovitz, the nephew of my mentor Sam Herschkovitz, who almost dragged me out of the store."

"Of course. Dr. Edmond. He was one of our compatriots. I had forgotten how lucky I felt when he intercepted you. The store was full of Russian comrades who hardly understood the Hungarian language. Had you spoken in English a few of them would have understood."

Rebecca moved her chair closer to Janos. "How did you find mother, and where did you get the brooch?"

Janos smiled at her. "Except for a few years, I always knew where your mother was, though I could never tell her the truth. When she was old enough, I sent the brooch. Yvette wrote the letter, and in case it fell into the wrong hands, she wrote your mother that she was *returning* the brooch, making it seem to be a copy, something a college girl might own, instead of the real thing. Then she said some of the *diamonds* had been replaced, so that your mother would not think of the piece as merely costume jewelry."

"What was the purpose of that?" Rebecca asked

"Those of us who knew the value of the brooch didn't want it to fall into enemy hands. Also, your mother was not important to the Communist movement. If they had followed Yvette and found the brooch before she had a chance to send it, "Myra Grainger" would still have been unimportant. They would not or could not have checked out her past.

"You knew where I was? Why was I never told?" Myra asked

"My dear, your Aunt Margaret wrote me and told me why Berta had had to send you away. Jacob Singer had been molesting you, which made me sick. Then Margaret wrote me about Berta's murder, and that Jacob was caught and electrocuted for the crime. I knew you were safe somewhere in the middle of America. Then your poor Aunt Margaret was murdered."

"Why would you care about me? Are you related to me?" Myra asked.

Janos stood up and walked to the bay window. His back was towards them. They weren't sure if he was watching the ducks on the lake below or trying to tell them something so important he was searching for words. Then his shoulders began to shake and he reached into the back pocket of his pants and brought out a handkerchief.

Myra stood up and went to his side. He was crying and tears were streaming down his cheeks. "What is it? Are you ill?"

"No, I am fine. It is just . . . after all these years and all you have gone through, I finally am here to help you.

What happened to Miriam happened to your mother. We were in love. But I was a Catholic, and in our time there was no way in hell that we would ever be allowed to marry. So I watched my darling being given to a man twice her age in the Szeged Synagogue as my heart broke into so many pieces. Abraham Steinman was an Orthodox Jew. He followed the religious rules of his faith as closely as he could.

"I use to walk by their house sometimes, but it just broke my heart again. Mary was his third wife and he was sure she would produce a child for him. Abraham believed, as all Jews did at the time, that after a Jewish woman had her monthly period, she should go to the public baths and cleanse herself, and not sleep in his bed for ten days. So he set up a cot for Mary in a small room he had made in a back shed, and avoided her presence.

"It was during one of these cleansings that Mary and I came upon each other. She and Abraham had been married for three years, I think, and there was no child born. She was coming from the Synagogue that day, and I had no work to do. We talked and had coffee in a little cafe. We both knew and felt our love was strong enough that not even adultery could keep us apart. It was the most wonderful six months of our lives. We met every month in a small apartment of a good friend of mine, when it was Mary's time to stay away. When she became pregnant with you, Myra, Abraham was so pleased he bragged about his manhood to all the men who had teased him for being unable to have a child."

Myra

Myra knelt down besides his chair and took his hands in hers. "Abraham could not have a child?"

Janos shook is head. "One would not think so, but Mary was a very young wife. His boast could have been true. Still, I felt you were my daughter, and Mary did too, though we had no legitimate right to claim it. Doing so would only make matters worse for Mary and for you, not to mention Mary's family. As good Jews they would never be able to hold their heads up again. Family reputation was the only thing the Jews of that period could be proud about."

"Wait a minute. Back up sir," Myra said. "I am getting flashbacks now, and I am remembering my grandmother and a bus station."

"What, mother, what do you remember?" Rebecca asked

"I was terrified. I knew I was leaving my grandmother and the woman who was to take me away scared me. Then suddenly as we walked towards the train tracks, my grandmother yelled, 'Wait!' and ran towards us with a little white box. I think she said it was my birthright. Was it not the Star of David?"

Janos shook his head no. "When I picked you up from the bloody floor, the Star of David was underneath you. I think in her last breath Mary slid it to you. I picked it up and kept it, thinking if it were cursed at least you would not be affected as your mother and ancestors

460

had been."

"Is that why Gerta and Carl never showed it to me?"

"No. It is my belief that although Berta wanted you to know that you were Jewish, Gerta and Carl did not. They may have been very religious Catholics and reacted to what they thought would save your soul. They had you baptised Catholic. They did not know the brooch was a copy with glass Austrian crystals in a metal resembling silver. Most likely Gerta did know the Star of David was a Jewish symbol, and had heard of the heirloom's value. The Depression was a harsh time. She knew your Berta was dead, and she may have read about Margaret too--so why not sell the expensive Jewish symbol and improve their shabby lives, and yours, too?" Janos coughed into his hand. "I think that is what happened. I think when they discovered the brooch Berta had given you was not Miriam's famous piece, Gerta got angry enough to change your religion. Besides, most likely her priest would have said you should be a Catholic if she and Carl were to raise you."

"So, where do we go from here?" Rebecca asked them.

"Back to the beginning, I guess." Janos said to Myra. "I don't *know* that you are my flesh and blood, but, for now, would you mind if I thought so? You look and act so much like your mother."

Myra moved closer to Janos and held out her arms

to him. He quickly encircled her in his arms and they both started to cry.

"If it takes forever we will find out the truth. There must be ways we can find out, mustn't there?" Rebecca said. "For now, you are Mother's father and I have a real Hungarian grandfather. OK?" Rebecca circled her mother and Janos, and they rocked in each other's arms.

Chapter Forty-one

Myra wondered how a monstrous ancestor could have chosen to curse the life she now was starting to remember. She hoped she was the biological daughter of the gray haired man who had loved her mother so much. He had rescued her as a child and he had rescued her from the Szeged house as an adult. It had to count for something. Her heart soared to think her life had traveled so many different paths, though now she often felt that it was ending. She had loved two wonderful men and lost them in turbulent deaths. Was that part of the curse that old Furst had bestowed on her bloodline? Rebecca would be next if she didn't do something now in this generation. A crazy thought entered her mind. If she died would the curse die too? She shook her head no. The curse had survived other deaths. Besides, she was not a selfish person to leave her children and grandchildren in devastating grief by ending her own life. She had been in the deep caves of grief and the blue skies of happiness, fleeting as they were if counted in years. She was not about to give up. She would find solace somehow in her family and go on as Michael would have wanted her to live in the future.

Janos had returned to Vienna promising to keep in touch. Rebecca flew back to her New York home to cut the horrible fringes of her wedding day from the future for herself and Julien, hoping their love would erase those memories. It was then that Myra came to her own decision about how to erase the curse from her life and the lives of her descendents. She called Mathew in California and told him what to do. He knew of the offers to display or buy the diamond Star of David, and she wanted him to sell it immediately and donate the profits to Jewish and Catholic charities. Shocked, Mathew asked for a family conference, but Myra was adamant. The sooner the jewelry was sold, the safer she would feel about their future. Since the Catholics had taken care of her when there was no else, she wanted a substantial fund set up in Sister Bernadette's name, set aside for scholarships. Other than that, the charities should do with the money whatever they saw fit to do. She did not want a penny from the sale. Her instructions threw Mathew into a turmoil. He knew the value of the brooch and argued again that the family should vote on it, but Myra would not hear of it. It was her property, and Michael had left her enough money. The family had all they needed and she was sure that when her time came, there would still be plenty for them all to inherit.

Mathew arrived the following week after Myra's call. He had informed his siblings, and although there were doubts about giving the money away, all of them trusted their mother to know what was best. They had seen and felt the curse Myra talked about and although it seemed like a resolution out of a horror movie, they agreed for the sake of their mother's health. Rebecca was more than pleased. Although the least wealthy of the children, she believed   the curse had caused the night-mare of her wedding and the loss of her father. It would not bring back her father, but with the brooch gone, maybe the dreadful memories of her wedding would vanish like a fog on a dreary day.

A month later, Myra was packing up Michael's clothes, her heart heavy inside her. How was she going to go on without her love? She had known that she would live beyond Eric with his terrible wounds and depressions. But Michael was supposed to grow old with her. He had appeared in a dream years before she met him. She had been in Estes Park on her first honeymoon, and she and Eric had driven the Trailridge Highway to the top of the pass. She had felt the enormous height and space, almost above the clouds, and the fresh crisp air had blown around them. That night, in her dream, she had been searching for Eric up there on the top of the path, but he had shaken his head, no, and pointed to a man standing down on the path dressed as a doctor. It was a Michael she had yet to meet. What caused some of her dreams to come true? If she had dreams these days she didn't remember them.

Her sleep that night was light and full of twists and turns until at last, the dawn started to light the sky, and she got up to another day of loneliness.

On this day, she knew the Star of David would be sold and she would be free at last from the curse of the brooch. The price was astronomical and Mathew had tried for a month with all his lawyerly persuasive tactics to convince her not give all the money away. But she would not concede. She wanted that brooch eliminated from her family once and for all. If she kept one cent of its price, she believed, the curse would linger. If she sacrificed it, then the curse on whichever descendent *inherited* it would certainly be ended; and she hoped that the broader curse on all of Miriam's descendents would also be removed. She had told Mathew about both curses, but he was neither superstitious nor a dreamer. He saw this sale and gift as folly, but since it was what she wanted he had searched for the highest bidder and contacted the charities his mother had named. He knew Myra's financial situation was secure and he loved her dearly. If this sale would bring that smile back to her face and the sparkle to her eyes, it would be worth the loss of a fortune. He had noticed gray hairs in her lovely thick black hair, though her face was almost as wrinkle free and smooth as Rebecca's.

So he flew to New York, prepared to sign away the brooch and the fortune it represented. As he put his pen to the paper, however, his hand began to shake uncontrollably and the carefully prepared papers flew in all directions. The buyers, the major beneficiaries, and their lawyers thought they were feeling a small earthquake, which was unusual for the area. They scrambled to pick up papers and set the chairs around the round table as they had been before the rumble.

At that moment, Myra was drinking a cup of tea at home in Baltimore, thinking that the sale should be done by now and that Mathew would call her soon to say it was over. Suddenly her hand began to shake and her teacup fell to the floor. Her windows rattled although there was no wind and the pond below with the ducks was as placid as ever. She stood up and watched her kitchen curtains blow wildly as a few glasses jumped from their place in the cupboard and smashed on the floor.

She knew it was the Furst curse, and she determined at last to stop it. She stood up and walked to her silverware drawer in the kitchen. She picked up the sharpest knife she could find. Then she held her arms upward, and, remembering what Janos had told her of Sandor's oath, she spoke her own oath: "I swear from this moment on, in God's name, the curse of the Furst family has ended. I swear by God that the ghosts of the past will no longer direct their anger at my descendants or me in any way, lest I, the immediate descendant of the Furst anger, condemn Sandor to hell, now and forever. To guarantee this, I am willing to give my body and soul to God at this moment."

Myra meant what she said, and the power of her oath was immediately felt all through the house. She sliced her left wrist and watched the blood ooze from her arm. The wind stopped and all was quiet. She looked around, and knew that what she had just sworn to do had been an honest confrontation with Sandor Furst. He would have no "inheritor" to curse now with the brooch sold; and his other descendents—especially Miriam's look-alike, Rebecca—would be freed from his horrible curse. Myra sliced her other wrist and fell to the floor.

And at that moment, Matthew's struggle to control his writing suddenly ended. He was able to sign the various papers, finish the sale, and allot the proceeds. When it was done he went to call his mother. There was no answer. A chill went through him, and he felt something was wrong. He called the police and asked them to check on his mother. Half an hour later, he was informed that Myra had been taken to Walter Reed Hospital with cuts on her wrists and a lot of blood lost. Mathew rushed to the hospital. In a very few hours, he was with Myra in the white room with nurses and doctors swarming in and out. A blood transfusion was in process, and her wrists were wrapped. An hour after he arrived, Myra opened her eyes. She looked at Mathew and asked, "Why is it starting all over again?"

"Mother. It is all done. You no longer have the Star of David."

Myra looked around the room, "Where are Gerta and Carl? Why is the room so white?" Myra turned her head to Matthew. He smiled at her and she tried to reach out to him, but her wrist was too heavy to lift.

"Am I dreaming again? Who are you?" she asked, glaring at him.

"Mother, I am Mathew, your son. You are not dreaming. You hurt yourself."

She smiled at him, and the long-absent twinkle re-

"I do know you. You are my son Matthew, my oldest and loving son."

"Yes Mother. There is no Gerta or Carl here. You are years from the first time you woke up in a hospital room and your memory had left you. You are now free of the Furst curse."

She closed her eyes and said, "Ah, yes, now I remember. I swore to God I would give my body and soul if it was needed, to send Sandor Furst's to hell along with his curse."

"You cut your wrist to kill you self?" Mathew asked.

"I had to my darling. The glasses were falling from the cupboard; the curtains were being blown to pieces. I knew you could not sign away the brooch unless I made an ultimate sacrifice." Myra looked at him. "I didn't die, did I?"

"No, Mother your meaning must have been clear, because I too felt the shaking and the impossible control of my hand. The whole office shook and scared the people surrounding me. Then, as suddenly as it started, it stopped, and they thought how strange that a small earthquake had interrupted us."

"Mathew, there have to be good spirits who have directed me all these years. At last, I have saved my family." She closed her eyes and slept peacefully. Mathew

Myra

went into the hallway outside her room and called the rest
of the family.

Chapter Forty-two

The train rumbled along the track passing villages and farms on the flat land of the Great Hungarian Plains. Many years had passed since she and Rebecca had traveled this route. The Hungarian borders had opened last year so that the dissidents and Freedom Fighters who had survived the revolution could come back to their homeland. It was a poor country now, Myra thought, trying to regain its place in the world. How many times had wars shrunk its borders and tried to destroy its people? But Hungarians are strong and deeply loyal to their roots, she thought. She envisioned the country rising again, staying solvent and strong, and maybe becoming a leader in the changing world. It had disturbed her to see at the border crossing that the young Hungarian guards, men and women, were still wearing those awful dark green uniforms of the communist days, still looking like robots, stiffly doing their duty, only their duty. No smiles or flexibility in their body language. Instead, blank faces had looked at their passports and visas, faces which indicated that they didn't care who you were or what time is was; it was only another day of work.

For most of her life Myra had wanted to belong to someone related to her biologically. Now she knew for sure. Morgan and Rebecca had urged her to try the new DNA method of identifying people through blood samples. Last year she had gone to Morgan's office and submitted her blood. In Hungary, Janos Peto did the same at Edmond Herschkovitz's clinic. Edmond had sent the sample to New York to be tested. The DNA test was a new procedure, headlined in almost every newspaper in the nation. Myra had doubts about it, but when the blood samples were examined in the labs, they proved that Myra was the daughter of Janos Peto. The information spun around in her mind and dreams. She was stunned at first, and then happy.

When Janos called her from Hungary, he reminded her that in his heart he always knew she was his daughter. He had wanted so much to take her away when Mary was murdered, but the laws of the land and the traditions of the Jews both stopped him from exercising what he knew to be his moral right. He would have shamed Mary's family and they would have bcome like outcasts. How could he do that to his beloved's family? Instead, he kept track of Myra by asking questions of Mary's father, Jacob Goldman. Berta knew his secret, as Mary had told her that Myra was his child; so after she moved to New York in 1928, Berta often wrote to him. To get around the restrictions on immigration imposed by the National Origins Act, Berta had claimed to be a widow and said that Myra Goldman was her granddaughter. After Berta's death, Janos tried vainly to discover what had happened to his child. Margot wrote that Berta had sent her away with an old friend to live out west. Margot was murdered too be-

Janos explained to Myra that he had then learned what he could about Berta's childhood and close friends. After some time, he realized that Gerta was probably the one who had taken Myra in. It took a couple of years more to find that Gerta and Carl Grainger had been living in Salida, Colorado. But by then they had either moved or died; he had not been able to determine which. He started reading the English language newspapers in the Szeged public library, looking for the latest news from Colorado. It was there that he read about Myra Grainger's scholarship to the University of Colorado. By then the war was raging in Europe, though the United States did not become involved until later. He had kept the Star of David brooch hidden for those thirteen years, not quite believing that it carried a curse strong enough to hurt his love child further. Had he known, he told Myra, he would have destroyed it. But he was not a believer in superstitions, or that a dead spirit could carry through with a curse for five generations. How could it?-- he'd asked himself, then sent the brooch to Yvette, who'd sent it on to Myra.

The conversations between Myra and her father had answered questions she had lived with for as long as she could remember. Now Myra agreed that they should meet in Szeged since Janos' health was not very good. He had suffered a slight stroke and his heart seem weak, his doctors told him.

There was one more mystery to uncover, though, Myra thought. Where was the famous painting of Miriam? She had other questions to ask Janos, too. Eric had been so sure the portrait was of her. She thought of Rebecca and her identical twin girls. They were safe now from the curse, though all three had the mark of Miriam's beauty. The curse had marked the death of her mother, Eric, Michael, and the weddings of Morgan and Rebecca. Now looking back, it seemed just one of her dark dreams.

The train passed by the columns of trees planted like soldiers in a row. She remembered them, first from her dreams and then from her first trip, when Sam was riding with Rebecca, who was asking so many questions. It had been hard for Sam to tie things together for a little girl to understand. Myra smiled as she saw a farmer chasing his chickens around the yard of his home. He was a tall thin person and he waved a large black cloth over his head as he ran back and forth trying to catch one of the chickens. "I am truly home," she thought.

The train station in Szeged was smaller than most depots but it didn't matter to Myra. There, sitting on a wooden bench, was Janos. He looked so much older than the last time she saw him in her Maryland condo. An old woman besides him helped him to a standing position and walked him forward to greet Myra. They embraced and he kissed Myra's cheek. In all of her memories of him, Janos was a tall, strong and determined man. Even in Maryland when he introduced himself, he had stood straight and his gray hair had curled around his face like the hair of Cupids in paintings. He was so handsome that Rebecca and Myra agreed that they too would have loved him like Mary did. Now, he could not stand straight. His shoulders bent over and his legs seem to be shorter. He held tight to his ebony cane with the silver top of a dog's head. Myra was so happy to see him. At last she held her father in her arms and felt his fragile body.

"This, my darling daughter, is Anna. Do remember her? You and the child stayed at her house the last time you were here," Janos said as he reached for Anna's support on the side opposite his cane.

Myra could hardly believe her eyes. This was the nice lady who with her brother had given them such a lovely room and home-cooked meals before she got sick. Of course it was the brother who was whispering to Janos in the garden that one night.

"Of course. I do remember you. How are you and your brother?" Myra asked.

Anna looked at Janos as though waiting for his permission to answer. Janos nodded to Anna and she said, "My brother is dead."

"I am so sorry Anna. Was he sick for very long?"

"No, madam. He was executed by our former government." She looked away then and Janos continued her sentence.

"It is a long story Myra. I will tell you about it later. Let us head for the car. I no longer can drive and Anna never did, so we have hired a young man to chauffer us around the city." That was when Myra noticed the wheelchair besides Janos. As Anna helped him into it, Myra reminded Janos that she must get the rest of her luggage.

"Of course, I forgot." Then he flagged a man in a black outfit whom Myra thought to be an agent from the railroad agency. Janos slipped the man a roll of forint and told Myra to accompany him to pick out her luggage. He would bring them to the car.

The ride to Anna's home showed some buildings going up, but the large apartment houses the Communists had built on land taken from homeowners still dominated the city's landscape. How ugly they were! Tenents had to walk up five or six stories if they lived on the higher floors. They had no elevators, Myra remembered from her past visit, and no improvements were visible.

At last, the building of white stucco with its brick archway came in view. It had changed too. It needed re-painting as chips of the outside walls were clearly falling off. The large wooden doors under the archway were also showing their age and squealed from the hinges as they drove through. The sad sight of a garden gone to weeds made Myra want to cry. It had been so beautiful, and the fountain, which had stood in the middle of the pond, now stood like a rustic ruin.

"We have so much to do getting this place like it was when you last saw it," Janos said as he noticed Myra looking around.

"What happened?" she asked, but he only shook his head and headed for the doorway.

Inside of the house, things Myra remembered were now missing. Furniture and china and the lovely white linen tablecloth were gone. The drapes in the large room were discolored and had been mended. The stairs also bent in the middle and were worn to the grain in the wood. The hall carpet had disappeared and the room Myra had shared with Rebecca had lost it charm, though Anna had managed to add a few colorful items around the room and clean lace curtains.

After Myra settled in, she joined Janos and Anna in the kitchen for a light supper. It was then that Janos told her what happened to Joseph. The Communists had been told that he was a spy. Janos and Anna did not know who had reported him, but they had some ideas. Joseph worked as a handyman for the commander of the KBG in Szeged. It seems someone had warned one of freedom fighters working underground that he and his family were to be arrested. Luckily the man and his family were able to hide out and eventually cross over to Austria. Joseph was the likely person to blame since he was not a communist party member.

"You see, my dear, Joseph and Anna are distant cousins of mine. I could not reveal that fact for fear of putting our underground in danger. After the outcry over Joseph's death calmed down, I asked to move into this home. It is an old house we all enjoyed as children."

"I thought you owned that large home Rebecca ran into, the one where she was met by that horrible German woman," Myra commented.

"Yes, I did own it, as it had a number of secret rooms in the basement where we organized our plans. The woman was not a German, but a Jew who had escaped from Germany before they sent her family away. She hated the Communists and had seen too much tragedy in her lifetime. She was not a pleasant lady, but a very loyal one."

"Why did it frighten me?"

"Because the house had belonged to a very rich Jew and relative of Abraham. He would hold the Seder every year. Of course you and your mother came with Abraham. There had always been a suspicion that you did not belong to Abraham since his wives before Mary could not bear him children. Why, people wondered, would a young girl like Mary be able to give him a child within three years?"

Anna interrupted. "You see, the rich Jew who owned the house at that time was becoming mindless."

Janos laughed and added, "He was getting very old and his mind was set on Jews never mixing their blood with Gentiles. I was told later that he once scolded you when you reached for a Matzo cracker before his reading from the little book was done. He was reading the section about tasting the bitter and the sweet in the history of the

Jews."

Myra remembered how the room had scared her when, as an adult, she ran in to get Rebecca. "I dreamed about that, and I remember what was said in the dream. He yelled that I was not Jewish and should not handle the matzo at all. Then my mother yelled back at him and picked me up. We left, didn't we?"

Janos was surprised by Myra's memory. "That is what I was told."

"Once we were at home she and my father, or Abraham, had a terrible fight. He screamed at her and I thought it was my fault because I wanted the cracker. Abraham pointed his finger at me and said I had ruined one of the holiest days of our religion. I felt I had betrayed my mother. It was a memory I must have stored deep in my subconscious mind to dream about as an adult."

"I was shocked to see you there in my house and later followed you to your old home where I found you trying to wipe up the blood on the floor, just as you did as a child," Janos said quietly. "I picked you up again, as I had done before, and carried you to Edmond's car. I later learned that you became very sick for a few years and were in a clinic or hospital."

"Yes," Myra answered. "I learned there to accept that I might not ever know who I was. I came to terms with the world I lived in. I had so many good things on my side with the children and Michael; it gradually stopped being important who conceived me. I learned to enjoy happiness without knowing a blood relative or remembering my early years."

Janos smiled at her. "I cannot believe you are here. You fill my heart with a happiness I never thought I could feel since I lost your mother."

"What was my mother really like?" Myra asked.

"Tomorrow, my daughter. It has been an exciting day for me and I am tired. I have Joseph's old room and Anna is in the bedroom next to mine. I cannot climb the stairs any more, so here we are on the main floor."

The kitchen door opened, and a young girl in nurse's uniform walked in.

"Oh it is Beth, our home care nurse," Anna said, and got up to clear the table.

"I see your daughter has arrived, Janos," the nurse said. "I can see why you are so excited. She is lovely." Then she turned toward Myra and held out her hand, "I am Elizabeth Heiney, the nurse assigned to these lovely people. They call me Beth for short, so you may do so too if you like."

Myra shook her hand and introduced herself. Beth scolded Anna about picking up the dirty dishes and began

Myra picked up the rest of the dishes saying to Anna, "Here, Anna, let me do this. You go help Janos and Beth. I can do dishes, you know."

The next morning Myra woke early. She sponged off her body and dressed in slacks and a blouse with tennis shoes for comfort. She had planned to walk around the town again to places she might once have known and later dreamed about. Perhaps she would remember them as real places now. She had found that she could converse a little with Anna in her native language. At 68, Myra was beginning to spend more of her thinking time in the past, and that meant recalling more about her childhood. She wanted to see the house where her mother was killed.

Anna was already in the kitchen brewing coffee and the smell of biscuits in the oven filled the room. "You are up so early, Myra. Did you not sleep well?"

"Yes, I did Anna. I just want to walk around the neighborhood to see if I can remember what was lost to me as a child."

"You should have some coffee first, and the rolls are almost done. There are thin sausage slices for the rolls, and the cheese and jam is on the table. Do have some before you leave."

The smell was a memory coming back, and Myra could not refuse the offer. "Very well, I shall have some coffee but only a half of a roll. I know it is a traditional breakfast in Hungary, but I only want a little jam, and no cream in the coffee."

Anna quickly produced the order and set another place for herself. "Your father is not awake yet. Beth gives him medicine that makes him sleep more now. He is not in good health, my dear."

Then Anna sat down and picked up a quilt that was folded on the chair next to her.

"What is that, Anna?" Myra asked.

Anna looked at her and smiled, "It is my hobby. It is a patchwork quilt. I have made many over the years. I made one for you too."

Astonished, Myra asked, "Why? You didn't know me, did you?"

Anna got up and poured some coffee into her cup and added cream and sugar. "Oh yes, my dear. I knew your story well. Joseph and I lived on the same street as your parents. There was no certain district that Jews or Christians could not live in when we were young. We were a much smaller village then, and we all got along just fine."

"What did you make for me? I see you have Janos' face in one patch of this quilt, and there is Joseph. What are you trying to make of it?"

"I started yours when you were born," Anna

replied, "since Joseph and I both knew you had to be the child of Janos. He had told us about his love for Mary, and I must say she was a beautiful lady. One could not stop looking at her, meeting her on the street."

"But why make me a quilt if you did not know my family other than what Janos told you?"

"I didn't care about that. I thought that one day when you grew up I would give it to you. That way Janos would be happy. He was so quiet, different from his usual self. Of course, when all the trouble started and you moved into your Grandfather's house, I thought better of it. I put it away until you came here with your little girl."

"I can't believe you would do such a wonderful thing. What is it like?"

"Oh, it is far from finished because I had no idea what your husbands looked like, or the people you grew up with. I just stitched three more patches on and waited until I would know your life story."

Beth came through the back door again and smiled. "I see you are up for the day, Myra. Did you sleep well?"

"Yes, thank you, I did. Anna, here"--and she felt Anna kicking her leg under the table--"made me some breakfast. I want to walk around for a while this morning." Anna let out a sigh of relief.

"Well, I will get Janos up and ready for the day too.

Is there hot water, Anna?" Beth asked as she walked down the hall toward his room. "I want to scrub him good today. He loves to be clean."

Anna did not answer her but thanked Myra for not mentioning the quilt. "It is none of her business," she said, "and she is known to gossip. She must be the busiest gossiper in town, and I bet anything I own she has had plenty of inquiries about you."

Myra stepped into the courtyard and through the arched wooden doors. Anna said she would have the quilt in her room by the time she got back. The sun was bright and the air smelled moist from the Tiza River a few blocks away. She circled the blocks looking for familiar places, and suddenly she was standing in front of the house Sam had pointed out to her all those years ago. It was his childhood home. It had fresh paint on the front, and one of the large doors was open under its arch. Myra could see fruit trees that Sam had talked about. His mother had made wine and jams from them, he'd said. But when she was last there, only skeleton trees with empty and dead branches could be seen. "Oh Sam, you would be thrilled to see someone has started to restore your home," Myra whispered. A small rose plant next to one of the trees moved as if waving to her. She blinked her eyes to be sure of what she saw. The bush moved again and she heard something weird. Was it a whisper? And again, barely a whisper, "Myra." Was it Sam? No, she was past the time for dreams and illusions.

She turned away and continued her walk up the

street to the Grey Friars Catholic church. School children were being led by hooded monks into their classroom across the street from the church. Myra walked into the church and saw that it was very old, with watermarks high on the painted walls indicating where the great flood had reached back in 1879. The colors of the paintings on the walls, especially the reds and blues in the icons of saints, were amazing. Ancient art of every color adorned the walls. Myra took water from the basin in the vestibule and made the Sign of the Cross, because years ago she had forgiven Jesus, there in St. Catherine's Church in Denver. This Jesus looked down at her with a slight smile, and she knew that he had been born a Jew, and also that he welcomed everyone who entered his house. She said a prayer for Janos and Anna, put a coin into the tall, altar-shaped box near the door of the church, and walked back the way she had come.

CPSIA information can be obtained at www.ICGtesting.com
Printed in the USA
LVOW041838201211

259764LV00007B/1/P

9 780981 790251